§ blood [...] book one: §

# the TURNING

*Watch for*

BLOOD TIES BOOK TWO: POSSESSION

*Coming February 2007*

# JENNIFER ARMINTROUT

## blood ties book one:

# the TURNING

MIRA

ISBN 0-7783-2298-X

BLOOD TIES BOOK ONE: THE TURNING

Copyright © 2006 by Jennifer Armintrout.

**Printed in U.S.A.**

Much love and thanks to:

The FNMS. Michele, for eye rolls and encouragement. Chris, for loving my characters (and me) enough to read revised scenes for the nth time. Cheryl, for your advice on shameless self-promotion. Marti, for the [expletive deleted] advice from that [expletive deleted] book. You know which one. Derek, for keeping the adverbs and alliteration at bay. And Mary, even though you weren't part of the crowd then, you deserve a mention for being Cyrus's biggest fan.

Peggy, who let me pretend to be a writer on her typewriter when I was four years old.

Shannon, for still liking the book after viewing my lame attempt at dancing.

My editor, Sasha Bogin, and my agent, Kelly Harms, for being enthusiastic about this book and me.

Joe, for believing I could do this and subjecting yourself to the ups and downs of living with a writer.

# One

### The End

I read a poll in the newspaper once that said the number-one fear of Americans aged eighteen to sixty-five is public speaking. Spiders are second, and death a distant third. I'm afraid of all these things. But most of all, I'm afraid of failure.

I'm no coward. I want to make that perfectly clear. But my life turned from nearly perfect to a horror movie in a matter of days, so I take fear a lot more seriously now.

I'd followed my life plan almost to the letter, with very few detours. I'd gone from plain old Ms. Carrie Ames to Dr. Carrie Ames just eight months prior to the night I now refer to as "The Big Change." I'd broken away from the sleepy, East Coast town I'd grown up in, only to find myself in a sleepy, mid-Michigan city. I had a great residency in the E.R. of the public hospital there. The city and surrounding rural communities provided endless opportunity to study and treat injuries inflicted by both urban warfare and treacherous farm equipment. Living my dream, I'd never been more certain that

I'd found the success and control over my destiny that had always seemed to elude me in my tumultuous college years.

Of course, sleepy mid-Michigan towns get boring, especially on frozen winter nights when even the snow won't venture out. And on a night exactly like this, after only having been home for four hours from a grueling twelve-hour shift, I was back at the hospital to help deal with a sudden influx of patients. The E.R. was surprisingly busy for such a forbidding evening, but the approaching holiday season seemed to affect everyone with a pulse. Thanks to my rotten luck, I was charged with attending trauma cases that night, patients with serious injuries and illnesses that put them in imminent danger of death. Or, more specifically, carloads of mall-hoppers who showed up in pieces after hitting black ice on 131 South.

After I'd admitted three patients, I found myself in great need of a nicotine fix. While I felt guilty for sticking the other doctors with a few extra cases, I didn't feel guilty enough to forgo a quick cigarette break.

I was heading for the ambulance bay doors when John Doe arrived.

Dr. Fuller, the attending physician and most senior M.D. in the hospital, ran alongside the gurney, barking instructions and demanding information from the EMTs in his no-nonsense Texan accent.

Distracted by the fact that Dr. Fuller's smooth, Southern speech had been replaced by an urgent, clipped tone, I didn't notice the patient on the gurney. I had never seen my superior lose his unflappable calm before. It scared me.

"Carrie, you gonna give us a hand here or are you on a one-way trip to Marlboro country?" he barked, startling me. The cigarette between my fingers snapped in half when I jumped, reduced to a fluttering shower of dry tobacco. My break had been officially canceled.

I brushed my hands clean on my lab coat and fell into step beside the gurney. It was only then that I noticed the state the transport was in.

The sight of the patient paralyzed me as we entered the cubical and the EMTs were squeezed out to make way for the R.N.s who rushed in.

"Okay ladies, I want splash guards, gowns, goggles, the whole space suit. Quickly, please," Fuller snapped, shrugging off his blood-smeared white coat.

I knew I should do something to help, but I could only stare at the mess on the table in front of me. I had no idea where to start.

Blood might be the one thing I'm not afraid of. In the case of John Doe, it was not the blood that made working on him, touching him, even approaching him unthinkable. It was the fact that he looked like my dissection cadaver on the last day of Gross Anatomy.

Puncture wounds peppered his chest. Some were small, but four or five were large enough to fit a baseball in.

"Gunshot wounds? What the hell was he shot with, a god-damned cannon?" Dr. Fuller muttered as he probed one of the bloody holes with his gloved finger.

It didn't take a forensic-science degree to tell that what had caused the wounds in John Doe's torso had not caused the wounds in his face. His jaw, or what was left of it, hung skinned from the front teeth to the splintered end, where it had been ripped from the joint to dangle uselessly from the other side of his skull. Above the gaping hole in his cheek, one eye socket stood empty and crushed, the eye itself and optical nerve completely missing.

"I'd say someone used an axe on his head, if I thought it were possible to swing one with enough force to do this," Dr. Fuller said. "We're not going to get a tube down this way, his trachea's crushed all to hell."

I couldn't breathe. John Doe's remaining eye, clear and bright blue, fixed on mine as if he were totally alert.

It had to be a trick of the light. No one could endure this kind of trauma and remain conscious. No one could survive injuries of this magnitude. He didn't cry out or writhe in pain. His body was limp and completely void of any reaction as the attending staff made an incision in his windpipe to intubate him.

He never looked away.

*How can he be alive?* my mind screamed. The concept destroyed the carefully constructed logic I'd built over three years of medical school. People did not live through something like this. It wasn't in the textbooks. Yet, there he was, staring at me calmly, focused on me despite the flurry of action around us.

For a sickening moment, I thought I heard my name from the mangled hole of his mouth. Then I realized it was Dr. Fuller's frantic voice cutting through the haze of my paralyzed revulsion.

"Carrie, I need you to wake up and join us! Come on, now, we're losing this guy!"

I could continue to stare at John Doe or turn my face to Dr. Fuller, to see him silently lose his faith in me. I don't know what would have been more distressing, but I didn't get to make a decision.

I mumbled a feeble apology, turned swiftly and ran. I had barely escaped the grisly scene before I noticed the sticky splotches on the floor that stained the pristine tile a deep, glossy red. I was going to be sick. I fell to my knees in the congealing blood and closed my eyes as the bile rose in my throat. I rocked back and forth on my knees, my vomit mixing with the blood on the tiles.

A sudden hush came from the cubicle behind me, followed by the insistent whine of the heart monitor protesting the cessation of pulse.

"All right, he's gone. Pack him up and get him to the morgue," I heard Dr. Fuller say. His cool, Texan confidence crept back into his voice, though it was tainted with weariness and resignation.

I scrambled to my feet and ran to the staff locker room, unable to face my failure.

I was still in the locker room an hour later. Fresh from a shower, dressed in clean scrubs from central processing, I stood before the mirror and tried to smooth my wet, blond hair into something resembling a ponytail. My mascara had run in the shower and I wiped at it with my sleeve. It only served to darken the circles under my eyes. My bone-pale skin stretched sharply over my cheekbones, my blue eyes were cold and hollow. I'd never seen myself look so defeated.

*When did I become so pathetic? So cowardly?* Cruelly, I taunted myself with memories I couldn't push aside. The way I'd snickered with the other students when the skinny foreign guy had tossed his cookies on the first day of Gross Anatomy. Or the time I'd chased Amy Anderson, the queen bee of the eighth grade, from the bus stop by sticking earthworms in her hair.

It appeared that I'd become one of those people I'd despised. To the entire E.R. medical staff at St. Mary's Hospital, I had become the squeamish nerd, the shrieking girl. It cut so deeply, I'd need emotional sutures to heal.

A knock at the door pulled me from my self-pity. "Ames, you still in there?"

The door swung open. Steady footsteps carried Dr. Fuller to the end of my narrow bench.

For a moment, he didn't say anything at all. Without looking, I knew that he stood with his head hanging down. His hands would be in the pockets of his crisp white coat, his elbows tucked in at his sides, giving him the appearance of a tall, gray stork.

"So, hangin' in there?" he asked suddenly.

I shrugged. Anything I said would have been a lame excuse for my poor performance, one akin to those uttered by countless med students who stopped showing up for class soon after.

"You know," he began, "I've seen a lot of doctors, good physicians, crack under pressure. You get tired. You get stressed, maybe you're having personal problems. Those things happen to all of us. But some of us leave it in here—" he pointed to the lockers behind me "—instead of taking it out there. It's what makes us capable doctors."

He waited for me to respond. I only nodded.

"I know you've gone through a lot this year, losing your parents—"

"This isn't about my parents." I hadn't meant to cut him off, but the words were spoken before I had a chance to think about them. "I'm sorry. But really, I'm over that."

He sighed deeply as he sat next to me on the bench. "Why do you want to be a doctor?"

We sat there for a long time, like a coach and a star player who had fumbled the ball, before I answered.

"Because I want to help people." I was lying. Badly. But even I didn't know the reason, and he didn't want a real answer, anyway. Real doctors lose the capacity for humanity and understanding before they grab their diplomas. "And because I love it."

"Well, I love golf, but that doesn't make me Tiger Woods, does it?" He laughed at his own joke before he became thoughtful again. "You know, there comes a time in everyone's life when they have to carefully examine the goals they've set for themselves. When they have to admit their limitations and look at their capabilities in a more realistic way."

"You're saying I should be a dentist?" I asked, forcing a laugh.

"I'm saying you shouldn't be a doctor." Fuller actually patted me on the back, as though it would take the edge off his harsh words. He stood and walked toward the door, stopping suddenly as if he'd just thought of something.

"You know," he began, but he didn't finish his thought. Instead he shook his head and walked out the door.

My fists balled with anger and my breath came in noisy gasps as I struggled to regain my composure. I'd failed the Great One's test. I should have told him I liked the money. It was considerably better than a stick in the eye. Though they were both reasons people entered the field, neither financial security nor desire to help others were my true motivation for becoming a doctor.

It was the power that drew me to it. The power of holding a human life in my hands. The power of looking Death in the face and knowing I could defeat him. It was a power reserved for doctors and God.

I'd pictured myself a modern-day Merlin, a scalpel for a wand, a clipboard my book of spells. I cringed at the ridiculous thought.

I could have changed into my street clothes, slunk out of

the hospital and never come back. But then I thought of my dead father and remembered one of the rare pieces of paternal advice I'd ever received from him.

"If you're afraid of something, face it. Fear is irrational. The only way to conquer your fear is to put yourself next to it."

Just as quickly as it had come, my self-doubt subsided. This was a test of faith in myself. I wasn't going to fail.

I got onto my feet and made my way through the packed E.R., blind and deaf to my coworkers and the patients that crowded the cubicles around me. I left the emergency and trauma ward altogether, pushing through the doors that led into the central part of the hospital.

The offices I passed were closed, their windows dark. The main lobby was empty, with the exception of one custodian who leaned on the deserted information desk, idly reading an old newspaper while his cleaning cart sat neglected in the middle of the room. He barely glanced up as I elbowed the cart in my reckless flight and knocked a stack of paper towels to the floor.

I continued to the elevators, pressed the button impatiently and tapped my foot. After what seemed like an interminably long time, the dull metal doors slid open and I entered. I pushed the button for the basement.

An irrational determination took me down the long hallway to the morgue. I had only been through there once, during my orientation tour. It was a simple route, though, and I located the unlabeled door again without much difficulty. I ran my hospital ID through the badge reader and heard the sharp click of the releasing lock.

I grabbed the handle and stopped, wondering for the first time what I intended to prove to myself. I feared I was a bad doctor, and I had come to confront my fears and view John Doe in all his mangled glory. What if I couldn't handle it?

Terror gripped me at the thought that his body might not be as damaged as I remembered. I recalled Amy Anderson's horrified face as she'd held the wriggling earthworm in her palm, her fear making the harmless thing a monster. Had my panicked brain exaggerated John Doe's wounds?

*No, you weren't hysterical. You know what you saw.* I entered the cool, antiseptic room before I could change my mind.

Hospital morgues are much different from morgues in the movies. They aren't cavernous spaces with stark lighting. In fact, the morgue at St. Mary's was small and cluttered. The on-duty attendant had left a rumpled fast-food sack on the desk, a reassuring sign of life in a room devoted to the indignities of death.

Before I approached the task at hand, I walked the perimeter of the room. I examined the cabinets, the plastic tubs of all sizes that held murky shapes of organs preserved for further study, and the autopsy tables. I avoided the one that appeared occupied.

"Hello?" I called. I winced at the volume of my voice. The room was so quiet you could hear the buzzing of the fluorescent lights. The phrase "wake the dead" sprung unpleasantly to mind. I expected to see an orderly emerge from one of the back rooms, but no one came. The lucky SOB was probably on a smoke break. I would have to do the dirty work of locating John Doe myself.

The morgue freezer held six gurneys. With the high volume of patients today, it would be full, maybe even sleeping double. Not a pleasant thought.

I stepped into the cooler and immediately wished for a

jacket. The thermostat on the outside read thirty-five degrees, warm compared to the temperature outside, but it hadn't occurred to me just how cold thirty-five degrees really was.

Shivering, I looked over the six shrouded gurneys before me. They all faced the same direction, their occupants' feet pointed at the back wall. I glanced down at my shoes and saw a dark stain on the sticky, unwashed floor. My skin crawled as I speculated exactly how long it had been since someone disinfected this room. Not that these particular patients were in any danger of disease or infection.

I started with the body farthest to the right, not bothering to uncover them to search for their toe tags. I opted instead to read the more detailed tag on their shrouds.

The first body was a female, age sixty-eight. The second was male, age twenty-three. So it went, each tag displaying the one thing I wasn't looking for: a name. I didn't see any bearing the big, red "unidentified" stamp, and it seemed that my field trip would prove useless.

I rubbed my hands across my face, stretching tired skin as I pondered my next step. Where had he gone? It was unlikely that the medical examiner would have come at night for an autopsy that could wait until morning. Even if they had identified him, they couldn't have released the body before the police finished with it.

*He has to be here somewhere.* But as I doubled-checked, I had to accept the fact that he was gone.

I would have to go back upstairs and face my embarrassment much to the delight of my colleagues. I'd missed the opportunity to confront my demon, but life would go on, as it always had. With the same resolve that brought me there, I left the cooler without a backward look. Someone would make a snide comment, or even pity me no matter what I did.

I'd had enough experience with criticism that I could shoot down my detractors without actually having to go through the experience of looking at what was left of John Doe's body.

My hand was on the door handle when I stopped again. From the corner of my eye, I glimpsed the sheeted figure on the autopsy table.

For all my bravado, I'd felt some relief upon finding John Doe's body missing. To look or not to look. It had been an easy call with no body to see. An uneasy feeling crept over me as my initial relief fled. There was no doubt in my mind that John Doe lay beneath that sheet on the autopsy table.

*If you leave now, you'll always wonder,* a tiny voice nagged from the back of my mind. For a fraction of a second, it seemed the gnawing fear would win. I would just walk out of the morgue and forget the whole incident ever happened.

But my father's words and Dr. Fuller's hurtful evaluation of my abilities bounced around in my brain. I didn't want to be the failure I'd been in my father's eyes. The failure I'd become in Dr. Fuller's. It spurred me toward the table.

I was no coward.

Before I gave myself a chance to change my mind, I whipped the sheet completely off the cadaver.

Every second passed in slow motion, frame by frame. The very instant I pulled the covering off the body, I saw a brightly colored sole of an athletic shoe poking from under the sheet. There wasn't time for this to register as I ripped away the shroud, revealing hospital-issue scrubs and the face of the morgue attendant, his features frozen in terror.

I didn't scream right away, either from shock or the fact that the scene didn't make sense. John Doe was supposed to be here, not this young man. The sight transfixed me.

His neck had obviously been broken. The flesh of his throat had been torn the way it would look after a dog attack. Extreme blood loss left his dark skin ashen, though the table and most of his clothing were spotless. His eyes were open. One was missing.

I saw the telephone perched on the gleaming steel counter, but it seemed miles away as I ran to it. My hands shook so badly that I could barely punch the numbers to issue a code blue. But no reassuring calm came over me when I hung up. I was still stranded, still isolated in this weird nightmare. I picked up the phone again.

I was dialing the number for the night security office when something brushed my shoulder. The touch was so light I barely noticed it, but I wound up inexplicably on my back.

The force of my landing knocked the wind out of me. Confused and frightened, I scrambled to my knees, but that was as far as I got.

In the next instant, I was airborne again. Shattering glass crashed, the consequence of my impact against the cabinets. I had flown into the glass with enough momentum to break it and splinter the wooden doors. Pain ripped down my spine. The shelves collapsed and the plastic tubs within slipped to the floor, overturning and spilling their contents. I fell to my hands and knees in a mire of formaldehyde and human livers, unable to efficiently crawl through the slippery mess.

A hand grabbed my hair and dragged me upward. When I tried to regain my footing I slipped to my knees again and writhed painfully in the grasp of my attacker. I looked up.

John Doe looked down at me.

His once-mangled face showed only the faintest remnants of injury in the form of purplish scars. His pale chest bore no marks at all, save for a long, straight scar that bisected it, obviously an old wound. His jaw was no longer torn, but had twisted, along with the rest of his features, into a demonic visage with a crumpled snout and weirdly elongated jaws. Dried blood stained his long blond hair, though his skull had neatly closed. The clear, blue eye that had stared so intently at me as he lay helpless on the gurney in the E.R. was piercing and ruthless. The other, formerly empty socket held a brown eye, the white occluded with blood.

The missing eye of the morgue worker.

John Doe bared his teeth, revealing needle-sharp canines.

"Fangs," I whispered in horror. *Vampire.*

He laughed then, the sound distorted by his changed facial structure as though it had been slowed on a tape recorder.

Everything about the creature suggested the calculated fury of a predator who killed not from necessity, but from love of carnage. He stroked my cheek with one talonlike fingernail. He was a cat playing with a mouse, a thief admiring his stolen prize.

I would not be that prize. My hands groped the floor and seized a piece of broken glass, and I stabbed the shard into his thigh. His blood sprayed across my face. I tasted the coppery wetness on my lips and gagged.

Howling in rage, he wielded his free hand like a claw and slashed my neck. The burning pain followed seconds later, but I didn't care. I was free. I held one hand to my throat, desperate to stop the warm blood that flowed between my fingers. It was hopeless, and I knew it. I would bleed to death on the morgue floor before anyone found me.

Then I saw the white shoes of the code team as they entered. I raised my free hand weakly to signal them. Only one moved toward me. The rest stood petrified by the scene.

"You're going to be all right," the young nurse said as he pried my fingers from the wound at my neck.

It was the last thing I remembered.

# Two

### A Few (More) Unpleasant Surprises

I spent nearly a month in the hospital. Detectives visited me on several occasions. They took down my description of John Doe, fangs and all, but no doubt wondered what kind of pain-killers I was on. The first to arrive on the scene didn't see him. The last police interview was short, and though they assured me the case was still being investigated, I didn't hold out much hope for justice. Whatever John Doe was, he was probably smart enough to evade capture.

A few nurses from the E.R. came to see me. They looked uncomfortable and didn't stay long. We joked about the Day-After-Thanksgiving sales I'd missed and the frantic shopping I'd have to do if I got out in time for Christmas. I didn't bother mentioning I had no one to buy gifts for.

The bright side of the interminable visits were the news-paper clippings that people brought. While I wasn't about to make a scrapbook of them, the articles offered more details of the crime and investigation than the vague answers I'd been given by the cops.

According to the press, the morgue attendant, Cedric Kebbler, had been attacked and killed by an unknown suspect, possibly an escaped mental patient. I had walked in on the murder in progress and had been attacked myself. I'd struggled, and the murderer fled through the morgue's only window. I wasn't interviewed due to my "critical medical condition" and "acute anxiety and post-traumatic stress," the latter affliction diagnosed in a rush interview conducted by the staff psychiatrist while I was in a morphine-induced haze.

None of the articles mentioned John Doe's missing body or the bizarre way the attendant's body had been found. Either the police had neglected to mention these details, or the hospital had a crackerjack P.R. staff.

The most uncomfortable visit had been Dr. Fuller's. Apparently, it wasn't enough for him to have written me off as a doctor. He had to write me off as a living person, too. He'd come to the end of my bed, my chart in his hand, barely acknowledging me as he read the details. Finally, he snapped the chart shut with a deep sigh. "Doesn't look good, does it?"

He was right. In the first week after my encounter with John Doe, I'd needed two surgeries. One repaired my damaged carotid artery, and the other removed the shards of glass embedded in my skull. In the recovery room after the first surgery, I flatlined, something my doctor noted later with a breezy wave of his hand, as though his disregard for the seriousness of the situation would somehow put me at ease.

I'd also endured a delightful course of precautionary inoculations, including tetanus and rabies vaccinations. I didn't think John Doe had attacked me in a fit of hydrophobia, but no one asked my opinion on the matter, and I certainly hadn't been in a position to argue.

During my lengthy hospital stay, I began to suffer strange

symptoms. Most of them could be explained by post-traumatic stress, others as common side effects of major surgery.

The first malady to show itself was a body temperature of one hundred and four degrees. This struck the night of my heart failure and subsequent resuscitation. I was still heavily sedated, and I can't say I'm sorry to have missed it. After forty long hours the fever broke and my body temperature lowered beyond the normal range, leaving me a cool 92.7 degrees.

It wasn't until I read over my medical files that I determined this was the first indication of my change. It baffled the doctors. One doctor noted such a thing wasn't unheard of and cited evidence of low resting temperatures in coma patients. It was the equivalent of throwing his arms up in defeat, and it seemed to be the end of the matter as far as they were concerned.

The second symptom was my incredible appetite. A nasal-gastric tube fed me without disturbing the repairs made to my throat. Still, every time the pharmaceutical fog lifted, I requested food. The nurses would frown and check their chart and then explain that while I received adequate nourishment through the tube, I missed the chewing and swallowing that accompanied the act of eating. And when the tube was removed, my voracious appetite didn't show signs of decreasing. I ate astonishing amounts of food and, when I was sent home, smoked nearly a carton of cigarettes a day as though I'd been possessed by some nicotine-craving demon. Conventional wisdom held that smoking after major soft tissue repair was a bad idea, but conventional wisdom wouldn't sate the maddening hunger. The masticating emptiness that plagued me was never satisfied. And the more I consumed, the wider the void became.

The third sign didn't become apparent until I had been discharged. After weeks of being immersed in the submarine-like interior of the hospital, I expected natural light to irritate me. But nothing could have prepared me for the searing pain that burned my skin when I stepped, blinking and disoriented, into the blazing white sunlight.

Though it was mid-December, I felt as if I'd been tossed into an oven. My fever might have returned, but I wasn't about to spend another night in a hospital bed. I took a cab home, shut the blinds and obsessively checked my temperature every fifteen minutes. Ninety, then eighty-nine, and it kept falling. When I realized my temperature matched the one displayed on the thermostat in the living room, I decided I'd lost my mind.

Whether it was a subconscious need to protect myself from further shock or a conscious decision to suppress the reality of my situation, I refused to acknowledge how odd these things seemed. It became necessary to wear sunglasses during the daylight hours, inside or out. My apartment turned into a cave. The shades were closed at all times. I stumbled around in the darkness at first, but I eventually adapted to it. After a few days, I could easily read by the flickering blue light of the television.

When I returned to my duties at the hospital, my strange habits did not go unnoticed. Because of my sudden light sensitivity, I requested night shifts. But focusing on anything amid all the beeping monitors and endless intercom pages proved impossible.

But too many things defied explanation, too many questions science couldn't answer. I wasn't sure I wanted the most obvious explanation, either.

I couldn't hold out forever, though. It would only be a matter of time before I exhausted the knowledge available in medical journals and textbooks. Eventually, I came to accept the conclusion I'd dreaded.

I paced in front of my computer for a full hour. What was I thinking? Grown people didn't believe in the things that went bump in the night. Maybe I really did need the psychologist my doctor recommended.

As a child, I'd never been allowed the luxury of watching *Dark Shadows* reruns, and any reading I'd done was strictly of an academic nature. Flights of fancy were discouraged in our household. My Jungian-analyst father considered them a warning sign of an underdeveloped animus and they were a red flag to my career-feminist mother who taught these things would lead me to become another foot soldier in the unicorn-lover's army. I sat down and fired up the modem. If they were looking down on me from the heaven they'd insisted couldn't logically exist, I'm sure they shook their heads in disappointment.

In a bizarre way, it was their fault I had the courage to explore the possibility that I was a vampire. Occam's razor was a theory my father constantly spouted around the house. God forbid an expensive item in our museum of a home ever be broken or misplaced. I'd always lie and say I wasn't there, it was a statistical anomaly. Whenever I did this, my father would fix me with his best stare of paternal disapproval and quote, "One should not increase, beyond what is necessary, the number of entities required to explain anything."

In other words, if it looked like a duck, et cetera, I probably broke that lamp. Or, in the current case, if it looked like I'd become a vampire…

"Thanks, Dad," I muttered as I lit another cigarette. I'd accepted the fact they did nothing for me physically, but the routine soothed my jagged nerves. I typed *vampire* into a search engine and held my breath.

Marginally more reliable than tea leaves or a magic eight ball, the Web offered possibility and anonymity, two crucial components to my quest for knowledge. Still, I felt a little silly as I clicked the first link.

The number of people interested in—and even claiming to be—vampires astounded me, but the amount of information their Web sites offered was negligible. I found one promising lead, a professional-looking site with an area to post messages. Figuring it was as good a place to start as any, I began to explain my predicament to the dispassionate white text area.

I'd never been good at expressing myself with the written word, and I felt sillier with each one I wrote. After several frustrated drafts, I gave up and shortened my entry to two fragmented sentences.

"Attacked by vampire. Please advise."

I didn't have to wait long for a reply. Before I could get up for a bathroom break, my e-mail program chimed.

The first response informed me I was a psycho. The second suggested I might be watching too many late-night movies. Another tried to lovingly counsel me away from my obviously abusive relationship. For people who were supposed to believe in vampires, they sure didn't seem very open to the possibility one might actually exist.

I began deleting responses as they rolled in, until one subject line caught my eye.

*1320 Wealthy Ave.*

I recognized the street. It wasn't far from where I lived. Just outside of downtown, it was a street where the college students spent money from home on Georgia O'Keeffe prints in poster stores next to bodegas where migrant families bought their meager groceries. I'd driven through the neighborhood, but I'd never stopped.

The content of the e-mail was simply this: *after sundown, any night this week.*

The digital clock in the corner of the computer screen's display read 5:00 p.m. After sundown.

I didn't have to go to work for six more hours.

I only had to get in my car and drive.

But it seemed a dicey proposition. Curiosity had nearly killed this cat already. The sender could be a deranged groupie or vampire fanatic. Sure, he or she might be perfectly harmless and just having a bit of fun, but I didn't relish the thought of spending another month in the hospital.

How could I go to an unknown address at the advice of an anonymous e-mail? Well, it wasn't exactly anonymous. *Zigmeister69@usmail.com* wasn't exactly the most common e-mail address I'd ever seen. I logged on to usmail.com in hopes of finding a user profile, a Web page, something to give me a line on who had sent the message to me. I came up with nothing.

That sparked another, more terrifying proposition. What if the sender was John Doe himself, quietly monitoring my activities? Though it seemed a long shot that the creature of my nightmares would give himself such a ridiculous online moniker, I didn't exactly know what he was. He could have been cleverly crafting a trap for me, finding out where I lived, how to contact me and lull me into a false sense of security.

"Fuck it." I vigorously stubbed out my cigarette in the ashtray beside the keyboard before entering the address into the search engine.

*The Crypt: Occult Books and Supplies.*

There was a phone number and driving directions.

Nothing could happen to me in a public place, in a busy neighborhood. I used that line of reasoning as I grabbed my keys and headed out the door.

Though it was an hour after sunset, the sky was still bright enough to make my skin feel tight and itchy. I wore a baseball cap as a disguise. If John Doe was waiting when I got there, I wanted to see him before he spotted me. I popped a painkiller and one of the pills prescribed for my light sensitivity, then wrapped up in my wool trench coat to guard against the December cold.

The 1300 block was only about five miles from my home. It was in the middle of three crisscrossed streets and housed a cluster of eclectic storefronts and trendy restaurants. There were women in broomstick skirts and crocheted coats scurrying through the snow next to men in Rastafarian hats and corduroy pants. Most of the footprints on the sidewalk were made by Doc Martens.

I found a place to park in front of a crowded coffeehouse. With my jeans, cap and ponytail, I felt rather conspicuous. I stepped onto the sidewalk and tried to ignore the stares of the ultrahip art majors huddled behind the steamy windows. I must have looked like a mascot for the capitalist culture they all gathered to complain about.

It proved difficult to find 1320 Wealthy. I passed it several times before I spotted it. A vintage clothing store and a corner grocery, 1318 and 1322 respectively, jutted up against each other with nothing but a sandwich-board sign between them. Had I been patient enough to read the sign in the first place, I would have saved myself much frustration. "The Crypt: Occult Books and Supplies, 1320 Wealthy," the silver lettering fairly shouted at me from the sign's black background. A large red arrow pointed to a staircase that descended below the sidewalk in front of the clothing store.

I peered down the dubious-looking hole. The steps were wet but not icy. I took a deep breath and started down.

The door at the bottom of the stairs was old and wooden, with a window in the top half that bore the name of the shop in gold paint. Bells jingled when I entered.

The sights and smells of the place immediately overwhelmed me. Incense burned, a particularly noxious scent, and the air of the place was hazy with it. New Age music played softly, some peaceful Celtic harp composition punctuated with birdsong. I didn't know if it was the smoke or the flaky music that made me gag.

The shop wasn't horribly bright, but enough candles were lit to cast flickering shadows along the rows and rows of bookshelves.

I covered my nose with my sleeve to avoid the heavy smell of incense that rapidly formed a metallic taste in my mouth. I looked toward the sales counter.

The shop seemed empty. "Hello?"

I heard the heavy thunk of the door scraping shut. When I turned toward the sound, something struck me hard in the chest. Lifted off my feet, I landed flat on my back on the unfinished wooden floor.

Muscles all over my body that still weren't used to movement after such a long recuperation screamed in agony, but an instinct completely foreign to me forced me to move. I quickly rolled to my side just as an axe blade splintered the floor right where my head had been.

With strength I hadn't realized I possessed, I arched my back and pushed off the floor with the palms of my hands, springing to my feet in a move like something out of an action movie. Only then did I come face-to-face with my attacker.

If I had to guess, I would have placed him at about fifteen years old. But the tattoo on the back of his hand and his multiple ear and eyebrow piercings told me he must have been at least eighteen. His long, greasy-looking hair was shaved into a thin strip down the middle of his head, and despite the temperature in the shop, he wore a heavy overcoat.

I held my hands up to show I meant no harm, but he swung the axe again, this time breaking the glass display window of the counter. "Die, vampire scum!"

Like any sensible person would, I ran. Though he was fast on his feet, I managed to get past the baby-faced psycho and gained the door just as it swung open. I couldn't raise my hands in time to protect myself. The heavy wood door smashed into my face and knocked me off balance. I hit the floor again in time to see the axe sail through the space I'd just inhabited.

"Nate, look—"

Two thoughts went through my mind when I saw the man who'd stepped through the door. The first was *holy crap.* He'd stopped the axe that was just centimeters from striking his very broad chest, catching the blade between his palms before the juvenile delinquent who'd thrown it could finish his shouted warning. My second thought was also *holy crap.*

The man was sex walking. Wide shoulders, flat stomach, wavy, dark hair… I suddenly realized the appeal of those firefighter calendars that the nurses ogled in the coffee room.

"I'm so, so sorry," he said to me.

I took the hand he offered, nervous electricity zinging up my arm at his touch, and got to my feet. I almost said "It's all right," before I realized it definitely was not. My hands shook as I reached for the door.

"What the hell were you thinking, Ziggy?" he raged at the younger man before turning back to me. "Are you hurt, do you need anything? An ambulance?"

He put his hand on my shoulder, and I shrugged it off angrily. "Do most customers leave in an ambulance?"

Ziggy pointed his finger accusingly at me. "She's a fucking vampire, man! Don't let her out of here!"

With a ferocity that startled me, the man yelled at the boy. "Get her a compress for her head!"

Ziggy sputtered in disbelief. "Maybe I should get her a cup of my nice warm blood, too? Sprinkle some marshmallows in it?"

"Upstairs, now!"

The kid pushed past us as he mumbled furiously under his breath, slamming the door behind him so hard the glass in the window rattled.

"I don't think he's coming back with the compress," I observed dryly.

"No, I don't, either." The man laughed quietly, holding out his hand. "I'm Nathan Grant."

"Carrie Ames."

*Get out of here, you moron,* my brain screamed. *He's still got the damn axe!* Yet my feet stayed rooted to the spot, completely under the control of the morbid curiosity that had brought me this far and the ruthless attraction that urged me to stay as close to this man as possible.

Nathan cocked his head and regarded me with sparkling gray eyes. Clearing his throat, he leaned the axe against the doorpost and crossed his arms over his chest. "Ames. You're the doctor from the newspaper?"

His voice was deep and seductively masculine, his words pronounced with a distinctly Scottish accent. I had a hard time concentrating on his question, distracted as I was by his perfect mouth. "Uh…yeah. That would be me."

He smiled, but it wasn't the friendliest expression I'd ever seen. It reminded me of the way the dentist looks right before he says you have to come back for a root canal. "Then we've got a lot to talk about, Doctor. I apologize for Ziggy. He's got it in his head that he's a vampire hunter. How'd he find you?"

"Find me?" *Zigmeister69.* I'd been set up. "E-mail."

Nathan chuckled. "Figures. Nightblood.com?"

I coughed deliberately to hide my answer. "Yes."

He shook his head. "Rule number one, don't go public."

"Rule number what? What are you talking about?"

As if he had all the time in the world to explain himself, he turned away. He stepped behind the counter and pressed a button on the CD player, cutting off the annoyingly soothing New Age droning.

"What are you talking about?" I demanded, tagging after him as he walked through the shop and snuffed the candles. "Would you stop and talk to me?"

He sighed and dropped his head, bracing his arms on a table that looked far too dainty to support his weight.

"The rules you have to follow. The rules every vampire has to follow."

My hand was on the door before I realized I'd intended to run.

"Wait!" he called after me. He caught my arm and gently turned me around to face him just as my hand found the lock. "If you run out of here, this will only end badly."

His grip on the sleeve of my coat unnerved me, as did the tension in his voice. My words sounded thick and strange as I spoke. "Is that a threat?"

"Listen," he began, some of the urgency of his tone gone now. "I know you have some questions. Otherwise you wouldn't have run into Ziggy."

"Yeah, I have questions." I spat the words in my anger. "Who the hell are you? Why did I get attacked when I walked through that door? And what the hell makes you think I'm a vampire?"

I yanked open the shop door and stepped into the pitiless cold, fishing in my pocket for my half-empty pack of cigarettes.

He followed me to the threshold and let me get halfway up the steps before he spoke again. I was struggling with my lighter when he called after me.

"What makes *you* think you're a vampire? That's why you were trolling the vampire message boards, right? That's where Ziggy found you. It's his M.O." He moved up the stairs with a grace I'd thought reserved for animals and put his hand over mine. His skin was ice cold. "No matter how many you smoke, you'll never feel satisfied. The food you eat no longer fills you up, and you can't understand why."

The cigarette suddenly looked ridiculous where it rested between my fingers. I trembled, and not entirely due to the cold.

Nathan spoke again, but he sounded disconnected and far away.

"Come upstairs," he said. "I'll try to explain."

I took a few more steps and tried to convince myself to keep walking, to get in my car and never come back, to avoid this side of town altogether. If I never saw this place again, I could pretend none of this had ever happened. There was always the hope that I'd never actually woken from surgery, and that I lingered in a coma in the ICU. As much as I wanted that to be true, I knew it wasn't. I dropped the cigarette and watched it roll to the next step. "No chance I'm dreaming here, huh?"

"No," he said quietly. "We can, uh, tell our own kind."

I looked up sharply. The blood drained from my face, and I could tell by the way his expression softened that my fear was visible. "You're a—"

"Vampire, yes," he finished for me when my voice trailed off.

"Well, that settles it," I said, feeling oddly relieved despite the fact I stood in a dark stairwell with a guy who claimed to be a vampire. "I'm crazy."

"You're not crazy. We all go through this, when we change." He looked up nervously as a pair of feet shuffled across the snowy sidewalk above us. "But this really isn't the place to discuss this. Why don't you come up to my apartment and we can talk."

"No—thanks though," I said, unable to help my laughter. "It was really nice meeting you, Mr. Vampire, but I've got to go. I have to work tonight, and I just might be able to get a call in to my psychologist first. With any luck, he'll give me a nice, fat prescription for some antipsychotics so I can get back to my normal life."

I turned away, but Nathan caught my arm. Faster than I could think to scream, I was pinned between his hard body and the harder brick wall. His hand clamped firmly over my mouth, muffling my terrified cry.

"I didn't want to have to do this," he said through gritted teeth. Then he dipped his head, and his body went rigid against mine.

When he moved his head back up, my heart stopped. The chiseled, handsome planes of his face were twisted, the skin stretched tight over a sharp, bony snout. Long fangs glinted in the dim light. He looked the way John Doe had, just before he'd ripped my throat open like a birthday present.

Only his eyes held a glimmer of control. Until the day I die, I will remember Nathan's eyes, so clear and gray and heartbreakingly honest behind that horrific mask.

"Now do you see?" he asked.

My heart pounding, I nodded. He pulled away and covered his face with his hands. When he looked up again, his normal features had returned into an expression of kindness and compassion. It disturbed me more than when he'd been a monster.

"Come on. Let's go inside and I'll tell you anything you want to know."

Numb with cold and fear and hopelessness, I let him guide me up the steps to the sidewalk. "Anything?"

"Sure," he promised, pulling a set of keys from his pocket.

"Okay." I swallowed the lump in my throat. "Why me?"

# Three

### The Movement

Nathan's apartment was small, with too much furniture. The walls were lined with bracketed shelves, the kind you'd buy in a home-improvement store and put up on a weekend. Some were so laden with books that they bowed in the middle. Notebooks and legal pads, all scribbled on in barely legible handwriting, littered the coffee table. It was cluttered but not dirty.

"Excuse our mess," he said with an apologetic smile. His gaze flitted to the hall. A Marilyn Manson song blasted at full volume behind one of the closed doors. "Turn it down, Ziggy!"

The music dropped a few decibels. Nathan and I stood awkwardly by the door for a moment. I suspected he was as uncomfortable as I was.

"Kids," I said with a shrug, looking in the direction of what I assumed was Ziggy's room.

"Let me take your coat."

I watched Nathan's face as he helped me out of the garment. He looked awfully young, in my opinion, to have a son

Ziggy's age. But then, for all I knew, Nathan could be hundreds of years old.

After he'd hung my coat on a hook by the door, he seemed to suddenly animate. "Have you fed?" He started for the kitchen and motioned for me to follow. "I've got some A pos."

I lingered in the doorway and watched as he retrieved a plastic collection bag of blood from his refrigerator. Then he lifted a teakettle from the dish rack next to the sink and ripped the top of the bag with his teeth as though he were opening a bag of chips. Snapping on the burner of the gas stove, he emptied the blood into the teakettle and set it over the flame.

The process seemed so natural that I had to remind myself normal men didn't keep blood in their refrigerators. Of course, most normal men didn't own teakettles, either.

"You're not going to drink that, are you?" Med school warnings of blood-borne pathogens flashed through my mind.

Though he didn't look at me, I saw amusement on his face. "Yeah, you want some?"

"No!" My stomach constricted. "Do you know how dangerous that is?"

"Do you know how dangerous I am if I don't drink it?" He leaned against the counter and wiped his hands on a kitchen towel. For the first time, I noticed how truly tall he was.

According to my driver's license, I stood five foot eight, and though my hospital stay had stripped some pounds from my frame, I was no wilting flower of a woman. Still, Nathan looked like he could easily rip me into pieces with his bare hands if he got the inclination.

But his voice held a note of sadness. His eyes met mine briefly, but before I could understand the pained look in them, he turned away.

"I'm sorry. You haven't had anyone explain all this to you. Blood-drinking is just one of the realities of being a vampire. You've got to do it sometime, and there's no time like the present." His voice was hoarse. "Besides, if you hold out too long, you'll snap and do something…regrettable."

"I'll take my chances." The kettle had begun to give off a warm, metallic smell. To my horror, my stomach actually rumbled. "So, am I going to live forever?"

"Why is that the first thing everyone asks?" he mused. "No, you probably won't live forever."

"*Probably?* That doesn't sound reassuring."

"Wasn't meant to." He tossed the towel over his shoulder. "We're not susceptible to the ravages of time or disease, and we have a healing ability that increases with age. But the list of things that can kill us is a mile long. Sunlight, holy water, hell, even a bad-enough car accident can take us out."

He poured some blood into a chipped ceramic mug and motioned toward the dinette table. "If you don't want this, can I get you something else?"

"No, thanks." I sat in the chair he pulled out for me. "Do you keep human food in here?"

"Yeah," he said as he sat across from me. "I like it every now and then. I just can't live off it. And Ziggy needs to eat."

I frowned. Ziggy had clearly lured me to the shop in order to kill me. It didn't make a lot of sense, considering he lived with a vampire himself.

"Um…does your son know you're a vampire?"

"My son?" Nathan looked confused for a moment, then he laughed, a deep, rich sound that warmed me. "Ziggy's not my son. But I can see where you'd get that impression. He's a…he's a friend."

A friend? I was hip. I could read between the lines. It figured that the first decent guy I'd met in this city was gay. "He's a little young for you, don't you think?"

An embarrassed smile curved Nathan's lips. "I'm not a homosexual, Carrie. Ziggy's my blood donor. I watch out for him, that's all."

That was the first time he'd used my name instead of addressing me as Doctor or Miss Ames. In his thick accent—I was fairly certain he was Scottish—my generic, first-pick-from-the-baby-name-book moniker sounded exotic and almost sensual. I wondered if he could sense the attraction I felt, the heat coursing through my blood.

If he did, he had the courtesy not to comment on it. I was grateful for that. "So why did he try to kill me? I mean, if you're a vampire, and he knows it and gives you his blood and everything, what's his beef with me?"

Nathan sipped from his mug. "It's complicated."

I glanced at the clock on the wall. "I've got a few hours."

He seemed to consider his response for a moment. Setting his cup aside, he braced his elbows on the table and covered his face with his hands. "Listen, you seem like a real nice girl, but there's something I have to ask you, and it's a little personal."

Despite the ominous tone of the question, I nodded. At this point, I wanted answers. I'd fill out a complete medical history if he asked. "Shoot."

"I followed your story in the papers very closely and I have some concerns. Namely, why you were in the morgue that night." When his eyes met mine, I saw the real question there.

"You think I did this on purpose?"

He shrugged, all compassion and friendliness gone from his face. "You tell me."

I had spent the past month in a haze of depression, deprived of normal life by a mysterious illness I couldn't shake. My bones ached twenty-four hours a day. My head throbbed at the faintest glimmer of light. If I was indeed a vampire, I certainly wasn't living out the posh existence of a Count Dracula or a Lestat de Lioncourt. I was in a living hell, certainly not by choice.

"Please," he said quietly. "I need to know."

I could have slapped him. "No! What kind of freak do you think I am?"

He shrugged. "There are some people out there, sick people, who want to escape their lives. Maybe they've had some sort of trauma, an illness, the loss of a loved one." He looked me dead in the eyes. "The loss of your parents."

"How do you know about my parents?" I asked through tightly clenched teeth. I hadn't spoken about them since the car accident that had killed them. They'd been on their way to visit me at college. Guilt had kept me from opening up about them. No one, save my distant, remaining relatives in Oregon—many of whom I'd met for the first time at the funeral—knew anything about them or the circumstances of their death.

"I have connections," he said, as if we were discussing how he'd obtained courtside Lakers' tickets instead of how he'd invaded my privacy. He actually had the nerve to reach across the table and take my hand. "I know what it's like to lose someone. Believe me. I can see why you'd want—"

"I didn't want this!"

I hadn't meant to scream, but it felt good. I wanted to do it again. The ugliness and horror of the past month seemed to swell inside me, pushing me beyond the limits of my self-control.

"Carrie, please—" he tried again, but I ignored him.

My knees bumped the table as I stood, and Nathan's mug toppled over, splashing warm blood across the tabletop. The sight held a sick fascination for me, and in a flash I saw a clear image of myself leaning over and licking it up. I shook my head to destroy the vision. "I didn't want this!"

Jerking the collar of my sweatshirt aside, I jabbed a finger at the barely healed scar on my neck. "Do you think someone would ask for this? Do you think I went down to that morgue and said 'Hey, John Doe, why don't you rip my fucking neck open? Why don't you turn my life to absolute shit?'"

The volume of the music from Ziggy's room drastically lowered. *Good. Let him hear.*

"Do you think I wanted to sit here and watch some guy I've never met fucking drink blood? I just want my life back!"

No, what I wanted was to scream until my throat was raw. I wanted to stamp my feet and throw things. I wanted to be empty of these feelings of despair and frustration.

Instead, I cried. My legs buckled and I slid to the floor. When Nathan knelt beside me and put his arms out to comfort me, I pushed him away. When he tried again, I didn't fight him.

I couldn't control my sobs as I cried into his firm chest. His wool sweater pricked my cheek. He smelled good, distinctly male and slightly soapy, as if he'd just gotten out of the shower. So what if he was a complete stranger? I'd never been able to cry and let someone comfort me like this before.

"I know you didn't," he said softly.

"Do you?" I demanded, looking up at him. "Because you were sure acting like the vampire police or something."

He gently took my face in his hands to force my gaze to his. "I know because the same thing happened to me. At the hands of your John Doe."

His words seemed to magically patch the dam that had broken within me. My chest no longer heaved with sobs, and my tears miraculously dried.

Nathan helped me to my feet. I took advantage of the moment, resting against him as long as I could without seeming weird. I pressed my hand just below his rib cage in the guise of steadying myself and felt the solid ridges of a perfect stomach beneath the wool.

He picked up my chair—a casualty of my sudden rage— and helped me sit. Then he got me a glass of water and began cleaning up the spilled blood.

The silence between us was stifling, but my questions overwhelmed me. I started with the obvious. "How did it happen?"

Nathan stood at the sink, rinsing the blood from the kitchen towel. "He took some of your blood, you took some of his. Then you died. That's the way it happens."

"No," I began. I'd meant to ask how he'd been made a vampire, if John Doe had attacked him without provocation, as he had me. Instead, I focused on his statement. "I didn't drink his blood. I don't think he drank mine."

"Did his blood get in your mouth? In your wounds?" He leaned against the counter. "All it takes is one drop. It's like a virus, or a cancer. It can lie dormant for decades, waiting for the heart to stop beating. Then it corrupts your cells."

"Yeah, but I didn't die. They got me to surgery to stop the bleeding—" But that wasn't exactly true. "Oh, God. I went into v-tac, in the recovery room. I flatlined."

"That's when it happened." He pointed to the living room. "Let's go in here. We'll be more comfortable."

I sat on the couch while he went to the bookshelves lining the wall. He pulled a volume down and handed it to me. "This should answer some questions."

The book, bound in burgundy-colored leather, had gilt-edged pages and seemed incredibly aged. The cover was bare, save for small gold lettering stamped in the lower right-hand corner. *"The Sanguinarius,"* I murmured, running my fingertips across the letters. I recognized the root word, Latin for blood. I opened it, but the usual publishing information wasn't printed. The title page lent the only clue to the age of the book.

*The Sanguinarius,* it read in large print. Beneath that, in smaller type, *A Practical Guide to the Habits of Vampyres.* The font was uneven, as though the pages had been printed on an ancient press. The book must have been at least two hundred years old.

I flipped a few pages. "A vampire handbook?"

"Not exactly. More like a training manual for vampire hunters."

No sooner than he'd finished his sentence, I came across a graphic woodcut of a man sinking a pitchfork into the round stomach of a raging she-demon.

"Oh." I slammed the book shut.

"Roughly translated, the title means 'The Ones Who Thirst for Blood.'" He smiled. "This is complicated. I'll start from the beginning."

I nodded in agreement, though it didn't seem I had a choice. He sat beside me, a little closer than I'd expected. Not that I was complaining.

"For more than two hundred years, there has existed a group of vampires dedicated to the extinction of their own kind for the preservation of humanity. In the past they were known as the Order of the Blood Brethren. Today, they are known as the Voluntary Vampire Extinction Movement.

"There were fourteen clauses under the Order. But the

Movement enforces only three. No vampire shall feed from any unwilling human. No vampire shall create another vampire. And no vampire shall harm or kill a human."

"Those don't sound like such bad rules," I observed.

"Vampires today have it easy compared to the old days." He sounded nostalgic. "The Movement headquarters are in Spain in some refurbished Inquisition dungeons, but Movement members are spread all over the world. I'm the only member on this side of the state, but there are assassins in Detroit and Chicago. The Movement has a fleet of private jets, in case a member needs to travel abroad. Otherwise, it would be pretty hard to get around."

"So, I take it they're not a nonprofit organization if they can afford jets."

That brought a small smile to Nathan's face. "Most of the Movement funding comes from generous benefactors, very old vampires who've had centuries to amass their fortunes. The Movement has been around a long time, and those donations add up. Plus, I believe they dabble in real estate on the side."

"I've always said my landlord was a monster, but I never thought it might be true." I tried to hand back the book. "Okay, no eating people, making other vampires, or murder. I've been able to follow those rules great up till now, and I don't foresee any problems in the near future."

"Good," he said, pushing *The Sanguinarius* toward me again. "Because if you do, the penalty is steep."

"How steep?" I tried to sound unconcerned.

"Death. Cyrus, the vampire who sired you—"

I snorted. "Cyrus? Is that his real name?"

Nathan looked mildly annoyed at the interruption. "Cyrus has been on the run from the Movement in America for more than thirty years, longer in other parts of the world. The injuries that brought him to your emergency room were incurred during an attempted execution."

I sobered as I remembered John Doe's horrific injuries, and my mouth felt dry. "Which of the rules did he break?"

"All of them. Long before he attacked you. We just haven't been able to finish him off."

"No one deserves that." I tried to force the image of John Doe's maimed body from my mind. "If you'd seen him, what they did to him…"

"I did see him," Nathan said matter-of-factly. "I was the one sent to execute him."

*"You?"* The wounds in John Doe's chest. The missing eye. The splintered, destroyed bones of his face. The man sitting beside me had done it all. "How?"

"I started with a stake to the heart, and when that didn't work, I thought I'd chop him into little pieces and bury him in consecrated earth, but he got in some good hits. I'm lucky to be sitting here right now. Someone must have seen us fighting, because the police showed up. The rest—"

"Is history," I whispered.

Nathan shifted uncomfortably beside me. "Not really. He's still out there. That's why Ziggy's been on the prowl for vampires. We know Cyrus is in town, and he's the only outlaw vampire in the area. I keep an eye out for any new fledglings that pop up. I find them, kill them and report back to the Movement." He stretched his legs to get comfortable. "They give me six hundred dollars a head. Figuratively, of course. I don't have to bring them actual heads."

I had to remind myself he was talking about ending people's lives, despite the casual way he mentioned it. "You kill them? Why?"

He looked at me as if I had antennae growing out of my head. "Because they're vampires."

"So are you!"

"Yes, but I'm a *good* vampire," he explained patiently. "Good vampires get to live, bad vampires get a one-way ticket to wherever it is we go when we die. It's not rocket science."

I shot to my feet. "Did you ever think maybe some of them might be good vampires? I mean, do you even check first or do you just go all kill-happy on them?"

"I give them a chance to change my mind but they all turn out the same way. It's just not possible for them to be good vampires," he insisted.

"And why not?"

"Because they weren't made by good vampires." Releasing a huge sigh, Nathan picked up *The Sanguinarius*. "Every fledgling I've encountered so far has gone the way of their sire. The blood tie is incredibly strong, which makes it nearly impossible for a new vampire to fight the will of the blood in his veins, the will of his sire. The book will explain it a lot better than I can."

"Well, I'm here now, so why don't you give it a shot?" I arched a threatening brow and put my hands on my hips to show I wasn't moving until he answered my question.

"You're a very aggravating person, you know that?" He set the book on the table. "The Movement doesn't want any new vampires made. We're trying to whittle our species down to nothing. Hence the extinction part of the Voluntary Vampire Extinction Movement. Some vampires aren't so into the idea. So they start creating new vampires.

"When a vampire exchanges blood with a human to create another vampire, their blood stays in the new vampire's veins. Forever. It builds something called a blood tie. For the sire, it's a way of controlling their fledgling, like an invisible leash. The tie weakens as time goes by, but the fledgling and sire will still feel each other's emotions, physical pain and hunger. The fledgling will always be ruled by the sire's blood, and most of them don't want to change. It lasts after death. Even if the sire dies, he can still wreak havoc on the world through his fledglings. The fledgling, forever influenced by his or her sire's blood and whatever bent morals were handed down to them, could go out and keep making new vampires. Pretty soon, it's goodbye human race. The way the Movement sees it, the only way to keep somebody like Cyrus from making his own vampire army and taking over the world is to kill his progeny. It's not fair, but that's the way it is."

I swallowed. "You sound like you're pretty hard-core about the Movement."

"I have to be. When I was turned, I swore my allegiance to them in order to keep my life." He stood and advanced on me, though for what purpose I couldn't tell.

"It sounds like these Movement guys hold a lot of sway. How do you know they've really got your best interests at heart?" I was tempted to take a step back, but I held my ground. I was not going to let him intimidate me. Not after all I'd been through. If he wanted to kill me, he'd have to…well, he'd have to go through the new me first.

He didn't answer my question, but he didn't try to grab me or shove a stake through my heart, either. He pushed my hair aside and gently touched the scar Cyrus had left. "He really got you."

A chill raced up my spine at his touch. I leaned into his hand. I couldn't help myself.

Something changed in his eyes, as if an iron gate were

slamming shut. He dropped his arm and turned away. "You're going to have to make a choice, too. Whether you want to pledge your life to the Movement, or lose it."

I snorted. "Where do I sign in blood?"

"This isn't a joke." He turned to face me, and I saw from his irritated countenance that it certainly was not. "I can't guarantee the Movement will even accept you, but it's your only shot at surviving. Your sire's death sentence extends to you."

My heart pounded and my legs tensed in anticipation of running. I took a step back. "You'd really kill me, wouldn't you?"

"Yes." He looked away, then sank onto the couch. "It's nothing personal. But I don't know you well enough to tell whether you're going to play loyal fledgling to Cyrus or not. You seem like a nice girl, but I'm not willing to take that chance."

"Nothing personal." I laughed bitterly in disbelief. "You know, it *is* personal. When I get lured into a trap and almost get decapitated, it's personal. When some guy I just met tells me he's going to kill me, it's personal. Because it's my life. You're out of your mind if you think I'm going down without a fight."

The corner of his mouth twitched and I thought he was going to laugh. I would have punched him in the face if he did.

Good thing he didn't. "I can respect that. But it doesn't change my position. You need to make a decision. Ask the Movement for mercy and hope they grant it to you. You won't get it from me."

"Why not just kill me now?" I asked, hoping he wouldn't take this as an invitation.

He merely shrugged and said, "Because without a kill order, I don't get paid."

"A kill order?" How much more like a bad horror movie could this possibly get?

"If you decide not to ask the Movement for membership, I'll report you. You'll be processed in their system and a kill order will be issued a few days later." He shrugged again, as if he couldn't care less about the conversation. "I suppose you could make a run for it, but until I have that order in my hand, I'm not going to do anything to you. I don't work for free."

I was about to argue that he could just kill me, then report me. Luckily, the common sense which seemed to have deserted me in the past few weeks found its way back, and I held my tongue. "How very Han Solo of you."

He didn't smile or laugh. In fact, he looked even more grave than before. "It's up to you. Petition for membership or die. I can get them on the phone right now."

"Fine." I ground my teeth over the words. "Can I make an informed decision at least?"

He frowned and cocked his head, studying me from the corner of his eye, as if this were a trick. "What do you propose?"

I chose my words carefully. "Give me a chance to read *The Sanguinarius* and have some time to let all this sink in. I didn't believe in vampires or monsters before tonight, and I'm in what we in the medical field call 'a state of shock.' It's only fair to know what I'm getting into. Besides, I'm a smart girl. I'm not going to join up with some organization just because you claim they're the good guys."

"They are the good guys." There was no amusement in his tone, just absolute conviction in the truth of his words.

I rolled my eyes. "Yeah, well that's what the Nazis said about themselves."

He slowly rose to his feet. Power, dark and barely leashed, emanated from him. And that, combined with his physical presence, made him more terrifying than John Doe had been as he'd sunk his claws into me.

Of course, John Doe hadn't been this hot. Somehow, my physical attraction to Nathan made him seem more dangerous.

But he didn't attack me. He just invaded my personal space and shattered my comfort zone. He leaned down so our noses practically touched. "How do I know you're not stalling so you can get back to Cyrus and gain his protection?"

"Because until you mentioned it, the thought hadn't crossed my mind." I don't know if he expected me to cower or cry or melt into his arms, but I could tell by the pronounced blink of his eyes that I'd surprised him. "Give me a couple of weeks. You can even check in on me. I'll give you an answer at the end."

"Or you'll run screaming." He tried again to frighten me, but I was confident he wouldn't kill me tonight. Something in the way he raked his eyes over my body, like he did now, raw and hungry, told me he had something of a soft spot for women. Or a hard spot, depending on how you looked at it.

A deliberately slow smile played across my lips. "Do I look like the kind of girl who runs away from trouble?"

He folded his arms across his chest. "You ran away from Ziggy."

*Touché.* "Yeah, but Ziggy had an axe. Are you going to kill me with your bare hands?"

He grinned. "I'm good with my hands."

*Holy hormones, Batman.*

The door to Ziggy's room burst open, and Nathan instantly stepped away. The teen stalked angrily into the kitchen, middle finger raised toward Nathan as he passed.

"I know, I know, I've got an early class, I should get my

rest," the boy called. "Psych 101, I so need to be awake for that. I'm just making a sandwich before bed."

"Bed?" I asked stupidly, checking my watch. Ten after ten. "I have to go."

Nathan followed me to the door. "Have you thought of what you'll do should Cyrus come looking for you?"

I hadn't. "I'll tell him to go away, that I gave at the office," I said, my uneasiness at the prospect betrayed by my forced laugh.

I couldn't stand the thought that I shared a plasma-level connection with the monster who'd attacked me. It was bad enough he'd invaded my nightmares. His blood had become part of me, too.

Nathan studied my face for a moment, and I stared back, unable to discern a single emotion. He'd probably practiced hiding his feelings for so long that even he couldn't find them. He looked away and handed me my coat. "If you need anything, you have my number. And this," he said. He held out *The Sanguinarius.*

I took the book in one hand and awkwardly tried to slip into my coat with the other. He moved behind me to help, and it took all my self-control to keep from leaning against him. What could I say? It had been a long time since I'd engaged in threatening, pseudo-sexual banter with anyone.

"Thanks," I said quietly, putting my hand on the doorknob.

"One more thing," Nathan said. "If you need blood, please come to me. I always have some to spare. Just don't go outside afterward. In the daytime, I mean. In fact, you should probably start avoiding it entirely. I'm sure after a while, even if you hold out from feeding, the change will complete itself on its own. I'm always here, if you need...help."

"Thanks, but I don't have any desire to drink blood."

"You'll feel it soon," Nathan warned as I descended the stairs.

"Feel what?" I was more concerned by the prospect of the snow on the ground outside than his ominous tone.

"The hunger. You'll feel the hunger."

# Four

### When Carrie Met Dahlia

I didn't give Nathan's warning much thought until the night the hunger came over me.

I'd spent the week doing my best to live life as though nothing had changed. Faced with what might be the last fourteen days of life before submitting myself to the Movement's judgment, I was going to savor them.

Of course, I read *The Sanguinarius*. It was as dry and Victorian as *Lord of the Rings*. I reminded myself that the course of my existence was dependent upon finishing *this* particular book.

Nathan called to check in on me every night. I cursed myself for having a listed number. Sometimes his call came after I'd gone to work, and soon I found myself actually looking forward to the end of my shift so I could hear his voice on my answering machine. But by the end of the week, my spare thoughts—no, my every thought—had turned to blood.

To get through my night shifts at the hospital, I snacked constantly. Coffee, pizza, popcorn, anything with a substantial aroma that covered the smell of blood. A few nurses made envious remarks about my ability to eat so much and never gain weight. I barely heard them. The obnoxious thumping of their pulses was all I could hear.

Blood became an all-consuming distraction. I took numerous, drastic measures to ensure the safety of everyone around me. On my frequent breaks, I locked myself in the staff bathroom and used a razor blade to make small, shallow cuts on the inside of my arm. Then I licked away the blood that welled up. It did little to slake my thirst, but the resultant marks piqued the interest of the psychiatry resident. I spent a great deal of time avoiding him and his softly spoken invitations to talk about my "recovery."

Despite my hunger, I couldn't stomach the thought of drinking human blood. Once or twice, in desperation, I'd snuck a vial drawn from a patient and brought it home with me. But the threat of tiny viruses just waiting to take up residence in my body made my skin crawl. I poured the blood down the sink and destroyed the vials.

My weight dropped dramatically. I lost ten pounds in three days. I was tired and sick. Everywhere I went, the sound of human hearts pumping blood through fat, blue veins absolutely maddened me.

*The Sanguinarius* recommended feeding captive vampires raw steak. Whoever wrote it had obviously never seen a *20/20* expose about slaughterhouse contamination and E. coli.

My nights off were almost worse than the nights I had to work. At least at the hospital I had to force myself to concentrate on something other than the hunger. I was struggling through a particularly bad night at home when I finally gave up and went back to Wealthy Avenue. Tears streamed down my face as I shook uncontrollably behind the wheel, like a drug addict in desperate need of a fix.

Nathan hadn't called me that night, and it hadn't occurred to me to call him before I showed up at his doorstep. I needed blood. I needed it badly. My hands trembled as I rang the bell to his apartment.

There was no answer. The window of the shop was dark, and no one responded to my frantic knocking.

Young men and women hurried up and down the sidewalk. The pumping of their blood drowned out the words of their conversation. Most of them looked young enough to have a curfew, but some could have been college students.

College students from other states, perhaps, with few acquaintances in their new surroundings. Like me, if they went missing, no one would look for them for days, possibly even weeks....

I was horrified at the thought, but I needed blood. Since I wasn't up to hijacking a bloodmobile, I would have to find a donor.

I didn't go back to my car. I needed to walk in the fresh air and open space.

I don't know how long I searched. I was selective. One bar looked too dank and blue-collar for my tastes. It would be crowded with middle-aged men in flannel shirts watching sports on television. I wanted someone young. Someone beautiful.

I spotted her on the street.

She crossed against the light. Her pale, blond hair flew behind her like a banner in the wind. The way she clutched her coat to her chest accentuated her skinniness.

I had never felt this sort of attraction toward anyone before, let alone a woman. It was not an attraction in a sexual sense. It was an animal instinct, as pure and natural as breathing. I wanted her blood.

The girl in the black coat pushed through a small cluster of young men and women loitering on the sidewalk. As I approached, I read the name of the building she ducked into.

The covered windows of Club Cite were framed by blue neon tubes. The brick building had been painted black, but the paint job had not been kept up, revealing flecks of the original red brick. The place was dirty and run-down.

Once inside, I followed her down the stairs. The walls around us vibrated with a muffled bass line. She pulled open the door at the bottom and the entire corridor flooded with noise. The club was packed with young people, all dressed in black. Some were Dickensian, with top hats and walking sticks. More were swathed in torn fishnets patched with electrical tape. They all looked at me as though my blue jeans and freckled face disgusted them.

I couldn't have cared less. I'd lost sight of my prey. Finding her tragic figure in this writhing mass of self-pity would be impossible.

"She went into the bathroom," a voice said close to my ear. "But I wouldn't go after her if I were you. She doesn't know what you are."

My heart could have stopped beating. My chest tightened, and the excitement of the chase vanished. I was caught.

I turned slowly, expecting to face a uniformed officer. Instead, I found myself looking down at the smirking face of a very confident young woman. She wasn't slender by any means, and she swayed to the music with an innate grace that erased any notion she found her body bulky or unwieldy. The standard Robert Smith makeup of heavy eyeliner and deep red lipstick decorated her pale face, and a thick riot of red curls hung to her shoulders.

"You're surprised?" she asked, putting her hands on her ample hips. "You were being so obvious."

"Obvious?" My mouth felt dry.

She looked me over with her head cocked to one side. Her curls bobbed as she laughed. "Yeah, obvious. But don't worry, most of the kids here wouldn't know a real vampire if one came up and bit them on the ass. They're here because their parents just don't understand."

The pulsating music, combined with the sound of beating hearts all around me, made me feel as if a speed metal drummers' convention was getting into full swing in my frontal lobe. I squinted against the swirling light and movement of the room. "How did you know what I am?"

"You must be new to this whole vampire thing, huh?" she asked. She smiled a perfectly mischievous smile, as if she'd practiced it in a mirror for years. "That girl over there, she'll scream like a banshee before you get two drops out of her, and then where will you be? In a whole heap of trouble, that's where."

Before I could protest, she grabbed my arm. Under her hand, my skin felt warm and alive, as though I'd absorbed her energy. Over the din of a hundred human pulses I could hear hers loudest of all, but I didn't feel compelled to feed from her. She was warm and alive, but she didn't seem wholly human.

Danger was here. Tension seethed beneath her sweet words. She moved like a dancer despite her round shape, her every movement charged with urgency.

The hunger gnawed at me, so I followed her.

As we walked, she told me her name was Dahlia. She led me from the club and down a few alleys, through an abandoned rail yard adrift with snow.

"There." She pointed to a squat stone building that had been gutted by fire some time ago. A cement barrier separated the area from the expressway. I heard the cars racing past.

"The cops never come here," she explained. "And if they did, they wouldn't come back."

The interior was large and open, as though the space had once been a warehouse or factory. In the very center, the ceiling had caved in. Someone had been industrious enough to cover it with plastic tarps. It was dark and cold. Ominous shapes huddled in every corner.

I heard heartbeats, coughing and quiet moans. The smell of fear in the room was as thick as the unmistakable odor of hopelessness.

"What is this place?" I whispered.

Dahlia shrugged off her coat and spread it on the ground. "A donor house."

I must have appeared not to understand her, because she rolled her eyes and sighed as though I were incurably stupid.

"A place for vampires to go and get a quick bite," she said. "A quick bite, get it?"

I nodded dumbly. "I get it...but who are these people?"

"The donors?" She plopped down cross-legged. "Who knows? Maybe they're homeless and just need some shelter. Maybe they're freaks that get off on the thrill of it. Or maybe they're like me."

"Like you?" I asked.

A skinny girl with a dirt-smudged face and greasy brown hair pushed past me. One of her bony shoulders slipped from her threadbare jacket as she shoved me aside.

"I need the money," Dahlia said as she motioned for me to sit down. "The point is, these people are desperate enough to give you what you want. Those Goth freaks at the club don't know shit. You're better off trolling under bridges for homeless people than going back to that hole."

I wanted to leave. The place reeked of sweat and smoke and despair. But I needed blood, so I knelt beside her on the crumbling cement. My heart beat faster and I shuddered in anticipation of sinking my teeth into supple pale flesh.

"Fifty dollars, cash." She produced a wooden stake from the pocket of her coat. "And you stop when I say, understood?"

The stake quenched the animal fury building inside me. I didn't know specifically what would happen if that thing touched me, but my imagination was fueled by the memory of the gaping wounds in Cyrus's chest.

My numb fingers fumbled for my purse, and as I tugged on the zipper, the contents spilled onto the floor with a clatter. A compact fell open as it dropped to the ground. Through a miniature mushroom cloud of powder dust, I saw my eyes reflected in the mirror, wide and scared and excited. *I thought vampires didn't have reflections.* It struck me as hilarious that I hadn't thought of that before. I handed Dahlia the money with shaking hands.

She counted it, smirked in satisfaction and tucked the bills into her bra. "Okay, then." She placed the point of the stake above my heart, swept her hair back and bared her throat.

I traced the line of one blue vein down her neck to her collarbone with my finger. My breath came in gasps. I thought my heart would explode the way it beat so wildly in my chest.

I felt the point of the stake as I leaned down to fasten my aching mouth to her skin. Her neck was warm and soft. I bit down. The flesh yielded crisply like the skin of a ripe peach, and her blood gushed into my mouth so fast I nearly choked.

The reality of my situation suddenly overwhelmed me. A moment ago I had not been a vampire. At least, not as far as I was concerned. Now, as I greedily gulped down the blood of this strange girl, I was truly initiated. She moaned, and the sound vibrated through me like an electrical current. The implications of what I'd done made me nauseous. The possibility that I might not really be a vampire at all flashed through my mind. Maybe I made the whole thing up. Tearing my mouth from her neck, I struggled not to vomit.

"Hey! What's wrong?" Dahlia shouted.

I didn't answer her. From the shadows, someone ordered us to keep quiet. I couldn't control my sobbing. I frantically grabbed the spilled contents of my purse and tried to stuff them back inside with shaking hands.

"Where are you going?" Dahlia asked, one hand on her neck. I expected to see blood flowing from the wound, but when she moved her fingers there was nothing but a faint bruise.

I wiped my nose on the back of my hand and winced in pain. My whole face was sore.

My compact lay innocently on the ground. I picked it up and checked my reflection.

My face, usually pretty by most people's standards, was twisted into a vision of horror. Cruel eyes peered out under a flattened brow. My cheekbones sloped down, forming a snout with my bizarrely elongated upper jaw. I pulled back my lips. My teeth were unevenly spaced in their roomy new setting, my canines lengthened into sharp points.

I'd seen Nathan transform this way, and my nightmares were filled with visions of John Doe's monstrous face, but I'd never considered such a thing could happen to me. I screamed and scrambled to my feet.

I fled from the donor house, gulping the fresh air as if it were water and I a lost traveler in the desert. Dahlia followed me. She leaned against the scorched cinder blocks and watched me check and recheck my face in the mirror. The demon was gone. A frightened woman stared back. My breath escaped in great white puffs of steam.

"Poor baby." She put on her long black coat and hugged it tightly around her waist. She wore the same coat, I realized, and used the same gesture as the girl I'd followed into the club. But I hadn't followed Dahlia...

She shook her head, laughing. "You guys never learn. You think you're so smart. 'Oh, we're at the top of the food chain.'"

She pulled out a pocketknife and idly ran it up and down her neck. "The fact is, there's power out there your kind can't understand."

I stared at her in fascination. "What are you talking about?"

She smiled. "Poor baby. Daddy didn't bother to tell you anything, did he? Just ran right out after he got what he wanted." Her mouth formed a momentary picture of disgust. "That's so like him."

With a flick of her wrist, she punctured her taut skin with the knife. A drop of blood welled and shivered on the surface of the wound before it broke and rolled down her neck.

My tongue grew thick. My body ached for more blood, though the thought repulsed me. I forced myself to look away. "Who are you talking about?"

I wanted to watch her face when she answered, but the scent of her blood was too tempting. I feared what would happen if I looked again, so I fixed my gaze on the streetlights above the highway.

"Cyrus, you silly goose. Don't you know your own sire?"

I'd known something wasn't right when we left the club. Maybe I'd known from the moment I saw the phantom girl on the street. But instead of following my intuition, I'd followed Dahlia. Right into a trap.

"I can't believe how stupid some of you can be," she shouted, suddenly agitated. "Your stories are splashed all over the papers, and yet you have no clue that someone might recognize you. I don't even know why he let you have his blood." She let out a sigh and appeared to calm herself. "Now you've made me lose my temper, and that really pisses me off."

I watched her as she slapped her forehead with the palm of her hand and muttered to herself, pacing back and forth. She stopped and faced me. Her expression was blank.

"Your little bookstore friend took care of the last one for me. But sometimes, if you want to do something right, you have to do it yourself." She pointed at me with the knife.

Suddenly, I was so weak I couldn't stand. I fell to my knees, wincing as I hit the dirt.

"Good girl." She threw the knife at me. It pierced the frozen ground inches from my knee. She took another deep breath, laughing. "I just don't know what's wrong with me tonight. Do you ever have days like that, where you just feel—"

"Crazy?" I eyed the blade. It was so close. I should have been able to grab it and get to my feet before Dahlia could reach me, but my body was limp and heavy. "What do you want?"

"What do I want, what do I want?" she singsonged, scooping up the knife before I could stop her. "You sound just like the last one I took care of. You guys always try to bargain."

She held the point of the knife to my throat. "I want to kill you."

"Why?" It was barely a whisper. I imagined the tip of the knife puncturing my skin the way my fangs had split hers.

She leaned closer, twisting the blade against my neck but never breaking my skin. "Because you took what's mine."

"What? What did I take?" I wanted to swallow, but I was afraid it would kill me. "I don't even know you."

"You're right. You don't know me, bitch." She lifted the knife and, without hesitation, plunged it into my stomach.

I gasped from the pain. I'd seen numerous stab wounds in the E.R. Never in my wildest dreams had I imagined they felt like this. The burning and tearing, coupled with the invasion of an object all my muscles tensed to reject. I couldn't think. Couldn't breathe.

Dahlia pulled the blade out of me and wiped it clean on the front of my shirt. "I don't know why he keeps doing this. He knows you all die."

"You're not making any sense," I wheezed, clutching my abdomen.

It was the wrong thing to say.

"I'm not making any sense?" She brought the weapon down again, piercing my side. "No! *He's* not making any sense! He says he loves me. He promises to give me power. But it's not time, Dahlia! It's not time! Then he wastes his blood on a piece of trash like you! Look at you. You can't even stand up."

She kicked me. It was a dangerous thing for someone to do to a wounded vampire, and this knowledge was apparently as much of a surprise to her as it was to me.

Leaping to my feet, I lunged for her, fueled purely by agony and instinct. I wrestled the knife from her hand and brought it to her throat.

"I didn't take anything from you," I whispered into her ear. "He didn't mean to make me. I was an accident. I've got no interest in you, your vampire boyfriend or any of this fucking vampire crap."

I threw her to the ground. She peered up at me through her disheveled hair. Her eyes were hard and furious.

"Yeah, you were an accident all right!" she screamed. "But it doesn't matter! You'll be dead by morning!"

My anger deserted me, and the weakness returned. Dahlia's voice was too loud, too shrill. Blood flowed freely from my wounds. I knew I needed to stop the bleeding, but I could think of nothing but getting away from Dahlia.

I staggered through the rail yard. Every step I took felt as though I were descending into a dark, warm pit. My pulse thrummed in my ears. It was slowing.

The impact of my footfalls on the uneven ground jarred my ankles and sent shock waves of pain up my legs. When I reached pavement, my body seemed to know where to go on its own. I moved in slow motion, but I must have been running because I reached Nathan's apartment in a matter of minutes.

I stood stupidly on the sidewalk, unsure what to do as I pressed my hands feebly against my torn flesh. I knew my car was parked nearby, but I didn't have my keys. I looked helplessly up and down the street, shivering. I yearned to be at home in my bed. I settled for Nathan's doorstep. At least there I would be shielded from some of the biting wind. Dahlia might have followed me, but the more pressing desire for warmth and sleep outweighed my fear. If she did come to kill me, my exhausted brain reasoned, I would finally be able to rest in peace.

I don't know how long I lay there before the snow began to fall. Big, fluffy flakes, straight out of a Christmas movie, floated to the ground. I watched a few land in my palm, where my lack of body heat allowed them to gather without melting. I started counting them, but when the storm picked up I couldn't count fast enough. I contented myself by watching the swirling patterns of snow and wind on the sidewalk. My eyelids grew heavy. Unable to fight sleep and not sure why I'd tried in the first place, I closed my eyes.

A familiar voice woke me. It was Nathan. It took a moment before I realized he had hold of my shoulders. He shook me frantically. He shouted at me and clapped his hands in front of my face, but I was too exhausted to respond.

My head lolled to the side. A brown paper bag lay forgotten on the sidewalk. The contents rolled across the snowy concrete.

"Your shaving cream…it's getting away," I mumbled, trying to follow the canister with my eyes.

"Don't worry about that." He turned my face to his. "What happened?"

"I don't know," I said as I tried again to give up and sleep.

Nathan shook me the moment my eyes slid closed.

"What?" I whined, and tried to push his hands away.

He cursed and gripped me tighter. "Wake up!" he yelled. When I didn't, he slapped my cheek.

My eyes flew open and I sputtered in shock. "What? Just let me go back to sleep!"

"I can't! You've lost a lot of blood. If you go to sleep, you'll die."

Then I felt the pain, a twisting, pinching feeling in my gut. As if I'd eaten broken glass. I clutched his arm, writhing in misery. He shrugged off his coat and quickly wrapped it around me. "I've got to get you inside," he murmured. He scooped me into his arms and carried me through the door, up the stairs to his apartment.

# Five

### Decisions, Decisions

I woke to the gentle sound of someone humming Pink Floyd's "Brain Damage." My eyes snapped open in alarm.

Judging from the clutter around me, I was in Nathan's apartment. I couldn't remember how I got there. My stomach growled, and my memory slowly returned. I'd been hungry. I'd gone in search of blood. Then I'd met Dahlia.

Being stabbed, now that's something I definitely remembered. I lifted the blanket that covered me. My wounds were carefully bandaged. Dried blood stained the gauze wrappings, but I resisted the urge to poke at them. It didn't take much to upset a fresh wound, and I didn't want to start bleeding again.

I reached up and gingerly felt my face. Completely monster-free. Aching all over, I sat up. My torn sweatshirt had been carefully folded on the arm of the couch. I pulled it over my head quickly, trying not to dwell on the fact that Nathan had seen me in my ratty, laundry-day bra.

"Feeling better?" he asked as he entered the living room.

I could smell the blood in the mug he carried. My throat was a desert and my stomach was trying to digest itself, but I turned my face away.

"Drink," he said, holding out the cup to me. He must have sensed the reason for my reluctance. "Don't worry about it. I've seen a few vampires in my time."

"Not like me."

"Exactly like you." He knelt in front of me, and I hid my face. My bones shifted under the mask of my fingers as he pressed the cup against the backs of my hands. "You need to drink this."

I heard the resolve in his voice and knew I wasn't going to win.

"Don't look at me," I whispered.

"Okay." He moved to the farthest corner of the room and turned his back.

The blood was warm, as Dahlia's had been, but thicker, as though it had already begun to clot. It coated my tongue and left a faint taste of copper in my mouth. It was like drinking penny-flavored Jell-O that hadn't set. This repulsed me, but instead of gagging, I gulped half of it down. I felt gluttonous. If I were drinking straight from someone's neck I probably wouldn't have thought of manners, but it was much different sitting in Nathan's living room, drinking from a mug like a civilized vampire.

I sipped the blood self-consciously and studied him. It was my experience that people weren't nice to strangers. In med school it's every student for his- or herself. In fact, most of us went out of our way to intimidate the "competition." The eat-or-be-eaten attitude had become so ingrained in my psyche, that I'd come to expect such behavior from everyone. But Nathan had been nothing but helpful from the start, which was surprising considering he was a week away from killing me if I didn't join his vampire cult.

It didn't seem right that a man so attractive would be such a complete stickler for the rules. He must have worked for the IRS in a past life.

Of course, I didn't know much about Nathan's current life. In the brief phone conversations we'd had during the past week, he'd revealed only generic information about himself and hadn't given me much room to ask questions. If I was going to trust anything he told me, I needed some answers.

There was no time like the present.

"How old are you?" I asked.

"Thirty-two."

"I meant including…" I didn't know how to phrase the rest.

"Oh, *that,*" he said, and it sounded as if he didn't care to dispense that information. "I've been a vampire since 1937."

I tried to conceal my disappointment. I had expected to hear he was hundreds of years old, that he'd walked the battlefield with Napoléon and discussed the mysteries of the cosmos with Nostradamus, like the vampires in the movies. "That was the year 'The Star-Spangled Banner' became the national anthem, you know."

"I didn't know that. I wasn't an American at the time." He glanced over his shoulder, and I immediately covered my face.

"It's okay," he assured me. "You're back to normal."

I leaned over a clear patch of the glass-topped coffee table to check my reflection.

"It's the hunger," he said as he straightened up the room. "The worse it is, the worse you look. The same goes for anger, pain and fear. It's very animalistic."

How anyone could be blasé about his entire head morphing into a Harryhausen-esque special effect was beyond me.

"The scary part is that it gets worse with age. Some of the real old vampires even get horns when they change, or cloven feet. But you can control it, with practice. You just have to calm yourself, find your center, all that New Age crap. It's very Zen." He took the empty cup from my hands and headed to the kitchen sink.

*New Age crap?* This from the guy running the witchcraft minimart?

"Now, how about telling me what happened tonight?" he called over the sound of running water.

I shuddered. "Can't we start with what the weather's been like?"

"No."

"It was nothing, really," I said, trying to sound casual.

"'Nothing' rarely stabs people." He came in and sat next to me on the sofa. The scent of him teased my nostrils, and I rather seriously debated whether or not to lean against him and inhale deeply.

*I really need to get out more.*

"I needed blood."

Nathan frowned. "You didn't hurt anyone, did you?"

"Okay, even if I had, did I look like I won that particular fight?"

He looked relieved that he wouldn't have to chop off my head.

"I followed a girl into a club downtown. One of those…Goth clubs." I lowered my voice, as if *Goth* were a dirty word.

"Club Cite?" he asked, and I nodded. "That was very dangerous. Clubs like that are full of all kinds of undesirables.

People who think they're vampires, wannabe vampires and vampire hunters. Amateurish vampire hunters, but with enough knowledge to kill you, even if it is just a lucky accident."

"I know that now," I said bitterly, remembering the metallic taste of Dahlia's blood on my tongue. I took a deep breath. "I met a girl there. She told me she'd let me—" I stumbled over the words. "Drink her blood. I paid her."

Nathan sighed and shook his head, reaching for one of the notebooks on the table. "What was her name?"

"Dahlia." I looked over his shoulder as he flipped through the pages. There were crudely drawn diagrams and notes in the margins. A paper clip held a Polaroid in place at the top of one page. He handed the photo to me.

"Is this her?"

I looked at the photo. The woman did look like Dahlia, but a black Betty Page wig covered her red curls. The eyes were the same. Hard and crazy. I wondered how I hadn't noticed that before. I told him it was her and returned the picture.

He stood, cursed and threw it down on the table. I shrank away, surprised at his sudden vehemence.

"I told you to come here if you needed blood! Why didn't you come to me?" he shouted.

"I did! You weren't home!"

"You should have waited!" He glared at me and braced himself for my next retort.

Raising my voice had calmed me considerably. When I didn't respond, he swore and turned away, running a hand through his hair.

"Are you finished?" I asked.

He sighed angrily. "Yes, dammit. But you should have waited."

"Maybe I should have. But I wasn't thinking clearly at the time." I scooped up the picture. "Do you know her?"

"Who?"

I rolled my eyes and held up the photo. "Dahlia."

When he sat beside me, he seemed to take up more of the couch than before. I didn't want to give him the impression that I was intentionally trying to be close to him, so I moved to the armchair.

"I know *of* her," he said, examining the notebook. "She's a very powerful witch."

"A witch?" I laughed.

Nathan stared at me in annoyance before turning his attention back to the notebook. He laced his fingers together and brought them to his mouth, and his eyes glazed in deep concentration. Watching him, I realized why I'd been so disappointed to hear he wasn't centuries old. Everything about him seemed anachronistic, as though he'd stepped from the Middle Ages into the present. He would look less out of place standing on a blood-drenched battlefield than sitting on a secondhand couch in an apartment full of musty old books. I imagined him charging into battle, face grim with purpose, his strong arms wielding a sword with both hands, his muscular thighs—

"See something you like?" His voice jolted me from my lusty historical imaginings. I was caught.

Nathan smiled that arrogant, knowing smile all males produce when their ego has been thoroughly stroked.

"Sorry, I guess I just zoned out." Even I wasn't buying that lame excuse, so I quickly changed the subject. "Why do you think she attacked me?"

He pushed the book aside. "I have no idea. She's been trying for years to hook up with different vampires in the area, without much success. She isn't someone to be trifled with. She has a lot of power."

His grave expression worsened my growing unease. I didn't know just how powerful Dahlia really was, but she'd been violent and dangerous enough without the aid of any spells or tricks. "She was really pissed at me. For taking Cyrus's blood. Do you think she's, you know, with him? Or just bat-shit crazy?"

"I've known Cyrus for a long time. He likes people who are easy to manipulate, and she definitely has powers he could exploit." His brow furrowed as he considered his statement. "But I don't think he would turn her. He's not that stupid."

"She said it wasn't time. Or that he said it wasn't time." I threw up my arms in frustration. "So, how, exactly, do we proceed from here?" I glanced nervously at the window. "Can you kill her? Or is she off-limits because of that human thing?"

"Off-limits," he answered automatically. "Besides, I don't have any reason to kill her. I keep an eye on her, sure, but nearly every vampire hunter around here does. I've seen her around, but the vampires I've seen her with usually disappear after a while. As long as they don't turn her, I don't care where they go."

"She kills them!" I triumphantly jabbed my finger in the air. "She said she'd killed Cyrus's other fledglings before, so you've got to be able to—"

"No, Carrie, the goal of the Movement is to rid the world of vampires. She's actually doing us a favor." He looked away from me. "But it does trouble me to hear he's been making fledglings we haven't heard of. If Dahlia were a vampire…but I can't imagine Cyrus would be foolish enough to turn her."

"He was foolish enough to turn me," I reminded him.

"Yes, but you're not a witch." His tone was the vocal equivalent of a condescending pat on the head. "A vampire's blood is very powerful. Combine that with a witch's abilities and you've got spells to raise the dead, summon armies from hell, et cetera. But as it stands, I think it would be safe to assume Dahlia merely wants to become one of us for her own selfish reasons. Is there anything else she said that might give us a clue why she targeted you specifically?"

I thought hard, but the entire evening was still a blur. "Just my ties to Cyrus."

He looked helplessly around the apartment, as though an answer hid in the bookshelves. "Well, if she assumes you're dead, at least she won't come looking for you. That's something."

Cold, sick realization made my stomach constrict as I remembered everything in my purse spilled all over the dirty floor of the donor house. "She has all of my identification. I left my purse behind."

Nathan frowned. "Well, that was careless of you."

"Yeah, I guess I should have gone back for it after she stabbed me!" I snapped. I was too tired to keep up the sarcasm for long. "What am I going to do now?"

He went to the window and lowered the shades. "The sun is going to be up soon. I don't think you'll make it home before dawn, and I'd rather have you where I can protect you. Why don't you stay here until dusk?"

I looked doubtfully around the cluttered apartment. There was one dead bolt on the door. It seemed a far cry from the safety and security of a building with a night watchman. Especially since a crazed witch was out to get me.

His eyes darted to the door, then back to me. "I swear, nothing will happen to you as long as you're here."

As if to reassure me, he stood and opened the door of the

coat closet, revealing an impressive array of medieval-looking weapons.

"Beats a night watchman," I said in awe.

Nathan suggested I take his bed. "I'm going to wait up for Ziggy, make sure he gets in okay."

Glancing at the couch, I realized I shouldn't argue. It didn't look comfortable, and since it lived in the company of two men, it didn't look very clean, either. I didn't mention that. "You look out for him, don't you?"

"Ziggy?" he said the name with genuine fatherly affection. "Yeah. Well, he hasn't got anyone else."

"Neither do you."

I'd said the words without thinking, but their impact was visible. Nathan's faint, unguarded smile faded. I glimpsed a flicker of pain in his eyes before the emotionless mask was back in place and he returned to being the polite acquaintance that held me at arm's length.

I had no idea why it bothered me, but it did.

"Listen, you've had a rough night, and those wounds aren't going to heal without some rest." He pointed toward the hallway. "The bedroom's straight back."

I knew a dismissal when I heard one. I was halfway down the hall when he spoke again. "There are some T-shirts in the bottom dresser drawer. You can borrow one if you want."

I went mechanically to the bureau. I'd just met Nathan. Spending the night in his bed was intimate enough. I didn't need to wear his clothes, too. But the thought of sleeping naked didn't appeal to me, either. I undressed, grimacing at the pain that tore through me when I moved. When I eased into the bed, I hissed in agony.

Loud footsteps charged down the hall, and Nathan burst

into the room just seconds later. "Are you okay? Do you need something for the pain?"

His immediate reaction to a sound I didn't think he'd been able to hear unnerved me. So did the sincere concern etched on his face.

He didn't give me a chance to answer him. With a speed that surprised me, he left and reappeared with a large metal toolbox. Sitting on the bed, he placed the box in his lap and sprung the latches. "Okay, what do you want? We've got morphine, meperidine, Vicodin… I've got local anaesthetic, but I'd really like to save that." As he continued to rattle off drug names, I peeked around his arm. The man's first aid kit was better stocked than the Pyxis medicine cabinet in the E.R., but I was willing to bet he didn't come by the stuff legally. "How'd you get all this?"

"Connections in the Movement." He lifted out a bottle of pills and squinted to read the label.

"I thought you guys were all about the extinction of your species." I reached for a syringe and the vial of meperidine. "This should put me right to sleep. Got a tourniquet?"

He handed me the stretchy strip of latex. "The rules state we can't save a vampire's life, not even our own. If our healing abilities don't take care of things, that's the end of it. Nothing in here is going to save me if I get in a bad way. There's no rule against keeping yourself comfortable for your last few hours. Do you need a hand?"

I had the tourniquet between my teeth and tried to wind it around my arm the way I'd seen them do it in *Trainspotting*. I'd started enough IVs in my time that it should have been a piece of cake, but doing it yourself wasn't as easy as it looked. When I shook my head no in answer to Nathan's question, the stretched length of rubber shot from my lips, snapping me painfully in the face.

"Here, let me." He chuckled as he deftly tied the tourniquet and thumped the fat vein on the inside of my forearm. "That looks like a good spot."

I watched as he carefully filled the syringe. This obviously wasn't the first injection he'd given. "Did the Movement teach you how to do this?" I asked.

He tapped the air bubbles toward the needle. "I picked it up somewhere. Now, hold still."

I felt the needle slide into my unsterilized arm. I remembered what I'd read in *The Sanguinarius* regarding disease: *The humors that delight in causing sickness and death will not touch the vampire. He will not be affected by the plagues of Pandora.*

I could only assume the same went for modern-day germs and bacteria.

The medicine stung as it entered my vein, but Nathan's touch was gentle and reassuring. Even so, I fixed my gaze on his face to keep from looking at the needle in my arm—I was never good at being the patient. "So we can heal from serious injuries on our own?"

"The depth of severity is determined by age. If someone had done to me what I did to Cyrus, I wouldn't be sitting here right now. I would've healed from your stab wound in an hour, whereas you're lucky you didn't need stitches. By the time I found you, though, you'd already started to heal. It's a good thing you'd fed some." He held his thumb over the injection site as he withdrew the needle, then reached for a Band-Aid. "There. That should take the edge off, and it will help you get to sleep."

"What about me? How long will it take until I'm completely healed?" I really hoped the answer wasn't two months.

"You'll be fine in the morning," he said as he recapped the needle.

I snatched it from him. "Don't do that. It's a universal hazard."

He looked amused. "A what?"

"A universal hazard. It's been in contact with body fluids, which transmit diseases that cause death. You could stick yourself in the process and end up dead. It's a universal hazard, and not recapping needles is a universal precaution." Realizing I sounded like one of my old professors, I pinched the bridge of my nose in embarrassment. "I can't believe how easily I just rattled that off."

"It was very educational." Nathan laughed. He had a great laugh, deep and genuine. It was the best thing I'd heard all day.

He shrugged. "But I'm not worried about diseases. I'm more worried about a stake to the heart or an axe to the neck."

"Is that all?" I teased. "I would have thought a strapping lad such as yourself would be concerned about his cholesterol levels."

Suddenly serious, Nathan caught my chin in his hand and forced me to look at him. "Your heart and your head. Lose either one and you're dead."

*How will you kill me?* I thought. "What about burning? Can you die from burning? Or drowning?"

As if horrified by the morbid conversation—or the realization that he'd started it—he removed his hand apologetically. "The short answer is yes, you can die from anything that causes more damage than you can heal in a feasible amount of time. But let's not talk about this now. You need to rest."

I wanted him to tell me more, but I just cried gratefully. "Thank you. You didn't have to do all this."

He didn't look at me as he began gathering up the medical debris from the bed. "No one ever died from being too polite. Besides, you need help. The next couple of months will be rough."

"I can't imagine it will be any worse than it already has been."

"You're going to have to say goodbye to your family, your friends. Everyone." He stood. "It's lonely being one of us."

"I don't have any relatives I talk to anymore. I mean, my parents are dead, and I haven't seen any of their family since I was little, except for at their funeral. I only moved here eight months ago, so I haven't had time to make any friends." I stopped myself. "Well, except for you, I guess. You're the closest thing to a friend that I've got so far."

He didn't look pleased to be drafted into the role. "You're going to have to quit your job. You can't continue to work at the hospital. The people there are too vulnerable to you."

I couldn't argue with that. I'd stolen their blood, not exactly a move in the best interest of patient care. But the thought of giving up being a doctor was, well, unimaginable. After four tedious years of college and three grueling years of med school, I'd finally gotten the prize I'd been striving for. I'd sacrificed my personal life in pursuit of my goal. If I let it go, I'd have nothing. I wasn't about to let fate, or anyone else, take away the one thing left that I cared about. "I'm not even going to discuss this. It's not your call to make."

He sighed. "You're right. It's not. But how are you going to explain to them that you can't work day shifts or attend morning meetings? How are you going to play off the fact that in twenty years you'll still look…how old are you?"

"Twenty-eight."

"In twenty years, you'll still look twenty-eight. What are you going to tell people?"

"Botox?" I yawned. The drug was taking effect. "Can't I wait and work this out in a week? If I join your club they'll tell me to quit, anyway, and if I don't, you're going to kill me."

The words appeared to surprise him, as though he'd forgotten he wasn't yet on my side. He opened his mouth to speak but turned away and snapped off the light. "Get some sleep. We can talk about this later."

Like I had a choice. Within minutes of Nathan leaving the room, I dropped off and slept like a log.

When I woke, I blinked sleepily and tried to remember when I'd gotten a goldfish.

The creature stared expectantly at me from his little castle in the bowl on the bedside table. An odd feeling of loneliness swelled under my ribs. As messy and small as Nathan's apartment was, it boasted homey, lived-in touches that were decidedly lacking at my place. I imagined going home to my high ceilings and bare walls, and the idea was too awful to contemplate. I buried my face in the pillow and pulled the covers over my head. It had been a while since Nathan had laundered the sheets. They smelled like him, and I shamelessly took a deep breath. I visualized him lying naked where I lay now. Did he bring women here?

I couldn't see the Nathan I knew forming a relationship with anyone. Yes, he cared for Ziggy the way a father watched over a son, but familial love came with ready-made boundaries. I'd only met him a week ago, but it didn't take a genius to deduce that *emotional intimacy* and *Nathan* were not terms that went hand in hand. It was probably a miracle he even had a fish.

The sun hadn't set. No sounds of life came from the living room. Forsaking my bloodied sweatshirt, I slipped my jeans on under Nathan's T-shirt and padded quietly to the bathroom. Despairing at my lack of a toothbrush, I brushed my teeth with my finger before venturing into the rest of the apartment.

Nathan was sprawled across the armchair with a book in one hand and a loaded crossbow in the other. A thin line of drool hung from the corner of his mouth. On the floor at his side were two wooden stakes and the axe Ziggy had attacked me with.

"Expecting company?"

He startled awake. "I wasn't sleeping!"

I jumped aside as the bolt shot from the bow and stuck in the door.

"For Christ's sake, I could have killed you!" He leapt to his feet. "Do you always sneak up on people like that or just when they've got a deadly weapon in their hand?"

I stepped back. "I've never happened upon a sleeping person with a weapon before."

He stretched his arms wide and yawned loudly. Apparently, he'd slept well enough when he was supposed to be protecting me. "How're the stab wounds this morning? Healed?"

I rolled up the edge of the T-shirt. Nathan pulled the tape from the gauze pad over my belly to reveal a faint pink scar.

"Holy crap," I breathed, poking the spot with my finger. The tissue wasn't even bruised. My body had mended while I slept. "How the hell did I do that?"

"*The Sanguinarius* says that humors in the blood we drink sustain our tissue and imbue it with a potent healing ability. I'm sure that's not very scientific, but it's the best answer we've got so far." He paused as an idea came to him. "You're a doctor. If you join the Movement, maybe you could work in their research department."

*If.* It hung between us again, destroying the friendly truce of the morning. We stood, staring at each other as potential enemies instead of a host and houseguest.

A knock at the door broke our awkward silence. Nathan grabbed one of the stakes and motioned for me to stand back. Just as he reached for the dead bolt, the door burst open.

Nathan lunged forward, tackled the intruder and brought him to the ground. His arm was raised, poised to thrust the stake into the man's heart.

"Hey, hey!" the trespasser shouted. He rolled out from under Nathan.

Ziggy got up and brushed off his clothes. He smoothed back his long, greasy hair and looked me over. "Sorry, Nate, I didn't know you had company."

Nathan snapped at his young ward with barely restrained anger. "Where the hell were you?" He turned his puzzled gaze to the door. "And I could have sworn I locked that."

"So much for protection," I snorted. Nathan's warning glare stifled further comment.

"Hanging out," Ziggy said, answering Nathan's first question with a shrug. "I slept in the van and went to class this morning. I'm just here to donate, then I've got an art history night class. So, what's up with her? Is she like, your new girl or something?"

"New girl? What happened to the old one?" I asked Nathan, raising an eyebrow.

He wasn't amused. "There hasn't been an old one for a while."

I couldn't imagine somebody who looked like Nathan going without a date for long. Then again, most women I knew—the nurses I overheard gossiping in the break room, anyway—weren't looking for vampires as potential mates.

Nathan hung up the heavy overcoat that Ziggy had discarded on the floor. "I don't like you going out all night, especially with Cyrus in town. And you forgot to use the special knock. I could have killed you."

"That's a phrase you seem to be using quite a bit today," I interjected, but Nathan ignored me.

Ziggy went straight for the kitchen, with Nathan and I trailing behind. He pulled a can of soda, marked with a territorial *Z* in black marker, from the refrigerator and swallowed it in one long gulp. He wiped his mouth on his sleeve and coughed. "Once, then twice, then once again. Yeah, I know. I did it. You just went all Rambo on me."

"You knocked four times," Nathan said. "That's not the same thing."

While Ziggy consumed another soda, Nathan retrieved sterile packets of IV tubing and needles from the cupboard.

The younger man sniffed the air and made a face. "Damn, Nate, you reek."

Surreptitiously, I leaned a little closer to Nathan. He did smell a bit like the bedsheets, but I'd thought it was a sexy smell. There's pheromones for you.

Nathan looked mildly offended, but his expression quickly changed to amusement. "I'd value your input a lot more if you hadn't just admitted to sleeping in that crusty old van of yours." He handed Ziggy the medical supplies. "If you have any trouble, Carrie here is a doctor."

Ziggy's face blanched as he looked from Nathan to myself. "Oh, yeah, new vampire, fresh, tender Ziggy flesh. Like I'm going to let her near me when I've got an open vein."

I rolled my eyes. I wouldn't shake hands with someone who looked like Ziggy, let alone suck blood from him. "You're totally safe, I assure you."

Nathan headed toward the bathroom. "I paid for two pints, I want two pints."

"Two pints!" I exclaimed once the bathroom door was closed. "You can't give him two pints of your blood!"

Ziggy settled comfortably in a chair and tied a rubber tourniquet around his arm, much in the way I'd tried the night before. He was a bit too proficient at it.

"Sure I can. In case you get hungry, you should know I've got a stake in my pocket with your name on it." He took a few trial stabs with the needle, missing the vein each time. I didn't know what to say. I was a little insulted he thought I was some wild, uncontrollable animal. "Here," I said gruffly. "You're turning yourself into a pincushion." I took the needle from him and slid it smoothly into the only undamaged vein I could find.

"Heroin?" I asked, casting a disapproving look at the track marks on his wrists and the backs of his hands.

"Not that it's any of your business, Doc, but no. I'm the cleanest donor in the city. And Nate's not my only customer."

In my opinion, his cleanliness was debatable. I didn't say so and resisted the urge to wipe my hands on my jeans after I touched him.

"You should be more careful with the needles," I said, trying to sound as concerned as I possibly could. "You can't just poke around in your arm like that."

"Duly noted," he replied, too distracted with the intricacies of plastic connector tubing to pay my warning much heed.

I dropped onto the couch and averted my eyes. I didn't trust myself to catch sight of his blood. I heard the water running in the shower and muffled singing.

"So are you and Nate like special friends now or something?" Ziggy asked.

"No," I replied, "and if we were, I don't think it would be any of your business."

He laughed. "Hey, no offense or anything. I just wondered because you're, you know, wearing his clothes and all."

I looked down at the T-shirt and wrapped my arms around myself. "My shirt had blood on it."

"Listen, I don't care. I was just trying to make conversation." He lit a cigarette then, and noticed my expression of utter longing, he held the pack out to me.

"No, thanks." I waved them away, knowing I'd get no satisfaction from them. "It'd be a waste."

"Suit yourself," he said, tossing them on the table. "But a lot of vampires smoke, you know. It doesn't matter much what you do when you're dead. You can't get cancer or anything."

"Yeah, but you can't get anything out of it, either," I said, my voice wistful. The acrid smoke smelled better than baking cookies.

"Not true." He held the cigarette out.

I took it and inhaled experimentally. He was right.

"It's the blood," he said. "Blood rules all."

I passed the cigarette back. "But it didn't do anything for me before."

"Because you were craving blood," he explained, prodding his arm where the needle entered his skin. I cleared my throat noisily, and he jerked his hand back with a grin. "It's like if you were craving chocolate cake, and you just kept eating SpaghettiOs. The SpaghettiOs aren't going to do it for you, you know?"

I hadn't even known that vampires existed until I suddenly became one. Now some smart-assed kid was telling me, a doctor, the ins and outs of my own physiology.

The collection bag filled. He kinked the tubing and

switched to an empty one. I motioned to the bag. "Do you want me to put that in the fridge?"

He nodded. "So, how long have you been a doctor?"

"Less than a year." I hesitated. "I'm not sure I'm going to be a doctor much longer. Because of the vampire thing. After I worked so hard for it… I can't believe it's over."

"That's a bitch." He sounded genuinely sympathetic.

The sound of the water stopped, and my mind briefly diverted to a vivid flash of Nathan emerging from the shower. I tried in vain to force the image from my thoughts.

A loud crash, followed immediately by a yelp and a dull thud, snapped me back to reality. For a moment, I thought Nathan had fallen out of the shower. Then I noticed the brick rolling awkwardly across the floor. The window behind the armchair was broken. Sunlight streamed in, and Ziggy slumped to his knees, unconscious.

Nathan rushed from the bathroom, a towel wrapped around his waist. He hurried to Ziggy's side and felt frantically for a pulse.

"What happened?" he shouted, looking from Ziggy's lifeless form to me.

I tried to focus on the emergency at hand, but it was hard to ignore a half-naked man standing in front of me, regardless of the circumstances.

His chest was well defined and droplets of water still clung to his broad shoulders. I felt heat rush to my face as I imagined gripping those strong arms and raking my nails across his back.

Yelling from the street snapped me back to the present. "Come out, come out, wherever you are!"

I knew that voice.

"I know you're up there! So does Cyrus! If I were you I'd

come down here and burn before he gets to you!" She laughed. It was the same crazy sound she'd made the night before.

"Nathan?" I whispered, paralyzed with fear.

Ziggy tried to stand. As soon as he was upright, he crashed back to the floor and clutched his head.

"What the hell happened?" He looked the room over through barely opened eyes.

Nathan raised a hand, shiny with blood, and motioned frantically for me to help him. "I don't know where he's bleeding from."

"Oh, shit!" Ziggy's eyes grew wide at the sight of his blood on Nathan's hands. He struggled to his feet. The window shade had nearly been torn down during the brick's dramatic entrance. A few rays of sunlight spilled into the room. Ziggy was careful to keep those beams of light between Nathan and himself.

When the smell of the blood hit me, I understood his reaction. I felt the muscles and tendons of my face rhythmically clench, and my fangs began their aching descent.

"Not now, Carrie!" Nathan snapped.

His sharp tone surprised me, and my transformation stopped instantly.

Ziggy looked from Nathan to me, as if trying to judge the best escape route. Nathan approached him cautiously. "Remember who you're talking to, Ziggy. I would never hurt you. I know you're not food."

Dahlia was still in the street, but she appeared to be running out of steam. "Are you waiting for sunset so you can come out and kick my ass? I'll have a lot of backup by then."

"Get out of here, Dahlia, or I can't be responsible for my actions!" Nathan roared.

"Oh, I'm so scared," she yelled back. "What are you gonna do, bookstore man? Read me to death? I'm going. I was just supposed to deliver the message."

"What message?" Nathan asked.

Just then the shade fell completely from the window, flooding the room with sunlight. Nathan cursed and dropped to the floor. My reflexes weren't as good.

Words can't accurately describe how sunlight feels when it hits vampire skin. The worst sunburn couldn't compare with the searing pain that rocked through me. My skin bubbled then burst into flame anywhere the light made contact with it. My shirt caught fire from my incinerating skin, spreading the flames to the rest of my torso. The only thing I could think of was that my burning flesh smelled like hot dogs. Nathan leapt up and grabbed me, smothering the flames as we tumbled to the floor.

Ziggy grabbed the blanket from the back of the couch and draped it across the window. "I'll try to rig this up so it doesn't fall again."

"Are you all right?" Nathan asked, his face hovering mere centimeters above mine.

"I'm fine," I wheezed, unable to take sufficient breaths. "Except for the third-degree burns."

Nathan actually smiled at that. He didn't seem in much of a hurry to move, and despite the fact that I couldn't breathe, I didn't really mind. Until I remembered Ziggy had an open head wound.

"And I can't breathe. Will you let me up?" I squeaked, shifting slightly beneath him. I realized too late what effect my wriggling might have on a half-naked man.

He looked embarrassed and apologetic as he rolled off me, clutching his towel closed.

While Nathan tended Ziggy, I sat up and gingerly inspected the burned patches on my arms and chest. The skin was blackened. When I ventured an experimental poke it flaked away, revealing tender new flesh beneath. "Why didn't I burn up?"

"Because I saved your ass with my mad blanket-throwing skills," Ziggy answered.

Nathan made a sound in the back of his throat. I couldn't tell if he was annoyed at Ziggy's comment or upset by the gash in his skull.

"This is going to have to be stitched up," he said with a sigh of resignation as he examined Ziggy's wound.

"I can do that," I offered, but Nathan shook his head.

"I don't have the supplies on hand, and you don't have enough control yet to be around this much blood." He turned to Ziggy. "It'll be safer if you go to the hospital. Do you mind?"

"Better than hanging around here," he said with a shrug. "It's like swimming in a pool of sharks with a paper cut in here."

Nathan went to his room. He returned with pants on his body and a roll of cash in his hand. "Take this," he ordered. "Go straight to the E.R."

Ziggy stuffed the money in his jacket. "Where else would I go? Denny's?"

"Knowing you, anything is possible. But I'm not kidding," Nathan warned. "Stay off the street tonight. I want you in by curfew."

"No problem," Ziggy said. "They'll probably give me some wicked pain medication at the E.R."

Nathan watched him descend the stairs, then closed the door and turned to me. "Here we are again. Just you and me, alone together. Not completely dressed."

The comment was so playful and unexpected, I didn't know what to say. I wrapped my arms around my chest to cover the burn holes in the T-shirt and tried to force a laugh. "I'm not having much luck with shirts lately."

"Well, I'd loan you another but I saw what you did to the last one." His voice sounded weary, but he smiled, anyway. "Besides, I like the view."

I rolled my eyes. "If you're going to be a smart-ass, I'll just ignore you."

Nathan clearly dealt with stress through humor. As long as I had to deal with him, I hoped he had enough stress to cause an ulcer. He was much more pleasant when he was using his coping mechanisms.

The fading sunlight that had peeked from the edges of the blanket over the window disappeared. If Dahlia's brick had broken the window five minutes later, it would have already been night. I checked my scorched flesh again. It had nearly healed.

"Why did that happen?" I asked, holding up my seared hand.

"Because you're a vampire. Haven't you seen *any* movies?" Nathan asked.

"I'm more of a werewolf fan, for your information."

He made a face. "You wouldn't be if you ever met one."

"Werewolves are real?" I smiled in spite of myself. I'd always liked the idea of wild guys who were animals in bed. Not that I'd ever actually experienced said animalism for myself, but a girl can dream.

Sighing deeply, Nathan stretched out his legs. "Why is it you women find them so damned attractive? Is removing ticks from a guy such a turn-on?"

"I never said I was attracted to them. I just said I favored them to, well, humanoid leeches, for instance." I spied Ziggy's cigarettes that lay forgotten on the coffee table, and snuck one from the pack. "Anyway, why did it happen now? It's been nearly two months since the attack, and I've been in the sun since then."

Nathan pushed an ashtray toward me. "You hadn't drunk any blood yet. You might have been light sensitive before, but after feeding, the sensitivity turns deadly. It's in *The Sanguinarius*."

"Yeah, but I haven't finished it yet," I confessed sheepishly. "But it makes sense. After I started…feeding, artificial light doesn't bother me as much as it used to."

"You were going through a prolonged transition into vampirism. Once you stopped denying your hunger, the change completed." He snagged the cigarettes from me. "Are these Ziggy's?"

Biting my lip, I considered the answer to that question. I didn't want to get Ziggy into too much trouble.

I decided the best course would be the parental guilt trip. "You shouldn't let him smoke. It's not good for him."

Nathan slid out a cigarette and lit up, another surprising development. "I know. These things will kill you."

"Har, har." I rolled my eyes. "You can make a joke about it because your lung function isn't going to be seriously compromised in twenty years."

"I don't believe all that crap they say on television. I smoked when I was much younger than Ziggy, and it never hurt me."

"Yeah, because you didn't live long enough to get emphysema or cancer." For the first time, I realized how wide the gap in our age really was. People from his generation hadn't worried about carcinogens and tar and nicotine addiction. He was a century old. He was probably more concerned with the danger of women wearing pants.

He studied me, an amused smile on his face. I felt naked, and not from the gaping holes in my shirt. I plucked at them self-consciously. "Would you mind?"

He headed into the bedroom. He playfully tossed me a new T-shirt as he returned.

There was a dull thud and he yelped in surprise. He bent down and picked something off the floor. It was the brick Dahlia had thrown. She'd tied a scrap of paper to it.

"Did you see this?" Nathan asked, dropping into the chair to nurse his stubbed toe.

I shook my head. "It must be the message she was talking about."

As he scanned the paper, his eyes lit up with alarm. He held out the note and I took it.

"'*Lady bug, lady bug, fly away home. Your house is on fire…*'" I read aloud. The rhyme wasn't complete. "You don't think…Nathan, my whole life is in that apartment!"

"Not to mention *The Sanguinarius*." He wrenched open the closet door and pulled his leather trench coat on over his bare shoulders.

"You didn't give me the only copy, did you?" I imagined my eyes bulging from my head as I spoke.

"No, but it's the only copy I have. The last thing I need is some firefighter finding it in the rubble and showing it off. Besides, we don't know if this is Dahlia being vindictive, or if she's done this on Cyrus's orders. He might have someone waiting for you, and if he does, I can take them out."

"I can't see Dahlia doing anything that was going to bring me closer to Cyrus, even if he ordered it. She definitely doesn't want me around." I noticed that Nathan had pocketed several stakes while I spoke and had yet to hand one to me. "Planning a road trip?"

He nodded. "Yup."

"Where?"

"To your apartment." He turned back to his arsenal and strapped a leg holster to his denim-covered calf, dropping another stake into it.

I waited expectantly as he pulled out Ziggy's axe. "Um…were you going to give me something to protect myself, too?"

"You're right." With an embarrassed smile, he headed down the hall. When he returned, he pressed something into my hand. "I'm sorry, I don't know where my head was."

I frowned at the cell phone in my palm. "So…is this a James Bond type of device that shoots fireballs or sprays acid or something?"

"Not exactly." He took the phone and pressed a button, lighting up the screen. "But it does speed-dial Ziggy's pager. If you have any trouble, call him."

My jaw dropped. "What? Ziggy's at the hospital and you told him to stay off the streets."

I wanted him to be annoyed by my protestations, but he remained perfectly calm as he prepared for battle. "Ziggy is better equipped to handle an emergency than you are. I trust him to keep you safe. Besides, there are plenty of weapons in the closet that you can use, and I really doubt that Dahlia will be back."

I couldn't believe what I was hearing. "Hey, it's my apartment burning down! I'm coming with you."

"No." Nathan shook his head adamantly. "Too dangerous."

"Too dan—" I sputtered in my anger. "You're supposed to

want me to die! Hell, if you're so loyal to the Movement, you should be shoveling vampires into burning buildings by the truckload."

"This isn't open for discussion. You don't know how to fight, and you'll be nothing but a distraction to me." When I opened my mouth to argue further, he held up a hand. "I'm leaving. If you want to live through the night, you'll stay here."

Grabbing the axe, he stormed out of the apartment, slamming the door so hard the walls rattled.

"Well…fuck you!" I shouted, kicking one of the couch cushions to the floor.

How dare he! As if I were somehow incapable of looking out for myself in my own, albeit probably on fire, apartment. And what did he mean when he'd said I'd be a distraction? Did he think I was going to get in his way, asking questions with painfully obvious answers and twirling my hair while looking on with a vapid expression?

*Jerk.*

I tossed the cell phone on the table. It slid across the glass top, colliding with the notebooks piled there. Papers cascaded to the floor. Frowning, I knelt to straighten them. I lifted the papers one sheet at a time and shuffled them into a uniform stack. When I laid the pile aside, I noticed the top page was an Internet printout of a map. It was a map of the very affluent neighborhood on the east side of town, with a big red *X* drawn on in marker.

Now, this was interesting. I flipped the paper aside to examine the sheet underneath. It was a fax, dated three days before John Doe had attacked me. Sent from VVEM to N. Galbraith, the letter contained only an address. The same address on the map.

"I thought his last name was Grant," I muttered to myself. I was about to flip to the next page when the cell phone rang.

"Nate, it's me. I'm stuck in this emergency room. They put me in this curtained-off little room and haven't been back since. I think they're calling the police."

I cut Ziggy off when he stopped for a breath. "Nathan isn't here. Dahlia set my apartment on fire. He went to check it out."

"No shit? And he left you there?" He sounded as surprised at Nathan's actions as I was.

"He thinks I can't defend myself." I looked over at the computer desk in the corner. "Listen, a fax came after he went out. From VVEM? Is that the Movement?"

His curse resonated down the line, and no doubt through the stark, sterile emergency room. "Yeah. That's them. I wonder what they want."

"I didn't read it," I said, compounding my lie.

"It's probably another kill order." He cleared his throat. "Just stick it on the fridge. It's the first place he goes after a fight."

"Thanks, Ziggy." I bit my lip. "When exactly did the order come down for Cyrus?"

"The original one? I don't know, he's got like forty by now. Hey, somebody's here to take my blood and they're not happy I'm on a cell phone here, so—"

"No, the last order for him," I practically shouted into the phone. "When did that come through?"

"Why?" Ziggy's tone was suddenly suspicious. "Maybe you should ask Nathan when he gets back. I have to—"

"Ziggy, wait!"

The line went dead. I threw the phone to the floor in frustration. This was too much of a coincidence, I concluded as I stared at the map. Three days. What were the chances he'd gotten this message about a different vampire three days before he'd attacked Cyrus?

I flipped a page. There was my answer, in black and white.

From: VVEM
To: N. Galbraith
Re: Case #372-96 Part 9Y
Assassination Order: Simon Seymour, aka
Simon Kerrick, aka Cyrus Kerrick for Crimes
against Humanity.

Well. There it was.

I glanced guiltily at the door and wondered how long Nathan would be gone. But did I really care if he found me missing?

Remembering his condescension earlier, I decided that I definitely would not care. This wasn't any of his business, and I only had a few precious days left to make my decision about the Movement. I deserved to know the truth about my undead birth. As much help as Nathan had been, it wasn't his blood flowing through my veins.

A curious ache filled me at the thought of Cyrus, and I wondered if this yearning was a symptom of the blood tie. And if it was, would this strange link protect me from more harm at the hands of my sire?

Without allowing myself to dwell on fear, I stuffed the map into my pocket. I called in to work to say I wouldn't be in. When I hung up, a vaguely empty feeling came over me, the realization that I might not return to the hospital. I forced the thought aside and opened the closet.

Though there were plenty of weapons at my disposal, I took a stake, the smallest and easiest to conceal of the bunch.

Besides, I knew what to do with a stake. The spiky-ball-on-a-stick thing looked considerably more complicated to operate. Of course, a stake wouldn't protect me from Dahlia, if she was still waiting for me. But Nathan was a vampire hunter, not a witch hunter. I suppose I could douse her with water and melt her like in *The Wizard of Oz,* if it came to that.

I almost left a note for Nathan but decided against it. I realized there was nothing I could write that wouldn't seem like I'd turned my back on all of his help. There was no way to soften the truth.

As helpful and considerate as he'd been, there were some questions Nathan couldn't answer. For those, I'd have to face my fear the way I had that night in the morgue.

I had to meet my sire.

# Six

*John Doe*

The day obviously hadn't been a warm one. The twilight air was cold enough to steal the breath from my lungs.

I'd found my wool coat hanging over the towel rack in the bathroom. It appeared Nathan had spot-cleaned the blood from it. But it didn't keep me warm as I walked the miles from Nathan's apartment to the address on the paper. Being dead had some serious disadvantages, like constantly assuming room temperature, no matter what that temperature might be.

While my car still sat at the curb outside the bookshop, the keys were probably still on the ground outside the donor house. There was no way I'd go back there. I preferred walking.

I was familiar with the posh neighborhood. When I'd been new to the city, I'd often drive through the winding streets and marvel at the modern mansions and fairy-tale châteaus. They looked completely out of place in the sparsely wooded area. Tall brick walls and elaborate gates wrapped around the lots. Some had privacy hedges with formidable-looking security cameras that glared at passersby with cold, glassy eyes. From the shelter of my car, I'd daydreamed about the people living in these houses and imagined living in one myself ten years down the road. The fantasies had always featured a handsome yet oddly faceless husband and our adorable, ambiguous children. Only one house had ever been the feature of a horror story in my mind.

That one turned out to be Cyrus's.

A severe Edwardian manor, it sat far back on a lawn surrounded by a stone wall. The wrought-iron gate at the drive looked as though it hadn't been opened in centuries. There was no intercom or bell. I gripped the iron bars and gave a push. The hinges didn't creak, and the gate swung open to admit me.

I'd never felt so exposed in my entire life as I walked toward the house. The driveway cut a paved swath through the lawn, which glowed an eerie green in the moonlight. Any moment, they'd release the dogs, I was sure. And I hated dogs.

Lucky for me, no one seemed to notice my presence, even as I neared the front door. With every footstep my confidence built, until I got close enough to grasp the doorknob.

The door was open.

I froze. I'd believed no one had seen me coming. As I looked over my shoulder at the broad expanse of lawn, I realized how foolish that assumption had been. The full moonlight might as well have been stadium lighting. Not to mention someone was probably watching me through the security camera mounted above the lintel. I swallowed my fear and stepped inside.

"Hello?" I called, my voice sounding like the dumb female protagonist of a slasher flick. "Your door is open."

"I know."

Before I could turn to find the source of the voice, strong arms wrapped around me. The echo of the slamming door sounded final, like the felling of a judge's gavel.

Whoever held me was not a vampire. I don't know how I knew. I just did. Maybe it was the smell of his blood, or the surge of power I felt at the realization I could easily overcome him and make my escape. But the foyer was completely dark, and I had no idea where I'd find the door. Healing abilities and heightened reflexes were cool and all, but I really wished we came equipped with night vision. I cursed the total unfairness of it.

"The Master doesn't like that kind of language," the man holding me admonished.

My captor shoved me with surprising strength. I collided painfully with a set of double doors, which opened under my weight and spilled me into the next room.

I wiped a trickle of blood from my nose, sickened at my compulsion to taste it. My eyes adjusted to the dark, and I saw the room was very lavish. Leaded windowpanes stretched from the gilded ceiling high above all the way to the marble floor where I lay sprawled. A fresco was painted on the wall. I couldn't make out the figures distinctly, but there was a lot of nakedness going on. It was like I'd died and been sent to a really Baroque version of hell. Somehow, though, I couldn't imagine Satan having bad enough taste to hang red velvet drapes.

Six black-clad men stood guard around the room, two stationed at each door, including the one I'd just been thrown through. The thrower stepped in. He was dressed the same as the guards.

"Watch her," he ordered the two closest men, and all the sentries nodded their heads.

When the thrower left, I climbed to my feet and took a few steps to the right. Each of the guards' heads swiveled slightly to follow me. I stepped to the left, with the same results. I had an overwhelming compulsion to boogie a little and see if they copied that, too.

Just then a door opened to admit a shadowy figure.

Though the sliver of light spilling in distorted my vision, I could tell from her scent it was Dahlia. My mouth watered at the memory of her blood.

One of the guards reached out as if to prevent her from entering, but she raised her hands and he inexplicably dropped his arm. A tremor of fear seemed to go through all the sentries. It was as tangible as a tidal wave crashing over my head. They were afraid of Dahlia.

She crossed the room slowly and waved a hand at the darkness.

"Illuminate," she commanded, and light flooded the room.

I forced myself not to retreat as she advanced. "Nice trick. I prefer the clapper, but to each his own."

"I can't remember where I picked it up, but it's handy," she said casually. "Not as useful as my other ones."

She walked in a wide circle around me. "So, you lived. I would have thought there was a lesson in that experience."

I shrugged. "Maybe I'm a slow learner."

"Really? Then perhaps you need a visual aide." She waved her hand again and mumbled a long command in a language I didn't recognize. Nathan's lifeless body appeared on the floor, his blood in a dark pool around him.

The sight stole my breath. I opened my mouth to scream, but no sound came. But Nathan wasn't dead. *This is just a trick,* I told myself. *Don't let it rattle you.*

The vision evaporated as quickly as it had appeared.

Dahlia laughed like a child with a new toy. "You bought that? For a doctor, you're not very bright."

I rounded on her and felt the change come over me. For a moment, I thought I saw fear in her eyes, but she stood her ground and didn't utter a noise when I tackled her to the floor. I wanted to rip her throat out, not to feed, just to kill. The thought of her harming the one person who'd bothered to help me made me insane with rage.

A series of loud claps interrupted me before I could deliver a killing blow. I looked up, and Dahlia kicked me away with more force than I would have expected.

Cyrus himself strode toward us. His blond hair seemed longer, falling almost to the floor. He wore an ancient-looking brocade robe the color of blood, and his bare feet peeked out below the hem.

This was the monster who'd made me a vampire. He didn't look like the creature who'd attacked me. His face was young and handsome. Only his mismatched eyes hinted at his true nature. That, and his facial expression. He looked furious.

"If you don't want to be the next meal on my table, you won't harm her again," he warned Dahlia in a deep, sophisticated voice.

But he didn't spare her a glance as he approached me. His every step resonated with predatory grace. A tremor surged through my body as our gazes connected. A smirk of satisfaction twisted his lips as he reached out to pull me to my feet.

Dahlia sniffled pathetically. Cyrus turned and pointed one finger in her direction. The deadly sharp nail gleamed in the light, manicured to elegant perfection.

"Get out!" he shouted, and she scrambled to her feet, running from the room as fast as her plump legs could carry her.

"Disobedience, you'll find, is the one thing I cannot tolerate from my pets," Cyrus said, turning to me with an apologetic shrug. "Please, allow me to introduce myself. I'm—"

"We've met before."

He arched an exquisitely sculpted brow. "Have we?"

With lightning fast precision, he pinned me against his chest. My veins burned at the physical contact, and I held myself absolutely still, afraid that at any moment I would writhe against him shamelessly like a cat in heat. This was the blood tie Nathan had spoken of. It was terrifying and exhilarating all at once.

Never in my life had I felt as if I were spiraling out of control the way I did at that moment, nor had I felt such absolute relief as I did with my sire's arms around me. The loneliness of the past months vanished when he touched me, as though all I had needed to satiate the agitated emptiness in my soul was to be with him. He made me feel so strangely complete that I wondered if I would ever be truly happy again without him or if I'd miss my old life if I never left this room again.

Cyrus leaned his cheek against mine and sniffed me.

I heard the blood singing in my sire's veins, compelling me not to struggle. I can't say I would have wanted to escape even if I could.

"Oh, yes. I know you now." His voice was a rich, awed whisper in my ear. "You're even more beautiful than I'd remembered."

He ran his hands up and down my arms. I trembled. My knees buckled and I sagged backward, relying on his strength to keep me up.

Now I knew why the Movement thought of the tie in such absolute terms. It was better than love, better than success. The blood tie was the culmination and fulfillment of all human desires. I couldn't imagine how anyone would want to resist it.

"What's your name?" Cyrus's cold breath teased my ear as he spoke.

"Carrie," I answered without hesitation.

"The cards suggested I had a surprise coming. I had no idea it would be so...exciting." He pushed his pelvis against my backside, his cock stiff and straining through the robe. His fingertips brushed the back of my hand, and he laced his fingers with mine.

A dizzying buzz forced my eyes closed, and I was overwhelmed with the unpleasant sensation of rushing rapidly forward. I forced my eyes open, and my vision swam. When it cleared, the room was gone. Instead, I saw the E.R., and my own panicked expression. I was inside Cyrus's mangled body as he lay on the gurney. I saw myself staring in abject horror at the patient before me.

I jerked my hand from his and found myself in my own body, in the present time.

"My very own angel of mercy." I felt his tongue, surprisingly hot, against my neck. "You tasted so good."

Suddenly, my memory of the demon who'd carved me up broke through. The claws that had ripped my flesh. The sadistic eyes staring down as I'd cowered, terrified and unable to defend myself. I broke free. "Get away from me!"

Though he looked much different than he had in vampire form, all I could see was his resemblance to John Doe. He folded his arms across his chest as he regarded me. "Oh, you have fire in you. I'll have so much fun with that."

From his perversely satisfied tone, I gathered it wasn't good, clean, car-bingo-type fun he spoke of. "I'm not interested. And speaking of fire, burning down my apartment isn't exactly the way to a girl's heart."

"No," he agreed with a frown, closing the distance between

us. "I find the more effective route is directly through the rib cage."

"What do you want?" I demanded.

Looping his arms around my waist, he drew me closer. "You came to me, Carrie. It seems you are the one who desires something."

He nuzzled my neck, rubbing his lips across the scar there. I closed my eyes, too willing to give in to the sensations coursing through my veins. "I want answers."

"Yet you haven't asked any questions." His teeth grazed my skin. "But you don't really want to talk."

"Yes, I do," I insisted, trying to pull away from him.

He held me fast. "Your body tells me something entirely different. You want me. I can smell it on you."

I ground my teeth. "It's the blood tie. If you were any other guy, I'd have slapped you by now."

"If you were any other woman, you'd be dead by now." Despite his menacing words, he let me go. "I slept quite late this evening and I haven't had my breakfast. Would you care to join me?"

"Will you answer my questions?"

"That depends on what you ask. But yes, Carrie. I will give you the answers you've so bravely sought." He held out his hand for me, and I bit my lip, considering his offer. Was this a trick? A trap? But he couldn't have known I was coming. He hadn't even known who I was when he'd first seen me. There would have been no time to plan anything devious. At worst, I'd spend an uncomfortable meal trying to fight the effects of the blood tie. At best, I'd get a better understanding of what had happened to me. I slipped my hand into his and let him lead me to another room.

The dining room was large and windowless. It was even

more ostentatious than the ballroom, if that were possible. Dark wood paneling covered the walls, and the only light came from candles held in ornate silver sconces.

Cyrus pulled out a chair from the long dining table and motioned for me to sit. Then he sat at my right, at the head of the table.

The table was long enough for twenty people, but it was only set for two. Crystal wineglasses took the place of plates. The largest covered platter I had ever seen dominated the center of the table. I wondered who he'd planned on sharing his meal with before I arrived.

"Dahlia." Cyrus replied to my thought as he gracefully smoothed a napkin over his lap. A dainty crystal bell lay by his left hand, and he rang it. It unnerved me that he could read my private thoughts so easily.

A distinguished-looking black butler entered, followed by two of the guards. The butler reached for the shining silver dome over the platter and hesitated at the sight of me. One of the guards made a noise. The butler glared at them and whisked away the cover.

"Your breakfast, sir," he said, a look of distaste on his age-lined features.

The nude body of a young woman lay on the platter. She was obviously dead. Her blank eyes stared sightlessly at the ceiling, one hand propped limply on her breast. Her other arm stretched high above her head, mimicking the curve of the platter. Someone had thought to garnish her with rose petals. The woman was displayed beautifully before us like a Renaissance goddess. I was horrified by my reaction. This woman was dead, her remains exploited for aesthetic purposes.

To please the man sitting beside me.

The terror I should have felt from his presence fought to the surface, then was quickly drowned once again by the blood tie. Despite all the harm he'd already done to me, it seemed absurd that he would ever hurt me again. I caught myself yearning to touch him, desperate for the security of a physical connection, and I squashed the feeling down.

*He's a monster. A murderer. You're smarter than this.*

"Thank you, Clarence, that will be all," Cyrus said with a polite nod.

The butler and guards departed. Cyrus stood and reached for my glass. He lifted the dead girl's arm and flicked his razor-sharp fingernails across her wrist. Dark red blood poured from the wound. She hadn't been deceased for long.

The calm, matter-of-fact manner in which he handled the corpse made it seem perfectly normal to be dining off a dead body. I stopped reminding myself to be horrified—what good would it do me?—and concentrated on the questions I wanted answers to.

He filled his glass next and lifted it to his nose, savoring the scent. I ignored my glass, but he didn't seem to mind.

"Now, what were we talking about?" he asked after he sat again.

"You mentioned Dahlia. Were you reading my mind?"

He drank deeply from his glass, then dabbed his lips with his napkin. "Of course. You wondered who I had planned on dining with since the table was set for two. Dahlia sometimes likes to consume human blood, and I indulge her."

"Is she a vampire?" It was a silly question. I knew I would have recognized his blood in the taste of hers.

As I expected, he shook his head. "No. Dahlia is very sweet, one of my favorite pets, actually. But I'd never make her one of us. She's not…special? I suppose that is the word for it."

"And I was special?" I felt a surprising sympathy for the girl. She thought I'd taken her place when there had actually been nothing to take. But that's not what concerned me most. "Can you read my mind all the time?"

"If I want to." He smiled. "And to answer your first question, yes, you're special."

"But I was an accident," I said as I fixed him with a piercing stare. "I remember that night, or at least, most of it. You never fed me your blood. It got into me when I stabbed you, but you didn't mean for it to happen."

Sighing heavily, he leaned back in his chair. He studied me for a long moment before speaking again. "You have my blood, Carrie. Even if I didn't intend to share it with you, it still flows through your veins. It makes you precious to me."

I glared at him. "You attacked me and left me for dead. I wasn't so precious to you then."

He raised his hand to stop me. "Please, excuse me. These damned eyes, they dry out so quickly."

He lifted a small knife and plunged it into his borrowed eye. The organ fell to the table with a soft, squishy sound and flattened. A gruesome image of the dead morgue attendant flashed through my mind.

Cyrus leaned over the face of the dead girl and carved out one of her eyes. When he'd inserted his replacement, he freed the second eye from the corpse and dropped it into his glass. It sank to the bottom like an olive in a martini.

"I had two perfectly good eyes before I returned to this city. Fresh ones are hard to come by, and they wear out before you've gotten much use from them."

My physician's curiosity took over then, distracting me from our earlier line of conversation. "How does it work?"

"I don't know." He blinked a few times, as though he'd just

put in new contact lenses. A thin line of blood ran like a tear down his cheek. "I'm assuming it has something to do with the regenerative humors in human blood."

"There's no such thing as humors. Does it work with other body parts? Limbs?" I scooted forward in my chair. "What about teeth?"

"How do I know? Carrie, I understand your thirst for knowledge, but there are questions even the blasted *Sanguinarius* can't answer." He sipped from his glass. The eye inside rolled around to stare at me.

I was going to barf.

Cyrus either didn't notice or didn't care. "I'll have the servants prepare your room, but I fear it won't be ready before dawn. You can stay with me today. I'm sure we can find some engaging activity to fill the boring daylight hours."

"Whoa, whoa." I waved my hands in front of me as though I were signaling a plane. "I'm not staying."

Not that I wasn't tempted. The blood tie was an incredible aphrodisiac, despite the fact I'd just watched him pick over a dead body as if it were a rotisserie chicken. But I had only come here in need of information, not an unfathomably dirty one-night stand.

Cyrus's expression darkened. "I thought you said your apartment burned down. Surely you need a place to stay."

"I have other options. Did you do it so I'd have no place else to go?"

"I didn't do it at all. If Dahlia harmed your property, then I'm sorry. The drama of fire seems to hold some fascination for her. I can't undo what she's done. All I can offer you is a place to stay. And a few amusements." He reached across the table to stroke my hand.

I rolled my eyes. "That's a lovely sentiment, but there's

this organization who'll want to kill me if I stay here with you."

"The Movement?" His rich laughter filled the dining room. "They'd like to cage us all and let us die."

"You don't think much of them," I said.

"No. I don't. I've longed for a companion for years, but because of the restrictions in place by the damned Movement, I have been unable to retain any of the fledglings I've sired."

So he didn't know about his *pet* and her penchant for off-ing the competition. I couldn't believe he would be so dense, but if he was really lonely, perhaps he purposely overlooked her transgressions. Maybe a murderous companion was better than none at all.

Cyrus stood and moved behind me, placing his long fingers on my shoulders. "Fate has put us in a unique situation. Why not come to an arrangement that will be beneficial for both of us? You become the companion I've been seeking, and I'll teach you to use the full extent of your power, power the Movement would deny you."

"What kind of power?"

He smiled like a used-car salesman. "The power to rule, of course. The power over life and death and the strength to wield it to your advantage."

A pang of longing washed over me. I'd loved the seemingly God-like powers I'd believed I'd held as a doctor. But that illusion had been ripped apart the night Cyrus had destroyed my perceptions of death and accidentally set me apart from both.

"I thought I had that before. I ended up bleeding to death in the morgue," I said, shaking my head. "Why should I believe you? I don't know you that well. You might just kill me again."

"I might," he said finally. "I'm not generally regarded as someone to be trusted."

I looked over the rapidly purpling body on the table. "No kidding?"

He knelt at my side. "Search your heart, Carrie. I have faith you'll make the right choice."

*Some choice.* I could live only if I pledged my allegiance to the Movement, or I could live to be Cyrus's little wifey. Either way, I was a slave. A prisoner. A prostitute.

"I've made my decision. Us meeting, that was an accident. I'm not fated to be your companion, or whatever the heck you're looking for."

"Tell me, Doctor, do you follow many of your patients to the morgue?" he asked with a knowing smile. "You followed me. You wanted me."

"You were dead. That's not my bag. Sorry."

He reached out his hands again, but I dodged them.

"If that's what you believe, I can't change your mind," he said, gesturing to the door.

I stood and headed for it, but Cyrus called after me.

"Dahlia is useful. She's only alive because she amuses me. Not because I love her. And she doesn't love me." His voice was quiet and sad.

"I'm sorry if you're unhappy." And I was. I could feel his desperation, his hurt, his anger. But I could also feel the cool edge of manipulation. He was confident I would cave in.

He continued, and his sorrow sounded genuine. "I only want to protect you."

"I don't need protection, Cyrus. I need time to think." I walked away. "If I go through that door, will the guards stop me?"

Cyrus shook his head. "Will you return?"

I thought of Nathan and his undying loyalty to the Movement. Would I ever become so indoctrinated to their rhetoric? Was I even susceptible to such brainwashing? "I don't know. Maybe."

His sorrow instantly changed to anger. "I'm your sire, Carrie. You belong to me."

So this was the true nature of his game. He would coerce me into staying.

"I don't belong to anyone." The words gave me courage as I spoke them. "I don't belong to my job, I don't belong to a man, I don't belong to the Movement, and I sure as hell don't belong to you. I have five days left to make a decision. If I choose to return to you, I will. But I'm not stupid, Cyrus. You didn't make me on purpose. You didn't make me out of love. You meant to kill me in the morgue. I was an accident. And I don't owe you anything."

I walked out the door and didn't look back.

# *Seven*

*June 23, 1924*

Cyrus's word was good. No guards accosted me as I left the house.

My head swam with a tremendous mix of emotions. The rage came from Cyrus. I could still hear his screams of fury and the crash of things breaking inside the house as I crossed the lawn.

My sadness weighed heavy on me as my feet hit the sidewalk. I didn't know what I'd expected to find in Cyrus. A mentor? A friend? An ally against the shadowy threat of the Movement, which demanded I live for them or not live at all?

What I'd found was another dead end. Cyrus would rule me as surely as the Movement would, and that wasn't something I could accept. My whole life, I'd been ruled by one thing or another. First, my father, who'd been so busy planning my future career, I'd wondered how he'd found time for his own.

*"You're my job, Carrie. It's my duty to see you do well in life."*

How disappointed he'd be in me now. But then, I'd been

just as bad as him, pushing aside adolescent dreams of romance for study and determination, until medicine consumed my life and any relationship that wasn't a calculated career move seemed like a waste of time. I'd let so many trivial things get in the way of my own happiness that I couldn't remember what the things that might have made me happy were anymore.

My body grew numb as I walked back to Nathan's apartment. I hadn't left a note, but I'm sure the hastily riffled-through faxes would give him a hint as to where I'd been. Tension coiled like electricity in the air as I crossed the street. The windows of the apartment were dark, but the shop's easel sign was on the sidewalk. I steeled myself against the unavoidable stench of incense and headed down the stairs to the bookshop.

There was no need for the precaution. The air was clear and no peaceful music soothed me as I entered the room and leaned against the counter. I heard muffled cursing, followed by the distinctive thud of books hitting the floor.

"Need some help?" I called.

Swearing followed a startling bang. Nathan emerged from the shelves, one hand pressed against the top of his head.

"You're back," he said flatly, wincing as he ran his fingers through his hair.

"Sorry. I had some stuff I needed to do." I couldn't tell him, I decided. If he asked, I wouldn't lie, but it would be suicide to volunteer the information.

He didn't say anything. He went behind the shelves again and continued doing whatever I had interrupted.

I followed him. He slammed the books into their places on the shelf and walked past me to the other end of the shop, where he fussed with a display of tarot cards that didn't look as though it needed rearranging.

"So, are you going to talk to me or what?" I asked quietly as he fanned out an open deck as if they were a row of magazines on a coffee table.

"I'm sorry. I'm being rude. How was your evening? Did you have a nice time with your sire while I rummaged through your burning apartment?" The sarcasm in his voice was like a slap in the face.

My temper rose. "You went to that apartment all by yourself. I didn't ask you to go. All you wanted was your precious book!"

"This isn't about the fucking book!" He slammed his fists on the table. A sealed deck of cards bounced onto the floor. "How long did you wait before you went snooping through my stuff to find his address? Did you give any thought to what you were going to do? No! After everything I told you, after what you lived through at his hands, you went after him unprotected. He could have killed you!"

"But he didn't. I can handle myself," I said.

"You don't know what he's like!" Nathan yelled as he put a display of candles in order.

I hoped he broke every damned one of them. "And you do?"

"Yes!" He turned to face me, a handful of orange candles still in his hand. "He's capable of things you can't imagine. Things you wouldn't want to know."

"He's a killer. It's in our blood to be killers. It says so in your freaking vampire bible!"

"Is it in our blood to torture? To maim? Is it in his blood to prey on the weak and exploit kids like Ziggy? Because I've got the same blood in my veins that he does, and I've never had the urge to rape and murder a sixteen-year-old girl!"

I couldn't believe my ears. Cyrus was definitely evil. In the short time I'd known him I'd heard him refer to humans as pets and seen him casually feast on a corpse as though it were a fine cut of beef. But I knew myself, and I would never have been so attracted to someone capable of such a heinous act. "He couldn't have done that."

"Are you so sure? Because it was on the last order. I've got a newspaper clipping about her disappearance upstairs. He was awfully proud of her. Apparently, the fun for him is in killing the girls as he's violating them. He likes to watch them die while he's inside them."

Nathan's description of the obscene act made my stomach churn. I covered my mouth with my hand. "I don't want to hear any more."

"No, you want to experience it for yourself." He exhaled noisily. "But you go ahead and do what you want."

"That's not what I want."

"Hey, I really don't care. Apparently, nothing I say is going to matter." He went back to his candles.

His calm fed my growing anger. "What's that supposed to mean?"

"It means no matter what I say, you're going to do what you damn well please."

"Why shouldn't I?" I shuffled the artfully arranged cards into a single pile on the tabletop. "The only words out of your mouth are 'don't do that, Carrie,' and 'it's dangerous, Carrie' and 'I'll kill you, Carrie,' but you never tell me why!"

"I dispense information on a need-to-know basis!"

"You sound like my goddamned father!" I shouted, stamping my foot.

Nathan made an exasperated sound and threw his hands up in the air. "What the hell are you talking about?"

"If I ask questions, you get all evasive. You don't want to share anything about your life, but you seem to want me to just blindly trust that you know what's best for me." I pointed at him. "How do I know you're not just as dangerous as Cyrus?"

He stepped so close to me that our shoes touched. "Oh, believe me, I'm the most dangerous thing in this room right now."

"Oh, yeah?"

"Yeah, and you're about to see just how dangerous."

I tilted my head so I could look him in the eye. "Is that a threat?"

"You tell me." His breath was cold on my face.

We glared at each other in silence, tension dancing between us like a ballerina with a broken leg. I don't think I'd ever been more infuriated.

He turned away, but neither of us had spent our anger. This was merely the eye of the storm.

He faced me again, his arms folded across his chest. "Fine. Prove to me you can take care of yourself."

I hesitated. "What?"

"Attack me."

"You're not serious." I laughed.

"The hell I'm not!" He stepped back and braced himself for a fight. "I'm angry at you. You're angry at me, right?"

"Yeah, but I'm not about to indulge in mindless violence with a vampire."

"Would it be better if I was a human?" He rolled his eyes. "This will work out some of that aggression. And you can prove to me that you can stand up to Cyrus. It's a win-win situation. Besides, right now, I'd really like to kick your ass."

"Kick my—" My mouth dropped open as I sputtered in resentment. "Oh, I'm going to put the hurt on you so bad!"

I charged him with no specific plan of attack. My shoulder collided with his midsection. He tumbled backward, and I fell to the floor on top of him. We upended the table on the way down, tarot cards fluttering around us as we struggled.

My flying hair and our flailing limbs obscured my vision. I swung at him blindly. Pain reverberated down my arm as my fist connected with his jaw.

Nathan pinned one arm behind me and rolled me onto my back. The hard floorboards bit into my knuckles, and I arched my back to relieve the pressure. Unfortunately, this motion pushed my breasts against his chest, and it was more than a little arousing.

I used my free hand to yank his hair, pulling as hard as I could. He grabbed my wrist, squeezing brutally, and I released my grip. He forced my arm above my head and held it to the floor.

The anger between us dissipated, abandoning us with only the raw, primal sound of our heavy breathing. I stopped struggling the same time Nathan loosened his grip. Painfully aware of how close our bodies were, I looked into his eyes.

He pressed his hips against mine. Apparently, I wasn't the only one affected.

"You suck at fighting," he rasped. He leaned forward, his mouth a millimeter from mine. I closed my eyes and tried to stop my body from trembling. His breath teased my lips, and I shivered.

The bells above the shop door chimed. Nathan sprang to his feet, using a book from the nearest table as a shield to hide his obvious state of arousal. I rose clumsily beside him and hoped I didn't look too flushed.

The customer who entered was about fifty years old and had long, graying hair. She looked us over with knowing brown eyes. "I've come at a bad time. I'll be back later." She gave the overturned table and scattered merchandise a pointed glance before turning toward the door.

"No, no." Nathan reached down to right the table. "What can I help you with tonight, Deb?"

The woman looked from him to me with an expression of uncertainty. I coughed and smiled, trying—quite unsuccessfully—to hide the guilt written all over my face.

At Nathan's urging, the customer rattled off a long list of ingredients she needed to make a protection charm. He directed her to the herb pantry at the back of the shop and promised he'd be with her in a moment.

"Deb is a regular," he explained, almost apologetically. "You might as well go upstairs."

"Not to my apartment?" I asked hopefully.

He stared at the ground. "Yeah, I was meaning to tell you about that."

"It's completely gone." I could tell by the look on his face.

He couldn't meet my eyes. "I'm sorry, Carrie."

I went to Nathan's apartment, my head still spinning. What had I been thinking? I'd met this man just over a week ago, and now I was rolling around on the floor with him. And after his tall, dark and surly act. Had I really become the wilting Southern-belle type, just waiting for a big, brooding Rhett Butler to come and dominate me?

I wandered around, absentmindedly picking up clothes strewn around the living room. Once the dirty laundry was folded, I moved on to the coffee table.

I straightened the hopeless pile of books and papers. Not too thoroughly, lest I be accused of snooping again. Thinking of everything he'd said downstairs only made my blood boil, so I gathered stray dishes and dropped them unceremoniously into a sink full of soapy water. I meant to wash them, until the coffee mugs turned the water a soft pink and I lost my stomach for the task.

My manic cleaning spree continued through the house. In the past nine days, I had become homeless, hunted and, soon, unemployed. I probably had enough money in my bank account for a few months' rent and utilities, but the point seemed moot since I didn't have an apartment anymore.

Did the Voluntary Vampire Extinction Movement pay a salary?

Nathan had offered blood, shelter and protection. The least I could do was tidy up the place. *Because he's not getting anything else.* My behavior downstairs might have raised some of his expectations. I'd have to nip that situation in the bud.

Moving to his bedroom, I stripped the sheets from the bed and threw them into the corner that appeared to be his dirty-laundry hamper. Vampire or not, it appeared men just couldn't clean up after themselves.

A pang of sadness washed over me as I realized I no longer had a home to clean. Or clothes. Or major appliances.

How had my life suddenly become so complicated? How would I survive as a vampire? *How long has it been since he's flipped his mattress?*

I eyed the goldfish bowl on Nathan's bedside table as I wrestled the heavy mattress off the box springs. I'd read somewhere that goldfish had a memory span of three seconds. Every three seconds, that poor fish had to come to grips with a new and frightening reality. I could definitely identify with that.

I lifted the bowl, pressed my face against the cool glass and counted to three. "Surprise."

I sighed as I set the container back in its place. It didn't seem to phase the little orange guy. He just kept on swimming. Another three seconds passed as I wrestled the mattress over and back onto the box springs. Panting and sweating, I looked to the fishbowl. No reaction.

Fish were survivors.

I opened the closet doors to look for clean sheets, on the off chance he owned some. There were assorted bare hangers and a few shirts that hadn't been worn in so long that the shoulders were dusty. Three mismatched tennis shoes huddled together in the corner next to a dried-out, curled-up object that resembled a dead mouse.

I found a set of sheets on the top shelf and pulled them down. Something heavy and sharp came down with them and landed on my foot. I said a few choice words and leaned over to pick up the offending object. It was a small picture frame, weighty for its size. The picture was yellow and faded.

A pretty young woman beamed at me from the photograph. She wore a simple white blouse and a long tartan skirt. She clutched a bouquet of wild flowers tightly to her chest. A young man in a plain-looking suit stood next to her. The couple posed on the stone steps of a small country church. I squinted at the man. He bore a remarkable resemblance to…

I flipped the frame over and carefully removed the photograph. There were no names, but someone had recorded the date. June 23, 1924.

I stared at the picture. Nathan, just twenty years old, stared back.

"Carrie? Sorry I took so long, but you wouldn't believe how that woman can talk about her cats."

I put the photograph back into the frame, replaced it on the top shelf and slammed the closet doors shut.

"Wow, this place looks great," Nathan called from the living room, veritable appreciation in his voice. He came into the bedroom and laughed when he saw me. "You're making the bed, too? Do I have to pay you?"

"And I flipped the mattress. That'll be twenty bucks." I eyed the shopping bags he held. "Or whatever's in that Victoria's Secret bag."

He laughed, a tight, embarrassed sound, and dumped the bags on the bed. "I didn't know what size you are, so if these don't fit, we'll return them."

Nathan had thought of everything. There were sweaters and T-shirts in safe, neutral colors from Old Navy, jeans, and pretty silk panties courtesy of Victoria's Secret. "I saved some of your clothes from the fire, but they were so full of smoke, I didn't think they'd ever come clean."

A lump formed in my throat. "Nathan, you didn't have to do this. I—"

I didn't realize I was crying until my voice grew too thick to speak.

"I didn't mean to make you cry. I just thought you could use some stuff." He cleared his throat and handed me another bag. "If I give you this, do you promise to stop?"

I snorted through my tears. "I'll try. When did you buy all these things?"

"When I got back from the fire. You were gone and I was pissed off, so I went shopping."

"You went shopping because you were mad at me?" I took the bag from his hands. "Remind me to stay on your bad side."

He chuckled at that. "Must be some lingering feminine influence from a past life. If you ever catch me watching *The View,* go ahead and kill me. I just figured you might come back, and I wanted to make you feel really guilty."

"Don't worry, I do," I said, reaching into the bag. It was

plastic, stamped with the logo of a local grocery chain. I froze when my fingers closed on a familiar object. "Nathan… what?"

With trembling hands, I pulled out the small framed photo of me and my parents on graduation day. It had been on my dresser when I'd last seen it. "Oh, thank you."

Appalled at the sight of my fresh tears, he backed away. "Whoa, whoa. I thought you were going to stop doing that."

"I'm sorry. Nobody's ever done anything so nice for me." It wasn't a lie. I'd been raised to believe that nothing came easy, nothing was free, and the only person I could depend on was myself. I reached into the bag again. "Is this my…this is my diploma."

"I figured you might want to keep it, for nostalgic purposes." He scuffed his shoes on the carpet. "You know, this fire might be the perfect way to break ties with your former life. People die in fires all the time."

Former life. My photo album. My journals. Everything I'd valued as irreplaceable was gone. My father used to say our society puts too much value on the past. I wished I could scream his words back at him now. *My past was all that was left of you. Now that it's gone, so are you.*

"Let's not talk about this right now, okay?" I said as I dabbed my eyes on the back of my hand. Before Nathan could protest, my stomach growled loudly.

A look of concern crossed his face. "How long has it been since you've fed?"

I cringed at the memory of the dead girl. "Cyrus offered, but I couldn't…feed. Not the way he did."

Nathan's jaw tightened, but he said nothing. He headed to the kitchen, and I followed.

"So, did you get *The Sanguinarius* back?" I watched as he

pulled a bag of blood from the refrigerator and poured it into the teapot on the stove.

He shook his head. "I didn't have time to look for it."

Surprisingly, I found myself savoring the metallic smell of the warming blood. "But you had time to look for my diploma, and the picture of my parents?"

Shrugging his shoulders, he poured me a mug and left the rest on the stove. "I had priorities."

Why was I a priority? Nathan had only known me a handful of days. "Your priority should have been getting the book."

He turned to the sink and began halfheartedly washing the dishes. "The book can be replaced. Memories can't. I know if I lost all those pictures I have of Ziggy... See, one time, when he was eleven, I took him to Disney World. We could only go out at night, of course, but we went in December, so the sun set earlier—"

"I hope you don't think I'm going to sleep with you just because you're being nice," I blurted.

There was a crash and Nathan hissed. When he pulled his hand from the water, he was bleeding. He looked from his torn thumb to me, his gaze murderous. "What the hell, Carrie?"

The logic I'd used to work the accusation up to a full-fledged fear in my head suddenly seemed incredibly silly. Still, I soldiered on. "Well, you bought me clothes, you rescued my diploma from a burning building at the expense of your precious book, you're feeding me...what am I supposed to think?"

"Maybe you're supposed to think I'm an idiot for doing all that shit for someone who clearly doesn't appreciate it!" He stuck his thumb in his mouth and sucked away the blood, his face contorting into the freakish features he'd displayed the night we'd first met.

I cringed, fervently hoping he didn't notice. "People don't just do things for other people without wanting something in return. Sorry if that offends you, but it's a fact."

"Is it?" He watched me for a moment with an expression of bitter amusement. "How on earth did you get so jaded?"

"Hey, you've lived on earth longer than I have, buddy. You can come up with a better answer than I can." I took a swallow of blood.

Nathan chuckled and turned back to his dishes. After a long pause, he spoke without looking at me. "You can stay here as long as you need to. I don't mind. But don't think I expect anything because of what happened downstairs. It was just one of those weird things we can forget about."

"Thanks," I said softly. I managed to drink more blood without dwelling on the repulsive things I'd seen that night, like Cyrus's choice of cocktail olive replacement. Unfortunately, all that was left to dwell on was Nathan's comment. I didn't consider myself the hottest tamale in the enchilada, but almost kissing me was something he could just *forget?* I couldn't help but be insulted.

He continued. "And I'm sorry about what I said. And I shouldn't have fought with you. We don't know each other very well, but what I do know of you, I like. I want you to make good choices so we don't have to be enemies."

"Nathan, I'm not like him. That's what I found out tonight."

"Good." He didn't look up.

I stood next to him so he couldn't avoid me. "He didn't have anything I wanted. I'm not interested in that kind of life."

When he looked at me, his gaze burned through me. "And what kind of life is that, Carrie?"

"A life without consequences." I turned away and went to

sit at the kitchen table. "But that doesn't mean I've made a decision. I won't spend my life trying to prove myself to some shadowy organization because they think they can choose whether I live or die. The only person with power over my life is me."

"I respect that. But it doesn't change anything."

I sighed. He would never bend, and I knew it. We were five days from being mortal enemies, and I'd come to rely on him as a friend. An incredibly touchy, downright rude friend, but the only one I had.

I didn't want to think about it tonight.

Nathan finished the dishes without further conversation. When the last one rested in the drying rack, he washed his hands and wiped them on the dish towel. I handed him my mug with a sheepish smile, and he made a face in good-natured annoyance as he dropped it in the empty sink. "Feel like a drink? A real one, this time?"

"I could definitely use one." I followed him to the living room where he ordered me to sit.

He pulled a large book from one of the shelves and opened it. It was hollow, the pages carved out to form a niche for a gleaming metal flask.

"Here I thought you were a bookworm, and you're really just an alcoholic." I yawned. "So the shop is just a clever front for a bootlegging operation, right?"

He handed me the flask. "Scotch. Aged thirty years. I only hide the good stuff." He motioned for me to drink. "Ziggy helps himself to the liquor cabinet and replaces what he takes with water. He thinks I haven't noticed."

I took a cautious sip. It was smooth and warmed me almost as much as the blood I'd drunk.

My thoughts strayed to the mystery woman in the picture.

Obviously, it was a wedding photo. But Nathan didn't wear a ring. He didn't even have a tan line from one. *Now, that's a stupid thought,* I scolded myself. *He can't go out in the sun.*

There had to be some way to bring up the subject, an innocent question I could ask that would lead him to spill the whole tale.

He sat on the couch next to me, and his thigh brushed mine. I didn't move away. Neither did he.

"Do you ever get lonely?" It seemed the best way to get the conversation started.

It was also intensely personal, judging from the look on Nathan's face. He took the flask and swallowed deeply. "Nah. Ziggy's here, and when he's not, I like being alone."

"I meant, does immortality get lonely?" I reached for the flask, deciding the best way to kill the sour aftertaste was with another shot of the stuff.

"Well, after the first decade or so, time seems to fly by. I have to admit, it gets boring every now and then. And yeah, lonely, I guess. Especially when I read about someone having his hundred and eighth birthday, or something like that. It drives home the fact I'm really, really old. I'm just not getting any older." He gave a little laugh and looked over at me. "I'm not making sense, am I?"

"You are," I assured him. "Though it might be because I'm slightly tipsy."

He smiled sadly. "It's hard to believe one day I'll be the only person left who remembers what it was like to be alive in my time. Sure, people will remember the major things. They've got them written down in history books. But only I'll be left to remember the price of eggs and milk in 1953. I'll be the only one who remembers what Mrs. Campbell's blackberry jam tastes like, or that Mrs. Campbell ever existed."

I had no idea how old my sire was. Had Cyrus endured too many years of that kind of solitude? Is that what made him so desperate for a companion? My heart ached at the thought, and the tender emotion surprised me. "So it stands to reason you'd want to find someone to be with when the people you love die."

He nodded. "I suppose. But I haven't felt that way for a while. Maybe because Ziggy's so young I feel like I have some time before I have to think about it again."

I could tell from his tone that this was as close as I was going to get to the bottom of this particular subject. "So, where are you from?"

"All over." He took another sip of Scotch. "I was born in Scotland, lived there until…" His voice trailed off for a second. "I went to Brazil in 1937. That's where I was turned."

"Oh?" I wasn't sure how I should respond.

"From there, I moved to London, then Canada when the war broke out—"

"You were a draft dodger?" I interrupted.

"No." He arched an eyebrow at me. "The Second World War. Eventually, I ended up here."

"That's a lot of moving." I wondered if I would have to move that much. The idea didn't hold any appeal.

He sighed. "That's what happens. If you live too long in one place, never getting any older, people get suspicious. Believe me, it's a real pain in the ass getting a new birth certificate and social security card."

I mimicked a redneck drawl. "Especially when you're obviously not from round these here parts."

He chuckled, then did a pretty fair imitation of a Midwestern accent. "I don't know who you're talking about. I was born in Gary, Indiana, in 1971."

"Seriously, though, how do you do it?" I took another swig of Scotch.

He leaned back, resting his long arm behind me on the back of the couch. "It's not hard, especially in a town like this. There are a lot of illegals running around, so there are plenty of connections for forged documents. It's all about networking. Once you've got the birth certificate and the social security card, you go down to the Secretary of State office and say, 'I'm here to apply for a driver's license, please.'"

He'd finished the last part of the statement with his ridiculously good Midwestern twang. I frowned. "Don't do that."

"What?" He half lifted his arm.

"The voice. I like your accent."

Nathan looked at me as if he'd never seen me before. His eyes searched my face but provided me no clue to what was going on in his head.

"In the bookstore tonight…if I had kissed you, would you have let me?" His voice sounded deeper than usual and rough from the alcohol.

My mouth went dry. I had some more Scotch, but it didn't help. "I don't know."

"Would you let me now?"

A feeble noise escaped my throat.

He took it as a protest. "No expectations. Just a kiss."

I nodded.

His lips were soft but cold. He brushed them lightly over mine, and butterflies the size of B-52s took up residence under my rib cage. I closed my eyes. I felt dizzy, either from the Scotch or the scent of Nathan that surrounded me. Probably both.

I opened my mouth under his. The tip of his tongue slipped past my lips, and I put my arms around him, one hand rest-

ing against the soft hair at the back of his neck. Excitement
tickled my stomach every time I inhaled.

Without warning, Nathan pulled away. I opened my eyes
in time to see him slump sideways and fall to the floor.

Dahlia glanced over his motionless body with a surprised
expression that gave way to a satisfied smile. She shrugged
her round shoulders. "Just as good, I guess."

Before I could ask her what she meant, she clapped her
hands and disappeared.

# Eight

### A Bargain

I knelt beside Nathan's unconscious body and rolled him onto his back. He was breathing, but just barely.

"Open your eyes!" I shouted into his face. I hoped whatever Dahlia had done was only temporary. "Nathan, open your damn eyes!" His eyelids opened a fraction and a slow smile formed on his lips. I sighed in relief.

"Marianne?" he whispered. His eyes closed again and his body went limp. As if someone had flicked a switch, my relief turned to immediate dread. I called his name again, but he didn't respond.

Looking frantically around the room, I spotted the cell phone on the table. Ziggy.

My hands shook as I punched up the speed dial. Ziggy's number was the only one listed. Once the call was sent, all I could do was wait.

I'd never felt so helpless in my entire life. I tried to summon the impartiality and calm I'd had when working on a patient, but I couldn't. Not when the patient in question was someone I knew.

I sat by Nathan's side, unable to offer anything but my presence. Was he still breathing? Did he look a little blue in the face? I was checking his pulse rate against the cell phone's clock when Ziggy's call came through.

"What?" was the unceremonious greeting I got when I pushed the connect button.

"It's Carrie. I'm at your place." I glanced down at the unconscious body beside me, not sure how to deliver the bad news. "Listen, where are you?"

"Just about to leave the hospital. It's a good thing I wasn't mortally wounded. I could have died six times before they bothered to help me. What do you need?"

"Nathan's hurt." I figured saying it really fast, like ripping off a Band-Aid, would make it easier. "Dahlia sort of poofed in here and zapped him, then poofed out again."

"Shit!" He was so loud I had to hold the phone away from my ear.

I could only imagine the looks he was getting as he stood in the E.R. lobby swearing at the top of his lungs. "Calm down. Can you get here, fast?"

There was no answer but a dial tone. I swore and tossed the phone across the floor. If he'd stayed on the line he might have been able to tell me how to help Nathan. Now all I could do was wait for him. Again.

I didn't want to just sit there and watch Nathan die, but it appeared I had little choice. His breaths grew more shallow, and his chest jerked with every inhalation. I hadn't been paying much attention to my own breathing, but it suddenly seemed stifled. In fact, the air in the little apartment had become hazy.

With smoke.

"What is it with her and fire?" I wheezed. Jumping to my feet, I grabbed Nathan from under his arms and struggled to drag him. Nathan hadn't included lack of oxygen as a potential cause of undead fatality, so I assumed smoke inhalation wouldn't kill us, either. But even with increased vampire strength, I had no hope of getting him down the stairs if I couldn't breathe. At least, not without dropping him and breaking his neck in the process.

I searched for an escape from the acrid smoke and I finally decided on the bathroom. The tiny, windowless room had an exhaust fan, so I flipped the switch and wet a towel to shove under the crack in the door. It kept the smoke out, but unless Ziggy hurried, Nathan and I would burn to death.

No sooner than the thought crossed my mind, I heard the front door slam open.

"We're in here!" I called, realizing too late that the heavy footsteps clomping toward the door could belong to a fireman and not Ziggy. Though I wouldn't turn down the help, I couldn't come up with a convincing enough lie to keep Nathan out of an ambulance. If he lived to make it to the hospital, I doubted they'd be able to help him. He'd wind up in the morgue like John Doe had, only more dead.

Luckily, it was Ziggy who called through the door, already choking on the smoke. "Are you guys, uh, decent in there?"

"Of course," I snapped. "He's unconscious."

Ziggy pushed the door open, coughing. He pulled the collar of his T-shirt over his nose. "That fucking pyromaniac bitch set the bookshop on fire. I beat the trucks here, but they're coming. We need to get him out."

"It's only a couple hours till dawn. Where are we gonna go?"

Ziggy stooped and lifted Nathan by the arms. "My van. Get his legs."

I complied, and we shuffled toward the door, Nathan hanging between us like a jump rope.

Ziggy hacked against his shoulder. "This reminds me of the scene in *Return of the Jedi* where the Ewoks take Han and Luke and Chewie prisoner and tie them to those big sticks."

"Conserve your oxygen. I can't carry you both out."

The night air had turned freezing. The phrase "too cold to snow" sprung to mind. I slid on the sidewalk and collided painfully with the brick wall of the building. Ziggy eased Nathan to the ground and opened the back of the van.

I peered over the iron railing to look down at the bookstore. The glass in the door had been broken, and foul-smelling smoke poured out. My mind raced with thoughts of the building burning to the ground and where we'd go to wait out daylight. We didn't have time to gather Nathan's things. His goldfish. His wedding picture.

I thought of how Nathan had rescued my diploma and the photo of my parents from my burning apartment. Those were still upstairs, too. But the sirens of approaching fire engines squashed any notion of knickknack heroism.

"Get him in the back," Ziggy urged, picking Nathan up by the shoulders. With a count of three, we swung him into the van and slammed the door.

"Click it or ticket," Ziggy reminded me, pointing to the seat belt as I climbed into the passenger seat.

As the fire trucks rounded the block, he started the engine and guided the van down the street at an inconspicuous pace.

"What did she do to him?" he asked, jerking his thumb toward the heavy tarp curtain that sectioned off the back of the van.

"I don't know. He just fell over. Bam." I threw my hands up in despair.

"I don't get it." Ziggy eyed me suspiciously. "Dahlia showing up in his living room isn't the kind of thing Nate would miss."

I shifted in my seat. "He was preoccupied."

"Ah." He at least had the courtesy not to reach back and high-five Nathan's motionless hand.

"So what do we do now?" I asked, looking fearfully at the lightening sky. "Can we fix him?"

"Not if we don't know what it is she did to him." He kept his eyes on the road. "Do you know where to find Dahlia?"

I did. Behind the divider, Nathan moaned in pain. I closed my eyes. "Turn right at the next light."

I found my way back to Cyrus's mansion with little trouble. The wrought-iron gate was shut. "Let me out here."

"Does the guy I think lives here live here?" Ziggy asked as he put the van in Park. "You want me to wait?"

I pushed the heavy door open and stepped onto the curb. "Yeah. If I'm not back before sunup, get someplace safe."

"Why, it's not like he can come out and get me or anything."

Casting my gaze up the lawn, I saw five of Cyrus's bodyguards filing out the door. "No, but he's got those guys."

"Holy shit." Ziggy's jaw dropped as he watched them through the driver's-side window. "You're not really going up there, are you?"

"I have to," I said, sounding braver than I felt. As I turned away from the van, the strangest urge came over me to look at Nathan one more time. I forced it away.

*Here goes nothing.* I kicked the iron gate open and headed up the driveway. The guards didn't move, letting me come to them. But once I got near enough, I was ready.

Two of the goons came toward me with arms outstretched. I stood still until they got close enough to seize me.

I didn't think. I just moved.

Lunging forward, I drove the heel of my right hand as hard as I could into the first guard's nose. There was a sickening crunch sound followed by a rush of blood that cascaded down his lips as he doubled over. While he clutched his face, I brought my knee up forcefully into his crotch. He howled in agony and fell to the ground.

The second one tried to grab me from behind. His hands closed on my arms and I flipped him forward, over my head. Then I twisted his arms in opposite directions until I heard bones snap.

I had no time to regroup before the third guard came at me. I dropped down and swung my leg in a wide arc, sweeping his feet from beneath him. As soon as he stumbled to the grass, I wrung his leg and popped the knee out of joint.

The other two guards stood frozen in shock. The scent of blood from the first guard's injuries stung my nostrils. My face shifted and I snarled at them.

"Either come down here so I can kill you, or go get Cyrus!"

But my request proved unnecessary. Cyrus stepped from the doorway, clapping his hands.

"Wonderful," he said like a proud parent. "A little predictable. Not enough blood, but overall a fine debut. I can't wait to see what kind of a killer you'll become." He motioned to the two uninjured bodyguards, then to the three who lay groaning on the lawn. Two more came out and helped the injured back inside.

"I hate to disappoint you, but I'm not here for an evaluation," I said, my features morphing back to normal. "I'm looking for Dahlia."

"I thought I'd see you again tonight. Please, come in." He gestured to the door and I followed him cautiously.

The foyer was pitch-black. The only guide I had was the soft slap of his bare feet hitting the marble floor.

I felt empowered by the battle outside, and weird fantasies of carnage ran through my head. I realized that if I made my move now, I could kill Cyrus before he knew what was happening. I took a few silent steps closer.

"I wouldn't do that if I were you."

His words jarred me. "Do what?"

His laughter filled the darkness and sent a chill up my spine. "You've just gravely injured three of my employees. I'm sure you think you're a real hero, but they were human. Fighting a vampire is another thing entirely, and I can assure you I'd come out on top." He turned, and though there was no discernible light source in the room, his eyes glittered. "But I can promise you, you'd enjoy it."

*Moron.* Of course he'd heard my thoughts through the blood tie. As charged up as I was, he probably sensed my adrenaline from across town.

I heard the clank of metal on metal and the scrape of a door as it opened. Light spilled through the wide double doors and we entered what appeared to be a study.

A fire burned in the massive stone fireplace and a Persian carpet dominated the floor. Cyrus moved around the room and lit a pair of Tiffany lamps with a pull of their chains.

"Very art deco."

He smiled. "I'm glad you like it. Please, sit down."

I sank into the leather couch in front of the fire. "I didn't say I liked it."

He laughed and sat next to me. Too close. He put one arm companionably around my shoulder and stroked my neck with his long fingernails, tracing my scar. My pulse quickened, but not from fear.

*Get it together, Carrie. You managed to resist him before. Stay focused.*

"Don't you love this carpet?" he asked, pointing to the ornate rug beneath us. "When they weave these, they always put one intentional mistake in. Do you know why?"

I didn't answer.

"Because only Allah can make perfection." He sighed softly. "I've studied this one over and over, and I've never been able to find the imperfection."

"What's your point?"

"The rug reminds me of you. You would be perfect, were it not for one minor flaw." He tickled my ear with a long talon and I shivered.

"What's that?" I asked.

He leaned in, his icy breath hissing in my ear. "Your humanity."

Drawing back, he tented his fingers in front of his chest. "Have you given any more thought to my offer?"

"I have." I wasn't lying.

"And?"

"And I'm still undecided. But I'm not going to give up my humanity, even if I choose you."

"Why not?"

"Because it's wrong. Killing for pleasure is wrong." I fixed him with a cold stare. "I heard what you did to that little girl."

"Which one?" He winked at me. "I wonder, have you even bothered to seek out others of our kind to ask them what they think of your idealistic Movement? There's a war coming. Do you honestly think you're on the winning side?"

"I'm not going to be on the side that gets off on murder. That's all that matters to me."

His face became solemn. "Carrie, you're making yourself a martyr when I could make you a queen."

His distress seemed real. The look in his eyes was enough to make me promise I would reconsider. I wiped a bloody tear from his cheek and a smile touched his lips.

"Stay with me, Carrie," he whispered against my palm.

I quickly moved my hand away from his face. My fingers burned from our contact, and I shuddered with rage. "I'm here for Dahlia."

"What on earth would you want with Dahlia? Aside from that deplorable fire incident, for which she's been thoroughly punished, anything she's done, she's done under my orders. If you want to punish someone, then by all means, punish me." A wicked grin lit his face.

I didn't give him the pleasure of a reaction. "You sent Dahlia to kill me?"

Rage contorted his face. "What?"

"I'm sorry, did I stutter? She tried to kill me. And I don't appreciate it."

His frown deepened, this time in confusion. "If she'd tried to kill you, you'd be dead by now. She's very good at what she does."

"Well, she missed." I stood and crossed to the floor-length windows. The curtains were not yet drawn, so he wasn't concerned about daylight any time soon. I'd never actually watched a sunrise, so I had no idea how long they took. Or, more important, at what point it would kill me. *I've got to get back to Nathan.*

"Ah, you've met Mr.—what is he going by these days? Grant?"

I silently cursed myself. I hadn't meant to think of him in Cyrus's presence.

There was no point in lying. "Yes."

"And I presume he's told you about our past…involvement?" Cyrus fought to control his anger as he spoke, but I still felt it through the blood tie. "No wonder you're on this…pro-human bent."

I held firm, despite the volatile emotions invading my mind. "He told me he was sent to execute you. He told me you have the same blood."

"We do. I didn't sire him, but I was there when my sire turned him. We're hardly on brotherly terms now." Cyrus stood and paced the room. "So Nolen is dead, is he? I'm glad to hear it, even if I didn't do it myself."

*Nolen?* "He's not dead. But I need Dahlia to reverse whatever she did to him."

Cyrus laughed as though I'd told a clever joke. He pulled two cigars out of a mahogany humidor and offered one to me. I refused. "I want him dead, Carrie. Why on earth would I help him?"

"Because it's the right thing to do." My reply sounded embarrassingly weak to my ears.

"But, Carrie, didn't you just accuse me of killing for pleasure?" He lit the cigar and took a few puffs.

I tried not to gag as the sickly sweet smoke assailed my nostrils. "Change my opinion. Give me Dahlia."

He moved toward me. I sensed what he was about to do and braced myself.

He reached out too fast for me to step aside, his cigar dropping to the expensive carpet. One arm wound around my waist and brought me up tight against his chest. He pulled my hair, jerking my head back sharply.

"I want to make something clear so we don't have any further misunderstandings. I don't care what your opinion of me is. At the end of the day, it's still my blood in your veins. I own you."

"No!" My instincts told me to get free, but I wouldn't give him the satisfaction of knowing I feared him.

He leaned forward, nuzzling my throat with his lips. The cigar still burned at our feet. It gave me something to focus on besides the feeling of his tongue against my skin.

"Your carpet is going to catch fire."

I stepped back, and to my surprise, he let me go. I didn't know if I'd have had the will to fight him. Without even looking at it, he ground out the cigar with the ball of his bare foot.

Swallowing hard, I looked him in the eye. "If you let Nathan die, the Movement will send someone else, someone stronger. They'll hunt you down like a dog. And I don't want that to happen."

"Don't you?" A menacing joy spread across his face. It did nothing to calm my nerves.

"No, I don't." My mouth went suddenly dry at the realization I meant what I said. "You're my sire."

He shrugged as if it were out of his hands. "Well, we can't have Nolen coming after me. You saw what he managed the last time. And I don't like fighting. It's ungentlemanly. Can you think of anything that could entice me to take such an ugly risk?"

Of course I could. I just didn't want to offer it to him. "Just say it, Cyrus."

He closed his eyes as if savoring a delicious meal. "I love the sound of my name on your lips. It's like music."

"I don't have time for this, just say it!" My vehemence startled me.

He clucked his tongue. "You have no appreciation for the dramatic. Fine. Promise you'll return to me, to stay, and I will help your precious 'Nathan.'"

I stuck out my hand in an attempt to appear confident. Instead of shaking it, he drew my fingers to his mouth and kissed the tip of each one. He might as well have set my hand on fire, for the scorching feeling that raced down my arm.

"Then it's settled." He strode to the doors and threw them open. "Dahlia!" His enraged call echoed through the dark foyer. Within moments, the room beyond the door flooded with light.

"You wanted me?" I heard her purr over the click of shoes on the marble floor. Then she screamed.

His hand tightly gripping her red curls, Cyrus yanked Dahlia into the room. She was dressed much the same as she had been the night I'd met her, in a tight black shirt and long skirt. The only difference I saw now was an abundance of jewelry, rings and necklaces all bearing silver pentagrams. Cyrus threw her to the floor, and she scrambled away as he kicked at her.

Normally I would have turned my head from such violence, but it was hard to feel pity for her after what she'd done. Especially since she'd intended to kill me.

She didn't beg for mercy when he grabbed her again and pulled her head back, exposing her throat. His face changed and he bared his fangs.

Dahlia didn't recoil, but I did. That face summoned the memory of glass piercing my skull, the slippery pools of human organs under my knees, and the sensation of being powerless in the grasp of a killer. I covered my mouth to stifle a gasp.

Cyrus's eyes flickered over my face for an instant. His grotesque face actually registered some emotion then, and I thought it was regret. He didn't like that he'd scared me.

He dropped Dahlia and let his features shift back to normal. "You tried to kill her!"

Now she did whimper, as though she knew her lies would prove useless. "I'm sorry."

"You're sorry? You're lucky this turned out so well for me, you sniveling bitch. Else I'd hand you over to the Fangs when they arrive." He stalked a circle around her as he spoke.

"No!" She reached for him, clinging to his leg. "I killed that bookstore guy for you! You should be happy."

He pulled away from her grasp as if he'd been touched by a leper. "You're not allowed to kill whenever you please! How can you expect me to turn you when you have no self-control?"

Her face paled. "What do you want me to do? I'll do whatever I have to. Just tell me what you want me to do!"

Cyrus rocked back on his heels, feigning consideration. "If there was a way to reverse what you did to him, what would it take?"

"An antidote," she said as she wiped her nose on her sleeve.

"And where would I find this antidote?" he asked patiently.

Tears shone on her face. "In my room."

"Why don't you go and get it, then?" He dismissed her as easily as telling a child to run along and play.

"Thank you," I whispered when she had gone.

"This is not a gift, Carrie. Don't mistake it as such."

"It's not a gift, but it's the decent thing to do. Even if you are being paid for it." I glared at him, hoping to make him feel the true weight of my words.

He crossed to me and cupped my cheek in his palm. "Poor little girl. Is the Big Bad Wolf taking advantage of you?"

I tried to turn my face away, but he grasped my chin and forced my lips to his. I opened my mouth beneath his, my blood both searing hot and prickling cold as it coursed through my veins. His excitement fed my own. His sharp claws raked my back through my shirt, tracing the column of my spine. I couldn't get enough of his tongue against mine, his breath against my lips.

He drew away, leaving me panting and flushed while he was as unaffected as someone who'd just received a dental exam. But when he lifted his hand to brush back a strand of his long, nearly white hair, his hands shook. "Believe that all you want, Carrie. But when you needed help, you didn't call the Movement first. I wasn't a last resort. I was a choice."

My body shook with the violence of the truth.

We glared at each other in antagonistic silence until Dahlia entered. She cleared her throat at the doorway and shot me a murderous glance. "I've got your fucking antidote." Cyrus reached out a hand to take the vial from her and she practically threw it at him. He pressed a kiss to her cheek and turned away. "Now, be a good girl and move your things to one of the servant's rooms. Carrie will need the guest suite."

I expected an outburst, but all she did was watch Cyrus. The full realization of his words—that I was usurping her place—hadn't yet dawned on her. I didn't want to be around when she made the connection.

Returning to my side, Cyrus slipped the vial into the palm of my hand. I stared hard at it. This was the price of my freedom. I could smash it on the floor and never have to come back.

"But you won't." He arched a knowing brow at my thought. "Your word means too much. You'll take this to Nolen, see him safely recovered and return to me tomorrow night after sunset."

"How do I know this won't do him more harm?" I called to Dahlia. I don't think she even saw me, though she looked right at me.

Cyrus drew my attention back. "It won't. She knows what will happen if she's lied."

She broke then, her back shaking with muted sobs as she covered her face with one hand. I'd never seen anyone cry so gracefully, and I'd seen plenty of tears in my life. But Cyrus didn't seem to notice. He kissed my forehead and gave me a push toward the door. "Go now, the sun will be up soon."

He didn't follow me. I hesitated as I passed Dahlia. I don't know if I meant to offer comfort or rub salt in her wounds, but when she looked up with hate-filled eyes, I kept walking.

The foyer blazed with light as bulbs crackled and shattered with the force of Dahlia's anger.

"Sunset," Cyrus called after me. "Don't make me come get you."

# Nine

*Antidote*

I left the house as a shower of sparks exploded from the electric fixtures in the foyer. This time, I did run down the lawn, but only to buy us a little time. With no knowledge of how Nathan would react to the antidote, I wanted to get him to a safe place before it took effect.

Ziggy had left the driver's seat, presumably to tend to Nathan. I pounded on the back doors and stepped away as they flew open. Ziggy crouched over Nathan's body, a wooden stake aimed straight for my heart.

When he recognized me, he dropped the weapon. "Sorry. Can't be too careful."

"It's all right," I grunted, pulling the doors closed behind me as I climbed into the van. "How is he?"

"Alive, but that's not saying much. What'd you find out?"

I showed him the antidote, which gleamed a muddy blue in the glass vial. "Drive. I'll pour it down his throat, and hopefully it won't kick in until we're back at the apartment."

"What do you mean?" Ziggy pulled the canvas partition back and slid behind the wheel.

"Because I have no idea what it's going to do to him."

As the engine sputtered to life, I carefully made my way to Nathan's head. The van lurched away from the curb, tossing me flat across his chest.

The contact was sudden and startling. Even unconscious, with no blood tie connecting us, I was still attracted to him. Despite the fact he'd lied about his identity. Or that he didn't tell me he was vampiricly related to my sire. I reminded myself of what I'd sacrificed for this *favor.*

I opened the vial and poured the contents into his half-open mouth. *I hope it tastes terrible,* I thought with a petulant frown. Then I rocked back on my heels and waited. Why had I done this? When I'd set out to help him, I'd felt I'd been doing it for a friend. And when I found I barely knew him after all, I still plowed on ahead.

I didn't want to acknowledge the fact that Cyrus might have been right. Nathan's—or Nolen's—predicament could have been handled by the Movement, but my first instinct had been to run to my sire.

I knelt over Nathan and felt for a pulse. Nothing. No breath. No reflexes.

Defeated, I lay down next to him, out of necessity more than familiarity. My body ached with fatigue. My emotions were a mess. The one person I'd thought I was safe with, well, not safe exactly, but safer, wasn't who I'd believed him to be. That he was dead was icing on the worst cake in history. Tears rolled down my cheeks as I tried to cry without Ziggy hearing me.

Then, like a miracle, Nathan groaned and mumbled something that sounded like "get off" as he swatted at me. He gagged and choked, sputtering a little of the antidote over the front of his shirt. But he'd swallowed enough. He was alive.

I sat up in shock. "I thought you were dead!"

"I wish I were," he said when he could finally speak. He rose on his elbows and clutched his head. "What happened?"

"We were…" I paused. "Um, what's the last thing you remember?"

His answering grin made my face grow hot.

"Well, you just suddenly sort of passed out."

He rubbed his temples. "Why would I go and do something stupid like that?"

"You didn't. Dahlia did."

He flopped back onto the goldenrod shag carpeting and closed his eyes. "We're in the van?"

"Yeah, we had to get you out of the building. It was kind of…" I trailed off as I tried to tell him his livelihood was gone.

"On fucking fire!" Ziggy supplied from the front seat. "Oh, man, am I glad you're awake."

An angry car horn pulled his attention back to the road as the van swerved violently. I sunk my fingers into the dirty carpet. It was the only thing to hold on to.

"Ziggy! Eyes on the road!" Nathan commanded, though his voice was still a little weak. He turned back to me. "The building is gone?"

I shifted uneasily. "Maybe not. The fire trucks were showing up just as we left."

"Great. Just great." He covered his face with his hands, and I saw the hard muscles of his stomach shake beneath his T-shirt. I really hoped he wasn't crying. But in the next instant, delirious laughter poured out of him.

"What's so funny?" He was taking this far too well.

"Nothing, nothing." He rubbed his hands down his cheeks,

stretching the stubble-dusted skin. "You know, up until about a month ago, things were completely normal in my life. All it takes is one fax from the Movement, and I'm knee-deep in chaos again." Nathan sighed. "So, Dahlia attacked me. She's never done that before."

"She was trying to do Cyrus a favor," I told him.

"Okay, folks," Ziggy called as the van squealed to a halt. "The sun is just below the tree line. I suggest you run like hell."

Within seconds, the back doors burst open. The dim morning light stung my eyes. Nathan recoiled.

"Take the keys!" Ziggy shouted.

I grabbed them and jumped out.

To my monumental relief, the building still stood. The flames had been extinguished, and soot covered the firemen that milled around their truck. Two police cars with whirling lights blocked off the sidewalk. It looked as if the bookstore took the extent of the damage.

A young, cocky-looking police officer swaggered over when he caught sight of us. "Getting in a little late, are we?"

Before I could respond, Ziggy stepped from the rear of the van, Nathan leaning heavily on his shoulder. "Whoo, we need to get him upstairs before he ralphs again. Oh, my God…what happened to the bookstore? We live right upstairs."

As I watched, Nathan lolled his head to the side like a passed-out drunk. The cop scowled at him. "There was a fire but we were able to put it out. Is your friend there gonna be okay?"

He'd aimed the question at me. Too tired to think of a lie, I opened and closed my mouth and made a few vague noises. Ziggy's urging stare burned into the back of my skull. It must have transmitted some connection in my brain so I could speak again, because words began to pour from me. "He'll be fine. I should know. I'm a doctor."

"O...kay." The officer reached into his coat pocket and withdrew a notepad. Apparently I wasn't going anywhere for a while. "I need to ask some questions."

The skin on the back of my neck began to blister from the sunlight. I heard Nathan do a bad impression of someone about to throw up. I turned, and Ziggy gave Nathan a shove, propelling him toward me.

"It's your turn to deal with the puke this time. I'll stay and talk to the officer. If he needs to ask you anything else, I'll bring him upstairs." Ziggy flashed a big grin at the policeman. "If that's okay with you?"

Nathan wretched again, this time more convincingly, and the cop moved back. "Yeah, get him out of here before I have to cite him for drunk-and-disorderly conduct. It's safe to go up. The fire marshall has cleared the building of any structural damage, and the apartment has been cleared, too."

With Nathan hanging awkwardly on my shoulder, we hurried for the door. As soon as it was closed, Nathan rushed up the stairs and headed straight for the bathroom.

Apparently he was a method actor.

"Holy hell," I said with a whistle as he clutched the toilet bowl and vomited. I pulled a hand towel off the rack and wetted it under the faucet. "That's a lot of puke."

I knelt beside him and held the compress to his forehead, putting one arm around his quivering back. "Don't fight it."

"You should have been a nurse instead of a doctor," he wheezed. His body trembled with the chills that inevitably follow vomiting. "Or a mom."

I laughed out loud. "Yeah. I'm not sure that was in the cards for me."

"Didn't you want to have kids?"

This didn't sound as accusatory as it might have coming from someone else, like someone who was pushing a stroller at the time for instance. I'd always been the woman explaining why she had no desire to have children. I was about to tell him this, when he spoke again.

"It's a moot point, anyway, since you can't now."

An icy pain knifed through my chest, stealing my breath. I stood and leaned against the sink. "What?"

His face went even greener, if that were possible, but I knew it had nothing to do with the potion. "I'm so sorry. I assumed you knew."

"No, I didn't. It's just…it's okay." I waved a hand in the air, hoping to look blasé. "I hadn't really thought about it. I never planned on being a mom. I probably wouldn't have been very good at it."

But now that the choice was taken away from me, I grieved for the loss of the possibility. *You're being ridiculous, Carrie.*

"I think you would have been a great mother." His words sounded pained, but it could have just been from the violent nausea.

"Yeah, well. Tell that to my last boyfriend."

Nathan sat back against the wall for support. Sweat beaded on his skin, but he didn't look as gray as he had moments before. His eyes searched my face. "Why do you say that?"

Turning to rewet the cloth, I shrugged. I shouldn't have mentioned Eric. Even though we'd broken up nine months before, the wound was suddenly incredibly raw.

To my surprise, I started blabbing the whole stupid story.

"Because he dumped me for not being a good-enough mom for his hypothetical children." Despite the painful truth of it, I could still manage a chuckle. "Basically, he seemed to be under the impression that when we graduated from med school, I was going to stay home and bake cookies or something while he had the career. He decided he was going to buy a house near Boston, I told him I was coming here for my internship, and he gave me an ultimatum. When I told him my decision, that I was going to go through with my internship, he said it was for the better. He wanted children, and he couldn't imagine me being a good mother. So that was it."

I'd been looking at my hands, the shower curtain, the towel rack, anything to avoid the sight of Nathan's face. But he stayed silent too long, and my eyes were drawn to his.

He didn't look away. "He's an idiot." Nathan said the words as though he actually believed them. And his eyes showed the truth of it.

I'd forgotten what it was like to feel valued by another person. It was nice, even if I didn't quite understand what had prompted such an emotional reaction from Nathan. Still, it was a feeling I wasn't used to. I cleared my throat. "Did you ever want kids?"

He didn't answer right away. When he did, his response was carefully measured, as if he'd calculated how much to tell without giving anything away. "Yes, I did. Having children of my own wasn't in the cards for me, either."

"I'm sorry," I whispered. Behind his mask of forced cheerfulness, his eyes were hollow and tired, and the agony I saw in them caused my heart to ache.

As quickly as I'd glimpsed his inner sadness, it disappeared behind Nathan's granite wall of self-control. "Don't feel sorry for me. I have Ziggy. I always did want a son."

It was the first time he'd acknowledged his true feelings for the kid. The look on Nathan's face told me he wasn't used to revealing so much. The angry panic that flashed across his features in the next instant told me exactly why. I recognized the expression because I'd seen it staring back at me from my own reflection too often to count.

Nathan truly believed that if he cared about something, it would eventually be taken from him.

I turned away. Unfortunately, I looked right into the vomit-splashed toilet bowl. "If I didn't know you were a vampire, I'd say you had an upper G.I. bleed. But I'm going to assume that was your dinner."

Nathan stood, still a bit wobbly, and rinsed his mouth under the tap before answering. "Tasted fine on the way down. Usually stale blood tastes like nail polish remover."

"You're familiar with nail polish remover? Did they have that in the thirties?" I dropped the toilet lid and flushed. I wasn't going to tell him about the antidote, or how I'd gotten it.

"Of course they did. And I had a girlfriend in the eighties. It was about twenty years ago, but you don't forget that chemical stench," he asserted, suddenly defensive.

"That still doesn't explain how you know what it tastes like. But I think you're right, you must have gotten sick from the blood. Wait about half an hour before you drink anything else, to make sure you don't barf it all up again."

Nathan laughed. "Barf? Is that a technical term?" He eyed himself in the mirror, and before I knew what he was doing, whipped his T-shirt over his head. "What did she hit me with?"

"A spell, or something." I knew I should be examining him with a clinical eye, but it was hard to do that when he was so…half-naked. My fingers flexed, itching to touch the chiseled ridges of his chest. I cleared my throat and looked away. "I guess."

"Whatever it was, it didn't leave a mark." He turned his head and twisted his shoulders to examine his back in the mirror, and my mouth went dry as the muscles of his torso moved beneath his skin.

In the living room, the apartment door opened and slammed shut, followed by the heavy fall of combat boots against the floor. "You guys aren't doing it, are you?"

Nathan gave an exasperated sigh. "Ziggy, manners!"

The young man appeared in the doorway, dark circles around his eyes. "I'm supposed to give you this." He handed Nathan a card with a police-shield emblem printed beside a name and phone number. "The cop said the books and merchandise are trashed. And they want the owner of the building to get in touch with them because they can't seem to locate him."

"The owner?" I looked from Ziggy to Nathan. "I guess I thought you owned the building."

"I do." Nathan slipped the card into his jeans pocket. "I'll call them later."

Ziggy let out a huge yawn. "I'm going to bed. I've got a big test tomorrow and I don't want to be involved in any other vampire shit today, got it?"

"Got it," Nathan replied with a smirk. "But I'm gonna need your help in the shop later tonight to find what we can salvage."

"Can do." Ziggy shot me a sharp and knowing look. "You feeling okay now, Nate?"

"Yeah, I must have grabbed a stale bag, gotten a little food poisoning."

His expression hard, Ziggy stared at me. "Yeah, that must be it. I mean, it couldn't have been anything else."

But he didn't mention the trip to Cyrus's place. I hoped he'd have the sense not to say anything. When I left, he'd believe I'd gone of my own accord. I would make him believe it.

Ziggy bade us good-night and retreated to his room. As soon as his door closed, loud rock music blasted away.

"When he gets moody like this, I just leave him alone." Nathan yawned and strolled into his bedroom. I followed him, not sure why. His upper-torso nakedness probably had something to do with it as he moved like an R-rated pied piper.

He opened his dresser and pulled out a T-shirt. *Gray, like his eyes*, I thought as I watched him pull it over his head. No. I didn't need to remember his eyes, or any other part of him for that matter.

Except for his beating heart. I could take some solace in the fact I'd added another saved life to my tally.

I tried not to think of the price that would cost me. "Nathan, who's Nolen Galbraith?"

He ran a hand through his hair, smoothing strands that had gotten mussed from the shirt. "That would be me. Actually, I should say that used to be me. Where did you hear that name?"

"It was on the fax from the Movement. And it's what Cyrus called you." I placed my hands on my hips. "He said he didn't sire you."

Giving me a crooked smile, he sat on the end of the bed. "Why all the questions?"

*Because I just traded my life for yours.* "You told me your name was Nathan Grant, and you told me Cyrus was your sire. Why did you lie?"

"I didn't lie." He reached into his back pocket and removed his wallet. "Look."

His driver's license, besides having a criminally unfair good picture, bore the name *Nathan Grant*.

"I have to change my identity every couple of decades, remember? I like to think I can pass for forty before I have to move again." He took his wallet back and tossed it on the dresser.

I shook my head in frustration. "But what about Cyrus? You said the same blood in my veins flows through yours. But he said he didn't sire you."

"He didn't. Our blood is connected because the same vampire who sired Cyrus sired me." Nathan cleared his throat. "I don't normally talk about it."

"Well, make an exception," I snapped, and instantly regretted it. "I'm sorry. I'm just really tired, and all of this still freaks me out. Does it ever get any less weird?"

He smiled. "It hasn't for me, so far. Maybe you'll get lucky." He must have realized he'd made the wrong word choice at the same time I did because an awkward silence lingered between us as we both tried not to look at the bed.

He stretched his arm behind his head and yawned to avoid eye contact. "Hey, about earlier tonight, when we—"

"Forget it," I said quickly. I knew I would. There was no reason to hang on to the memory when we'd be enemies this time tomorrow.

I thought I saw disappointment in his eyes, but he shook it off with a contrived laugh. "Yeah, that's probably for the best. We were just caught up in the moment and things got out of hand."

"Absolutely," I agreed. "It's a total nonissue."

"Well, then, I guess I'm going to go look over my insurance papers for the shop. Did you want to watch TV or something?"

"No, I'm actually pretty tired." I looked at the bed. "Do you want me to take the couch tonight?"

He pointed a finger at me. "Today, Carrie. Get on vampire time. But no, I'll be up for a while and I don't want to disturb you. We can work out better sleeping arrangements tomorrow."

"Tomorrow," I said, suddenly numb.

With a look of concern on his face, he reached out and gave my arm a squeeze. "Are you okay?"

"Yeah, I'm fine. I'm just tired." It wasn't a lie. But when we said our good-nights and he left me alone in his bedroom, I couldn't fall asleep. Instead, I looked around the room for a pen and paper. On the floor, between the bed and the wall, I found a sketchbook with a drawing pencil tucked into the coiled binding. It would do.

I flipped open the cover and paused. An incredibly beautiful, almost photographic-looking drawing of a sleeping child took up the first page. In the margin, in distinctly masculine handwriting that sharply contrasted the skilled lines of the drawing, was written, *Ziggy, age eleven.*

Turning the pages, I found a succession of similar drawings. They were mostly of Ziggy at various stages of his teen years, sleeping. From what little I knew of Ziggy, I realized the only time he'd hold still long enough to be sketched would be while he was unconscious. The few portraits of Ziggy awake were accompanied by photos paper-clipped to them. I flipped to the last pages, hoping to find some blank sheets. The final drawing froze my blood in my veins.

It was like looking at a photograph of the night we'd first met. He'd obviously drawn it from memory, as the coat I'd worn ended at the hips, not the knees, and my hair had been up, not curling softly around my shoulders. But it was unmistakably me.

I was flattered, but I couldn't help but wonder what kind of freak spent time in moony daydreams about someone they'd known for less than two weeks.

But then again, what kind of freak trades their freedom for the life of someone they've known for less than two weeks?

Trembling, I pulled the page free from the binding and folded it small enough to fit into the back pocket of my jeans. Something to remember him by, I supposed. Then I tore out a blank piece and started writing.

The first letter I wrote was easier than I expected. My resignation from the hospital was simple, professional and, as it was handwritten in pencil on notebook paper, probably the last nail in the coffin of my medical career.

But it really wouldn't matter. Nathan was right. Eventually, people would notice I didn't age. Unlike Nathan, there was no way I'd ever pass for forty. Judging from how often I've been carded buying beer, I could barely pass for twenty-one. I'd have to redo college and medical school every ten years just to keep being a doctor. It would be like hell, only worse.

I'd slip that letter under the door of Dr. Fuller's office before I arrived at Cyrus's house tomorrow night.

I took out another sheet and began the more difficult farewell.

Nathan,
I'm not going to pretend we'll ever see each other again, at least not on friendly terms. I've decided that the best place for me is with my sire. Please know that while I

*Jennifer Armintrout*

wish you only the best, I understand you have a job to do for the Movement. I won't take it personally if you try to follow that assignment through, but be aware that I will fight you with my last breath. No one has the power to decide whether I live or die. If you ever felt the slightest friendship toward me, you'll forget I ever existed.

Carrie

# Ten

*Sunset*

As much as I tried to ignore what I was about to do, I couldn't quiet my mind enough to sleep. Instead, I consolidated my clothes into a shopping bag and waited, staring at Nathan's alarm clock like a death row inmate. Soon, my time would be up.

For a while, I listened to Nathan puttering around in the living room. Though he'd claimed to be set on an evening of reviewing insurance forms and serious concentration, all I heard was the popping of microwave popcorn and Led Zeppelin. He listened to *Houses of the Holy* twice before I heard the springs of the couch creak as he settled in to sleep.

Ziggy left at about eight o'clock. When I heard him return at noon, I opened the bedroom door and waited for him to notice that I was awake.

It didn't take him long. His stocky frame filled the doorway, and he toyed with the huge skull ring on his index finger to avoid looking at me. "So, my guess is you're leaving."

"Yes." I sat on the edge of the bed, which was currently

experiencing the foreign pleasure of clean sheets. "I don't want to overstay my welcome."

"You made a deal with Cyrus." He didn't pose it as a question. The kid wasn't a fool.

"I'd appreciate it if you didn't tell Nathan about it. He doesn't need to know."

"And I'm going to lie to Nate because you've done what for me lately?" Ziggy demanded.

"I'm asking you not to tell him as a friend. I don't want him to get hurt."

"Why? Are you going to hurt him?" he asked as he turned to look into the living room, pulling a wooden stake from his back pocket. "Nate's my dad. He's taken care of me since I was nine years old. There's no reason not to kill you if you're threatening him."

"I'm not threatening him. I just don't want him coming after me. Cyrus would kill him."

Ziggy laughed. "Yeah, like you're not trying to save your ass the only way you know how. What the fuck do you want?"

I wanted to forget all this had ever happened and get some sleep. I wanted to wake up and help them salvage smoke-damaged dream catchers from the shop. I wanted anything but to go back to Cyrus's house. I'd spend an eternity in that house. But I just handed him my letter. "Give this to him after I've gotten a head start."

He didn't read it immediately, like I thought he would. "Fine. Anything else?"

I watched him slip the note into his pocket, and I closed my eyes. My throat suddenly went dry. "No."

"He likes you. This is really going to tear him up."

The softly spoken declaration should have surprised me.

But since I'd found Nathan's drawing, I'd come to that conclusion on my own. "I know."

"But you're still going?" There was cold judgment in his tone. "Look, it's not like he's going to be heartbroken or anything. But for what it's worth, the whole time I've lived with him, he's never shown this much interest in anyone."

"That's very sweet." I wished I knew how to make him understand. I'd never idealized romantic love as an adolescent, but maybe Ziggy had. From his standpoint, just the possibility of a relationship should have been enough to make me stay.

"Nathan has been a big help, but I don't think of him that way. I've given this a lot of thought. It's the right choice."

"He worked for fifteen years getting this place going. He knows you for a week and he's right back to the beginning. And you run straight to the bad guy. It's not fair."

"It was a trade, Ziggy. To get the antidote, to save Nathan, I had to make a trade."

The implication of my words sunk in and Ziggy looked like I'd slapped him. "Why would you do something like that?"

I shrugged. "I'm a doctor. I'm supposed to save lives and help people. And Cyrus needs me." I wished I could take the words back. Not because Ziggy had heard them, but because by saying them, I'd acknowledged the truth. "Nathan can't know about this."

"Are you nuts?" His young face lit up with relief. "All you gotta do is tell him what's going on. He'll take care of everything."

"No!" I said a little too loudly, and I heard Nathan roll restlessly on the couch. I explained more quietly, "If Cyrus kills him, what good was the deal I made? I'll still be stuck with him, and Nathan will be dead. It will all have been for nothing."

"Then why are you telling me?"

I chewed my lip. "I guess because...I don't want you both to hate me."

"If you're going to be with him—" he stopped and shook his head in disbelief "—if you're going to be like him, Nate *is* going to hate you. But I won't let him bad-mouth you too much."

"That's all I can ask," I said with a smile. The expression on Ziggy's face was nothing if not heartbreaking. I felt my heart fly apart like a body hitting the sidewalk from forty stories above.

"I won't give him the letter until sunup. That way, even if he wanted to do something rash, he'll have some time to cool off."

"Good thinking." I reached for Ziggy's hand and he didn't pull away. "Thank you."

He seemed embarrassed by my gesture and quickly withdrew his hand. "Yeah, well, if we ever meet up in a dark alley, do me a favor and don't eat me, okay?"

"Deal."

I lay down then and finally slept. When I woke, the apartment was dark and empty. It was time to go.

I picked up my shopping bag full of clothes, cushioning my diploma and the photo of my parents between sweaters, and made sure I had my letter to Dr. Fuller. Then I started down the stairs to the street.

On the sidewalk, I stopped at the railing of the basement stairs as I heard Nathan groan in disgust. "How many candles would you estimate have melted into this rose-scented mess?"

"Twenty?" Ziggy answered him.

There was a long pause before Nathan replied. "Yeah, that sounds right."

I took a deep breath to ease the ache in my chest as I walked away. They would be fine without me. I'd only just come into their lives. There'd hardly been enough time to form an attachment. But I'd never had such a longing for family, warmth, comfort. Being raised by emotionally distant parents had almost entirely eradicated any notions of familial love I might have had. But with Nathan and Ziggy, just for a moment, I'd felt like I belonged.

It hurt more to give it up than I would have expected.

After delivering my letter at the hospital, I soon found myself standing before the gate of Cyrus's mansion. In a few hours, my former boss would think I'd headed back to the East Coast. At least I wouldn't end up on any missing-persons lists.

Two armed guards approached me, muttering into their headsets. When they reached the gate, I took a step back.

"Dr. Carrie Ames?" one of them asked.

I nodded. They didn't offer to take my bag. The one that had spoken hitched his thumb toward the house. "Cyrus is waiting."

The other guard stepped forward and pulled the gate open. I noticed that his hands trembled.

When I reached the front door, it opened. But instead of Cyrus, a leather-clad couple emerged. They pushed past me as they descended the steps, and I caught the sound of loud music coming from somewhere in the house.

More tough-looking vampires loitered in the foyer. Some lounged on a sofa in the center of the room, their vampire faces on full display. A few played with dice in a corner. All of them were dressed to ride in a motorcycle gang, and all appeared to be very intoxicated.

A bodyguard stood in front of the doorway to Cyrus's study. Compared to the bikers, the black-clad guard looked like a Boy Scout, so I made a beeline for him.

"Is Cyrus in there?" I asked, juggling my bag to the other shoulder.

"I'll take you to him."

At the sound of the voice behind me, I spun and came face-to-face with Dahlia. My features began to shift and loosen. I bared my fangs.

"You'd be dead before you laid a finger on me." She snapped her fingers, and the guard at the door retreated.

A low growl formed in my throat, the sound animalistic and satisfying. "I'm a lot faster than you think."

She smiled sweetly. "You weren't so fast when I was killing your boyfriend last night."

I lunged at her. She raised her hands to form a spell, and I slashed them with my suddenly clawed hands. Droplets of her blood sprayed the marble floor.

The biker vampires stopped their carousing. I assumed the blood had drawn their attention, but they weren't staring at us. They were staring beyond us.

Cyrus stood in the study doorway, clad in a lush floor-length fur dressing gown. His hair hung in two long platinum braids that fell behind his shoulders. He smiled at the bikers.

"Gentlemen," he called over the sound of Dahlia's swearing, "I trust you are enjoying yourselves?"

A few of the vampires raised their beers and gave a raucous cry.

When they turned back to their amusements, Cyrus gripped Dahlia by the hair and pulled her into the study. He motioned to the bodyguard, who grabbed my arm and pushed me in, as well.

When the door closed, Cyrus threw Dahlia to the ground. "What to do with a disobedient pet? Especially one that has had so many warnings."

Dahlia wiped her nose on her bloodied wrist. "Cyrus, it wasn't my fault, she—"

He slapped her across the face. The sound of the impact made me wince. Leaning down, he grasped her chin in his hand and twisted her neck at an uncomfortable angle so she was forced to look up at him. "What did you call me?"

Fresh tears rolled down her face, mixing with the smeared blood from her hands and the layers of makeup that coated her face.

"I'm sorry. It won't happen again." She choked on her words. "Master."

He shoved her away and dusted his hands together as though he'd touched something dirty and unpleasant. He signaled to the guard. "Take her and get her bandaged up. Then lock her in her room."

He turned to me as the guard led Dahlia away. His beleaguered expression morphed to one of pure joy as he looked me over.

Fidgeting beneath his hot stare, I laughed nervously. "I hope you don't expect me to call you Master, because you'll be sorely disappointed."

Stepping behind me, he laid his hands on my shoulders. I could smell Dahlia's blood on them. "You might surprise yourself yet, Carrie. I can make you do things you've never imagined."

*It's the blood tie,* I reminded myself as a wave of pleasure buckled my knees. *He doesn't have any real control over you.* I clenched my fists so hard that my nails slashed my palms.

He pulled me back, slipping his hands beneath my shirt. His skin was warm, as though he'd just fed.

"Don't I?" The phantom desire that assaulted me was replaced by a hot, electric shiver as his fingers dipped into the cups of my bra. He snickered at my soft moan. "I'm not using the blood tie now, Carrie."

I writhed away, though my flesh cried out to be touched. "Let's get something straight. I came here to make good on a bargain. This, you touching me, wasn't in the terms of our agreement."

"I bet I'll change your mind before long," he said with a smirk. "In the meantime, let me show you around."

I adjusted the bag on my shoulder.

"I can have your things taken to your room," he told me.

"I'd rather keep them with me, if it's all the same."

"As you wish." His tone was gentle, but he obviously didn't take well to not getting his way.

We attracted a few curious stares as we walked through the foyer. Cyrus didn't acknowledge the group of vampires as he leaned over to whisper in my ear. "The Fangs," he explained. "They're a motorcycle club from Nevada. They've had some trouble with the Movement there and sought safe haven with me. Hence the appalling sofa in the foyer and the intolerable stench of, what are the kids calling it these days? Reefer?"

"Yeah, about fifty years ago." I sniffed the air. "It reminds me of college. You ever try it?"

His deep, rich laugh echoed off the polished marble floors. "Carrie, do I look like someone who'd indulge in such a filthy habit? I prefer more elegant intoxicants."

We entered a corridor. Long windows cast silvery squares of moonlight on the floor. Through the darkness I saw a painting on the wall that depicted the grim shape of a giant clutching a headless corpse.

"Is that…Goya?" While his subjects were gory, an original work by Goya was priceless. With a house like this, his decadent clothing, and round-the-clock security, I supposed I could have wound up with a worse sire. Remembering that Nathan was probably at that moment rooting through the ashes of his ruined shop, I instantly regretted the thought.

"You know your art, Doctor. Very good." Cyrus let out a melancholy sigh. "It's only a copy. The real one hangs in the Prado, despite my numerous attempts to purchase it."

"Well, it's a really good copy." I reached out to touch the surface of the painting, and he caught my wrist with an apologetic smile.

"Please, don't touch. A number of years ago, I had a pet of exceptional talent. He's also responsible for the bacchanalian orgy depicted on the walls of my bedroom." His thumb stroked the nearly translucent flesh beneath the cuff of my sleeve, sending a shiver up my arm. "Perhaps you'd like to see that next?"

I jerked my arm away. "Let's not press our luck, now."

He chuckled and slipped his arm through mine. "This way."

At the end of the hallway were large double doors. They opened to the ballroom I'd seen on my first visit, though we entered on a different side. The room had been converted into a makeshift garage, with rows of motorcycles parked on sheets of canvas laid out to protect the floor. Cyrus viewed the objects with some distaste. "I'll never understand the compulsion some people have to drive themselves anywhere."

"Had chauffeurs all your life, huh?" I asked, running my hand across the chrome tank of a motorcycle.

"Not quite. I was born six hundred years before the advent of the modern automobile."

"Six hundred—" I swallowed noisily. "So you were alive during the age of knights and armor and all that crap?"

"Yes, Carrie, all that crap." I thought I saw him roll his eyes, but he didn't make any further comment. Instead, he led me quickly through the room.

The dining room had been rearranged to accommodate a larger number of people and reminded me of a great hall from a medieval movie. I followed him to the kitchen where the huge, industrial stoves were cold. Pots and pans hung gleaming from the ceiling. The only person present in the room was the elderly black butler, who watched us intently as we entered.

"How can you afford all this?" I asked as we passed through the room.

"Good evening, Clarence," Cyrus tossed off casually, as though he didn't notice the man's apparent animosity. Cyrus turned to me and replied, "I've killed some very wealthy people in my time, and invested the profit wisely. Your room will be in the family quarters, of course," Cyrus explained as we climbed the back staircase, "but we'll go through the servants' area first so you'll know where everything is."

The servants' quarters were made up of two narrow hallways that were crammed with small rooms. A few of the Fangs roamed the hall. I heard the buzz of a tattoo needle from somewhere.

"They're leaving for Canada in a couple of weeks," Cyrus whispered, a tight smile pasted on for the benefit of his guests. He spoke through clenched teeth. "I can't say I'll be sorry to see them go."

"Why do you let them stay here, then?" I asked as we strode past a few of them.

He shrugged. "They're anti-Movement. I'm anti-Movement. We have to stick together. When the Movement falls, and it will, I'd like to be poised for a leadership position. It helps to grease the wheels now."

The second hallway was guarded by sentries armed with wooden stakes. I thought we'd breeze past them as we had all the household staff so far, but Cyrus stopped. "Gentlemen, this is Dr. Ames. I'm granting her full privilege to the cattle, any time she wishes. Please pass the word along."

"Yes, sir," the guards said in unison as they stepped aside to admit us.

"Cattle?" I didn't like the sound of that.

"Pets, if you prefer. They're humans that live here so I, and my guests, can feed."

Most of the rooms we walked by had their doors closed. The few rooms with opened doors were unoccupied, with two small beds in each with a nightstand between them. Dark squares stood out on the faded wallpaper, as though posters or other decorations had hung there and were only recently taken down.

A door opened, and a skinny, pale girl with dark rings beneath her eyes exited. She smiled nervously at Cyrus, and kept glancing at me as she spoke. "Hello, Master."

"Good evening. Amy, is it?" He reached for her, taking her chin in his hand to tilt her head to the side. Faded fang marks stood out against the thin skin.

"Cami." Her voice was barely audible as his fingers curled around the back of her thin neck.

"Oh, yes. Cami. I'm sorry. So many names to remember lately," he said, more to me than to her. "Cami, dear, how long has it been since I've sent for you?"

"A week." She looked down at her hands. "Was I…was I bad at it?"

I wanted to shrink into the wall, to become completely invisible and spare her the embarrassment of this conversation, but she didn't seem to care that I was there at all.

"No, no. I've just been terribly busy with…other things." As he spoke, Cyrus discreetly laced his fingers with mine, pulling me into his memory.

My vision clouded, and I stared down into Cami's terrified face from Cyrus's eyes. She struggled not to cry as he moved inside her. My stomach turned at the feeling of her young limbs and barely matured body beneath his. I pulled my hand away.

Suddenly out of Cyrus's thoughts, I returned to the present and saw Cami's face show the tentative beginning of a hopeful smile. "Today?"

"That is, unless you'd feel slighted?" Cyrus asked me with a rueful grin. His voice invaded my head. *If you refuse me, I'll take her to my bed in the morning and she won't live to the next sunset.*

The girl looked at me with something akin to jealousy and despair. I had no doubt Cyrus would make good on his threat. I leaned close to his side. I managed, "It's my first night here. Wouldn't you rather spend it with me?" Concentrating as hard as I could, I silently added, *You dick.*

A low laugh rumbled from his throat, and he spread his hands in a gesture of helplessness. "I'm sorry, Cami, the doctor has spoken. Perhaps you'll find company with one of my guests?"

She paled further, her eyes filling with tears. "Will they hurt me?"

"Of course not. I wouldn't allow it." He patted her on the

head. "Run along now, I have to show Dr. Ames the rest of the mansion."

We exited the hallway and entered a small sitting room. I glanced at the railing to one side and realized we were directly above the foyer. I heard the good-natured shouting of the Fangs below.

"You pervert," I said as soon as the door closed behind us. "She's only a little girl."

"She's fifteen. Just a year younger than my first wife."

"This isn't the Dark Ages anymore," I seethed. "There are rules."

"I find there is something beautiful in the forbidden."

"Beautiful?" I thought of the memory Cyrus had shown me, the way her knuckles had turned white as she'd gripped the bedsheets. "What about her parents? Her family? They're out there somewhere, looking for her, and you're planning to kill her?"

"She's a runaway, Carrie. Nearly all of my pets are. Now, if they don't suit you, I wouldn't miss a few of my guards as long as you're discreet about it."

"I'm not going to kill for blood. I want a willing donor."

"The cattle are willing," he said, pointing in the direction we'd just come from.

"Willing to die?"

He nodded. "Willing to endure a little bit of discomfort for what I give them. I kill them eventually, but for a few days, maybe even weeks, they feel like they belong. Like someone wants them. Surely you know how precious that can be."

I did. As a child, I'd worked hard to be the best, the smartest, the most accomplished in the hopes my parents would take notice. I'd savored every word of their praise like ambrosia. I knew what poor Cami had been looking for. She'd prostituted herself for love, or at least, a shadow of it. She would never know the difference.

I was infinitely thankful that no one like Cyrus had come along when I was fifteen. I would have been easy prey. I still was. I felt a gentle probing at the edges of my thoughts and pushed away the taloned hand that rested on my arm. "Stop it."

We began to walk again, toward a heavily guarded wing I assumed contained his room, and mine. I stopped and waited until he realized I didn't follow.

"I'm not going to sleep with you. I only agreed to spend the day with you so you wouldn't kill her."

"I know. And I won't. *Today.* Let me show you to your room."

The hallway was considerably wider than those in the servants' wing, though only two rooms appeared to open onto it. At the end, another set of bodyguards were stationed at double doors, but we stood at the only other entrance.

"Here we are," Cyrus said, leaning closer to me than was necessary to turn the knob. Ducking past him with a minimum of contact, I entered the room.

The suite was larger than the whole of Nathan's apartment. The first room was a parlor full of Edwardian furniture. A fire burned cheerfully in the oversize fireplace.

"If you don't like the decor, it can be changed." Cyrus walked slowly around the room. "Dahlia's tastes mirror my own somewhat, though I've never been able to stomach so much light blue."

I had a ridiculous urge to thank him, but I pushed it aside. "This was Dahlia's room?"

He lifted what looked like a Fabergé music box from a plant stand by the window, frowning. "Yes. For a while, anyway."

I dropped my bag and removed my coat, draping it over the back of the settee. "Why'd you kick her out?"

"Truthfully? I didn't like having her so close. The jealous witch monitored all my activities. It was a bit like being married again." He wound the mechanism of the box and an unrecognizable tune began to play. "Let me show you something."

He walked to the small corner hutch and slightly pulled on one of the shelves. The whole thing swung forward with ease. "This leads to my chambers."

I stared at the door as if it were ignited dynamite. "Any way we can wall that up?"

"I prefer to have unhindered access to you." He closed the secret passage. "But I'm sure you understand why I'd want to keep Dahlia elsewhere. Under heavy guard."

If I were him, I'd want to keep her in a different country. "She thinks you're going to turn her."

"Her power is beyond any I've ever seen." He paused thoughtfully. "But I fear how she'd wield that power with a vampire's strength behind it."

I sniffed derisively. "Because you're so moral."

"Because I'm a realist."

"Couldn't you just control her with the blood tie?" I folded my arms across my chest. "I mean, since you're so good at it."

"You're perfect." A wry smile formed on his lips. "Alas, she has more power than I. And I won't chance her ruling me."

"Well, I'm glad to know you're not a completely remorseless psychopath."

Cyrus sighed with theatrical weariness. "What you perceive as evil is only an acceptance of our true nature. I only do what I am built to do. That doesn't mean I'd want some complete nutcase steering the world toward doom."

"Could she do that?"

"Probably. That's the thought that keeps me awake during the day." With a look of feral hunger, he crossed to me. "But now it seems I have a better reason for my sleepless days."

He raised his hand and I trembled, alternately wishing he would touch me and cursing myself for wanting him to do so. When he dropped his hand, I turned away from him in embarrassment.

"I have some gifts for you. In your bedroom."

The last place I wanted to be with him was anywhere with a convenient horizontal surface, but I went, anyway. As I passed the open door, I noticed the key had been removed from the lock, the keyhole soldered closed. I had no way to keep Cyrus out should he decide to come courting in the middle of the day. *Would you want to keep him out?* As disgusting as I found his predilection for pubescent girls, my revulsion didn't dampen the power of the blood tie. I assured myself it was only the new vampire side of my nature, and that I'd simply learn to ignore it. I had no intention of acting out his perverse fantasies.

The bed was huge, larger than any I'd ever slept in, and was covered in a thick blue duvet with lace-trimmed edges. A mountain of pillows was at the head, and a half canopy with curtains brushed the high ceiling.

"This is like a fairy tale," I said, trailing my fingers over the soft bedspread. It was hard to imagine Dahlia, in her fishnets and heavy eyeliner, curling up to sleep here.

Cyrus closed the door and leaned against it casually. "I'm glad you like it. Of course, I hope you don't spend much time here. Look in the armoire."

The large mahogany wardrobe was already stocked with clothes. Rich fabrics in colors I'd never imagined myself

wearing crowded the space, and when I opened the drawers
I found a selection of jewelry that would put Tiffany's to
shame. I nearly choked on my surprise. I was so hypnotized
by the sparkling jewels that I didn't notice he'd stepped behind me until his arms clung around my waist. I jumped, startled, when he reached for a large, pear-shaped emerald
pendant.

"I've never had so many…liquid assets," I rasped as he
lifted the necklace to my throat.

Laughing, he brushed my hair aside. "Everything in this
house is yours." He fastened the clasp, then smoothed the
chain against my shirtfront.

I stepped away, immediately reaching to remove the bau-
ble. "As long as I'm obedient, right?"

"To a point." He regarded me with a calculating stare. "I
don't believe I need to press my will with you."

A chill crawled up my spine. "And why is that? Because
you gave me expensive things?"

"Because I don't want to create distance between us.
You're an intelligent woman. You'll realize soon enough that
fighting your true nature is futile. When you do, I will be
there." He turned to the door. "I'm sure you're tired, so I'll
leave you to settle in."

So he wouldn't require my company after sunup. "What
about Cami?"

Confusion sparked across his face. He'd already forgotten her name. Only after I angrily began to tap my foot did
he understand who I was referring to. "Oh, yes, the girl. No,
I think I'll get my rest, as well. However, if you wished to
join me after all—"

"I don't foresee that happening." I dropped the necklace
into the drawer and slammed it shut.

"No, of course you don't. But you know where to find me."

I stood in the doorway and watched him exit through the hidden passage. When it closed, a deliberate and ruthless wave of lust washed over the blood tie. I gritted my teeth and closed my eyes.

*God, help me,* I pleaded to a deity I'd never bothered to speak to before. *If you don't, my sins are on your head.*

# *Eleven*

### *A Sleepless Day, An Uncomfortable Night*

Although there were still hours before sunrise, fatigue forced me into the huge bed. I left the lamp on at the bedside table, as I found it slightly unsettling to be alone in the enormous room.

*You don't have to be alone.* The thought couldn't have been mine. I sat up, peering into the dark corners of the room to see if Cyrus had returned. But I was the only one present, and as much as I hated to admit it, curling up next to Cyrus was an appealing prospect compared to spending the night by myself in this museum of a bedroom.

It had to be the blood tie. Cyrus was a monster who preyed upon the weak and helpless. The attraction between us wouldn't have been so strong if he were anyone but my sire.

But even I couldn't believe that. I'd felt the excitement of sinking my fangs into a warm, human neck. I'd known the hot, heady feeling of blood rushing into my mouth from a tapped vein. That kind of gluttonous pleasure could be addictive. I'd done it once, I wanted to do it again, and Cyrus offered the very thing I craved.

I was attracted to Cyrus because my darker nature wanted me to give in and become like him. A predator, with no remorse or humanity to interfere with my base desires.

A horrendous scream tore through the still night. I ran to my window in time to see a half-naked girl racing across the lawn toward the dark shape of the hedge maze. Four of the Fangs followed her.

Her pale body cut a glowing streak through the darkness and I recognized her at once. Cami.

"Don't look back," I whispered, willing with all my might that she make it to the maze. She could hide there, maybe even until the safety of daylight.

But I knew my worry was in vain. I'd seen her kind many times in the E.R., souls so abused they were afraid to find help for their situation. Having escaped death, Cami would just slink back to the house, and death would find her again.

The vampires gained more ground. She looked over her shoulder, screaming again at the sight of her pursuers. The glass of my window muffled the sound and I was glad for it. I wouldn't have wanted to hear the full might of her mortal terror.

Looking back proved to be a fatal mistake. Her feet tangled beneath her and she sank to the ground. All four vampires fell on her. She didn't scream this time.

It took them only a moment to finish her. As they dispersed, I caught a glimpse of the body, or what was left of it. They'd ripped her apart and fed until not even her organs remained inside her mangled corpse. She looked like a rag doll whose stuffing had been ripped out.

I turned away from the window, my body shaking. My heart raced and my lungs burned with the exertion of my heavy breathing. But my reaction came not from horror. Not from disgust at what I'd seen. I'd liked it.

I'd wanted to be with those vampires. I'd wanted to feel her flesh tear beneath my claws, to rip skin and sinews with my teeth.

Now I, Dr. Carrie Ames, who took the Hippocratic oath before a crowded auditorium, vowing to never cause harm, never aid death, wanted to kill.

Sick to my stomach, I forced myself not to look at the grisly scene as I reached to pull the curtains closed.

I went back to bed, but sleep eluded me. Primal and raw, my hunger tormented me. The knowledge I could simply walk down the hall and pick out a tender, willing human to feed from made it ten times worse. Shuddering and sweating, I resolved to stay where I was. I could ask for blood— in a cup—after sunset.

But that seemed so very far away.

Through the day, as I lay awake, I heard the secret door to the sitting room open several times. I'd jolt upright and listen to footsteps cross the floor. They always retreated before they reached my door.

Exhausted, I fell asleep just before sunset. I'd only slept an hour when the footsteps returned.

Thinking to catch Cyrus creeping around my parlor, I pulled on my robe and headed for the bedroom door. The house was spooky enough without him lurking around. I was surprised to find that it wasn't Cyrus who was making all that noise, but the butler. He went about his business, opening the drapes and building up the fire. I didn't think he'd seen me enter until he spoke.

"Don't get any bright ideas or I'll push your demon ass into this fireplace so fast you'll be in hell before you know what happened."

I approached him slowly, not doubting he meant what he said. "I'm not that kind of vampire."

*If you say it enough, maybe you'll believe it.*

"Sure. I suppose you're a good guy, right? We get a lot of those around here, so you'll have to excuse me for not trusting you." He pulled back the collar of his tuxedo jacket and revealed a series of bumpy, keloid scars on his throat. "Bite me once, shame on you. Bite me twice, shame on me."

I sat in one of the stiff wing chairs and rubbed my eyes. "That's a good personal motto. Another good one would be 'don't work for vampires.'"

He straightened and turned to face me. His dark eyes glittered in the firelight, and I thought it might be humor I saw in them. "For future reference, most 'people' don't talk to the help. Just imagine that I'm invisible."

"Sorry. I'm new here."

The secret passageway opened, and Cyrus entered without knocking. I stood as though he were royalty. I'm not sure why.

He wore a silk dressing gown tied loosely enough to make me acutely uncomfortable. His torso was hard and well-defined. A perfect body, with the exception of the thick scar that ran from his collarbone to his stomach.

An injury like that would have been deadly six hundred years ago, so he must have been human at the time to keep a scar. A vampire would have healed. I touched the scar on my neck. Cyrus must have incurred the injury before he'd completely changed into a vampire.

He yawned and stretched like someone who'd had the luxury of too much sleep, and his unbound hair brushed the floor with the motion. "Rested and ready for the night?"

I shook my head. "Someone was creeping around my room all day."

"Clarence, I hope you apologized for waking Carrie," Cyrus admonished the butler.

"I don't think it was Clarence who woke me."

Like some kind of reverse genie, Clarence disappeared at the mention of his name. I heard the parlor door click softly shut.

"I did come in to check on you." Cyrus slipped behind me and stole my chair, pulling me into his lap as he did so. I yelped in surprise as I felt his ice-cold skin through my robe and tried to rearrange the fabric over my bare legs. Sprawled as I was over him, it was hard to maintain a ladylike appearance. He took advantage of the position and slipped his hand between the slightly parted fabric. "I felt your distress at the scene in the garden. And your excitement."

I swallowed as his fingers teased my inner thigh. "You saw that?"

"It was spectacular, wasn't it?" He inched his fingers up the hem of my T-shirt. "They're such vulgar creatures, but I love the way they feed, the pack mentality of it."

"Yeah, it's a regular nature special." I pushed his hand away and stood, whirling around to face him. "Did you tell them to do that? So I could see?"

Standing had been the wrong move. My wriggling had dislodged the tie of his robe completely, and he made no move to cover himself. I tried to look anywhere but where carnal curiosity forced me to. Not that I wanted to look at his immensely pleased face, either. He seemed delighted by my embarrassment. "Oh, I'm sorry, am I making you uncomfortable?"

"You forget, I'm a doctor. Or was," I added with a surprising twinge of guilt. "I've seen plenty of naked bodies before. They all sort of look the same after a while."

"Really?" He stood, far too close to me.

"Did you or did you not tell them to kill Cami?" His intimidation wasn't going to work. At least, I hoped it wouldn't.

"You're really no fun, do you know that?" he said. "No, I didn't arrange that little spectacle. I rather discourage the notion of feeding outside. As large as the grounds are, her screams probably carried to the neighbors. I find police investigations tedious at best, though I do harbor a fondness for handcuffs."

I rolled my eyes. "There's a cliché if I ever heard one."

"I couldn't resist." Cyrus circled me slowly, tapping his lips with his forefinger. "Something is off about you. I can feel it."

"I am a bit hungry," I admitted. "But I'm not interested in human sacrifice. Can you get any of your pets to donate blood?"

He stopped behind me and rested his hands on my shoulders. Before I could stop him, he tugged my robe backward. The tie came loose and I stood before him in only the dark blue T-shirt I'd worn to bed, the one Nathan had loaned me.

Leaning close to my neck, Cyrus sniffed at the collar. "That's what the problem is."

He spun me, grasping my upper arms so hard I knew I'd have bruises that would heal in a moment. "Go take this thing off and deliver it to Clarence to be destroyed, along with any other reminder of him you might have thought to bring along."

Though I didn't mean to, I flinched from the pain in my arms. "What happened to not pressing your will?"

With a snarl of anger, he pushed me. I landed hard on one of the delicately embroidered chairs, the impact of my fall skidding it backward.

Cyrus loomed over me, bracing himself on the polished wooden arms of the chair. "Do not abuse my patience and I won't need to display the force of my will."

For the first time, I felt utterly weak and vulnerable beside him. I knew he wouldn't kill me. He was too fond of his trophy. But that served little comfort when I knew exactly how much torture a vampire could live through.

I almost apologized, but as I stared into his cold, mismatched eyes, I saw nothing to compel my forgiveness.

With a firm shove to the chair, he stomped over to the secret door, his open robe trailing behind him.

"What about my breakfast?" I called after him, a little emboldened after my staring-contest victory.

"I'll have Clarence bring it," he growled. "But after this, you'd better learn to drink from a human, like a real vampire. Your behavior is a reflection on me, and I won't have anyone saying my blood is weak."

After he'd gone, I went to the bedroom to change. As angry as he was, I didn't think I'd see Cyrus again that night, but I wasn't going to take any chances. I dressed in clothes I found in the armoire instead of the ones Nathan had bought me. A black turtleneck and loose-fitting slacks were the closest items I could find to my preferred uniform of T-shirt and jeans.

Clarence brought my evening meal, a still-warm carafe of blood accompanied by a selection of fresh fruit, the B-movie version of a continental breakfast. I tried to make some cheerful conversation, but he only provided the minimum requirement of polite response. I eventually gave up and finished my meal in silence.

When I ventured from my room, I found the Fangs were out in full force. Curiosity brought me to the ballroom, where a new row of bikes testified that more vampires had arrived.

I expected some trouble from them, but nothing happened. On the contrary, the thugs saluted me with a fearful courtesy. I fully expected them to start bowing and genuflecting when they saw me.

The only person who seemed to want interaction with me was Dahlia. I discovered her lounging on one of the deserted sofas in the foyer, reading a magazine. She made a noise as I passed, presumably to get my attention. When I ignored her, she swept her hair back from her shoulder, revealing a fresh bite mark. She yawned loudly and stretched. "I am just so tired. But why shouldn't I be? I was up all day." She giggled and crossed her legs. Her already short skirt rode up, flashing a generous portion of white thigh. Fang marks scored her ample flesh there, as well.

"Do you think you're making me jealous?" I asked. For some insane reason I was, but I'd eat raw cactus before I admitted it to her.

She shrugged. "No. I just feel sorry for you. Your first day here and he sends for someone else to spend his time with. It's sad, really."

"I can think of sadder things." I dropped onto the sofa beside her and picked up a magazine from the stack at her side. "Ooh, hot spring beauty trends."

From the corner of my eye, I saw her raise her hand.

I clucked my tongue condescendingly. "I wouldn't do that if I were you. He'd kill you if you harmed me."

She snorted derisively. "Whatever. He thinks you're pathetic."

Though I doubted the validity of her statement, it called to mind Cyrus's earlier angry slur. I dropped the magazine and shifted to face her. "More pathetic than a vampire groupie hanging on to her last scrap of hope?"

Dahlia didn't rise to the bait this time. "If I were you, I would seriously avoid pissing him off. He owns you. He can make your life hell."

"I don't think I *can* avoid pissing him off." Quieter, I added, "Not if it means being like him."

With a sigh of obvious contempt, she tore her attention away from a page detailing the best cut of jeans for different body types. "Yeah, and what is he like?"

"What do you mean?" The realization we were having an actual conversation struck me as odd, but Dahlia seemed unperturbed by it.

"What is he like?" she repeated. "I mean, since you've taken the time to get to know him and all."

*Ouch.* She had a good point. I didn't know Cyrus. At least, not as well as she did. I tried to imagine what it would be like if I were in her shoes. She clearly had some affection for him, to stay after all the violence I'd seen him inflict on her.

I cleared my throat. "I suppose I meant evil. I don't want to be evil."

She rolled her eyes, not bothering to cover her impatience with me. "News flash, not everything is good or evil."

"I don't follow."

She tossed her magazine aside and twisted her body toward me, pulling one meaty leg up on the couch in a very lewd manner. "Okay, let's pretend there was a tornado, and it destroyed like, half the town. That's bad, right?"

I wasn't quite sure where she was going with this analogy, but I nodded in agreement.

"So since the tornado did something bad, by your logic, it's evil?"

"I wouldn't call a tornado evil, no."

"Why?" she asked in a way that suggested she knew what my answer would be.

"Because it's just a tornado. It's part of nature."

"Just like vampires are a part of nature." She didn't seem very pleased to prove her point, but more annoyed at having lost precious seconds of her life teaching me. "Some things aren't good or evil. Some things just…are."

With that, she stood and gathered her magazines. "Now, if you'll excuse me, I'd rather drive nails through my eyeballs than have to sit here and play nice with you anymore."

"Well, fuck you, too," I said under my breath as she charged up the stairs.

So we weren't bound to become Best Friends Forever, but at least she could talk to me without trying to kill me. And to be honest, if she got so sick of being polite that she *did* drive nails into her eyes, well, that would be a bonus.

I looked to the magazine in my lap, the one Dahlia hadn't bothered to collect on her way out. Beauty magazines didn't usually appeal to me, but I didn't usually have so much time on my hands, either. I flipped to an article about the bacterial hazards of tanning beds and assured my horrified brain that it was medical research.

I'd only read the first paragraph when the study doors burst open, admitting the sounds of male exertion and clashing steel. Cyrus glided into the room dressed in tight black leather pants and a billowy white shirt that was unbuttoned to the waist. His long hair was pulled back and he carried a fencing foil. All he needed to complete the ensemble was an eye patch and parrot. I tried not to laugh as the image formed in my brain.

Wiping droplets of bloody sweat from his brow, he tossed the foil to the guard that followed him. I pretended to be too interested in my magazine to notice their presence.

Cyrus sat next to me with an exhausted sigh as he tugged the black leather gloves from his fingers. "Good evening, Carrie."

"Ahoy, matey. Going sailing?" Although I was still mindful of his sudden change in temper earlier in the evening, I couldn't help but push it a little. That was *my* nature.

He put his arm around me, a gesture so familiar and strong that I had to force myself to pull away. He paid no mind to my reaction. "I was just brushing up on my defense. Roger is a wonderful fencer, aren't you, Roger?"

The guard nodded sharply. "It's Robert, sir. And yes, I am."

I didn't engage myself in the conversation and flipped a few pages in the magazine.

Cyrus leaned in close under the pretense of reading over my shoulder. "That's quite an interesting look. I've never cared for women with too much eye makeup, but it certainly would look striking on you."

"I'll have to remember that in case I ever feel compelled to impress you."

Despite my best efforts, I felt my body react to the pull of the blood tie. Everything about him seemed appealing, pirate shirt aside. He smelled wonderful. He felt even better pressed to my side. Then I thought of him with Dahlia. He'd been doing God knew what with her all day, slipping away periodically to "check" on me. I wasn't hurt by his unfaithfulness, and rather surprised myself for expecting fidelity in the first place.

I flipped another page, hoping to cover my emotions with sarcasm. "Captain Hook called. He wants his shirt back."

He raised an eyebrow. "You're angry with me."

There was no denying it. He could feel it through the blood tie. "Yeah, actually, I kind of am."

"Because of our fight?" He circled his arm around my shoulders again, holding me fast when I tried to shrug him off. "All couples fight. It's nothing to worry about."

*Couple?* "I was single last time I checked."

He smiled and twisted a strand of my hair around his index finger. "Then why are you so upset that I spent time with Dahlia?"

I sniffed. "Am I that transparent?"

"It's not hard to tell. Jealously is practically radiating off of you." He put his hand on my knee. "You're aware of the role Dahlia plays here."

"Executive knob polisher?"

"That's a rather crude way of putting it, but yes. There's no need to feel threatened by her. You're my blood."

"How can I help but be threatened by her? She's your favorite." I pushed him away and got up.

He looked me up and down, not bothering to disguise his lustful stare. Turtleneck or not, I felt naked. I covered my face in frustration. "Never mind. You won't understand. I hate being jealous and you aren't even listening."

"I am listening," he insisted.

"No," I said as I ran a hand over my hair. "I'm just being stupid. I've been trained since birth to be competitive and Dahlia brings out the worst in me. But you're not helping."

"I'm sorry you feel that way. Let me make it up to you," he suggested, standing to guide me back to the couch.

"How?" I'd expected him to pull me into his lap, but he sat a comfortable distance from me.

"Let me woo you. Give me a chance to show you how dear you are to me." He drummed his fingers on the arm of the sofa. "How about dinner? We can get to know each other better."

"I remember the last dinner date we had. I'm not interested in another postmortem."

"No bodies, I promise," he assured me with a smile. "For a doctor, you're awfully squeamish."

"It's not about being squeamish. It's about having an ounce of humanity left." Every moment I spent with him faded my anger, like a photograph exposed to sunlight. I tried to find reasons to stay mad at him, but it was difficult when I was this close to him. "Wouldn't that make Dahlia jealous?"

"I don't think she's the only one who's jealous." He lifted his hand and cupped my chin, turning my face to his. "Dahlia is a momentary distraction. I'll have you forever."

*Forever.* For the first time since I'd made the bargain for Nathan's life, I realized the ramifications of my promise. How long would I live? Cyrus had managed to stay alive for more than six hundred years. I'd fought the fiend lurking inside me for only a night, and I'd barely been able to stand it.

Perhaps my fall was inevitable.

Gently, Cyrus pressed his cold mouth to mine. I didn't resist. But not because I didn't have the willpower or because the blood tie was manipulating my response. I kissed him back because I wanted to prove to him, and myself, that he made me feel nothing. That I was still in control.

It didn't quite work out that way. I wrapped my arms around his neck and let him pull me closer. I sensed his surprise, but when he drew back he smiled as though he'd won a great battle. "Now, that wasn't so terrible."

It wasn't. He leaned in for another when I heard the forgotten guard clear his throat. Annoyance danced across my sire's face, but he quickly covered it with a smile as he stood and straightened his shirt. "Roger, what would you say to another match?"

"Robert, sir. I would be honored." The guard tossed him his foil.

Cyrus caught it and gracefully took up a ready stance. "Dinner, in my chambers, 5:00 a.m.," he instructed me. "Please be on time." With that, he and the guard parried and thrusted their way out of the room.

I closed my eyes. It would have been all too easy to blame my submission on the blood tie, but I couldn't lie to myself. There was a magnetism about him that had nothing to do with his being a vampire. Despite the horrible way he'd treated me this morning, for a moment he'd made me believe he cared for me as something more than a possession.

It was the most dangerous tactic he'd employed in this battle so far.

# Twelve

## A Gift

With 5:00 a.m. fast approaching, I paced my bedroom floor in complete indecision as to what I should wear. A chastity belt would have been nice, but he hadn't included that item in my new wardrobe.

The absence of modern noise in our wing of the house, which had at first been pleasant, was beginning to drive me batty. I didn't relish the idea of hanging with the Fangs to listen to the radio, but the idea grew more appealing with each passing hour. I hoped to negotiate a TV in my room if I played my cards right. After the tedious night I'd had, the idea of prostituting myself for my cable fix didn't seem as wrong as it should.

I had almost settled on a plain black skirt to go with the turtleneck I wore when there was a soft knock at my door. Before I could open it, Clarence entered. He bore a plastic garment bag, which he dumped without a word on the bed.

"What's this?" I asked after him as he left the room.

"Read the card" was his only reply before I heard the outer door click shut.

"Thanks for your help," I muttered, looking down at the bag. A small envelope rested atop it. I slid the card out and read the elegant script.

I hope the gown is to your liking. It would please me greatly if you wore it this evening. Clarence will come to retrieve you at five o'clock.

Bracing myself for what I might find inside, I unzipped the bag. The dress wasn't what I had expected—though my expectations weren't terribly specific. Lifting the length of blush-colored satin, I grudgingly admitted Cyrus had good taste.

I would normally feel a little silly for being so overdressed, but I liked what I saw when I slipped into the gown and looked myself over in the mirror. The color complimented my blond hair, and though my skin had paled since I'd turned, it wasn't as obvious against such a delicate shade.

I usually wasn't so vain, but I hadn't gotten dressed up like this since my high school prom, and the sight of myself in something other than a lab coat or jeans enticed me to the mirror. I snuck a pair of diamond earrings from the stash in the armoire and let my hair down, brushing it until it fell in soft waves around my shoulders. I looked so good *I* would have given myself television privileges just for standing there.

*Now I look like something worth drawing,* I thought, and instantly regretted it. After the T-shirt debacle, I'd taken care to hide Nathan's sketch, but it had felt like burying a dead friend. I wondered what he was doing now. If he missed me. Or if he was just biding his time until he got the chance to kill me.

I commanded myself to stop thinking of such morose

things. Whatever might have begun between Nathan and I was over now. I could continue to cling to the past, or I could try to be happy in my new life.

Staring in the mirror, I barely recognized myself. In the past, I'd been lonely and unhappy. I'd defined my life by my career, and my heart hadn't even been in it. I'd had no idea who I was or any plans to find out. But now I had the opportunity. I couldn't waste it.

Clarence entered my sitting room just as the clock chimed for the fifth time. His face was somber as he led me down the hallway. We stopped at the large double doors and waited while they were opened from within.

Cyrus's rooms were much larger than mine. The parlor boasted a painted ceiling where cherubs looked down from a sunny sky. It was a striking contrast to the marble statues of nude women in the grasps of winged demons that flanked the fireplace.

Cyrus was seated at a small table in the center of the room. There were no corpses, as promised. Two champagne flutes and a large crystal decanter full of blood were laid out before him. He stood when I entered.

"Look at you." His eyes glittered with genuine appreciation. "You're more beautiful every time I see you."

"You look pretty good yourself." It wasn't an empty compliment, though anything was better than his pirate outfit from before. He wore a simple, button-down black shirt and black pants, and his hair was tied back. He looked surprisingly modern, and I found it easy to imagine he was a different person from the man who'd wreaked so much havoc in my life.

Maybe that's what I'd have to do. Live in denial to stand living at all. But I'd been doing that for far too long already.

I cleared my throat. "I'm glad to see the leather pants couldn't make a return appearance."

Clearly, he interpreted this as an insult. "I beg your pardon? Leather is very fashionable."

"In 1997." I sat in the chair Clarence pulled out for me and spread my napkin across my lap. "And I must tell you I'm not really big on the whole 'Satan Goes to Versailles' vibe you've got going on here." He ignored me and poured some of the blood into my glass. It fizzed slightly as it hit the glass.

"Let me guess. Poison?" Knowing better than that, I took a sip and let the fluid roll slowly across my tongue, savoring its sweet flavor.

"Champagne. Think of it as a *bloody* mimosa." He laughed at his own joke before he went on. "I thought we had reason to celebrate tonight." He filled his glass and took a long swallow.

I eyed him incredulously. "What are we celebrating exactly?"

A wickedly satisfied smirk stretched across his face. "Your fall from grace."

"Hold on there, buddy. I haven't done anything yet." I'd learned from past experience that he would try to tempt me, to appeal to the monster in me. I also knew I was more receptive to the possibility now than I had been when he'd tried to lure me before. But he didn't need to know that. Then again, he probably already did.

Cyrus took another drink, his eyes never leaving me. "I do like that dress. You'll have to wear it more often."

"I don't know." I smoothed my hands over the silky fabric. "When I get the chance, maybe. It's not really something I can wear around the house."

"Why not?"

I laughed, until I realized he was serious. "Well, I'd feel overdressed, for one."

"No one would mention it." His champagne flute dangled from the tips of his fingers as he leaned back in his chair. "It befits your station."

I huffed in annoyance. "My station. Because you said you could make me a queen, right?"

"I can't *make* you a queen, that was a bit of a fib. More like a princess." He made the remark without a hint of humor. "You've read *The Sanguinarius?*"

"Only about half of it. My copy was lost when my apartment burned down."

"A pity. So, if I mentioned the name Jacob Seymour, you'd have no idea who I was speaking of?" Cyrus's eyes were fixed on my face, as if he were trying to register something in my reaction.

He'd find nothing there. "No clue at all. Why, is he someone important?"

"Yes, you could say so. He was my father."

I didn't know how to respond, so I merely waited for him to continue.

"My father was not a powerful man in life. He was an old man with two wives in the grave and ten grown children when he was turned. We were serfs, what you call peasants now. We farmed land owned by a wealthy lord and tithed most of our profit to the Crown."

"In England?" I took a sip from my glass, enjoying the effects of light-headedness from the champagne and satiation from the blood mixed with it.

Cyrus nodded. "The vampire who sired my father did so on the condition that he use all the powers gifted to him to grow strong and overcome those who would rule him. Father took it quite literally. First, he killed the noble family who enslaved us. Then he killed and fed from his sire, and finally, one by one, he sought out those of our kind already in existence. The oldest, the strongest, the most fearsome. My father slew them all. He drank their blood and stole their power.

"And then, of his seven living sons, he chose the one he felt was the most ruthless and calculating, and he sired him."

Cyrus straightened in his chair, pride transforming his face. "And while my brother slept, on the first day of his new vampire life, I killed him and stole his blood." He paused, and his brows furrowed as if he were trying to remember something. "Then I stabbed him in the heart and took a handful of his ashes to my father to show him what I'd done. That I deserved the place I'd been denied."

My heart racing, I reached for my glass and drank half of it down before I could speak again. "Why are you telling me this now?"

"Because my father has now successfully killed all the oldest known vampires. He is the leader of our kind." Though he said this in all seriousness, he shrugged it off rather quickly. "His blood runs in mine, and my blood runs in yours. We are royalty, Carrie."

I looked around helplessly as a tremor of—was that paternal affection?—passed across the blood tie.

"So, in a roundabout way, what I'm saying is that there's good reason for you to wear the dress again."

"I'll see what I can do," I breathed.

A new, frightening possibility entered my mind. What if Cyrus wasn't the man I thought he was at all, but merely a pawn under his father's control? How much of the evil he inflicted on others originated from his own brain? He'd been a vampire for so long now, perhaps he couldn't remember what it was like to be free from the blood tie.

Cocking his head, Cyrus regarded me with the amused

smile of a man viewing a prize that was nearly his. "My God, but you're lovely."

The sentiment was a bit too heartfelt to sit comfortably with me. "Why do you say things like that?"

He lifted one shoulder in a half shrug. "Because I mean them."

I filed his words away under "Ploys to Disarm Me."

He nodded to Clarence, and the butler stepped forward to clear the table.

Still hungry, I handed my glass over with some reluctance. "Are we finished?"

Cyrus stood and moved to take my hand. "No. This was just an appetizer. Now we're on to the main course."

He stepped behind me and covered my eyes with his hands. The feeling of him so close, his body brushing against my back as he led me from the room, set my nerve endings on fire.

"Where are we going?" I asked as if I didn't know the answer.

"Look," he whispered as he removed his hands.

A huge bed on a raised dais dominated the room. Elegant curtains of sheer gold-and-cream fabric hung from the dark wood canopy, and in the center lay a young man, bound, gagged and shirtless.

Although his hair was clean and trimmed, and he wore trousers instead of jeans, I recognized him immediately.

Ziggy.

"He's for you." Cyrus walked over to the bed and held his hand out to me.

*Don't react,* I urged myself, picturing a brick wall in an attempt to keep Cyrus from seeing my thoughts. *Pretend you don't know him. Deny you've ever met him. Just don't do anything to endanger him.*

But my panic clearly transferred through the blood tie. His face full of concern, Cyrus moved from my side. "He's completely harmless."

Ziggy's eyes were wide, pupils dilated, but he didn't struggle. I stepped closer. "What's wrong with him?"

"Drugged." Cyrus sat on the edge of the bed and motioned for me to join him. "They tend to gain strength when fighting for their lives, and I wanted tonight to be perfect."

I stepped up cautiously, trying to cloak my thoughts from Cyrus while I frantically willed Ziggy not to show any sign of recognition.

Was it possible Cyrus didn't know who this was? It would be unlike him not to gloat about his prize, especially after the way he'd acted this morning. But it made no sense for Ziggy to be in the mansion at all.

"Who is he?" I croaked, fervently praying Cyrus didn't already know the answer.

To my immense relief, he yawned and reached up to unbind his hair. "I don't know. Some runaway. He showed up here a few hours ago. Isn't he breathtaking?"

The day before I wouldn't have exactly agreed with that statement, but groomed and divested of his various piercings and odd metal jewelry, Ziggy recalled a Renaissance portrait of youthful, male beauty.

Hesitantly, I climbed onto the bed. "Why is he here?"

"For you to feed from, dearest," Cyrus answered distractedly as he popped off his cuff links and shook out his sleeves.

"But he's conscious."

My mouth went a little dry as I watched Cyrus work the buttons of his shirt. "Well, that's the point, isn't it? No fun drinking from a victim who can't feel it. But you'll have to hurry. The paralytic will wear off soon."

I frowned. Paralyzing drugs were nothing to trifle with. Ziggy could die of suffocation if his lungs were affected. In the guise of lazily stroking his chest, I measured the rise and fall of the flesh beneath my hand. His respiration was labored, but not seriously. "He can't be too paralyzed if he's breathing."

Cyrus reached for me over Ziggy's body, tracing a line up my arm, over my shoulder, to my neck. He pulled me forward. I rose on my knees and braced my hands against the smooth, cold skin of his chest beneath his open shirt.

I heard Ziggy's blood moving faster and faster through his veins between us. I remembered the rich taste of his blood and my stomach growled. Another hunger sprang to life in me, an ache that grew as Cyrus pushed my hair aside. He pressed his mouth to my neck, grazing his teeth over the surface.

"I should have bitten you that night," he rasped, one hand moving to cup my breast. "I should have ripped your flesh with my teeth and fed from you, rather than flee like a coward. If only I could have silenced your screams so I could have taken my time."

I moaned, dropping my head back to give him fuller access. Memories of the attack washed over me, some his, some my own. But now they were not horrific. Now, when I saw his hand twisted in my hair, saw myself kneeling and praying—had I prayed?—at his feet, the images were searing and erotic.

I reminded myself of the blood tie, of the control he had over me, but I didn't care. This wouldn't be something that happened to me. This would be something that I chose to do.

Ziggy groaned at our knees. Moving behind me, Cyrus eased me onto the bed so I lay beside the boy. With one arm draped over my waist, my sire leaned close to my ear and whispered, "Drink, Carrie."

And God, how I wanted to. But it was Ziggy. "If I do, will it kill him?"

Obviously misinterpreting the nature of my question, Cyrus chuckled. "Go ahead, take his life if you'd like. Or, let him live and we'll play with him later. Whatever you prefer."

When I hesitated, he reached over me to lay a lethally sharp fingernail against Ziggy's exposed throat. "Do you want me to cut him for you?"

I sensed his impatience through the blood tie and by the way his legs rubbed restlessly against mine. If he knew who Ziggy was, if he knew why I couldn't feed from him…

No. I could do this. All I needed to do was show Cyrus I was willing to perform the act. Even just a few drops would prove that. Then he wouldn't hurt me or Ziggy.

Yes, I could do this. To protect Ziggy's life, I could hurt him.

I ran my tongue over my fangs. I hadn't even felt the change take place. It was beginning to feel natural. I leaned close to Ziggy's throat.

"Yes," Cyrus hissed into my ear. He bunched a fistful of my gown in his hand, pulling it higher and higher until I felt his palm against my bare thigh.

Taking a deep breath for control, I bit down. I'd expected Ziggy's body to stiffen beneath my mouth, but he didn't react at all.

When the blood hit my tongue, I cried out with the most intense orgasm I'd ever experienced. The sensation was so overwhelming it took me a moment to realize I hadn't felt it at all. It was Ziggy's memory, seeping into me through his blood. His eyes opened and I saw through them as he collapsed, sated, against the bare mattress of his bed.

There was the click of a door opening, and Ziggy flipped onto his back, panic obliterating the peace that lingered from his climax. Nathan stood frozen in the doorway, covered in grime and soot from the fire. His eyes, clouded with fatigue, flamed to life with shock and sudden anger.

*He was masturbating, so what?* I thought, a little surprised at Nathan's reaction. Then I saw the third person in the room, a young man Ziggy's age, at the corner of the bed. He clutched the rumpled sheet to his naked body and rapidly tried to explain his presence before grabbing his clothes and pushing past Nathan.

I felt Ziggy's shame, but also his strange relief at being found out and his embarrassment at the knowledge I saw everything he remembered.

*I didn't know he was coming upstairs,* his thoughts whispered in my head. *I didn't know he'd be so mad. I should have told him. I want to go home.*

I jerked my head back, clamping my palm over the wound I'd inflicted to stop the bleeding. When no blood oozed between my fingers, I lifted my hand. The bite was neatly closed, but a telling scar remained.

"What's wrong?" Cyrus sat up and tried to slip his arm around me for support.

I pushed him away. "I can't do this."

His face contorted in anger, but he covered it quickly. "Why not?"

Quivering, I tried to pull down my skirt. "I can see his thoughts. I can feel his emotions."

"Oh, is that all?" With a laugh that sounded more condescending than comforting, he pulled me into his arms. "Darling, that's the best part."

"I didn't like it." I tensed a little, testing the strength of his hold.

His arms tightened around me solidly enough to prevent me from running. He licked the shell of my ear, and I felt some of my forgotten desire return. "There, there, dearest. You did very well, for your first time." His hand fell to my lap, seeking the hem of my skewed gown. "And the night is still young. There are plenty of other exciting things we can do."

The touch of his cold hand, separated from my flesh only by the thin material of my panties, sucked the breath from my lungs. I opened my legs for him and reached back to loop an arm around his neck.

When I heard Ziggy make another soft groan, I snapped back to reality. "Wait, wait."

"Now what's wrong?" His annoyance was unmistakable this time. Cyrus swung his legs over the side of the bed and stood, pulling his shirt off in one agitated motion. "Do we need scented candles and Barry White? How about mirrors on the ceiling?"

"Don't be angry," I said, a little tearfully, and I insisted to myself it was nerves and exhaustion that made me react in such a way. "This is just so…new."

With a deep sigh, he removed his belt and dropped it to the floor, kicking it aside. "I know. And I know I come across as a tad impatient. But I want you, Carrie. I'm not used to waiting for gratification."

"I'm tired," I admitted, not caring if it upset him. "Let me sleep today, and I promise we'll…you know, tomorrow."

He smiled. "I suppose I can wait one more day."

Biting my lip, I looked to Ziggy, who still lay paralyzed on the bed. "But you have to do something for me."

I'd expected him to be insulted, possibly enraged, but he seemed pleasantly surprised. "You want to make a deal with me? Fine. For what price will I buy a night of sin with you, my princess?"

I wished he wouldn't call me that, but now was not the time to argue. I pointed at Ziggy. "I want to keep him."

Cyrus arched an eyebrow. "Keep him?"

"As a pet. He was my first victim. I want a souvenir."

I held my breath as I waited for his reply. After a long moment, he finally spoke. "I don't see why not. You may have your trophy."

"Thank you." I kept my eyes downcast and let him kiss me on the forehead to seal our agreement. As I walked toward the door, I heard the rustle of the mattress sinking under his weight.

I turned to see him stretched out beside Ziggy, tracing the line of the boy's bicep with a clawed finger.

"We had an agreement," I said cautiously.

Cyrus laughed. "Don't worry, Carrie, I won't kill him. He's in good hands."

I didn't want to ask what those hands would be doing. I couldn't spare Ziggy from whatever perverse activities my sire had planned. I believed Cyrus wouldn't kill him, though, and that was all I cared about for the moment.

I went to the door and looked back once more. Ziggy's eyes locked on mine, pleading.

I could only leave and close the door behind me.

# Thirteen

*Revelations and Recriminations*

Back in my room, I practically ripped the gown from my body. My fingers shook and my chest ached with sobs as I struggled to hold them back.

What was Ziggy doing here? He'd had an awkward confrontation with Nathan, but that didn't explain why he'd come here. Not when he knew who lived here. Unless…

But he couldn't have been running to me.

I put on my robe and rang the velvet bell pull to summon Clarence. He appeared minutes later, looking crisp and pressed as always.

"Don't you ever sleep?" I asked as he nodded politely to me.

His face was humorless. "You needed something?"

I drew myself up as regally as I could manage in a bathrobe. "Yes. The Master—" I stumbled on the word. "He has a guest with him in his chambers. I'd like to be informed when he's…finished. And bring the young gentleman here."

Clarence shook his head. "I'm sorry, ma'am. I don't involve myself with the pets."

"He's not a pet," I snapped. "He's a friend. If you don't wish to do it yourself, tell the guards to deliver him to me."

I thought I saw a spark of admiration in his eyes, but he didn't smile. "Yes, ma'am. Will you require anything else?"

"Paper and a pen. Clean sheets. And medical supplies, any you might have. Gauze, disinfectant, clean towels—"

He cut me off. "I'm sure I can find an adequate first aid kit for you in the guardhouse."

I wasn't sure how to dismiss him. "You do that, then. Right now."

After he'd gone, I went to my bathroom and ran the tap water until it was as hot as it could get. I grabbed a hand towel from the rack and plunged it into the water, then hurried to the parlor. I wiped off the wooden arms and carved back of the antique sofa, making several return trips to the sink when the cloth got cold. I repeated the process with the marble end table, and covered it with a clean towel. It wasn't sterile, but it would have to do.

Clarence returned, and I nearly knocked him over to get at the medical kit he bore. I asked him to leave the folded sheets on the sofa. He surprised me by spreading them out carefully, skillfully tucking the corners around the odd shape.

I popped the latch on the beer cooler that contained my necessary supplies. Taking a seat, I examined the contents. There were all types of sutures, tape, gauze, vials of drugs, and even surgical instruments in sealed, sanitary packages. "This is what he gives the guards here?"

"He doesn't want them going to the hospital. Raises too many questions," Clarence said.

I looked up sharply. "What if they die?"

"Then some of the guards get burial duty."

I looked out the window. The sky was turning pink. "What about the pets?"

"They don't bury them out there. Guards go behind the guardhouse, that's out past the maze. Pets go in the cellar. That's my job."

"The cellar? In the house?" I imagined piles of bodies festering below us. It made my skin crawl.

"In barrels. I fill 'em with cement and every other week the guards go out to the lake and dump them," he answered.

"Like the mob." If Lake Michigan ever dried up, I was willing to bet they'd find hundreds of such barrels. And crates, and probably shoes perfectly preserved in bricks of concrete. "Well, thank you, Clarence. That was enlightening."

"I'll keep an eye out for your young man" was all he said. Then he left.

I took the paper and pen he'd brought and went to my bedroom. I didn't know how I intended to get the letter to Nathan, or what I should even say. "Hey, don't be so hard on your runaway gay son" didn't sound quite assertive enough, and "Get over it, you big, stupid baby" was more aggressive than I'd like to be.

Groaning in frustration, I went to the window. I'd have to close the curtains against the sunlight soon, but in this faint predawn, my gaze fell on something I hadn't noticed before. A slight gap in the ivy-covered rock wall that surrounded the property. A gate. There were no guards.

I wanted to run downstairs and check it out immediately, but bursting into flames didn't seem like the best way to start the day. I shut the curtains and went back to my letter.

Nathan,
Ziggy is with me. Wait for me at the gate in the side-

wall after sundown. Don't be late, I won't be able to
meet you after Cyrus wakes up.
Carrie

Dawn came, but I couldn't sleep. Not until I knew Ziggy
had survived. Eventually, exhaustion overtook me as I dozed
off in one of the parlor chairs. It was around nine when I woke
to the sound of labored footsteps coming through the door.
Ziggy hung weakly from Clarence's frail shoulders as the
older man guided him in.

"Give me a hand," the butler rasped, and I hurried to his
side. Ziggy whimpered as he leaned against me, and I felt his
nakedness through the sheet he'd been wrapped in. When I
laid him on the couch, I saw the fresh bites that marred almost every inch of his skin.

And I saw the one I'd made. My stomach soured.

"Ma'am," Clarence said, bowing stiffly as he handed a
bundle of clothes toward me. It was Ziggy's borrowed pants.
On top was a folded note.

I looked from the livid purple bruise of a hand print around
Ziggy's neck to the gleaming white paper and snatched the
clothing and note from Clarence's hands. Shaking with rage,
I unfolded the missive.

*I only said I wouldn't kill him. Enjoy what's left.*

I crumpled the note in my fist. "Clarence, if I needed you
to send something to someone, would you do it?"

"It depends on what that something is." He eyed Ziggy's
gray body as if mentally calculating his weight.

"No, not him. He'll be fine." I couldn't ask the butler to
risk his life freeing Ziggy, nor did I feel comfortable just turning the kid loose on the streets. I would hand him over to one
person, and one alone. "I need you to deliver a note."

He appeared reluctant. "You could ask the Master. He has messengers."

"No. Cyrus can't know about this." Almost without thinking, I smoothed back a damp strand of Ziggy's hair. His gaze darted over my face and his mouth moved slightly, but I could tell the drug hadn't yet worn off completely. Had he been given another dose?

I wanted to be able to smile, to give him some reassurance, but I couldn't. I turned back to Clarence. "Please. I want to notify this boy's father. I want to get him out of here."

Ziggy's body spasmed. *Great,* I thought, *he's allergic to whatever Cyrus gave him, and he's going to have a seizure.* To my relief, the twitches that followed were much tamer, a sign that his muscles were slowly coming back to awareness after their paralysis.

"Give me your letter," Clarence said somewhat reluctantly. "And tell me the address."

"1320 Wealthy Avenue," I said, choking back tears of relief. "The note's on the table there. Do you want me to write down the number?"

"No, ma'am. 1320 Wealthy Avenue. Will you require anything else?"

A declaration of loyalty like the knights gave Arthur in all those Camelot movies would have been nice, but I doubted I would get one from Clarence. The only guarantee I had was the fact he hated Cyrus and probably wouldn't go out of his way to make his master happy.

Clarence nodded as though he'd read and agreed with my thought, then he left without another word. Once he had gone, I knelt at Ziggy's side.

His eyes searched my face, and his mouth worked feebly to speak. I laid my hand on his chest, hoping the touch comforted him. "Ziggy, I believe the drugs he gave you are wearing off. Did he give you another dose? Blink once for yes."

With visible effort, his eyes closed briefly, then snapped open.

"You have some bite marks I think might need cleaning. Can I examine you?"

Two blinks and an angry glare.

I sighed. "I'm sorry I bit you. I really am. But I couldn't let Cyrus know who you were. He'd kill you. You know I wouldn't have done it in any other circumstance."

Two blinks.

"Ziggy, please. I don't want you to get an infection I can easily prevent."

After a long moment, one blink.

I went to the bathroom and scrubbed my hands thoroughly. Then, with the consideration I'd give a sexual assault case in the E.R., I began my examination.

"I'm going to take this sheet off of you, but I'll rearrange it so you're not completely uncovered. Right now, all I'm doing is evaluating the severity of your injuries."

And some were pretty severe. Long, but fairly shallow cuts latticed his chest. Hideous, purple bruises darkened his skin, and claw marks showed where Cyrus had gripped the boy's shoulders. When I moved lower, I saw bite marks, not inflicted by fangs, but blunt, human teeth, on the inside of his thighs. I turned my head away.

When I looked back, I saw a tear roll from Ziggy's eye. He wouldn't look at me.

A few hours ago, he'd been indulging in what looked like some pretty terrific sex. Then he'd run away from the only home he'd ever known, just to come here and be violated and humiliated by Cyrus. And me.

I debraded the bites and scratches and covered the worst with squares of gauze. "Do you hurt…anywhere else?"

He answered with two blinks, but croaked a barely audible "No."

I went to wash my hands and snag an extra blanket from my bed. When I came back, I tucked Ziggy in, then dropped wearily into a chair. He spoke again, with more strength behind his voice this time. "Thank you."

I heard the emotion in his words and tried to sound casual. "It's okay. If you need anything else, just let me know."

"Some aspirin would be nice. I'm sore all over." He swallowed with a wince.

I looked through the medicine kit and found a bottle of acetaminophen. "This will have to do. I don't want to thin your blood, with all those…wounds."

I couldn't say *bites*. I crushed the pills into quarters so they'd go down easier and got a paper cup of water from the bathroom sink. Slipping my hand behind his head, I helped him to ingest the pills. "Why did you come here?"

He choked a little on the water, and it roughened his voice. He sounded like a man, not the boy who'd attacked me in the bookshop. "You saw what happened. He kicked me out."

"That doesn't explain why you'd come here. You knew who lived here."

"I knew you lived here." His arm jerked in an effort to wipe away his tears, but he couldn't yet control his limbs. "I thought you'd let me stay. I didn't know you were going to feed off me and let him do w-what he did to me." The last part came out as a shamed whisper, and he closed his eyes. "I love irony, when it doesn't happen to me."

He felt he was being punished. I wanted to weep for him, trapped in his prison of self-loathing, but he didn't need that now. He would shun my pity and turn away from me. Then he'd have no allies left. "You didn't deserve this."

"Yeah, well. That's your opinion." He laughed bitterly, and more tears rolled silently from his eyes to wet the hair at his temples.

"It's not an opinion. It's a fact," I told him sternly. "You didn't deserve what he did to you."

He looked away, and I could practically feel the blame radiating from him.

I cleared my throat softly and decided to change the subject. "Ziggy, when you got here, did you tell anyone you knew me?"

"Yeah. The guards at the door. I told them I was looking for the doctor, that I knew you from the hospital." He sniffled. "Don't worry, I didn't mention the Movement. I figured they would have probably killed me."

Rage brought me to my feet. "I'll be back in a minute."

With enough strength to splinter the hinges, I wrenched the secret door open and strode into Cyrus's chamber. Two guards stood at his bedroom door, but they stepped aside and even opened it to admit me.

Cyrus was sprawled naked across the bed, the sheets and blankets in a tangled heap on the floor. Blood spattered the linen beneath him, and he snored in the depths of a contented sleep.

*I could kill him right now and he'd never see it coming.* The thought came before I had a chance to guard my mind from him, and I tensed, waiting for a response. His breath hitched, but he didn't wake.

I stepped to the side of the bed, intending to wake him, but his arm shot out and caught my wrist. He pulled me down and pinned me beneath him.

"You're mad enough to kill me, then?" he murmured against my neck. "You should have brought a weapon, because I can guarantee you won't be able to do it with your bare hands."

I didn't struggle. "How could you do that to him?"

"How could you lie to me?" He twisted a hand in my hair, wrenching my head back painfully. "'Who is he?' you asked, as though you hadn't the faintest clue that he'd come asking after you. As if I were stupid enough not to notice you'd cut yourself off from the blood tie, become so closed down to me that it was obvious you hid something. Who is this man to you, Carrie?"

I wanted to spit in his face. "He isn't a man. He's practically a child. And he's a friend of mine. He was looking for a place to stay."

"And I should just open my home to every derelict who wishes to show up?" He rolled off of me, and I pointedly ignored his nakedness.

"You do for your pets." He'd grown aroused as he lay on top of me, and I clenched my teeth to fight the mirrored feeling from our invisible connection. "Why should it be different for him?"

"It isn't." Cyrus reached for the crystal bell that lay on his nightstand and he rung it sharply. The door opened, and the two sentries moved into the room. Cyrus pointed to the bedding on the floor, and they wordlessly began to untangle it.

Cyrus reclined against the pillows, utterly shameless in his nudity. "I only did what I would have done with any of my pets. I took what I wanted from him, and in return he'll get what he wants from me."

The guards laid the covers over us both, and Cyrus pulled me into his arms.

Though I was still angry, his touch felt so good that I didn't resist him. I rested my head on his chest. "Promise me you won't do that to him again."

I felt his breath on the top of my head. "Fine. I won't touch him against his will. But I won't promise not to try to bend that will. He was a lot of fun."

"I don't want to hear about it," I snapped.

He chuckled and stroked the exposed skin at the neck of my robe. "You'd be disappointed, anyway. I don't kiss and tell."

I started to rise. "I'm going back to check on him. He's pretty beat up. But you already know that."

"Stay." It wasn't a request.

"You there," he called to one of the guards. "Blast, I've forgotten your name."

"Thomas, sir," the guard replied quickly.

Cyrus nodded. "Thomas. Go and see to the young man in Carrie's room. He's in your care today."

As the guard moved to do as his master bid, I called after him. "If he complains about the quality of care you give him, I'll kill you myself. Understood?"

Thomas didn't even blink at the warning, but I felt Cyrus's pride through the blood tie. "Very good, Carrie. If I didn't know better, I'd say you were enjoying your role as lady of the house."

His arm slipped around my waist and he cupped my bottom through the robe. I pushed his hand away. "Don't think you're going to get any. Ever."

He replaced his hand and pulled me tighter against his side. "Do you really think I could perform after the energy I expended with your friend?"

"I said I don't want to hear about it."

He laughed softly. "Sleep, princess. All I wanted was to feel you beside me. Where you belong."

His words were like a death sentence.

Though it was nearly noon, I couldn't sleep. I listened as my sire's breathing grew slow and even, and his gentle snore returned. I propped myself up on my elbow and studied him.

He couldn't have been very old when he'd been turned. Twenty-five at most. In sleep, his face was smooth and devoid of lines, unmarked by the volatile emotions that ruled him in wakefulness. His skin, though pale, stretched across a body hardened from years of physical labor. From what little I knew of the time he'd been born to, I guessed he'd worked hard as a human.

*This man is your sire. This man is the blood that pumps through your heart.* I pressed a kiss to his lips. No matter how much I tried to hate him, something defeated the effort. The blood tie? Or my own, insane attraction to him that grew despite his cruelty and depravity?

When I was near him, I wanted him. When he was out of my sight, I hated him. If I could just weed out my true emotions from those governed by the blood tie, I'd know how I felt. Maybe I'd be able to feel my own blood in my veins then, not just the scorching presence of his.

One of his arms secured me at his side as though he were afraid I would bolt. The other lay across his chest. I reached for that hand, surprisingly elegant despite the lethally long nails that tipped each finger. I remembered what Nathan had said about vampires looking different as they aged. If I lived long enough, what would I become?

I lifted his hand and wondered what I would see if I linked our hands the way he'd done before. If his defenses were down in sleep, would I be able to choose the direction of the visions? I laced my fingers with his and closed my eyes.

Before the rushing current took me, his body thrashed against mine, as if he were in a nightmare. Then a red film washed over me and an unimaginable pain tore through my chest. I opened my mouth, or rather, Cyrus opened his mouth, and a scream of agony burst from his raw throat. "Father!"

*"Hold still, boy. Your brother didn't carry on so!"* When Cyrus opened his eyes, the face that belonged to the stern voice sneered down at me. Though his skin was weathered with age and the lines of a hard life, he bore a striking resemblance to my sire. Blood stained the front of his shirt and the ends of his long white hair. His hands were inside Cyrus's chest, searching, pulling, ripping.

In a dizzying second, the vision changed. The face before me morphed into that of a young woman, her body limp, her eyes wide but sightless. The searing pain in Cyrus's chest began anew. He couldn't breathe—couldn't move.

*Couldn't pray.*

His father's laugh echoed in his ear. Cyrus's scream was harsh, his voice used up by his cries for mercy. A deafening roar propelled me out of the vision, and I sat up, panting, at the same time Cyrus woke from his dream.

His features transformed in his rage. "Did you get a good look?"

The Cyrus I knew was gone, replaced by the ruthless figure of John Doe. I cowered, and was ashamed of the motion. "I needed to know…" I had no idea how I would finish the sentence. "I needed to know how I really felt about you, and I thought I might get a clue by poking around in your head." That wouldn't leave me vulnerable to his manipulation or anything. My eyes searched the room, finally resting on the scar that divided his chest. "I wanted to see how you got that scar."

Wrong answer. He grabbed me by my shoulders and flung me from the bed. I hit the floor and skidded painfully, the soft carpet cutting like razors as it scraped my skin.

"Get out!" He leapt from the bed and snatched his robe, angrily thrusting his arms into it.

I stood, rubbing my tender knees. "Don't be mad. It's not like I—"

"Did you hear me? I told you to get out!"

He paced the floor like a caged animal. I thought he'd strike me, but each time he raised his hands they closed in frustrated fists and he dropped them to his side. Eventually, he gave up and stalked to the door. He called to the two guards who blocked it after he passed. "I'll be in my study. See that I'm not disturbed."

Aching with physical pain and rejection, I pushed one of the guards aside. "Don't worry, I'm not going to follow him," I snapped when they protested. I told the truth. The sun would set in a matter of hours, and I had a meeting with Nathan. I'd need to be strong.

Because I didn't know what Nathan would do to me when he saw me.

# *Fourteen*

### An Uncomfortable Reunion

The guard sent to watch over Ziggy had fallen asleep at his post. I dismissed him coolly and took a blanket from my bed to tuck Ziggy in with.

Fatigue penetrated me all the way to my bones, and I groaned when I saw the time on the clock on the mantel. I'd only get a few hours of sleep before I had to meet Nathan. And sleep would not come easily. I tossed and turned in the bed, agitated beyond my own nerves. Cyrus was still awake. I could feel his anger and his restlessness, but I didn't take it to heart. Whatever he was upset about had less to do with me and more to do with what had been going on in that vision.

I woke groggily from the little sleep I did manage to get and dressed quietly, wishing not to disturb Ziggy. As I passed through the parlor, I stopped to check on him. He didn't look like a boy anymore. His exposure to Cyrus's cruelty had wiped the last traces of childhood from him. If the thought broke my heart, I could only imagine how it would make Nathan feel. I made a conscious decision not to tell him what Cyrus had done.

For the most part, the mansion was still asleep. I got the distinct impression that this wasn't an "early to bed, early to rise" kind of place. A few guards scurried around, preparing the common rooms for the occupants who'd soon fill them.

With a fearful glance at the study, I stepped furtively out the back door. A fresh blanket of snow covered the lawn. I tried not to think of how the hedge maze, frosted with shimmering crystals of ice, reminded me of *The Shining*. I was creeped out enough without the threat of Jack Nicholson jumping out at me.

I reached out to Cyrus with my thoughts, hoping that I sent off an innocent "just going for a walk" vibe. But it was like hitting a brick wall with my mind. Cyrus was ignoring me.

For a moment, his neglect stung me. Then I had the good sense to remember I didn't want him to pay attention to what I was doing, anyway. I had enough to worry about without wondering if my sire would rip me to shreds for my betrayal when I returned.

Not to mention the fact I had no idea whether Nathan had even received my message, and if he had, whether or not he would actually show up. If I got caught, I was a goner. I couldn't even lie my way out of a parking ticket. What if Clarence had sold me out after all? He didn't like vampires, period. Why should I have expected him to help me?

I kept to the shadow of the wall. I was sure every step I took would be my last before I was finally discovered. My initial trepidation had mounted to full-blown fear by the time I reached the gate. My cover disappeared as the stone wall broke, and I gasped, startled.

On the other side of the weathered iron bars, Nathan jumped at the sound.

I hadn't given much thought to what my reaction would

be when I saw him. I guess I'd assumed I'd have to plead for my life or fight him, so I wasn't prepared for the concern on his face or the way he gripped the bars like a man in a prison cell.

"Where is he? Is he okay?" he asked, peering past me up the lawn.

"He's fine," I assured him. "He's just tired. He had a rough night."

Nathan's jaw set as he spoke through tight lips. "I swear, Carrie, if anything happened to him—"

"Hey!" I snapped. "Do you really think I'd hurt him?"

"Yes, I do."

It stung too much to let it go. "You don't know anything about me."

I started to walk away, but then I remembered Ziggy and my reason for meeting with Nathan in the first place. Before I could turn back, Nathan called my name, and the anguish in his voice cut me to the quick.

"Please. I'll do anything you want. Just get him out of there." He reached through the bars as if to draw me back. "If anything happens to him…Carrie, I don't know what I'll do."

I sighed wearily and went back to the gate. "Nothing is going to happen to him. I've made sure of that."

Without my permission, my eyes flitted over the dark windows of Cyrus's bedroom. I remembered my promise to be with him at dawn, and an unexpected shiver of desire raced up my spine. I turned back to Nathan, hoping he couldn't sense my distress. "The problem is, this place is like Fort Knox. I don't know how we're going to get him out."

Nathan stared up at the mansion, rubbing his hands as if he was trying to warm them.

"You're dead. Aren't they supposed to be cold?"

His gaze never moved from the looming edifice. "I'm thinking."

"Tell me how that works out for you." As I watched him study the house, I found myself wanting to touch him. Not from sexual attraction, although I knew at least one of us still felt it. This was an urge borne of homesickness. Seeing him made me feel as if I'd been on a long trip in a violent foreign country.

"Why did you kick him out?" I asked quietly, and his eyes darted sharply back to me.

"I didn't kick him out. He left."

"He said you kicked him out."

"I reacted badly. There was some yelling. A lot of yelling. But I never told him to leave." Nathan's voice was thick with emotion. "And I damn sure wouldn't have let him go if I knew he was coming here."

"I'm sorry you had to find out that way. I'm sure it wasn't easy." But no matter what I said, it wouldn't erase his regret. "He's afraid you hate him."

"That's stupid of him!"

"Is it?" I planted my hands on my hips. "In case you didn't notice, he was pretty embarrassed that you walked in on him like that. And all he got from you was judgment and the angry face!"

For a moment, it appeared my words had penetrated his thick skull. Then he shook his head, swore and took a step back. "Why am I even talking to you? I should be jabbing a stake through this fence right now, after you ran off like that."

I'd almost forgotten my letter. "Ziggy gave you my message?"

"Yeah." His voice was cold and impersonal.

"And?" I wrapped my fingers around the icy metal, hoping he'd touch my hand.

It was a foolish hope. "What the fuck do you want me to say, Carrie? You made your decision."

"Then why are you talking to me?"

He clenched his fists around the bars and gave the gate a hard shove. Then he kicked it and swore again. I looked frantically toward the house, sure that at any moment I'd see guards streaming down the lawn. But Nathan continued to rage. With a final, violent kick to the stone wall, he spun away from me. I took that as my cue. "Are you finished?"

He limped back to the gate and nodded.

"Fine. Then why are you talking to me?" I phrased the question in a softer voice than I had before.

"Because you're the only way I'm going to get Ziggy out of there alive." When I didn't respond, he reached into his back pocket. "Listen, I'll cut you a deal—"

"I don't need money," I said quickly.

He gave me a melancholy smile. "Yeah, I see your boyfriend has a nice setup here."

"He's not my boyfriend." I reached for the folded paper that he passed through the bars. "What's this?"

"Information. I'm paying you for Ziggy. Do whatever you want with them."

I scanned the paper. "Nathan, these are battle plans."

"Do whatever you want with them," he repeated. "But if I were you, I wouldn't be here on the thirtieth."

I frowned at the page. "January thirtieth?"

Nathan snorted. "Hasn't he told you anything?"

"No. There hasn't really been time."

He laughed humorlessly. "I'll bet."

"Not because of that." I couldn't meet his eyes. "We haven't. Yet."

He shrugged. "I really don't care. Look over those plans.

You can find out what you need to from your sire. In the meantime, start thinking of how you can get Ziggy safely out of there. How can I contact you if I need to?"

"I have no idea. Maybe through Clarence. He goes out every day. Food shopping." I just hoped he'd relay the messages he received. He'd obviously helped me this time, since Nathan had shown up, but we hadn't exactly become fast friends.

"The guy who delivered your message? The one who lives with and works for Cyrus?" Nathan looked at me with disbelief. "How about if I want to talk to you, I'll be right here, after sunset. Make it a habit to check every night."

"If I can get away." It was sort of an agreement.

He turned then, as if he was going to leave, and I called his name. The sound was desperate, almost pathetic as it passed my lips. I wanted to tell him why I stood on this side of the fence. I wanted him to know that the only reason he lived was because of the choice I'd made.

Instead, I just stared, my mouth frozen open in shock at my sudden exclamation. He stared back, his expression hard as some indiscernible war raged behind his eyes.

"Keep him safe, Carrie," he said. Then he turned and walked quickly away.

I went back to the house, numb from the temperature outside and the mood of our chilly encounter. Telling him what I'd done wouldn't have accomplished anything. Nathan would have rushed into battle as if I were some princess trapped in a tower by an evil magician. Then I'd be in the awkward position of explaining that this damsel hadn't exactly decided to be rescued.

As for the evil magician, he stormed past the princess

without a word when they crossed paths in the hallway outside their chambers.

"Good morning, sunshine," I called after him, greeted only by the sound of his slamming door.

Ziggy was already awake when I entered my quarters. Clothed in the pants he arrived in the night before, he leaned greedily over a bowl of cereal as Clarence looked on.

"Hey. Did you see Nate?" Ziggy's voice was light, though I could sense the desperate hope there.

I cast a wary glance at Clarence. It seemed awfully imprudent of Ziggy to speak so freely in front of a guy we barely knew. "Y-yes."

With a frown, Ziggy jerked his thumb toward Clarence. "Don't worry about him. He knows how to keep a secret, don't you, Clarence?"

"Like a dead man," Clarence confirmed, but I still felt a little uneasy about what he knew.

"What did he say?" Ziggy lifted the bowl from the marble-topped end table, and Clarence used the opportunity to wipe a condensation ring from the spot where it had rested.

I chose my words carefully. "He wants you to go home."

Ziggy slurped the milk from his spoon and glared at the coaster Clarence had placed on the table. "Is he still pissed at me?"

"He never was pissed." I dropped beside him on the sofa. "Nathan loves you."

As unobtrusive as a ghost passing by, Clarence decanted a glass of blood and pressed it into my hand. I thanked him, but my attention was still on Ziggy. "Do you want to go home?"

"Hmm…stay here with the crazy, sadistic vampire, or go home?" He paused. "To the cold, emotionally shut-off vampire who'll freak out if I ever bring another guy home."

"I don't think he will. He was just surprised. And I get the distinct impression he's not so pleased that you've grown up. He would have acted the same if he'd caught you with a girl." At least, I hoped he would have. Different generation or not, times changed and Nathan should have adapted. And he shouldn't have cared in the first place.

Ziggy mustered enough false enthusiasm to say, "Great. When do I leave?"

Clarence coughed softly. "It's not as simple as that." Ziggy and I stared at the butler in silence. How could he possibly know the details of my conversation with Nathan? Were there spies?

As if sensing my distrust, Clarence shook his head. "But maybe you don't want an old man's help."

He moved to collect the dishes, but Ziggy stopped him by placing a hand on his arm. "What do you know?"

Clarence gave me a frigid glare.

"What? Do you want me to leave?" I folded my arms across my chest stubbornly. "This is *my* room, you know."

"I don't want you to leave," Clarence explained, a little condescendingly. "I want you to stop acting as if I'm going to turn sides all of a sudden."

"I'm sorry, but how am I supposed to trust someone who's worked for Cyrus all this time? You are on his payroll," I pointed out.

Clarence seemed to roll this around in his mind for a moment. "I trust you a little bit, and you're a vampire."

Considering his stance on vampires, that was a pretty bold statement. Pulling Nathan's plans from my pocket, I motioned for Clarence to come closer. "Apparently, there's going to be some kind of attack here on January thirtieth."

I realized I'd been so caught up in my new vampirehood

that I hadn't noticed Christmas had come and gone. I supposed it had saved me from a particularly miserable holiday. I couldn't imagine snuggling up in front of the tree and listening to Bing Crosby records with Cyrus of all people.

I swallowed the knot of loneliness that formed in my throat and forced a stoic expression. "Do you know anything about this, Clarence?"

"I don't know about any attack, but January thirtieth is the Vampire New Year."

"Vampire New Year?" Ziggy's question echoed my own.

Clarence nodded, his face growing more serious, a feat I'd thought impossible. "Every damn year. And they always throw a big, disgusting party."

"What happens at the party?"

"A lot of people die." Clarence removed Ziggy's empty cereal bowl and placed it on the rolling service cart. "All except two of the pets will go on the ingredients list. The two Cyrus leaves off are the guests of honor."

"That doesn't sound too bad," Ziggy interjected, his voice hoarse.

"Unless you've been his guest of honor before," I pointed out, and his expression grew dark. "Clarence, how does Cyrus pick these guests?"

"I don't know. He just gives me the list. I'm not invited to the party. But I do know that only one of them comes back. He turns them. Sometimes his daddy does it if he's feeling up to it. I'm not sure what happens to the other one. If I were you, I'd get your young man out of here before then."

I had plenty of questions, but Clarence had apparently reached his talking quota for the day. I'd have to get my answers from Cyrus.

* * *

Cyrus had either forgotten to lock the door or hadn't expected anyone to interrupt him, but when I burst into his study, the look on his face was murderous.

"You weren't invited into this room," he snarled, glancing sharply up from the book in his lap.

I took in his uncharacteristically casual appearance, noting that he wore a black eye patch. "Where was that yesterday when you needed it?"

With an annoyed sigh, he closed the book. "For your information, I'm wearing this because I didn't take an eye from your friend, and I simply don't have the energy to seek a replacement tonight."

"Too tired for me?" Alternating stabs of disappointment and relief sliced through me.

"No, but I'm rapidly becoming tired *of* you. Is there any reason for this visit?" He folded his hands across his lap.

"Yeah. I've got a question."

"Well, are you sure you wish to ask, or would you prefer to sneak around in my mind while I sleep tomorrow?"

"Are you still upset over that?" I walked slowly toward him. Taking the book from him, I insinuated myself into its place. "If I had known it would make you so mad, I wouldn't have done it."

"Why do I have difficulty believing that?" But he smiled, anyway, pulling me against his chest. His skin seemed colder than usual.

I sat up. "You haven't fed."

Only then did I notice the dark circle beneath his visible eye, and the tired, pinched look of his face. He was weak, and it alarmed me.

With a shrug that came off more theatrical than carefree, he urged me to lean back against him. "I wasn't in the mood."

"Was it because of me?" The question came out before my mind could consent.

It seemed to take him off guard, as well. Maybe if he'd been feeling better he would have lied to me, but he nodded wearily. "There are things in my past that…put me off my appetite when I dwell on them."

He nuzzled my neck as though seeking comfort, and I couldn't deny him. I stroked his hair and tried to quiet my pounding heart. The contact was more emotionally intimate than any of the times he'd touched me before. I suddenly couldn't remember why I'd been angry with him.

It felt right, holding him like this. As if someone finally needed me. Not because I was going to save their life. Not because I was going to fulfill some long-held parental expectation. Cyrus needed me because I was me.

"You wanted to ask me something?" His words were heavy with sleep.

*Did I?* The question drifted lazily to the surface of my consciousness. "Right. What's up with Vampire New Year?"

He let out a low rumble of laughter. "Where did you hear about that?"

"Around."

To my relief, he didn't question further. "Vampire New Year is a tradition created by my father. You'll enjoy it, if you let yourself."

Cyrus gently moved me from his lap and stood, then walked to an intercom box beside the door. "Send for Clarence. Tell him I've changed my mind about breakfast."

Static crackled, followed by a "Yes, sir."

Cyrus smiled at me, but it was clear he'd wasted much of

his energy getting to the door. I made a move to help him, but he refused me. "So you want to know about the New Year?"

I did, but his weakened state worried me. "You fed from Ziggy. Why are you having such a hard time?"

"I didn't feed enough. I didn't want to anger you," he said, supporting himself on the heavy wooden arm of the sofa. "As you get older, you'll find you need more blood to function. It makes life rather difficult if you have to go a day or two without feeding."

I shifted into doctor mode. "If you don't feed, will you die?"

"Not right away." He eased onto the couch and patted the seat beside him. "But it's very uncomfortable after a while."

I joined him, fitting familiarly to his side. "How many days has it been for you?"

"The last time I drank my fill was the night we first met." He kissed my forehead. "I've been a bit distracted since."

And he hadn't fed tonight because of what I'd uncovered as I'd snooped through his brain. To assuage my guilt, I changed the topic. "You were going to tell me about the New Year."

"Oh, yes. A fitting topic, actually. You remember what I told you about my father?"

I nodded. How could I have forgotten?

Cyrus seemed to draw strength from talking about his father. "Though he hasn't been a vampire much longer than I have, the blood of the elders he drained seems to have sped up his—blast, what's the word for it?"

"Metabolism?" I supplied.

"Yes, exactly. Within fifty years of turning, he needed to feed from two, sometimes three bodies a night. It was too hard to keep his identity concealed for long. We moved from village to village, but suspicion followed us everywhere. Father discovered that if he ingested vampire blood, his hunger was sated longer.

"For a while, it was easy. I would turn them, and Father would feed from them. We left them with enough blood to live, but we didn't provide them with the guidance they needed to survive. We didn't expect so many of them to last as long as they did."

Clarence entered without knocking, but Cyrus didn't acknowledge him. "Carrie, would you be so kind?"

I poured him a glass from the decanter Clarence handed me, then returned to the couch. "If your father kept making vampires, there would be a lot more of them by now. What stopped him?"

Cyrus didn't answer until he'd gulped down the first glass and handed it back to Clarence for a refill. "Fear, I suppose. My father was a brave man, but he wasn't stupid. I think he knew that someday, one of his fledglings would do to him what he'd done to his sire.

"Now my father feeds only once a year. In the meantime, he goes into a sort of hibernation. The day will come when he can walk the earth again, but until then, I serve him at the New Year."

"Walk the earth again? What does that mean?" All this information overwhelmed me. "Where does he live?"

With a knowing smile, he waved his index finger at me. "It's a heavily guarded secret. For the time being, all we need to do is make sure Father is fed every year."

"Cyrus, that doesn't make sense. You're weak after a few days without feeding. If your father's metabolism has accelerated beyond that, how can he survive drinking blood only once a year?"

"Oh, he doesn't just drink their blood." A cruel spark of the Cyrus I recognized returned to his eyes. The blood he'd consumed flushed his cheeks. "He takes their very essence. Carrie, my father is the vampire other vampires fear most. My father is the Soul Eater."

# *Fifteen*

### *Consummation*

Cyrus's proclamation shook me to the core. Once I was sure he'd fully recovered from his fast, I left him alone to finish his reading or whatever the hell he did when he was locked away in his study.

*The Soul Eater.* Though I'd never heard the name, it struck fear into my heart.

Cyrus had given me a brief rundown of the New Year's festivities. They'd picked January thirtieth because of its proximity to Bride's Day, an ancient Celtic holiday celebrating the young Sun God's courtship of the Virgin Goddess.

"It's all about innocence," Cyrus had said smugly. "The point of the New Year's festivities is to choose someone with a pure soul and turn them. When Father kills them, instead of a frothy afterlife of clouds and harps, their souls have nowhere to go. Father collects those souls, and they sustain him for another year."

What would it be like to be forever trapped in another person's body? I prayed I'd never find out. I had yet another incentive to stay on Cyrus's good side. Not that staying on his good side would be any trouble after sunup, if his enthusiasm of the night before was any indication. I tried, and failed, to keep my hormones in check as dawn drew closer.

It was 6:00 a.m. when I finally decided to go to him. My senses were so attuned to his that I knew I'd find him in his bedroom. Occasionally, a thrum of anticipation shivered through the blood tie, but I couldn't tell if it was from his or my own desire.

I didn't change or put on any makeup. I didn't want to appear too eager. When I was stripped of my clothing, a cool facade was the only armor I'd have left.

Cyrus's room was much different tonight than it had been on my previous visit. The sitting room was dark and cold. No fire had been lit. Cyrus was nowhere to be seen, but the door to his bedroom stood slightly open, and warm, flickering candlelight spilled out.

If I'd had any illusions about my purpose for being there, I would have been put abruptly in my place. Still, a gentle seduction would have been nice. No one likes to know they're a sure thing.

My heart pounding, from trepidation or anticipation I didn't know, I pushed the door wide.

The canopied bed, cream-colored furnishings and wrought-iron accents all appeared the same. I noted with relief that no heavily sedated pet lay on the bed. The bedclothes were turned down, and black rose petals had been sprinkled liberally over the ivory duvet. Apparently tonight was all about me. I would have been more convinced if he'd bothered to acknowledge me when I entered.

Cyrus sat at his small writing desk beside the window, head bent in concentration. His hair was tied back and he wore his black silk robe. He was so absorbed in his task that I had to clear my throat to get him to look at me.

He didn't lift his face, but I heard the smile in his voice. "I'll be with you in a moment, Carrie. Please, make yourself comfortable."

"You make it sound like we're about to close on a house." Was that my voice, tight and nervous as it scraped from my throat?

"In a way, we are closing a type of deal. Doesn't this officially buy your little friend's life?" Unadulterated excitement radiated through the blood tie. There was no tenderness from him, only dark, perverse lust. The intensity of it should have frightened me, but his desire overrode my fear and left me trembling in its wake.

I watched him fold the sheet of paper and noticed his hands shook. He was struggling for self-control, I realized. In a purely antagonistic gesture, I conjured a vivid picture of us in my mind, of myself naked, on my hands and knees as he pushed into me from behind, head thrown back in pleasure.

He hissed as the image materialized in his brain, and his back straightened. I heard him take a few deep breaths before he stood. "You have a very creative imagination, Carrie."

With the deadly smile of an advancing predator, he moved toward me. His robe, open to the waist as usual, slithered against him like living skin in the candlelight. "Don't you think this would have been more interesting?"

Blackness, then a crystal-clear vision invaded my mind. A girl, probably no more than sixteen, lay in the center of the huge bed. My hands pinned her arms to the bed and she screamed in terror as I sank my fangs into her neck. Cyrus captured her wildly struggling legs and parted them, thrusting into her as the spark of life drained from her eyes.

I shook my head to be rid of the vision, only to see anger contort his handsome face.

"Don't ever forget whom you're dealing with," he warned, pulling me against him so I could feel his erection through the thin silk of his robe. "I am capable of things you couldn't begin to comprehend."

Just as suddenly as his sinister mood appeared, it faded. Kissing me on the cheek, he stepped back to look me over. He frowned as he took in my jeans and T-shirt. "I thought you'd wear something more…appropriate. Didn't I buy you anything suitable for this occasion?"

He had. In the armoire were several revealing outfits, including a Catholic school girl costume that I'd stuffed far back in the drawer in disgust.

I shrugged. "I assumed I wouldn't be wearing much for long."

His mouth quirked at my blunt words. "Very perceptive of you."

He motioned to the mantel above the fireplace. Just as in the outer room, no fire burned. "Would you like anything to drink?"

I eyed the green liquid in the crystal carafe and shook my head. The blood tie was intoxicating enough. I needed a clear head tonight. "No. I'd rather just—"

"Get it over with?" he finished for me, and I dared not reply.

He trailed a fingernail down my neck and followed it with his tongue. The sensation sent stabs of desire racing south, and I felt myself becoming wet. No living man had ever pulled such a response from me. I couldn't hold back my moan.

His tongue teased the lobe of my ear, his breath stimulating the moistened flesh as he whispered, "You're such a puzzling woman. This afternoon you were affectionate and caring. Now you hold back."

He drew away and cupped the back of my head with his hand, forcing me to look him in the eyes. His missing eye was still hidden by the patch, but the one that remained stared hard into mine. "What am I to you, Carrie?"

Though his touch was gentle, I felt his true intent. He wanted to break me, to make me as shameless with lust for him as Dahlia and the other simpering pets in his harem.

And from what I'd experienced so far, he was very good at what he did. I swallowed. "You're my sire."

"Is that all I am?" There was a note of sadness in his tone, but I didn't answer. He hadn't been asking me.

He reached beneath my shirt and dragged his nails across my stomach. My breath hitched. Then he turned away. "Undress and come to bed."

Wrapping my arms around my stomach, I could still feel his cold hands there.

Cyrus moved to the bed, not once looking at me. He shrugged off the robe, revealing a body so white and firm it could have been chiseled from marble.

My mouth went dry at the thought of him above me, filling me. I wanted to blame this new wave of longing on the blood tie, but I couldn't. I wanted him.

Maybe that was his first victory. But looking at Cyrus, the ripple of his muscles moving beneath tight skin, I wondered why I'd wanted to fight at all. There wasn't much left for me outside these walls. I couldn't go back to the hospital. I had no home, no friends, no family. Why should I run from the one person who truly wanted me?

I pulled my T-shirt over my head and stepped out of my jeans then climbed onto the foot of the bed and crawled toward him in nothing but my black satin bra and panties. His eye flashed in hungry recognition, and he pulled the covers aside to let me under.

The linen sheets were crisp and cool and far too real against my skin. I was about to do something forbidden, to surrender fully to something I was all too aware was wrong.

*But it's something you've chosen. You're in control.*

How easily I could lie to myself. I was as far from control as California was from Connecticut. Even the touch of my hair as it brushed my back turned me on.

Cyrus pulled me into his arms, his naked skin made somewhat warmer from desire. "You look better than I thought you would," he practically purred as he swept a hand down my back and over the curve of my buttocks.

Goose bumps rose on my skin. "How did you think I'd look?"

He traced lazy circles over the rise of my spine as his hands moved over my back. "I don't know. Perhaps harder, more manly. You always hide beneath such masculine clothes."

I pushed against him, my breasts spilling over the cups of the bra as they pressed against his chest. He dipped his head and ran his tongue across the seam between the fabric and my flesh. "But not tonight."

Sliding the straps down my arms, he leaned away, exposing my newly uncovered skin to the cold of the room. His eye darkened as he reached for the front clasp of my bra and released it.

I wanted nothing more than to yank the blankets up to my chin and hide from his severe evaluation, but he threw them aside so his view was entirely unobstructed.

He said nothing, unsure of what I expected to hear. He took his time looking me up and down until I thought I'd scream just to break the tension.

Slowly, deliberately, he glided a sharp fingernail from the hollow of my throat to the top of my panties. I arched my hips shamelessly, and he slid his finger beneath the satin, slicing the garment with his nail. Then he took the two halves of the fabric and ripped it completely away from my body.

"Do you know how long it's been since I've been with one of our kind?" he whispered, lowering his head to nibble my stomach.

I didn't particularly want to know about his past conquests, but I asked, anyway. "How long?"

"Over half a century." He parted my legs, running the tips of his nails leisurely up and down the insides of my thighs. "Sex with humans doesn't compare."

With a flick of his wrist, he made a shallow cut just above my knee. I hissed at the pain of it, then moaned when he lifted my leg and closed his mouth over the blood that welled there.

When he withdrew, red smeared his lips. He leaned to kiss me, and I zealously sucked my own blood from his mouth. How strange that such a short time ago I'd feared the consumption of blood. Now I thought nothing of it.

"You taste as good as I remember," he murmured against my cheek. His hand skimmed farther down my thigh, and he made another cut, this one deeper.

My body burned as he slid down to lap at the new wound. His hair brushed against my aching sex, a cruel tease.

This wasn't what I had expected. I'd never really enjoyed sex much before. It was a thing that naturally happened in a relationship, but I'd never felt I needed it. Not like this, feeling as though I'd die if he left me right now, or at least cling to his legs whimpering and begging for more. He set out to seduce, to savor each moment, and I found myself enjoying the sensation of his icy lips on my skin. His wicked fingers stroking my legs. His hard body against mine.

He made a cut in the sensitive seam where my leg met my body, and "accidentally" bumped his cheek against my mound when he moved to suck away the blood. My legs twitched and tightened around his head.

"Could it be you're actually enjoying yourself?" he asked in mock surprise.

I closed my eyes, unwilling to see his satisfied expression when I spoke. "Yes."

He nipped at my chin. "Tell me you want me."

Closing my eyes, I breathed, "I want you."

"Not the sex, Carrie. Tell me you want *me*." His words snapped my eyes open. His face was filled with pure, undisguised longing. He wasn't asking if I desired him. He was asking me to love him.

He needed me to say yes. His desperate fear of rejection saddened me. But the piece of me that was still unaffected by the blood tie held me back. It was the piece of me that hadn't been touched by anyone. I wasn't about to surrender it. "I'm sorry, Cyrus."

I thought he'd push me away, put an end to the encounter. Instead, he became more focused, kissing me harder and with more passion than he'd ever shown me before. His hands seemed to be everywhere at once, threatening pain with his razor-sharp nails and pleasure with his gentle touch.

He traced a path down my body with his tongue, until he reached the hot, slick entrance he sought. Parting me with his thumbs, he blew a gentle stream of frosty breath across my quivering flesh. I tried to lift my hips against his mouth, but he pushed me down on the bed. Before I could protest, he was on top of me, pressing the rigid length of his cock against me. He yanked my head back with my hair. "Tell me you love me."

I was speechless. I feared the actions that would be wrought by the fury etched on his face.

"Lost your voice?" He reached between our bodies and roughly shoved two fingers inside me. I shrieked in pain as his sharp talons plowed through my sensitive flesh, but he covered my mouth with his other hand. "Well, you can scream easily enough."

As suddenly as his touch had turned violent, he became gentle. His fingers, still buried deep within me, no longer tore at me. They stroked, as if seeking to repair the damage done. The fleshy pads of his fingertips massaged and delved, swirling over the hypersensitive spot that had eluded all the other men I'd been with. I bit down on the hand that still covered my mouth to keep from moaning.

I should have fought him, should have defended myself. But I couldn't. His excitement fed mine. He pulled his hand from my mouth to hear my sobs of pleasure.

He withdrew his fingers. I saw my blood on them, mixed with the wetness of my arousal. Cyrus brought his fingers to his lips and sucked them clean, holding my gaze as he did so.

*Tell him to stop,* my rational mind cried out as the prison of my body panted, waited, begged to come with words I'd never imagined saying. When Cyrus ruthlessly thrust into my torn flesh, I screamed in grateful agony.

His face was a study in blasphemous rapture as he flexed his hips, driving himself deeper. Cyrus was hard and cold inside me, like glass, and was nearly too much for my overloaded nerve endings.

"Bite," he gasped, leaning his neck close to my mouth.

I shook my head, trying to regain some of the control I'd lost. He slapped me across the face, and I flinched. "Do it!"

I opened my mouth, trying desperately to summon my transformation, but it wouldn't come. He growled in frustration, so to avoid another blow, I bit down hard on his neck with blunt, human teeth.

He yelped in surprise, and no wonder. I felt the force of the pain in my own throat, and it wasn't pleasant. A fresh surge of his lust seared my veins.

"Drink."

As the first drops fell to my lips, I came. My body shuddered and my legs twisted around his back. My mouth froze open in breathless pleasure while his blood dripped onto my tongue.

Then I was rushing forward, and though I fought it, my eyes opened and I was once again in Cyrus's body, looking into his past.

The images were disjointed. They flickered like a broken projector, some frames repeated over and over again. One by one they slipped into place, and the hazy, dizzy feeling in my head lifted.

Cyrus sat at a long table in a candlelit dining room. The air was hot and sticky, and stale cigar smoke made his eyes water. He wasn't seated at a place of prominence. Instead, he was grouped with a few wealthy-looking men and women.

Cyrus turned his head to gaze at the woman next to him, and just beyond her there was a man in a military uniform that was definitely not American.

A deep, accented voice cut through the chatter. "Ladies and gentlemen, before our guests of honor arrive, I'd like to thank you all for coming."

Cyrus turned his head toward the voice. A tall, thin man stood at the head of the table. His white hair was braided into plaits so long they nearly touched the floor in front of him. Though he appeared much more frail and withered than when I'd first seen him, the straight nose and cruel eyes were unmistakable. It was Cyrus's father.

*The Soul Eater.*

When the older vampire's gaze fell on his son, something that resembled love warmed his eyes. It passed all too soon, replaced by the calculating, predatory glare he gave everyone assembled.

"I also wish to remind you all of the rules. Only one of our guests tonight is the main course." He chuckled at his joke, and the other vampires in the room laughed politely. "The other is for me. You'll be able to tell, as they are clearly marked."

Cyrus's attention turned to the large double doors at the end of the dining hall. Two servants pulled them open. Framed in the cavernous wooden doorway stood Nathan and the woman I'd seen in the photograph from his closet. Nathan looked nearly the same as he did now, with the exception of his hair, which was shorter, and the healthy golden tone of his skin.

The woman at his side had lost all the youthful good looks I'd seen in the picture. Her cheeks were gaunt and dark circles ringed her eyes. She leaned on Nathan's arm for support.

Cyrus focused on the pendant she wore. It was a golden dragon coiled around an extraordinarily large diamond.

The doors slammed shut behind them and there was an ominous clang as a large bolt slid into place.

*"Bon appétit,"* the old vampire said wickedly.

The faces of those seated at the table transformed. Their

change was reflected in the horror on Nathan's face and the weak acceptance on the woman's. He stepped in front of her, as if to shield her, but the party guests descended on them, pulling them to the floor.

Cyrus stayed in his seat, and jumped when his father's hand touched his shoulder. "One day, we'll be finished with all of this," the Soul Eater hissed in his ear.

"Yes, Father," Cyrus replied, his throat dry. "One day, we'll rule."

Then he moved toward Nathan.

I wanted to manifest into some form I could control, so I could lash out at the Soul Eater and stop what was about to take place. But I knew what I saw wasn't really happening. It was a part of the past, already over and unchangeable.

A pain in my head threatened to tear me apart. My vision clouded, but I clearly heard Nathan's screams of anguish and terror as my senses tried to join me in the present. I saw twisted limbs, mangled torsos and flames, as though the earth had been consumed in them. Rivers of blood flowed through my mind.

I was back in my body, and Cyrus groaned as he spilled inside me. It was ice-cold.

I was going to be sick. With all my strength, I pushed him off me and rolled to the side of the bed. Blood, mine and his, was smeared all over the sheets. I squeezed my eyes shut to block out the sight. "What is your father?"

The sheets rustled behind me. I suppose Cyrus sat up. "I've told you."

"But you haven't told me, really." I wasn't sure if the chill creeping up my back was from the cold radiating from his skin or the drafty room. "What does it mean, that one day he'll rule?"

He heaved a sigh and flopped audibly against the pillows. "It's all very complicated. I'd rather sleep than talk about this."

"Sometimes in life, we have to do things we don't want to." I sat up so I could face him. "Why don't you just tell me?"

Cyrus obviously wasn't happy with my postcoital pillow talk, but I wasn't about to back down. He considered what I'd said for a moment, as if trying to gauge whether I was joking or not, then gave another exasperated sigh. "If you really want to know."

"I do." I hugged my knees to my chest, suddenly aware of how vulnerable I was to him.

"For years, my father has been searching for a way to recover his power. It's a very secret quest, and even I'm not privy to the rituals and texts he's reviewing." There was a note of bitterness in Cyrus's voice.

"Then how does he get them?" One day of consciousness per year didn't seem like a lot of time to scour the libraries.

Cyrus let out a resentful laugh. "He has an assistant who does most of the reading for him. I don't know who it is, but he's assured me it's someone he can trust."

I wasn't about to delve into Cyrus's father issues, so I let the comment slide. "You told me your father was a peasant before he became a vampire. What power did he have that he needs to recover?"

"It's not power he actually possessed. It's the power he believes has been reserved for him. It's locked away, waiting for him. He merely needs the key." With an elegant shrug, he leaned on one elbow, a sinful smile curving his lips. He reached to gently stroke my arm. "But we can discuss this later."

I shifted away from him angrily. "We can discuss it now.

What exactly is the Soul Eater trying to do?" But I'd pushed him too far. The easy dialogue between Cyrus and I dried up immediately, as though someone had dammed the flow of words.

He settled back and closed his eyes. "I'm tired. If all you're going to do is bother me with incessant questions, you may leave."

"I'm not going anywhere!" I realized how shrill my voice sounded, but I didn't care. "Tell me what's going on!"

"You want to know what my father is planning?" Cyrus sat up and leaned toward me, his face now mere inches from mine. "When the time is right, and all the pieces fall into place, the Soul Eater will rise to become the most powerful vampire this world has ever seen. Humans will be cattle to feed my father's minions. Any vampire who opposes him will be consumed. He will rule the world, and the world will perish."

The religious fervor with which he spoke chilled me to the bone. When I spoke, I could barely force a whisper from my clamped throat. "You would help him do this?"

"Carrie, you knew who I was when you walked through the front door." Cyrus looked almost wounded. "You can't hate me for it."

"No," I agreed. "That wouldn't be fair."

I stood and tugged the top sheet loose from the others, wrapping it around myself with nervous hands. "But life isn't fair, Cyrus. And right now, I don't like you very much."

He didn't try to stop me as I limped from the room.

# Sixteen

◦─◦⟋⟋⟋◦─◦

### Best-Laid Plans

In the days following, Cyrus didn't speak to me. I didn't know if he was busy with party plans—his frequent excuse—or if I'd honestly hurt his feelings. It shouldn't have bothered me if I did, but I was learning fast that where Cyrus was concerned, my heart wanted the opposite of what my brain knew was right.

The first few mornings, he called on Dahlia to share his bed. She strutted around the mansion proudly displaying her scars, but she never spoke directly to me. I wasn't sure if this was a blessing or a curse, as it seemed everyone in the house knew I was persona non grata with their master and followed suit. The days were lonely and dull, and it was no comfort to know there were centuries of them to come.

At nightfall, Cyrus ventured from the mansion accompanied by his bodyguards and sometimes Dahlia. I didn't know where they went or what they did, and I convinced myself I didn't care, despite the fact I was dying to get out. It would have been a perfect opportunity to meet Nathan, but he'd stopped showing up. I pushed my worry to the back of my mind. Nathan wasn't the person I had to protect.

What concerned me more was Cyrus's sudden interest in Ziggy. He kept his word and never harmed the kid physically, and after the first few visits to his chambers, it seemed Ziggy had grown to genuinely like my sire.

"It's not like we're dating or anything, Doc," Ziggy said when I cornered him in the kitchen one evening. He rooted through the large refrigerator of people food, claiming various items with a Sharpie pen. I didn't bother telling him that most pets didn't live to mooch off their host for long.

I leaned against the freezer. "I know, but Dahlia is going to kill you. And do you have to act like you're enjoying it so much?"

He shrugged. "He'd actually be a pretty decent guy if he wasn't an evil vampire. But more important, if I want to live through this thing he's got planned, I need friends in high places."

Was there more to the New Year's party? "Well, don't leave me hanging. What's he got planned?" I asked.

"The party," Clarence said as he emerged from the walk-in freezer.

I hadn't even known he was there, and his sudden presence gave me a start. "I knew about that. But I've been pathetically out of the loop for a couple of weeks now. Fill me in."

The butler didn't look at me as he slammed a block of ice on the countertop. He no longer watched me from the corner of his eye, but there remained a sliver of unease between us, most likely because I was still a vampire. But he'd continued to relay messages to Nathan when possible, and he'd dropped the stuffy butler act and refrained from calling me ma'am every second word.

"What the hell are you doing, boy?" he barked.

Ziggy grinned sheepishly and tossed a can of soda over his shoulder. The older man caught it in his nimble fingers and popped the top. "This shit will rot the teeth right out of your dumb head."

"I ain't gonna live that long," Ziggy replied as he drew a thick *Z* on another can.

My stomach lurched. I'd never believed all those stories from med school about patients who knew they were going to die and freely dispensed the information to everyone, but I didn't want to hear Ziggy make such predictions.

"Don't talk like that," I snapped. I tested the blood tie to see if Cyrus was listening in. All I felt was a vague, alcoholic haze before the tie seemed to evaporate between us. The fact that he could so easily ignore our connection created a sick, lonely feeling in my stomach. But if he closed himself off, I at least had some time to talk about the impending event without the risk of him knowing my thoughts. "Since Cyrus won't be back for a few hours, tell me what's going on with this party."

Clarence groaned and rolled his eyes. "Same as every year. A few human sacrifices and a whole lotta pain. That's sorta his thing."

"Human sacrifices? You mean the kids on the list?" I hoped he did.

Nodding grimly, he wiped his hands on his apron. "Them, and a few others he'll lure in from out of town. Can't get them all from around here or it'll look suspicious."

I shook my head. *I wish Nathan would get his ass back here.*

Every night, I'd faithfully checked for Nathan at the gate under the guise of walking the perimeter of the lawn. If I were still human, I would have considered the long distance as good cardio exercise. Now my only concern about my heart was whether someone would suddenly give it the Big Splinter. But Nathan hadn't returned, and as the time of the New Year drew nearer and nearer, my nerves were pulled tighter and tighter.

"Don't you worry about our boy," Clarence drawled lazily. "He got himself in good with the Master. He ain't on the menu."

He pushed a sheet of paper across the island and I snatched it up.

It was a list of names. Nearly every one of Cyrus's pets were on it, except two. "Ziggy and Dahlia are going to be spared?"

"Guess it's not so bad hangin' with the boss after all," Ziggy said as he slipped a brick of cheese into the pocket of his baggy black jeans.

I relished the thought of Dahlia being selected for the Soul Eater's consumption. But I guess she wasn't much of a "pure soul."

Two guards entered and I stepped away from Ziggy. "Excuse us, Doctor," one of the thugs said curtly. He turned to Ziggy. "The Master would like to see you."

"Duty calls," he said with an apologetic smile. "Hey, we gotta stop by my room on the way 'cause I've got a book C wants to borrow," he told the guards as they led him away.

*C?* I pulled one of the stools from the island and plopped myself down.

Clarence had gone quietly to work on the block of ice with a chisel and hammer, but he chuckled at my spite. "You still gonna help rescue him, even though he stole your man?"

"He did *not* steal my man." I made an appalled face, hoping it would fool the old man. But I knew it wouldn't. "I just don't understand why Ziggy would have such an interest, after what Cyrus did to him."

"The Master is a good one for winning somebody back after he's wronged them. Look at you. He wrecked your life, and you still came back to him." He turned the ice and started chipping away on the other side.

"That's different. There's a blood tie. You wouldn't understand because you're not a vampire. But it really makes a difference."

Clarence bobbed his head up and down in agreement. "You're right, I don't know about blood ties. But I do know you wouldn't be here if you didn't want to be. You're not that type. If you've got to tell yourself it's some magical thing keeping you at his side through all his bullshit, I'm not the one to argue with you."

His words cut me to the core. He was right. Yes, there was a blood tie, but that wasn't why I was here. Sure I'd made a promise to return to Cyrus in exchange for Nathan's life, but why hadn't I called the Movement, or even asked Ziggy for help? I'd been Persephone, eating the pomegranate seeds with delight and blaming it all on big, bad Hades. I knew what I was doing when I'd committed myself to this Underworld. I'd resigned myself to accept my plight, and now I wanted to explore the life Cyrus had offered me, but I feared his interest in Ziggy might do something to usurp my place.

It sucks when your little palace o' denial comes tumbling down.

The next night, Nathan waited at the gate.

"How's Ziggy?" he asked as soon as I was near enough to hear him.

"He's fine. Hello to you, too." I stamped my feet, trying to get some feeling back in them. It had snowed during the day, and the depth of the stuff almost kept me inside.

Nathan's hands were nearly blue where his gloveless fingers gripped the iron of the gate. "Is he on the list?"

"No." I thought relief would register on his face.

Instead, it twisted with horror. "Tell me he's not—"

"A guest of honor. I just don't know which one." I looked at my feet. "I know how you were turned."

A muscle in his shadowed jaw twitched. "He told you?"

"I saw it." I don't know why I felt the compulsion to tell him how, but I did. "I drank his blood...from him. And I saw it."

Nathan was repulsed, but I knew he was scared more than he was disgusted. Maybe he was afraid I wouldn't help him. Or that I'd throw Ziggy to the wolves.

He cleared his throat. "That's all in the past. I just don't want it to happen to Ziggy. Who's the other one?"

"Dahlia."

"Dahlia and Ziggy, and they need to pick the one with a pure soul? Oh, that's going to be a tough call." Nathan looked away, but not before I saw the suffering in his eyes. "Are the Fangs staying for the party?"

"They were supposed to leave a week ago. I think they're hanging around so Cyrus will have to invite them to the party. What's going to happen?"

"He'll probably invite them to the party."

I glared at him. "You know what I meant. When you and your little friends show up. What's going to happen?"

"We'll bust in, I'll grab Ziggy, and they'll kill all the vampires."

His pointed gaze added *including you.*

My heart constricted painfully in my chest. Did he really hold such a grudge? I'd thought we'd built a friendship of sorts.

*That was before you left.*

I cleared my throat. "That sounds dangerous."

"It will be." Still, he offered no assurance of my safety.

"Would it be easier to just sneak him out before the party? I could go get him. We could just boost him over the fence right now."

"That has crossed my mind," Nathan replied bitterly. "But I'm not allowed to do anything that might compromise the integrity of the mission. Movement orders. They think Cyrus would step up security if the compound was breached this close to the event."

"Compound? You make it sound like I'm in some weird religious cult."

That at least brought a half smile to his mouth, but it died quickly. "I've been playing host to a couple of full-time Movement guys. The terminology starts to creep in after a while."

"Is that why you haven't been showing up?" I sounded jealous, like a spoiled child whose playmate has made friends with the neighbor kids. It just crept into my voice on its own.

Nathan didn't appreciate it. "I'm sorry, but you're not a priority for me anymore."

*Anymore.* That stung. Not because his feelings for me were gone, but that he'd confirmed he'd had some in the first place.

It was much easier to be angry with him than regretful over our lost friendship. "So you're going to march in here on the night of the party and kill me, then?"

He shook his head. "Not me. I'm going to find Ziggy and

get him out. But watch out for the other guys. We've been ordered to kill any non-Movement vampires on the premises."

"You're not going to tell them about me?" I hated the fear in my voice. "I took care of Ziggy, that has to be worth something."

"It was worth the advance warning I gave you," he snarled. "You put yourself on the losing team, Carrie. It's a little late to back out now."

"You know what, I didn't come here because I wanted to!" I spat.

"What are you talking about?"

I hadn't wanted to tell him, but there was no avoiding it now. Some deranged part of me demanded honesty, as brutal as it might sound. And really, if I stood a good chance of dying on Saturday, I didn't have much to lose. "It was a trade, asshole. Your life for mine."

He stepped back from the gate. I could see in his eyes that he didn't want to believe me. "No."

I wasn't going to soften the blow. "I couldn't reverse Dahlia's spell on my own. So I went to Cyrus for help. This is what he asked for in return."

He ran a hand through his dark hair, mussing the strands. "I don't believe you."

"Fine, don't believe me." I was too tired to convince him of a truth I hadn't wanted to reveal in the first place. "Ziggy will tell you. He drove me here to get the antidote. And he'll tell you what I've done in here to keep him safe."

Whatever I'd said to make him change his mind, Nathan clearly felt like the jackass I thought he was. "Why didn't you tell me?"

"Because it was something I had to do. I didn't want you to die, and I didn't want you to get killed barging in here as if I needed rescuing." He looked so penitent, I couldn't help but ease his guilt a little. "Besides, I wanted the chance to know my sire. There's a reason he became the way he is."

I thought of the scar his father had inflicted on him and the pain he'd felt. Yet Cyrus still wanted to please the Soul Eater. Could he have been a good person before his father had tempted him with the promises of wealth and power? Then again, he did kill his own brother in his sleep.

Nathan blew out a long breath as he scratched his head. There were things I wanted to say, but I didn't know where to begin. Although I'd suffered abuse at Cyrus's hands, I didn't hate him. I certainly didn't want him to die, and a part of me desperately wanted him to pursue me again.

*Wow, it* has *been a lonely couple of weeks.*

But despite what I felt for my sire, I didn't want Nathan to leave without some sort of resolution between us. Perhaps what I'd dismissed as lust-at-first-sight had been a deeper connection than I'd been willing to admit. That terrified me more than the prospect of looming death.

Finally, Nathan spoke. "I've kind of been a jerk."

"Kind of. But maybe I should have trusted you. I mean, if I had said, 'I made this deal with Cyrus, now I've gotta go live with him,' you'd respect that, right? You wouldn't just come charging in to save me."

He arched an eyebrow sardonically in answer.

"Which is exactly why I didn't tell you." With every passing second, I became more aware of how much I'd missed Nathan, and more afraid that I'd made a mistake in coming to live with Cyrus. There was no blood tie between Nathan and me to inspire my feelings for him. Did that mean they were stronger than what I felt for Cyrus?

As if in slow motion, Nathan reached through the gate, and

I lifted my arm toward him. When our hands touched, a current leapt through me, different from any I'd felt from the bond I shared with Cyrus. There was no darkness in these feelings. Nathan's thumb stroked the back of my hand as our fingers entwined, and we stared at each other for some time before he spoke.

"Carrie, do you want to leave?"

My head snapped up. "For real?"

"For real." He laughed softly. "I can get you out the same time I get Ziggy."

I looked back at the house. The light in Cyrus's room was on. "I want to go, but—"

"But the tie is holding you back." Nathan gave my hand a squeeze.

A tear fell from my eye and landed on the back of his hand, freezing almost instantly on his cold skin. Why was I crying? I wanted to escape this place, didn't I? "I don't know if I'm strong enough to walk away from him, Nathan." I couldn't meet his gaze. "When I'm not near him, I don't miss him, but when I'm with him…I feel like he needs me. It probably doesn't make sense to you, but I like to be needed."

"It makes perfect sense. Why else would you have become a doctor?"

Nathan's words brought back the memory of sitting beside Dr. Fuller in the cold, impersonal staff locker room. My mentor's voice resounded like a requiem bell in my head.

*"Why did you want to be a doctor?"*

I'd thought I'd wanted power. Now I had that power and I didn't want to use it. Was Nathan right? Had I become a doctor not out of some heartless quest for control, but from a desire to be indispensable and valued by complete strangers? Did I only feel complete when other people needed me?

The most annoying part of this revelation was that some-one else had made it before I had. I must have been the most naive twenty-eight-year-old on the planet.

"Carrie, are you all right?"

I looked up at Nathan. "I want to leave."

He cocked his head, uncertain. "You mean that?"

Leaving such sure things as shelter and regular meals should have struck me with fear, but it didn't. When my parents died, I'd survived on my own. The only difference was this time I *wanted* to be an orphan.

"Yeah," I answered finally. "You'd run like hell, too, if you saw the window treatments in there."

Still holding my hand, Nathan reached through the gate and pulled me into an awkward and slightly painful hug. When he stepped back, a slight flush colored his face.

*So, vampires blush.*

"This is the plan," he said, clearing his throat. "Lie low when we get here, and whatever you do, don't fight anyone. Stick close to Ziggy. They're not going to hurt him. And for God's sake, stay away from Cyrus. He's a main target."

"Just don't do anything stupid." After the vision I'd seen, I knew he had a score to settle. It was a good thing he didn't know what Cyrus had done to Ziggy.

"I think it's too late for that." The intense way Nathan's gaze roamed over my face lent an uncomfortable meaning to that statement. But in the next moment, the intensity was gone. Nathan dug in his pocket and produced a tiny bottle. "Take this."

Without thinking, I stuck it in my bra for safekeeping. "What is it?"

"Holy water."

I fumbled to remove the vial. "Jesus Christ, you could have warned me!"

He laughed. "Sorry. I didn't know you were going to stuff it down your shirt."

"What do I do with it?" I asked as I held it in my hands.

"Be careful with it. It'll cause a nasty burn. But use it to defend yourself if you have to."

Hoping to ease his mind, I shook my head. "I'm not going to need it. He hasn't paid any attention to me for a while." Realizing I sounded wistful, I quickly added, "Not that I care, or anything."

"You do care," Nathan said softly. "That's why he doesn't deserve you."

"Nathan—" I began, but he cut me off.

"I've got to go. Keep in mind what I said, and go over the plans again. I'll see you Saturday." He turned, took a few steps, and stopped. He didn't look at me. "Thanks for saving my life."

I knew him well enough to realize that when Nathan got choked up, his accent grew thicker. It was almost impossible to understand his next words.

"And maybe after we get you and Ziggy out, you'll tell me how you liked the drawing."

When I returned to my room, I pulled the sketch from its hiding place. After the party, I'd have to tell him it didn't look anything like me. Because the woman on the page was a completely different person. Things used to happened *to* her.

This person was about to *make* things happen.

Making things happen proved to be more difficult than I expected. Cyrus was increasingly moody, constantly fretting over the impending fete and his seemingly permanent house-guests. A huge part of my plan to help Ziggy hinged on my ability to manipulate Cyrus, but it was hard to manipulate someone when they wouldn't talk to you. Saturday loomed like impending death. I grew desperate, and not just because my plan might fall through.

As sick and dishonest as it seemed, I wanted to spend one last day with him. It was a death wish, considering how adept he was at reading my mind, but he either had been too busy to uncover my deception yet, or he had figured it out and was waiting to punish me for it at a more convenient time. For reasons I wasn't willing to explore, I would risk being found out for just a few more hours with him, even after he'd made me feel so…used.

Eventually I decided that if I were to get myself back into Cyrus's good graces, I'd have to take the first step. Friday morning, I went to his bed without an invitation. Dressed in a white silk nightgown I'd found in my wardrobe, my heart pounding so loudly I thought it would burst from my chest, I stared down the guards at his door.

When I entered his bedroom, I'd expected to find him with Dahlia or Ziggy, but he lounged on the bed beside a slender girl with blond hair. Her back was turned to me as they lay sideways across the bed, and one of her arms draped across Cyrus's waist. He looked up with eyes of mismatched blue and the smile of a man who'd just learned he'd be having his favorite meal for dinner.

"I hope I'm not interrupting," I said, surprised at the smoky sound of my voice. It must have been the sexy lingerie, or the perfume, or the makeup, because I was really getting into character.

Cyrus gave the girl a kick. Instead of scrambling to her feet and rushing from the room, she fell limply to the floor at the foot of the bed. Her head lolled to the side on her broken neck, and I saw her missing eye.

I almost turned back. *No. Do what you came here to do.*

I called over my shoulder for the guards and they stepped through the open door. I gestured to the dead girl, trying not to look too revolted as they carried her away. "I didn't want an audience."

"She was boring, anyway. Kept crying about wanting to go home." He leaned up on one arm. "To what do I owe the pleasure of this visit?"

I approached him slowly, trailing my hands across the silk that covered my stomach, my breasts, then the bare skin over my collarbones. "I've missed you."

Suspicion clouded his eyes. "I thought you didn't like me very much. Those were your words, were they not?"

"Maybe I don't like you. I might just be here for sex." My body throbbed at the thought.

I looked down the length of his body and saw he was just as hungry for me, despite his previous encounter. "You want something more, I can tell."

I stepped to the edge of the bed, ignoring the blood on the carpet at my feet. "Maybe I do."

He smiled, flashing the tips of his fangs, which had not yet retracted since his feeding. The vampiric feature in his otherwise normal face made him seem more dangerous than usual. "Is this something I can give you?"

I feigned helplessness. "I don't know. It could be."

"Everything comes at a price, Carrie." He sat up, swinging his legs over the side of the bed.

Taking a deep breath, I hiked my nightgown above my knees with one hand and gently pushed him to the bed with the other. I straddled him, lifting the silk to my waist, and guided his erection into my body.

He moaned and I gasped as I sank down his cold length.

I lifted my hips, letting him slip almost completely out, and pressed my throat to his mouth.

The change came over him almost immediately as he pierced my neck. I forced myself to concentrate on the feeling of him inside me, the sensations that made my head swim, so he wouldn't see the true reason for the favor I would ask.

Or the pain that suddenly knifed through my heart.

This would be the last time we'd be together. I don't know why it bothered me so much. I blamed all the feelings I had for him on the blood tie. But maybe that blame had been misplaced. Maybe I really did care for him. But the decision had already been made. I'd promised Nathan, and I had a duty to protect Ziggy. There was no changing my mind now. If I grieved for Cyrus in the end, it would be my burden to bear.

I rose on my knees, letting just the tip of him rest against me. He strained up from the bed, trying to reenter me. I made a move to get off him completely, and he stopped fighting.

"You're trying to hide from me," he whispered, leaning up to run his tongue over the scar he'd created on my neck. "But you aren't strong enough. I can see what you want. Say it."

My hands shook as I stroked his hair back from his forehead. Was this a trick? How much did he really see? "I want to choose who the Soul Eater gets."

His body went still at the words, and for a moment, I thought he would turn me down. Or worse, reveal that he'd seen through my ruse and kill me on the spot.

Wrapping his powerful arms around me, he flipped me onto my back and filled me in one, brutal thrust. "Whatever my princess wants."

I suppose I should have felt like a total whore at this moment, but my relief was so overwhelming I almost laughed. I threw my head back and surrendered to the feeling of my sire's hands on me, his cock filling me. When I came, I shouted so loud I was sure I'd woken the entire household.

Cyrus finished soon after, collapsing on top of me with a smile.

"Saturday will be a night to remember," he rasped against my cheek.

A tear fell from my eye.

*You have no idea.*

# Seventeen

### Happy New Year

When I woke the next night, Cyrus was gone. I curled into the space he'd vacated, expecting warmth but finding none. *Of course. Vampire. No body heat.* I sat up, chuckling at my stupidity, but my good mood vanished at the sight of Dahlia leaning against the closed door.

"What are you doing?" I pulled the sheets up to my chest and groped through the bedclothes for my nightgown.

Dahlia's face was emotionless, and she didn't make eye contact with me. "Do you love him?"

I had no idea what to say that wouldn't set her into a flying rage. I hoped the truth was good enough. "No."

"Then why are you still here?" She kicked the door with a slow, deliberate rhythm.

"I can't leave."

"I wish you could." She laughed, not in the crazy way I'd heard before, but in a dry, bitter laugh of weariness. "I wish I could."

"You can." I felt a little guilty for lying to her. In less than twenty-four hours, I planned to have her fed to the Soul Eater. I bolstered my resolve by remembering the time she'd stabbed me in the gut, burned down my apartment, attacked Nathan, and the fact she was pretty much the reason I was stuck here.

She looked me straight in the eye. "Are you familiar with the Stockholm Syndrome?"

*Am I ever.* I nodded. "It's when the victim of a hostage situation forms an attachment to her captor."

"You probably think that's what's going on here, right?" She ran a hand over her mussed curls.

"Maybe," I said quietly, reaching for Cyrus's robe at the end of the bed.

Her eyes dropped to the black silk in my hands, and narrowed when I pulled the robe over my shoulders. But she didn't move from the door, or cease her cadenced kicking. "You don't know shit about why I'm here."

"Dahlia," I began, wetting my parched lips. I needed to feed, and soon. Her plump neck was beginning to look far too good for my liking. "Are *you* in love with Cyrus?"

"I didn't know he was a vampire. Not before." She pressed her palm to her forehead as tears slid down her face. "He told me he loved me."

I tied the robe and hurried from the bed over to her. I didn't know what else I could do but stand beside her and offer a shoulder to cry on in her misery. "He probably did—does—love you."

She sniffled. "He was fascinated with me, with my power. And now I'm trapped here."

"He's afraid of you," I blurted. Her face was the picture of hopelessness, and it broke my heart. As much as I disliked

Dahlia, I sympathized with her. "He's afraid of your power. That's why he won't turn you."

"I know," she snapped. "But that doesn't help me, does it."

"It could. There are going to be a hundred vampires here tomorrow night. If you could find just one of them to turn you, you could get away from Cyrus." The thought of Dahlia with unlimited power smacked me in the cerebral cortex about a half a second too late. But the words were already out there and I couldn't take them back.

To my relief, she shook her head and her old venom returned. "Right. Because it's so easy to just get a vampire to make a fledgling."

I couldn't help my sarcastic reply. "It was for me."

In an instant, her hand left a stinging impression on my cheek. Her eyes flashing with rage, she whirled around and waved at the air as though she were batting away a fly. The door flew back, practically tearing off the hinges, and she stalked into the dark anteroom.

Trembling, I pulled Cyrus's robe tighter around me. I couldn't shake the feeling that I'd either just performed an incredible act of mercy or made a huge mistake.

Saturday night arrived with a flurry of flamboyantly gay party planners and confused teenagers who thought they'd been invited to a rave. The former were led quietly around the side of the mansion to set up a garden party in nearly freezing temperatures, and the latter were lured into the house with promises of alcohol and social drugs. Ziggy and I stood on the balcony in the foyer and watched as guards herded a group of the hapless victims toward the cellar.

"So I'm basically toast, is that what you're telling me?" Ziggy wore a neatly pressed dress shirt and slacks, a stylish black tie draped around his neck. Even with the change in wardrobe, he looked antisocial and slightly intimidating. But not to those who knew him well. I could practically see the word *fear* written across his forehead.

I hoped he didn't share my keen insight. I wouldn't seem so reassuring if he could tell my insides shook like barren branches in the winter wind. "You're not toast. I get to pick who the Soul Eater takes. Cyrus will turn Dahlia, and then he'll throw you to the crowd. It's all very simple."

"Right." Ziggy stretched the word out. "Thrown on the mercy of hungry vampires. And yet I'm somehow missing the part where I'm not toast."

"You know how to fight, and Nathan will get here in time. Don't worry about it. I'm not." I was, but there was no point letting him know that.

"What about the secret service down there?" Ziggy pointed toward the guards below. "Nate and those guys can't touch them. They're human."

"Then they'll be easier to subdue," I pointed out. "Besides, there aren't many of them here tonight." It was a protective measure, Clarence had told me before he'd left for the guardhouse earlier in the evening. Fewer humans meant less chance of a feeding frenzy. Most of the guards had been dismissed already. The mansion now ran with a skeleton crew on hazard pay.

It seemed a little strange that Cyrus would leave the party so vulnerable. Of course, there was the Soul Eater's own security team. They were apparently scary enough that Cyrus felt comfortable entrusting them to guard a house full of Movement exiles on the most notorious night of the year.

Again, another fact Ziggy didn't need to worry about. "Now, get back to the room before somebody mistakes you for cattle."

His eyes were fixed on the herd in the foyer. "You'd think someone would miss these kids."

"I guess he moves the party around every year. He said he can't stay in one place for long without people getting suspicious." Then the sadness in Ziggy's words made me realize he wasn't referring to the teenagers below us. "Nathan does miss you. He loves you."

"Yeah, well. I guess we'll find out tonight, huh?" With a grimace, he shoved off the banister and headed toward the hallway.

I wanted to follow him, to go into my room, lock the door and sleep wherever I fell. I'd spent the day with a pillow over my head, trying to drown out the sound of Cyrus cursing and shouting in his room as he agonized over every new development, from parking to table decorations, until I was as stressed about the party as he was.

If he thought things were going badly now, I couldn't wait to see how he reacted when his uninvited guests showed up.

There was no telling how events would turn out. In just a few hours I could be safely away from this house and all the temptation inside. Or I could be dead. Ziggy could be dead. Cyrus could be dead. Hell, we could all be dead at the same time from some freak accident. I wasn't ruling anything out.

To get my mind off such grim meditations, and because guests had begun to arrive, I went to my room to dress in the new gown Cyrus had bought me for the occasion. When Clarence had delivered the garment, all my bad feelings about the night had multiplied. It was a floor-length, red-and-black ball gown with thin shoulder straps and a tiered tulle skirt. I'd quickly zipped up the garment bag and assured myself it wasn't so bad.

I was wrong. In fact, it was much worse on second observation.

"I'm going to look like a ballerina from hell," I whined out loud as I picked at the sequined bodice.

Not to mention the fact that running—hell, even standing—in the shoes he'd bought to match would be impossible, at best.

I pulled the offending footwear from the box with a frown. I slipped the patent leather pointe slippers onto my feet and wrapped the deep red ribbons around my calves. They would have been comfortable if it weren't for the tall spiked heel that ensured I stood on perfect tiptoe.

I teetered into the sitting room where Ziggy stood like a real gentleman, an expression of pure disbelief on his face. "You look really good."

"Thanks." I touched my hair self-consciously, checking to make sure the long, blond strands remained in the French braid I'd put them in. "I feel like a clown."

"You look like a Goth boy's wet dream. Hell, I'd go straight if you made an offer right now."

For a moment, his wicked smile reminded me so much of Nathan it seemed impossible they weren't blood related. "I'll take that as a compliment. And I'll pass."

There was a soft knock at the door. I called out permission to enter, expecting Clarence.

One of the guards opened the door instead. "The Master wants you in the foyer, so you can greet his father."

I wiped my suddenly sweaty palms on my skirt. "The Soul Eater is here?"

"Master *Seymour* is in transit," the man corrected me in a warning tone.

"Fine," I replied with an equally stony glare. "I'll be down in a minute."

The door closed, but I knew the guard waited outside. I motioned Ziggy closer. "When they bring you down for the party, stay close to me, because—"

"Because I'm your life insurance policy. I know, I know." He blew out a long breath. "You're not going to change your mind at the last minute and let them eat me, right?"

"I wasn't planning on it." My heart felt like a solid mass of lead in my chest, and I reached out impulsively to hug him.

His back tensed beneath my arms as his breath hitched. The little boy that still lived in some deeply buried part of him appreciated the comfort. But I wouldn't offer him empty reassurances. I had no idea what would happen, and I wouldn't pretend to. "I've got to go downstairs."

I wouldn't allow myself to look back as I went to the door. The guard waited to escort me, as though I didn't know the way on my own. He walked fast and didn't offer me his arm, so I kept up as best as I could without spraining my ankles.

Teetering precariously down the stairs, I caught a glimpse of the guests that were gathered in the foyer. Vampires of various ages chattered among themselves in excitement. Everywhere I looked I saw expensive fur and jewels in exotic styles. Even the Fangs seemed to have dressed for the occasion, though they probably would still be kicked out of higher-end truck stops for breaching the dress code.

Cyrus stood at the front doors. I couldn't see his face, but I felt his excitement at the prospect of reuniting with his father, and the nagging fear that something seemed out of place, that something wouldn't go right. I pushed through the crowd with an air of confidence. It wouldn't do any good to let him sense my own anxiousness and have all of Nathan's planning go down the drain at the eleventh hour.

I wobbled on my spiky heels and fell against a slender vampire with a bald head. Two small horns protruded from his forehead, and his thin black mustache quirked in annoyance. He looked like the cartoon devil on a package of Red Hots. "Excuse me," I said, struggling to right myself and not stare.

When I finally reached his side, Cyrus slipped his arm around my waist. He pulled me close and kissed my cheek. "You look lovely."

"Thanks. But maybe next time you could let me pick the footwear." I peeked distractedly at the vampires around us. "Who are all these people?"

He waved dismissively. "Friends of Father's, friends of mine. Allies, acquaintances. The Fangs."

I smiled at the disgust in his voice. "Aw, but they're wearing their Sunday best. Are they all vampires?"

"Yes, but some are mutts."

"Mutts?" I looked back at the horned man. "As in mixed with something else?"

"Mmm. The vampire you just collided with has some demon ancestry. There are some lupins here, as well." He wrinkled his nose. "Do take care around them, they're liable to hump your leg."

"Lupins?" I remembered something Nathan had told me. "You mean werewolves?"

Cyrus shushed me. "Werewolf-vampire hybrids. But that's not the politically correct term. Lupins are making great strides at becoming semicivilized, and they prefer not to be lumped in with their lesser wolven brethren. My God, those creatures are still living in the woods, running in packs. Who would want to be associated with them?"

A guard stepped forward. "Sir? They're approaching."

Cyrus took a deep breath and turned to me. "Are you ready?"

I wasn't certain what I was supposed to be ready for, but I nodded. Still firmly clamped to his side, I walked with him as guards opened the doors.

The night air was cold as it hit us on the top step. In the moonlight, I saw the gate at the end of the driveway open. A long sedan pulled up, followed by a hearse. Another sedan completed the motorcade. They rolled to a stop at the top of the drive, the hearse in position in front of the door.

Eight men, identical in height, features and their black suits, exited the cars. A chauffeur stepped out of the hearse. He opened the back door ceremoniously, exposing a gleaming, bronze coffin.

Cyrus straightened at my side. I thought I saw a tear on his cheek, but it might have been a drop of blood from his deteriorating replacement eye. He wiped it away with an unsteady hand.

The men lifted the casket on their shoulders and carried it to the house. Cyrus turned and guided me back inside. I glanced over my shoulder to see the pallbearers follow us.

The crowd parted and allowed our procession to pass. I saw some of them bow their heads as we walked by. Those who didn't either looked on in interest or boredom, and the Fangs lifted their beer bottles in salute as our weird caravan moved through the foyer.

Guards opened the study doors. Inside, the furniture had been removed to make a place for a large dais, ringed with tasteful arrangements of black and white carnations.

The pallbearers moved past us and slid the coffin gently into place.

"Thank you, gentlemen," Cyrus said quietly. "My guards will see that you are adequately fed."

The doors closed, leaving us alone with the Soul Eater. Cyrus knelt at the side of the coffin and laid his hands reverently on the bronze lid.

He bent his head, his hair falling forward, obscuring his face. He pressed his lips to the lid's surface, and I heard him whisper, "Welcome home, Father."

I felt guilty for watching this exchange. Cyrus was vulnerable, and I stood there as if I wasn't about to jab the proverbial knife in his back.

He rose and turned to me, one arm outstretched to invite me closer. "Carrie, come meet my father."

Wicked butterflies rioted in my stomach. I knelt beside the casket as I'd seen Cyrus do, and slid my trembling hands onto the lid.

Never in my life had I felt hate so strong. It radiated from the coffin beneath my fingertips and wound around me like tendrils of bloodred smoke. My arms shook as I struggled to pull them away. All I could hear were screams of death. When I closed my eyes, pain and torture surrounded me. Fangs and claws tearing flesh. Blood pumping from severed arteries. I opened my mouth to scream, and when no sound came out, I realized I hadn't been able to move my mouth at all.

When the insidious power released me, I jerked my hands away. Sweat beaded my forehead.

Standing next to me, Cyrus didn't appear to notice. He stroked the smooth metal of the casket as if hypnotized by its reflective surface. "Father, this is Carrie. My fledgling, and your new daughter. I hope you find her worthy of your blood."

Something told me my new father-in-law didn't think I cut the mustard. I bit my lip and silently prayed Cyrus wouldn't see what I had felt and kill me right there. But whatever he experienced when he touched his father's casket, Cyrus's expression of serene pleasure never changed.

"I'd like to spend some time alone with my father. Will you see to the rest of the preparations for dinner?"

I nodded slowly, my gaze fixed on the casket. I was pretty sure I wouldn't win Daddy Dear over by ensuring the napkins were properly folded, but anything was better than witnessing this macabre family reunion. "Sure. No problem."

I wandered around for a while, scoping out the attendees more closely. It was fun trying to figure out who was a vampire, who might be werewolves, and how much money they might have spent on their outfits.

The guests milled around the foyer and dining room, sipping blood-infused cocktails and chatting about politics and art. A row of chairs had been placed along one of the dining room walls, and a few unlucky pets were chained to them. They slumped over unconscious, and thirsty vampires dispensed blood from taps in their necks. The pets who'd already expired were tossed unceremoniously onto a pile in the corner, and guards wrestled replacements in.

The Fangs had already invaded the garden. Some lounged in the delicate chairs that were rented for the occasion and rested their heavy boots on the immaculate tablecloths. Another group had brought out a beat-up stereo and blasted heavy-metal music to drown out the string quartet playing on the terrace. I thought I should remind them of their manners, but then decided against it. I wanted to see Cyrus's face when he learned his elegant garden party had become the Head Banger's Ball.

By eleven forty-five it seemed the entire vampire population of the world had crammed onto the grounds. At least, the entire *evil* vampire population. Cyrus entered the foyer at five before the hour and greeted the assembly there. Then the guards ushered them into the garden. I was right behind them when Cyrus stopped me.

"Wait." He nodded to the only remaining guard, who then mumbled into his headset.

"You wanted the privilege of choosing. I won't deny you." Cyrus dropped something hard and heavy into my hand.

When I uncurled my fingers, I gasped. The dragon pendant lay against my palm, but the diamond had been replaced by a huge ruby.

"Do you like it? I thought it was time for a change." He pressed his lips to my cheek. "You have no idea how much it means to me, to have you at my side tonight."

Two guards escorted Dahlia and Ziggy down the stairs. She looked triumphant and sure of herself. He looked terrified.

"Hey," I whispered, giving him a small wave.

Cyrus stepped forward to inspect the pair. "Dahlia, you look lovely as ever."

She shot me a smug grin, and then turned back to admire Cyrus. He moved on to Ziggy. His dapper appearance clearly impressed my sire. "Are you nervous?"

Ziggy shook his head.

"Good," Cyrus continued. "There's no reason to be." He paced back and forth in front of them for a moment. "As you know, every year I must make a difficult choice. Of all my pets, two must survive this night to make our celebration complete. Still, only one may take the place of honor in our festivities. Until now, I've been charged with deciding who receives that honor."

Dahlia's eyes grew wide. "Until now?"

"Don't interrupt the man while he's talking," Ziggy quipped. I shot him a warning glance.

Cyrus paused. "As I was saying. Until now, I've had to decide who receives that honor. This year, I have the pleasure of seeing my fledgling perform this office. Carrie?"

I stepped forward, and without hesitation, pointed at Dahlia. "Her."

Cyrus raised an eyebrow. "Interesting choice."

"Why do you say that?"

But he had already pried the pendant from my hands. Dahlia squealed and clapped her hands, then leaned forward, lifting her hair. Cyrus slipped the chain around her neck and stepped back.

"Master, the first course is ready."

At the sound of the guard's voice, Cyrus turned to me. "We don't want to keep our guests waiting." He held out his arm and I took it, casting a reassuring glance at Ziggy. Cyrus faced forward and Dahlia was so preoccupied with her new prize, neither of them saw me mouth *stay close* to him.

We stepped onto the terrace to a round of applause. A guard stopped Ziggy and Dahlia from exiting with us. The glass doors swung shut, leaving them inside.

"Ladies and gentlemen," Cyrus called, his voice cutting through the excited chatter. "Thank you all so very much for coming. It warms my heart to share this night with such good friends."

There was a polite smattering of applause. I tried not to scan the garden walls for signs of the Movement. It had to be nearly time now. Nathan promised they would come tonight.

The cavalry didn't show up. Not during Cyrus's long-winded speech about the importance of tradition and the looming threat of extinction.

*God, it's like he's running for office.*

Finally, he ended with some sugarcoated platitude about old and new friendships, clapped his hands and signaled the guards waiting inside the French doors.

"As you know, our guests of honor will enter in a moment. Please remember that one of them is for the Soul Eater, and the other is our traditional first course."

Dahlia and Ziggy joined us on the terrace. As I looked at her beaming face, a pang of guilt shot through me. She thought she'd been chosen for a great honor. I'd condemned her to a fate worse than death, once Jacob Seymour consumed her soul.

Cyrus waved Dahlia forward. I expected him to bite into her, to start the process so she'd be turned quickly for the Soul Eater.

Two guards stepped forward and grasped Ziggy by the arms. I assumed they prepared to throw him into the crowd.

*Nathan, where are you?*

I felt sick to my stomach as I saw Cyrus's hand twine around Dahlia's hair.

"Ladies and gentlemen, *bon appétit!*"

Then he threw Dahlia off the terrace.

# *Eighteen*

### The Soul Eater

Confusion flashed across her face as the vampires surged forward and seized her. She fought their greedy, clutching hands as she looked toward us. "Cyrus? What's going on?"

My own panicked brain echoed her question.

"This was what you wanted," Cyrus snarled at me before rounding on Ziggy.

"I thought you'd feed her to your father!" I gripped his arm, but I didn't have the strength to stop him as he turned away from me.

"No fucking way!" Ziggy struggled against the guards and actually managed to break their hold. He fell to the hard stone, scrambling backward on his hands and feet like a frightened crab.

He didn't get far.

"No!" I shouted as Cyrus descended on him. There was a sickening crunch as muscle and vein gave way under fangs. Ziggy's agonized screams filled the air, a death rattle of blood gurgling from his throat.

I needed something, anything to use as a weapon. Ziggy's cries slowed, then stopped altogether, and his body hung limp in Cyrus's arms.

Dahlia faired much better. She shrieked a command and the vampires fell back in a wave. She ran toward the maze, never looking back. The Fangs followed her, whooping war cries as they disappeared into the dark hedges. The diners who were unaffected by Dahlia's flight murmured in surprise and looked around uncomfortably.

Cyrus rose and left Ziggy unconscious where he lay. I watched, sickened, as Cyrus wiped a rivulet of blood from his chin and raised his arms. His roughened voice and savage vampire face made him seem more evil, if that were possible. "Ladies and gentlemen, enjoy the hunt."

Behind us, the doors pushed open and a frantic group of humans flooded the terrace. They ran for their lives and would have trampled Ziggy, had I not knelt over him and shielded his vulnerable body.

"Ziggy, can you hear me?" I pulled him into my lap and pressed my hand to the oozing wound on his neck. Blood should have been spraying from his gashed throat, if there was enough blood left to spray. He opened his eyes, but they rolled back into his head as his body seized in my arms.

Most of the pets ran straight for the maze, herded toward it by the pursuing vampires. A few of the humans broke away from the crowd and were caught as they tried to climb the garden walls.

Cyrus watched for a long moment, something akin to pride on his face. Then he turned to us and raised his wrist. "Shall I turn him, or will you?"

"No!" I shouted again, trying to cover Ziggy by leaning

over him, but my answer was swallowed up by the pandemonium. "I made a mistake. I wanted him to live."

"Well, it's not bloody likely now, is it?" Cyrus asked dispassionately. "Look, we'll get you another one."

Tears rolled down my cheeks, stinging my cold flesh. "This wasn't how it was supposed to happen."

Cyrus frowned. "What are you talking about?"

He suspected something. Amid the screams and destruction around us, I let my guard down, my guilt and terror flooding the blood tie.

Over all this, a new sound emerged. The steady thump of rotary blades chopping through the air. I'd often heard the sound at the hospital, when accident victims were brought in by helicopter.

The medical chopper had nothing on the three sleek, black, military-style copters that dipped below the tree line. I stared up at the sky, transfixed by the whirling blades. My heart swelled with a mixture of dread and hope. The hour of salvation had arrived, too late for Ziggy.

Or me, for that matter. Without him, my safety wasn't assured. I wrapped my arms around Ziggy's chest and stood, half lifting him. He gasped and a cascade of blood poured over my hands. He wasn't going to last much longer.

Cyrus shouted frantically to his guards. New screams erupted from the hedge maze, the petrified cries of vampires trapped like foxes in snares, as one by one they realized what was happening. The helicopters' floodlights snapped on and pure UV rays drenched the lawn in artificial sunlight.

The heat and glare made my skin sizzle, but there wasn't enough direct exposure to kill me on the shaded porch where we were. Others weren't so lucky. The few vampires who made it clear of the maze exploded into flame and burned before they could reach the terrace. Only a handful made it to the house, pushing past us and charging through the glass doors.

Long ropes fell from both sides of each helicopter and dark figures dropped onto the lawn.

The assassins had arrived.

Twenty of them slid to the ground, covered in head-to-toe black gear. On their heads they wore black hoods and dark goggles. Leather gloves and boots protected their hands and feet. Not a centimeter of their skin was exposed.

They were impressively efficient. The vampires that didn't burn quickly enough were staked. A few were decapitated with long, studded knives.

It was gruesome. Headless bodies burst into fire, skin and muscle flaking to embers in the wind generated by the helicopters. For a brief second, all that remained of them was a flash of blue flame where their heart should be, just before their ribs turned to ash and crumbled to the lawn.

Cyrus fled past me, the right side of his face scorched by the lights. "I'll deal with you later! Run!"

But I couldn't leave Ziggy to die alone. I struggled backward to the door, dragging him with me, as my sire ran to cowardly safety.

The assassins surged up the lawn in a lethal wave. A thin line of smoke wafted off of the top of the head of one of the assassins. He lifted a walkie-talkie to his face, mumbled into it, and the lights cut off in sync.

I searched the lawn frantically for any sign of Nathan. How would I find him when they were all dressed the same?

One of them pointed in my direction as I gained the door. "Don't hurt him!" I screamed, dropping Ziggy to the marble floor of the foyer. I laid across him, wincing at the rattle I heard in his chest. "He's human! Don't hurt him!"

Without a word, the killer reached down and lifted Ziggy's legs before he barked at the others filing into the house. "I want a sweep of the grounds, and the house upstairs and down. Max, Amy, get the ground lights, and for God's sake, let's find the Soul Eater! Carrie, get him by the shoulders!"

It was Nathan.

Numb, I grabbed Ziggy under his arms. Seeing the doors were open, I nodded in the direction of the study. It was dark, but my eyes adjusted in time to guide Nathan to the corner farthest from the door. He eased Ziggy to the ground and whipped off his hood to examine the wound.

"It's pretty bad," I said softly. "Even if we got him in an ambulance now—"

"Shut up!" Nathan shouted, lifting Ziggy in his arms. "He's gonna be fine. Aren't you, kid?"

Ziggy's head lolled to the side, and he choked on his blood as he struggled to speak. Only two words came out clearly. One was *home*.

The other was *Dad*.

"Yeah. We're going home," Nathan whispered, smoothing Ziggy's hair back from his forehead. "Daddy's got you, and we're going home."

I covered my mouth as a sob threatened to tear from my throat. Outside the door, a war waged. No one knew that in this room, a father held his dying son.

*No one except us, and the Soul Eater.*

I'd forgotten his presence, had even run past his coffin as we'd entered the room without a second thought. Now dread overwhelmed me. My gaze fell on the casket. It was empty, the lid torn off the hinges. "Nathan…"

He would be no help, I realized, as I watched him cradle Ziggy close, half rocking on the hard floor. The sight was too painful. I had to look away.

The Soul Eater was somewhere in the house. Then I remembered the vial of holy water Nathan had given me. I'd tucked it into my bra as I'd dressed for the party. I'd just fished it out when the doorknob rattled. "Nathan!"

He was on his feet beside me, his face expressionless. "Ziggy's dead."

"I'm sorry," I whispered. "Is there anything I can—"

"There's really not time for that now." Nathan stepped in front of me. "Whatever comes through that door, run like hell."

"Excuse me?"

Just then the doors burst open. Cyrus stood in the doorway, rage twisting his burned face.

"I should have known," he hissed as his one remaining eye moved between Nathan and I.

Nathan strode forward. "Simon Seymour, son of Jacob Seymour, by order of the Voluntary Vampire Extinction Movement, I charge you with the destruction of humans, the creation of new vampires, and the crime of aiding your sire, the Soul Eater, in his own offenses. How do you plead?"

A cruel smile formed on Cyrus's lips. "I never plead for anything. Certainly not to a whelp like you."

Nathan stood his ground as Cyrus moved closer. He watched Cyrus warily, as though he were a deadly snake about to strike.

"Dear Nolen. Stupid as ever."

Nathan clenched his fists. "How do you plead to the charges, Cyrus?"

"Does it matter? I'm unarmed, and no match for you,

should you choose to strike me down in my weakened and vulnerable state." After a deliberate pause, he added, "Like you did your wife."

Nathan's body, tensed to the breaking point, snapped into motion. As his hands closed around my sire's throat, I wanted to kill him. My heart constricted in grief and horror at the thought Nathan might hurt Cyrus.

"Do you think she'll survive without me?" Cyrus wheezed. "The tie is too strong between us. But that doesn't matter, does it? You didn't even save the pathetic human boy."

"Shut up," Nathan growled, slamming Cyrus into the wall.

Faintly, through the frantic staccato of my pulse, I heard Cyrus laugh. "You don't really believe you've changed? Just because you've killed a few of the bad guys?"

Nathan crushed Cyrus's head against the wall, and I slumped to the floor, my chest tightening painfully so that I could only take fast, shallow breaths.

When Cyrus spoke, his voice was ragged, but the hate there was unmistakable. "Kill me then, Nolen. It will be worth it to see the satisfaction in your eyes. I'll die knowing you're worthy of our sire's blood."

Nathan's hands flexed, squeezing Cyrus's neck with fury, but Cyrus rallied one last time and shoved Nathan backward, hard. Nathan lost his balance and toppled to the floor. As he pulled himself up, he snarled, "I'm taking her with me."

Cyrus stepped aside, rubbing his neck as he leaned against the wall. "Fine. You're welcome to her."

Before Nathan or I could react, Cyrus lunged forward and grabbed me by the wrist, spinning me into his arms like a dance. "How many pieces would you like to carry her out in? Two?"

He twisted my arm until the long bones of my forearm snapped like dried twigs. I'd never actually broken a bone before. Man, did it hurt.

Screaming in pain and anger like a wounded animal, I flailed my free hand to break the vial I still clutched in my fist. If I had to, I'd spray us both with it.

"What's this?" Cyrus hissed into my ear. "A token of affection from your knight protector?"

He pried my fingers loose and snatched the bottle. Ferocious fingers seized my chin and squeezed my face roughly, forcing my jaw down.

"All this time you let me think I'd created the perfect companion, and you were just waiting to sink the stake into my heart." He popped the lid off the vial and tilted it. A single drop hung on the edge, poised to fall directly into my open mouth. "We're more alike than I thought."

"Don't do it," Nathan warned.

"Why? Because you'll kill me? You've already proved you can't. You'd enjoy it too much." Cyrus tipped the vial a little more. The suspended drop trembled and I closed my eyes.

I wasn't ready to die. I might not have anything to live for, but an empty life sounded a lot better than an uncertain afterlife.

"Please," I whimpered as best I could with limited movement of my jaw.

"Oh, shut up, Carrie. What a useless specimen you've turned out to be. Did you think you could betray me with no consequence?" His fingers gripped my face tighter. "What were you planning to do? Beg for mercy? Tell me you love me?"

Though it burned my soul to do it, I nodded a little, terrified my movement would bring the liquid onto my flesh. "I do love you." It wasn't completely a lie, but he didn't buy it. I couldn't exactly blame him.

"Do you think I'm stupid? Do you think I didn't sense your betrayal?" He licked my ear. "Every moment I was inside you, I felt your uncertainty. Your fear of me. You never made your choice."

Nathan sucked in a sharp breath, and hot shame flooded my face.

"Oh, does that bother you, Nolen?" Cyrus bit my neck softly. "I bet you thought you were rescuing a pure damsel. Don't let her fool you. She begged for it. She let me use her like a whore and she drank my blood as payment."

"Gentlemen don't kiss and tell," Nathan quipped.

*How can he joke at a time like this?*

"I never claimed to be a gentleman. Unlike others in this room, I don't deny my true nature."

Cyrus let the drop of holy water fall. I twisted away and it landed on the bare shoulder of my injured arm. The liquid burrowed through my skin and the flesh underneath like a scorching bullet. I bit my lip to stifle my cries.

"I do wish you'd scream, Carrie. You have such a beautiful scream." He sighed and tipped the bottle again. "Ah, well, just one of the things I'll miss about you."

The vial flew from his hand before he could spill the rest on me, and his grip released. I fell to the floor. I couldn't move my arm, and it felt as if it had been severed from my body while it hung lame at my side.

Nathan pinned Cyrus to the wall, his face changing as he flashed his fangs. The holy water splashed their legs, and smoke rose from the floor where it burned their feet.

Cyrus brought his knee up and kicked Nathan away. He

hit the floor and rolled out of reach. I saw Cyrus withdraw a stake from his sleeve. I shouldn't have been surprised that he'd lied about being unarmed.

I jumped on him, sinking my fingernails into his face. One finger slipped into his empty eye socket, and it was all I could do to keep from yanking my hand away in disgust. He twisted violently, dislodging me, but I landed on my feet. When he stopped to wipe the blood from his eyes I was on him again, locking my legs around his waist and pummeling him from behind. He threw himself backward, crushing me between his body and the wall. The breath rushed from my lungs in a great whoosh and I slid to the floor, clutching my chest. He stood over me, ready to strike.

Nathan got to his feet and slammed his elbow into the back of Cyrus's head, bringing him to the ground. Once he was down, Nathan delivered vicious kicks to the back of his head until he stopped struggling.

"Is he dead?" I gasped, using Nathan's proffered arm to climb to my feet.

He didn't look at me. His gaze was locked on Ziggy's motionless body. "No. And he won't be out for long. Let me get Ziggy and we'll go."

As soon as he uttered those words, the doors to the foyer blew off their hinges.

A forceful and foul-smelling wind blew us both against the wall in a shower of wood splinters. Ashes exploded from the cold fireplace as flames leapt up seemingly from nowhere, and the remaining furniture turned over from the magnitude of the blast.

A tall, sickly vampire slid into the room. His eyes burned red, and his long white hair trailed behind him as he floated effortlessly above the ground. Although he looked much older, and though I was nearly overcome by the stench of decay, I recognized him.

It was Cyrus's father.

The Soul Eater.

"Carrie, run!" Nathan shouted. He sprang toward Ziggy's body.

I grabbed him by the arm. "No, Nathan, there's nothing you can do for him!"

The ancient vampire slowly came closer, his bloody, dripping claws outstretched.

"Don't go. I'm so hungry," he said, the sound of many voices speaking all at once.

"Fuck you!" Nathan screamed, and for a moment I thought he'd charge him without a weapon. "You took everything from me!" He'd totally lost it. I'd never seen anyone so angry. All the resentment and rage that Nathan had been holding back from the world finally surfaced as he howled at the Soul Eater.

The vampire cocked his head, like a child who couldn't understand why he was being punished. "Just let me have a taste. A little taste."

The Soul Eater pointed to me. "You. Come to me."

"No!" Nathan grabbed my hand and ran for the door.

"Don't run from me, boy!" The Soul Eater's tone was like fire. "I smell my blood on you! Why do you not serve your master?"

"I will never serve you again."

The assassins poured down the stairs. Some had removed their hoods, and they high-fived each other on a job well done.

"Get out!" Nathan shouted. "The Soul Eater's awake!"

It had never occurred to me their plan might have hinged on the Soul Eater's vegetative state, but power had radiated from the old vampire. Logic and instinct collided in my brain, and I knew even this large number of assassins were no match for his awesome strength.

They knew it, as well. It didn't take them long to move. They ran for the back door, some jumping over the stair railing to save time.

But Nathan had a different exit planned for us. I tripped over my ridiculous shoes and wrenched my ankle. Nathan never missed a beat.

"Hang on," he ordered, scooping me up in his arms. He slung me over his shoulder like a sack of potatoes and ran out the front door, down the steps and onto the driveway, then across the snow-covered lawn.

"Just a little farther," he repeated over and over, a determined mantra more for his benefit than mine.

I held on to him for dear life with my one usable arm as he struggled to keep his footing on the grass.

*Please don't fall and break both of our necks. Not now, not when we're so close to getting away.*

The front gate was closed. "Can you climb?"

I wiggled my good arm. "I can try."

"Good enough for me." He boosted me up. I scrambled to the top, but slipped going over and fell to my feet on the pavement. The wicked heel of my shoe slid from beneath me, further twisting my injured leg. I swore loudly at the pain.

Nathan was at the top when he heard me. He jumped and landed next to me, rolling to his feet. "Can you walk?"

I shook my head. "I don't think so."

He lifted me into his arms and ran across the street, where Ziggy's van waited.

Nathan unlocked the door and dumped me onto the passenger seat. He hopped into the driver's side and started the engine, and I braced myself against the dashboard as he stomped on the gas.

I looked in the rearview and watched as we sped toward safety. Behind us, three black helicopters rose into the night air as the tiny, flickering lights of distant police cars approached.

"You're going to be okay," Nathan said hoarsely. "We're gonna be fine."

I took the assurance at face value, and since there was nothing left for me to do, I slumped against the seat and closed my eyes.

# Nineteen

### The Assassins

I woke beside Nathan in his bed. The last rays of sunlight were fading from the sky, and all around us the room glowed a rosy pink.

I sat up, careful not to disturb him or jostle my wounded arm. He'd taken the time to fashion a makeshift sling out of an old T-shirt before we'd both collapsed with exhaustion, but I still wasn't healed. I might have been in a lot worse shape if Nathan hadn't helped me.

His eyes were closed, his face smudged with dirt and sweat and blood. He still wore his black uniform, but the shirt had come untucked as he slept. His flat stomach was exposed, and I lay my hand there, taking comfort in the feeling of another body beside me.

"Please tell me you're in the process of giving me the best wake-up call I've had in a long time," he mumbled sleepily.

I smiled. "I'm sorry, I didn't mean to wake you."

"It would have happened sooner or later." He sat up and

swung his legs over the side of the bed, frowning at the boots he still wore. "You want some breakfast?"

"Maybe in a little while. I think I want to go back to sleep."

He got to his feet. "We've a busy night ahead of us."

I groaned and shuffled my feet as I followed him down the hall. My injured ankle caused me to limp pathetically. As we entered the bathroom, Nathan halted at the sight of two half-used bottles of blue and magenta hair dye.

The giddy relief I'd felt at escaping death had filled me so completely that I hadn't had room for anything else. But this reminder of Ziggy created plenty of space for sorrow, anger and, above all, guilt.

"I'm so, so sorry," I whispered. I wanted to touch Nathan, to comfort him. But as usual, he seemed untouchable.

With an unconcerned shrug I knew he didn't mean, he pulled his shirt over his head. His body looked less tempting than usual, as though pain and exhaustion had sapped him of some of his perfection. Or perhaps my body wasn't in any shape to fool around.

"We've got to meet with the assassins tonight. Cyrus is still out there." Nathan turned on the shower and unfastened his belt as if I wasn't there, as if he didn't care I was. Debating whether it would be more awkward to stay or make a fuss about leaving, I pretended to look for something in the medicine cabinet. His belt buckle jingled as he kicked off his pants, and I waited to hear the rattle of the curtain rings before I allowed my gaze to roam anywhere else.

"So, are you okay?" I said as I closed the cabinet door.

"Why wouldn't I be?"

"Because Zi—" I couldn't say it. "Because of what happened last night."

"People die."

"Yeah, they do, but he was kind of your only family."

"Let's not talk about it right now. I've got other things to worry about."

The hairs on the back of my neck prickled.

I left the bathroom without another word. The clothes Nathan had bought me were still at Cyrus's. I swiped a pair of Nathan's jeans and a sweater that required some maneuvering to put on over my injured arm.

I listened as the water cut off in the bathroom. Nathan came in to retrieve some clothes, a towel wrapped around his waist. He didn't speak to me, but eyed my attire with an expression that would have been amusement had his eyes not looked so sad.

I'd never felt so in the way in my entire life. If not for the dim light outside, I would have just made some excuse to leave. As it was, I had to settle for a different part of the apartment.

The living room looked cold and alien. A pair of Ziggy's shoes sat by the door. A stack of heavy metal CDs took up the corner of the coffee table, and a backpack full of college textbooks leaned against the couch. It was like a pharaoh's tomb, a museum of my failure to protect him and of Nathan's loss.

I went to the kitchen and pulled a bag of blood from the refrigerator. I was looking for something to cut the top of the bag with when Nathan's hand gripped my arm.

I jumped, dropping the bag. He caught it and cradled it against his chest as if it were a priceless artifact.

"What?" I demanded, rubbing my offended arm.

"It's the last one. I don't want to drink it." His voice was tight and he strained to get the words out.

My heart lurched at the full import of his statement. "Oh.

Oh, God." I stared, mesmerized by the shimmering liquid contained within the dull plastic. The millions of cells were the last physical evidence of Ziggy's life on earth.

Nathan opened the freezer door and unceremoniously dumped the bag inside. "How about we talk about this?" I said without thinking, and I was glad. I might not have said it otherwise.

"How about you mind your own business?" Nathan didn't exactly hide his face from me, but he didn't look at me, either, as he went through the cupboards, taking out pans, bowls and pancake mix. "You're not a vegetarian, are you?"

I planted my hands on my hips, cringing at the sting the motion caused. "It's kinda tough to be a vegetarian vampire. Unless you're Bunnicula."

He actually laughed at that.

I arched an eyebrow. "You know *Bunnicula?*"

He grew serious again. "I read it to Ziggy when he was younger. Will you get the bacon out of the freezer?" He turned away from me in an effort to hide his suffering. I couldn't believe that after all we'd been through together that he would continue to shut me out. I walked over to him and placed a hand on his shoulder, and he immediately jerked away from it.

Tears of anger sprang to my eyes. "You asshole."

Nathan turned around, his expression dark. "Fine. I'll make sausage instead."

I clenched my good fist. "You know what I'm talking about."

He opened the fridge and pulled out eggs and milk, pointedly turning the side of the carton labeled *Z* away from himself. "I do. And I told you before, I don't want to talk about it."

"Well, I do!" I stamped my foot.

Nathan poured the milk and the pancake mix into the bowl without measuring, the way a mother would after years of preparing breakfast for her family. Except I'd never seen a mother with such a murderous scowl. Nathan suddenly threw down the wooden spoon in his hand. It bounced off the rim of the glass bowl and splattered half-mixed batter everywhere. "Just because I don't want to stand here and have a Hallmark moment with you doesn't mean I didn't love Ziggy. I cared about him more than somebody like you could ever understand!"

*"Somebody like me?"* I hated the shrillness of my voice when I was mad. "What the hell is that supposed to mean?"

He folded his arms across his chest. "You tell me. What exactly did you have to do to keep him safe, Carrie? And so I can appreciate how indebted to you I should be, how much did you enjoy it?"

His remark twisted like a knife in my heart, just as he'd intended. Rage set my limbs trembling. I lashed out. "I did what I had to do! Unlike some people in this room!"

"What are you talking about?"

"Why didn't you give Ziggy your blood? You could have saved him. All it would have taken was a little of your blood! Why didn't you do it?"

The question had hung between us since the moment we left the mansion. It had been the cause for the tension we'd felt all morning.

Nathan looked at me, his eyes filled with confusion. "You think I let him die?"

The pain in his voice stole my will to fight. "Do you think you let him die?"

With a growl of fury, he shoved all the dishes and utensils off the counter. The glass bowl shattered at his feet, and the clang of metal nearly deafened me as the pans collided with linoleum. Nathan stalked forward, and I took a step back out of reflex more than fear. He wouldn't hurt me. No matter how tough he tried to appear, he wasn't the type to abuse someone weaker than himself.

"I would rather have him dead than be one of us!" he shouted, so close to my face that his cold breath stirred my hair. "You only know *your* change. You got to stay the same person you were before. Not everyone is so lucky. The blood has different effects on people. It does something to you, it makes you do things you wouldn't normally do."

I looked down, all too aware that I could have just as easily saved Ziggy with my own blood.

"You saw that, that *thing.*" Nathan spat the word, as though no reference to his sire could ever accurately describe his hideousness. "His blood is in mine. How could I put that into my son? How could I make him…"

He was running out of anger, and all that was left for him was despair. "How could I make him like me?" On the last word, his face went ashen and his shoulders sagged in defeat. He crumpled to the floor with a cry of anguish.

Faced with a man's tears, I reacted much in the way a male would to a woman crying. I stood silently and watched his misery, feeling helpless in the awkwardness of the moment. Then I realized I had to do something, so I knelt on the floor of the tiny kitchen and put my arms around him. "Nathan, you're nothing like them."

I thought he'd push me away, but he returned my embrace, clinging to me like a drowning man to a piece of driftwood. "You don't know me, Carrie. You don't know what I've done."

I wondered how long it had been since he'd let himself cry

or talk to anyone or, God, even feel. Unable to think of any better way to comfort him, I held him while his cold tears wet the front of my shirt and his back shook with unrestrained sobs.

A long time later, when he'd composed himself, we salvaged the dishes that had survived his wrath. As if nothing had happened, we set about making breakfast side by side in the tiny kitchen.

Because there was nothing else to talk about, I asked about Ziggy.

At first, Nathan resisted, giving short, perfunctory answers. I'm not sure if it was talking through the tragedy that soothed him, or making breakfast, but he soon fell into an easy pattern of storytelling. "Ziggy was a runaway. He left home when he was nine. Can you believe that?"

I shook my head sympathetically and let him continue.

"His mom was on drugs, his dad was in jail. His stepdad beat him so badly that he had two broken ribs when I found him. Every few months, I'd do the rounds at the Goth clubs. I'd look for wannabes and vampire hunters, and kids who got into the role-playing and took it too seriously. Usually, I'd give them a good scare and send them home." He motioned for me to flip the bacon I'd arranged in a frying pan, and leaned to turn down the heat.

"Ziggy had fallen in with some pretty stupid kids. They were in their early teens, but they let him hang around. They called themselves vampire hunters, but I'm glad I got to them before they could get in any actual trouble. These kids had no idea how to fight. They all ran from me. Except Ziggy. We stood in that alley for two hours, staring each other down. I even did the whole—" He waved his hands in front of his face. "He just kept insisting he was going to kill me and rid the world of, I think the term he used was 'hell spawn.'"

I imagined a nine-year-old Ziggy staring down a killer vampire, and it brought a smile to my face. "What did you do?"

"I would have washed his mouth out with soap, if I'd known he'd had a gift for that kind of language. I took him to Denny's to get some pie." He smiled at the memory. "He hadn't eaten in days. He was so skinny, you could have turned on a flashlight on one side of him and it would have shone through to the other. I asked if he had a place to stay, and he tried to play it off like he had all sorts of options. I told him he could stay with me, and he's lived here ever since."

He paused, clearly noticing he'd used the present tense. But he didn't correct himself. "You know, I feel like any second now he could walk through that door."

Before he could get too emotional again, he reached for a whisk and set to mixing the pancake batter. "He was only my donor for about a year. I don't want you to think I was taking advantage of him."

"I didn't."

"And I don't want you to think I didn't love him because of what happened before he left. I followed him. I looked all over town for him until the sun came up and I had to come back here. I had a hell of a burn."

"I'll bet."

Without saying anything further, I got two plates and laid out some silverware. I wasn't sure pancakes would hit the spot in the absence of blood, but cooking seemed to be therapeutic for Nathan. By the time we finished, we had pancakes, eggs Benedict, sausage and bacon. He had just gone rummaging through the cupboard, muttering under his breath about muffin mix, when I stopped him.

"I'm sure this will be enough. I mean, I don't know if vampires can gain weight, but I really don't want to take a chance."

He laughed softly. "I'm sorry. I'm used to cooking for a teenage boy. It'll take me a while to get used to this."

Not sure how he'd react, but needing the contact to reassure me, I laid my hand over his as he reached for a plate of bacon. "Nathan, you don't have to put on an act about this. Not with me."

"Hey, forget about it. But I'm glad to know you're there if I need you." When he smiled, I recognized the Nathan I knew. The calm surface stretched over a terrifying riptide of emotions. It was a depth he probably didn't visit, for fear of drowning in his past.

By the time eleven-thirty rolled around and we headed downstairs for the meeting, we'd sunk into an easy pattern of speaking without saying anything.

The shop looked much better than I'd expected. Last time I'd seen it, it had been full of burnt, smoke-damaged merchandise. Now it was a totally different store. New shelves were empty and draped with plastic. Sawdust covered the floor and made the air hazy, making it seem as if workmen had just left.

"It looks good," I said, touching the freshly painted trim. I wiped my hands surreptitiously on my jeans and hoped he hadn't noticed.

Nathan inspected the new countertop and ran his fingers over it. "The firemen said it was faulty wiring and I wasn't going to tell him that a crazy witch was actually responsible for the fire. Insurance covered the remodel. It'll be a shame to leave. This place looks better than it did when I first bought it. Maybe I should send Dahlia a thank-you card."

A lump rose in my throat at the thought of him leaving. He was the only friend I had in the city. "You're leaving?"

Nathan nodded. "I've been here fifteen years, Carrie. My customers are starting to comment on how well I've aged. It's one of the first signs that I need to go. That, and someone called offering to teach power yoga in the back room. Power yoga. I don't think I have the strength to put in another decade here."

"Where will you go?" I asked, willing myself to sound casual. "Back to Scotland?"

"No, not there. I haven't given it much thought." He quirked an eyebrow. "Why? Are you going to miss me?"

"Ha, ha." I tried to change the subject. "What do we have to do to set up this meeting? Do we need coffee and doughnuts?"

He smiled, a little wickedly, in my opinion. "How's your arm?"

I lifted it uncertainly. It was sore, but practically healed. "It's okay. Why?"

"We need chairs." He opened the storage room door and slid out a cart of folding chairs. "Get unfolding."

"Yes, sir," I said with a mock salute. "So, are they going to go ballistic when they realize I'm not a part of the club?"

"Maybe." He dropped a chair into place. "If anyone gives you a hard time, send them to me."

"Ooh, big man."

"You have no idea." The devilish grin that formed on his face eased some of the anxiety I felt. The comment, however, renewed the spark of another kind of tension I'd almost forgotten existed between us. I nearly dropped the chair I held.

The bells above the door jingled. They'd melted in the fire, so rather than merrily announcing the entrance of a customer, they sounded like the arrival of a satanic ice-cream truck.

Two men entered. Though they were dressed in casual clothes, they projected an aura of menace.

Nathan was unperturbed as he hurried to greet them. "Alex, Gary! Get rested up?"

They didn't respond. They were too busy staring at me. I wondered if maybe I had said something under my breath.

Alex spoke first. He was tall and dark-skinned, with a shaved head. "What's she doing here?"

Unfazed by the man's gruff demeanor, Nathan motioned me forward. "This is Dr. Carrie Ames."

"Hi." I extended my hand, hoping it didn't shake.

Alex didn't take it. But Gary shook my hand readily.

"Pleased to meet you." He had dark hair, olive skin and a Texan drawl. And he didn't appear to hate me outright, which scored big points in my book.

"Is she one of us?" Alex asked as he eyed me suspiciously.

Nathan smiled, a clearly antagonistic gesture. "Yeah, she's one of us. Not Movement, though."

Gary raised his hands as if surrendering as he stepped away from his friend.

Alex inclined his head toward me. "Any reason for that?"

Before I could answer, Nathan stepped in front of me, and in doing so, was almost nose to nose with the other vampire. "She's not sure about it yet."

"Not sure if she wants to be good or evil? That doesn't sound like a tough choice to me," Alex said, his voice liquid hate.

Nathan tried to remain calm. "She hasn't broken a single rule since she turned."

"Yeah, but you know the rules, man." Gary sounded nervous, as if they might all be struck down for consorting with a renegade vampire any second.

"And we all know how well you follow the rules." Alex stared right at him. The tone of his voice implied an intense dislike for Nathan.

292	*Jennifer Armintrout*

Gosh, if this guy thought Nathan was soft on the rules, I'd hate to think how he lived *his* life.

I saw the muscles of Nathan's back bunch beneath his shirt. More vampires would be arriving soon. I sent up a silent prayer Nathan wouldn't flip out and start throwing punches.

I cleared my throat and tried to sound authoritative. "This isn't about Nathan. It's about me. I'm all for law and order and keeping the peace, but I don't know where you Movement guys get off with your 'join us or die' rhetoric. I don't do anything unless I'm asked nicely."

I stole a glance at Nathan and saw quiet pride on his face.

"I think you better ask her nicely," Gary said with a laugh.

Alex sneered at me. "Pretty please, with a cherry on top, would you join the fucking Movement?"

"I'll think about it."

With a muttered curse, Alex walked to the cluster of chairs and dropped down heavily. I secretly hoped there would be a weakness somewhere in the chair's frame so that it would topple from under him.

Alas, it didn't. Gary regarded me with wide eyes and went to join his friend.

Nathan leaned close as he walked past me and whispered, "Think you can do that about fifteen more times?"

He wasn't kidding. Exactly fifteen more vampires showed up, offering fifteen lukewarm receptions. But most of them just ignored me as they socialized with one another. The situation harkened back to my high school days, when my friends would rope me into going to college parties and promptly disappear with their new frat-boy love interests. I'd just be standing there, holding a red plastic cup of two dollar beer, trying not to catch anyone's attention.

The variety of vampires surprised me. I like to think of myself as a forward-thinking woman with feminist leanings, but I was truly surprised when almost half the team turned out to be female. Some of the women looked like stereotypical vampire seductresses, with dark clothes and heavy makeup, but most of them were very normal looking. One of them even wore a pink cashmere twinset with pearls. She looked more suited to be an attendee at a meeting of the Young Republicans than a gathering of ruthless assassins.

The males in the group were just as diverse, some so young they appeared to be teenagers and one was old enough to have been my father. The older man shook hands enthusiastically with me, explaining he'd been a doctor as well. "Well, a doctor of psychology," he'd said, in the early 1920s. "We'll have a lot to talk about," he'd promised, and when he'd patted my hand, I couldn't help but think he might be coming on to me.

When the meeting came to order, only one person voiced concern at my attending, and that was Alex. He was overruled by the tall, slender female who seemed to be in charge.

The tall, slender female Nathan couldn't keep his eyes off of.

"I asked her to let you stay, as a personal favor," Nathan whispered, never tearing his rapt gaze from her willowy body.

"Try to keep your tongue in your mouth," I snapped quietly.

Ms. Gorgeous paced back and forth in front of us, and I tried hard not to hate her. She had legs that seemed to go to her neck, and a fashion sense I could never hope to cultivate. With a sad smile, she began to speak. "Thanks for coming tonight, guys. I know a lot of you have planes and buses to catch, so I'll keep this as brief as possible. As you know, we lost two members in our fight with the Soul Eater."

I looked around at all the grave faces.

The speaker continued. "And Nathan Grant lost someone very special."

She smiled tenderly at him, and I realized I was glaring at her. Behind me I heard quiet chuckling, and I turned to see a blond man with a friendly—not to mention adorable—face wink at me. I doubted it was Nathan's tragedy the man found amusing.

Nathan had heard the laughing as well. "Max, do you have something to share?"

Max sobered instantly. "No, man. We're cool. Sorry about the kid."

With a grumpy nod, Nathan turned in his seat.

"If we can all get back to the meeting," the alpha female said, frowning so sternly at Max I almost reminded her that Nathan had been talking, too. God, petty jealousy was turning me into a deranged tattletale. I wondered if it was a trait I'd inherited from Cyrus, or one that I'd had all along but never had a chance to use.

"While our raid on Cyrus's mansion was successful in that we eliminated a fair number of vampires, some of you were a bit kill-happy. Three Lupins and a half-demon were mistakenly killed. I don't think any of us wishes to increase the tension between the Movement and the Lupin council." She waited as if to let her remark sink in. "And we didn't achieve either of our goals."

"What does that mean?" I whispered to Nathan.

"It means we didn't kill Cyrus. Or the Soul Eater."

The blond vampire behind me leaned forward, his cold breath tickling my neck. "But some of us got damned close."

Nathan twisted around in his chair. "Cyrus is her sire. You really know how to put your foot in it, don't you?"

I almost snapped that I didn't care, that jerk could say any-thing he wanted. It certainly would have earned me some points with this crowd. But beneath my current tangle of confused emotions was a lingering ache from being separated from my sire. The pain I'd felt through the blood tie would be nothing compared to the emptiness I'd feel if he actually were killed.

I finally knew what my mother meant when she'd said, *just because you love a person doesn't mean you have to like them.*

Miss Thin Dark and Annoying stopped directly in front of us. Nathan was certainly appreciative of the view.

"Since our first mission failed and the council still wishes to see Cyrus exterminated, we've been ordered back in."

Angry shouts and groans of disbelief erupted around the room. Some people grumbled about nonrefundable plane tickets and jobs they needed to get back to.

Max actually stood up, like a character in a town meeting from an old movie. "Now that Cyrus knows we're in town, he's going to hightail it out of here. Not to mention the fact the Soul Eater is going to up his guards."

I couldn't tell if the outraged voices agreed with him or not.

The leader waved her hands to silence everyone. "Cyrus isn't going anywhere. The Movement has pulled passenger lists for upcoming domestic and international flights. None of his known aliases are traveling, passenger or cargo. As for the Soul Eater, he successfully shipped himself to…" She pulled out a Palm Pilot and punched a few keys. "Wash-ington, D.C. The council wants one volunteer to follow him—"

"Yo," Max said as he raised his hand.

She narrowed her eyes and keyed something in. "Fine. We also need a small group to infiltrate Cyrus's mansion and assassinate him."

Nathan tore his gaze away from the woman, finally, and turned to me. His eyes were so intense I thought he'd shoot lasers from them as he stared at me. I knew he was making a decision from the way he furrowed his brows.

A decision that obviously concerned me.

Not that he would consult me on it. "I'll go."

The woman smiled. "Thank you, Nathan."

"Then I'm going, too!" I claimed as I raised my hand, despite Nathan's persistent attempts to block it. We ended up looking like we'd engaged in a very sissy slap fight.

"Absolutely not!" He didn't bother to lower his voice. "He's your sire. You're too much of a liability."

Anger burned hot on my face. I'd had just about enough of people telling me what I could and couldn't do. I wasn't going to let Nathan face Cyrus alone, partly because I feared for his safety and partly because I needed to see Cyrus die with my own eyes. "Pardon me, but I do believe she said *volunteer.* I'm volunteering, and I don't think it's any of your business!"

The speaker cleared her delicate throat. "It doesn't matter. She's not Movement, so she's not eligible to take the assignment."

"Excuse me, I'm right here," I nearly growled at her.

"Ladies, ladies. Let's not have a catfight," Max urged, standing again. "Unless there's going to be torn clothing involved. If Cyrus is her sire, I say she's got the right to take him out herself."

"How do we know she won't fall to the blood tie and stab us in the back?" That bitch was becoming more irritating with every second.

"Hello!" I shrieked, rising to my feet. "I'm still right here. How do *you* manage to keep from going all feral and tearing people up? I haven't done it yet, and I'm pretty sure I can avoid doing it in the near future!"

"I don't want you going in there again!" Nathan shouted, grabbing me by the arm and tugging me back into my seat.

I wrenched out of his grasp. "You don't have the authority to boss me around, so drop the dad act!"

His face went ashen.

"Oh, God, Nathan, I'm—"

"You know what? Go ahead and come along. If you get killed, it's your fault, not mine. I don't give a damn anymore." He stood and stalked off, slamming the door behind him.

"Forget that D.C. thing. I want to go with *them*," Max said, waving his hand furiously in the air.

The woman scowled at both of us and ran after Nathan.

Max shrugged and addressed the group. "I guess that means meeting adjourned."

Tears stung my eyelids as the discordant bells above the door chimed. I don't know what bothered me more, that I'd hurt Nathan's feelings or that *she* was out there comforting him.

"Hey, don't worry about it, he's not really interested in her." Max's voice was so close to my ear, I jumped.

I turned to see he'd slid into the vacant seat beside me. "I don't care."

Max's smile was boyish and held just a hint of naughtiness, as though my obvious attraction to Nathan didn't remove me from his prospective bedding pool. "I know you don't. I just feel like talking about it. If you don't care, it shouldn't bother you."

I couldn't help my smile. "Fine."

"Rachel's a good girl. But Nathan's not her type, if you catch my drift."

I didn't, so I just stared at him blankly.

Max frowned. "Okay, let me put it this way. If Nathan were to actively pursue her, he'd have to get a major operation. In Switzerland."

"Now I get it."

"Good, I could tell you were a smart one. I'm Max Harrison." His handshake was firm, as if he'd been practicing for a job interview. I was surprised when he slipped his hand out of mine and tried to bump fists with me.

I laughed. "I'm sorry, I'm not that hip."

"Don't sweat it." He covered his soft laugh with a cough. "Rachel just looks out for her kids. They're the vamps she took under her wing when they were new to the Movement."

"You're not one of her kids?" I raised an eyebrow.

He sniffed and leaned back in his seat. "No. But enough about me. I want to know about the cutie in the Goth ballerina costume."

I blushed from the roots of my hair to the tips of my toes. "You saw me?"

"It was kinda hard to miss you." There was nothing boyish about his expression now. He was almost predatory, the way he looked me up and down.

The bells above the door jingled again, and I was grateful for the excuse to change the subject. "Sounds like they're back."

Nathan and Rachel entered the shop. I could tell he was still upset, but he managed to put on an amicable face. Rachel pasted on a fake smile and walked toward me with Nathan.

"Well, Doctor, I've heard a lot about you," she said, leaning casually against the counter. "Do you think you can live up to the hype?"

I smiled back sweetly, but narrowed my eyes at her challenge. "I'm sure I can, and then some."

"I hope so." She turned to Nathan. "I need to speak to you. Alone."

The last word was added like a bullet aimed at both Max and me. I folded my arms, some evil little urge to antagonize her compelling me to stay.

Max threw his arm around my shoulder. "Fine. We know when we're not wanted. Well, Miss—"

"Doctor," Nathan snapped.

I put on my best flirty smile, making sure he saw and understood why I'd done it before I turned to Max. "Call me Carrie."

He gave me a nod, as if to say "good play." "Well, Miss Doctor-Call-Me-Carrie, I have a fantastic room over at the Hampton Inn on Twenty-eighth Street, complete with a minibar. What do you say we get slightly buzzed on very small bottles of schnapps and paint Mallsville red?"

Despite his ridiculous come-on, it was hard not to like Max. I laughed and shook my head. "Actually, I'm kind of tired, after last night. I think I'll go upstairs to bed."

I said a brief, polite goodbye to Rachel and Max and headed up the stairs.

The night air was cool, but the day must have been warm. The snow had nearly melted. For once in the last few hectic days, I didn't feel as if I had to rush anywhere, or dread anything. In fact, I was actually looking forward to tying up the bathroom with a nice long bubble bath.

When I got to the door, I realized I didn't have any keys to get into the apartment. That's when the hair stood up on my neck, and I desperately wanted to get inside.

I didn't know what had spooked me, but every instinct in my body screamed *run*. I wasn't going to argue. I'd nearly gained the top of the stairs when something caught my hair and tugged me backward. I opened my mouth to scream, and a hand stifled the sound.

A cold, clawed hand.

A startlingly familiar hand.

My sire's hand.

# Twenty

### Transfusion

He wrenched my head back, hard. "What a nest of vipers you've fallen into."

I shuddered. "All I have to do is scream, and—"

"But you won't." His fingers slid across my shoulders, dipping into the neck of my shirt. "Because you don't want to fight me."

"You're right. I don't want to fight you." I clenched my teeth. "I want them to come up here and tear you to pieces."

The unmistakable chill of metal pressed against my throat.

"I don't think I'm the one who's going to go to pieces here." He drew the blade across my neck, and though I barely felt the sting of the cut, a warm cascade of blood wet the front of my shirt. Blood gurgled from my mouth.

"That should take care of your annoying talking problem."

I heard the door open at the bottom of the stairs, but my vision swam. I couldn't see who it was.

When I heard her call a farewell over her shoulder, I recognized Rachel's voice.

If I could have called out, I would have. But Cyrus quickly backed into the narrow alley beside the building, dragging me with him.

"Imagine that. They're all leaving." He lowered his head and lapped at the blood flowing from my neck. "And you don't have much time."

He raised the knife again, and I was too weak to dodge it. The blade split my sternum, and for a terrifying moment I thought he'd struck my heart.

"I wouldn't do that to you, Carrie," he whispered against my ear as he sawed the blade upward. "If I punctured your heart, you'd be nothing but a pile of dust. No fun for Nathan to find you that way."

As he wedged his fingers between my separated rib cage, his memories flashed through my mind.

The Soul Eater's sadistic face filled my vision. "Hold still, boy. Your brother didn't carry on so!"

My bones and cartilage cracked as Cyrus yanked my chest open. When I screamed in agony, I gagged on my blood.

The pictures in my head scrambled and jumped. I saw the face of the dead woman I'd seen before, the same one I'd seen beside Cyrus at the dinner party. She laughed and trailed her finger down the scar on Cyrus's chest. "And why would I let him do that?" she asked.

Her mocking wounded him. "So we can be together forever."

My vision cleared, and I saw Cyrus looming above me, his hands and clothes drenched in my blood. "And *you'll* be with me forever."

Those evil bells jingled again. I had no idea how long I'd been lying there. I couldn't see Cyrus, but I heard his voice from somewhere in the alley. "If you live through the night."

The blood on my shirt wasn't warm anymore. It was nearly frozen to my skin. In the gap between the buildings, I saw no stars in the cold, clear sky.

Dawn would come soon.

I closed my eyes, unable to worry or care what would happen to me when the rising sun touched my flesh. It seemed simpler than being rescued. If someone found me, how would they fix me? I'd been damaged beyond repair, gutted like a fish.

I thought about what Nathan would think when he went upstairs and found the apartment empty. Maybe he'd think that I'd turned my back on his friendship again. Or that I'd been so angry with him that I'd returned to the man who'd killed his son.

Would he spend the rest of his life hating me?

Something soft and cool brushed my ear, a breeze in the windless night. I opened my eyes. All around me, the alley grew dim. Colors bled together into shapeless blobs that darkened with the rapid deceleration of my heart. The pain in my chest ebbed into a warm, focused feeling that lifted my whole body from any sensation.

Then the space that separated the shapeless blobs got smaller and smaller as the darkness became absolute. In the distance, I saw a point of light. It swelled and spiraled toward me.

In medical school, we'd been taught the Kubler-Ross theories of death. A glimmering tunnel, all your relatives and the deity of your choice waiting to welcome you.

When I'd gone on to my internship, I'd heard the nurses talk about "The Man at the End of My Bed," a vision they claimed patients always reported on the night of their death.

Both versions of dying had been terrifying and alien to me,

looming in the future like a standardized test or a root canal, something unpleasant you couldn't avoid. What I was experiencing now was peaceful and gradual, my senses dropping away one by one as the intense light widened in my fading vision.

Instead of seeing heaven, I saw the alley and the street beyond. At my feet, I saw my lifeless body, torso splayed open like a macabre storybook.

I wished I could see the world around me all my life as it appeared now, painted in the washed-out tones of a watercolor. Suddenly, where the sidewalks had been empty before, pale shadow forms drifted aimlessly in an eerie ballet. A big orange tabby cat jogged down the alley, pausing to sniff my body.

The animal's vitality and life took my breath away. The shadows spotted it at once and reached their long fingers out to touch it before it hissed and ran back where it had come from. I wanted to follow it. I needed to touch the cat and feel the life there. But something held me down like an anchor.

A pull at my spectral chest reminded me that my body still had breath and life. I wanted to just die already.

*So this is what it's like to become a ghost.*

I heard Nathan's voice. When he passed the alley, he stopped, sniffed the air.

He howled in fury.

He dropped to his knees beside my body, arms spread as if he didn't know what to do first. Sadly—though not too sadly, because everything I felt seemed to come through a filter—I realized he wanted to save me.

I wanted to tell him not to bother. It was too much work, and I was just too tired.

The shadows shimmered and pulsed, but they didn't

swarm Nathan the way they had the cat. I didn't blame them. There was no life in him, no color. Just pale shades of sadness, and we already had those.

Nathan lifted my head in his hands and kissed my dead lips. A tear splashed against my cold skin. It couldn't have been mine.

The tenderness there made me feel something. Regret?

My new companions beckoned, and I reached out to them. Not with my hands. I had no hands. Neither did they. But they surrounded me, and their embrace was warm and comforting.

Nathan raised his wrist to his mouth and bit down. Dark blood dripped into my slack mouth.

The ghost people wavered and dimmed.

*No!*

I tried to fight, but piece by piece I came alive again. First I heard sounds more clearly. Then I felt a little pain, and the sensation of hot, sticky blood pooling in the back of my mouth. I swallowed, and the pain grew, until all I felt was agony and hunger.

I closed my lips over his wrist. When I drew more blood into my mouth, a tremor went through him.

"You're going to be okay," he rasped.

He held my broken body in his arms.

"I saw them," I whispered. I drifted away again, but this time there were no lost souls to welcome me.

I was stranded in the darkness.

# Twenty-One

❧❧❧

### Born Again (Not That Way)

I had no concept of time over the course of my recovery. It moved from darkness to light, and not at regular intervals. Sometimes I opened my eyes, but my vision was as soft and unfocused as a newborn's.

Occasionally, pictures splintered my mind. Some were unrecognizable, but a few were my own memories from a skewed perspective, as if I were watching myself in a movie. In the most frequently occurring flash, I saw my own lifeless body in the alley. It was like a scene in a horror film, and it repeated over and over.

The longer I slept, the worse my hunger grew. When it finally outweighed my fatigue, I woke, cranky and hurting.

Though my memory was fuzzy, I knew I was in Nathan's bed. His scent was all around me, and my body reacted with surprising ferocity. It demanded I find him.

At first I was afraid to move. I remembered my throat had been cut. With no idea how long I'd been asleep, I didn't know how much I'd healed. When I touched my neck, I felt only smooth, new skin.

"You're awake."

I knew Nathan had entered the room before he spoke. I sensed him. He looked haggard, as if he hadn't slept in days.

I glanced at the clock on the nightstand. "Is it really noon?"

He nodded. "How are you feeling?"

His eyes were ringed with dark circles; his face was drawn and pinched. When he spoke, it sounded like his vocal chords had been raked across a cheese grater.

"I hurt," I answered truthfully. "Very badly. And I'm hungry."

He scrubbed his face vigorously with his hands and blew out a long breath, much like a man who was faced with a task he was too exhausted to undertake would do. But he smiled encouragingly. "Let me take care of the pain first, then I'll see what I can do about getting you some blood."

I shifted carefully in the bed, white-hot spears of pain ripping through my torso as I did so. "How long have I been out?"

"Eight days. Nine if I give you enough meds."

"What about Cyrus?" I thought he looked angry at the mention of his name, and he had every right to be. But I had a right to know. "Did you kill him?"

Nathan looked away from me. "No, we didn't kill him. I suggested we postpone the mission in case you survived to bitch at me when you found out that we went without you."

At least he hadn't lost his sense of humor. Beside the bed, he'd set up a folding card table stocked with clean towels, the first aid kit, and numerous boxes of gauze and medical tape. Most of these were empty.

He lifted a needle and measured out an injection of something. I didn't care what it was as long as it took away the crushing feeling in my chest.

Gauze wrapped around my torso, giving me the appearance of a fashion-conscious mummy wearing a tube top. I pressed my hand to my ribs and another sharp ache pierced down my body. "I can't breathe."

Nathan sat next to me on the bed, carefully trying not to make any movements that would jostle me. "Yes you can. Take deep breaths. If you panic, you'll hyperventilate."

He pulled back the blankets and wrapped a tourniquet around my arm. I flinched when he sank the needle into my vein, and acute pain billowed through my limbs.

My memories played out like a rough cut of a movie I only knew half the plot to. The sound was bad, the visuals confusing. There were threads of a coherent story, but no pattern to weave them all together.

"What happened to me?"

Nathan's face, lined with tension, tried to soften. "What do you remember?"

"Sounds. Pain." And horrific, physical torment. But I didn't want to recall that now. "I remember coming back downstairs for the keys, and after that, nothing."

He shook his head. "You never made it downstairs, Carrie. I found you in the alley."

The alley. I remembered the sky, that it had been almost dawn and I couldn't move. "Did I burn?"

"No." Gently, he removed the needle and recapped it. Although I'd already lectured Nathan about this, I didn't bother correcting him.

*I'm a completely different person.*

A pang of sadness brought tears to my eyes, and Nathan looked up sharply. "What's the matter?"

And then he shrugged, as if answering a question I hadn't

voiced. "I think I've been cooped up with you too long if I'm starting to read your mind."

The lighthearted comment brought echoes of something to the surface of my consciousness. A medicated haze settled over me, and my words slurred as I spoke. "You should get some sleep. You don't look too good."

His hand was cold against my forehead. "Likewise, sweetheart."

I'd been dead. That was the important detail I needed to remember. I'd been dead, and he'd been there.

But I drifted off again, and it was two more days before I woke.

Nathan lay on his side next to me, curved protectively around my body. If I turned my face, I could snuggle against him, listen to his heart beat. It felt so comforting to have him there. His hand stroked my hair, and I opened my eyes.

The gauze around my chest had been replaced by a navy-blue T-shirt that had seen better days. There was blood on it, and vomit.

"You had a bad, bad reaction to the morphine. I'd been giving you the meperidine, since you'd had it before with no trouble, but I ran out."

His voice was hoarse. He still hadn't slept.

"Well, reaction or not, it must be working okay. I don't feel a thing." The pain of my injuries was a distant nightmare, and only the lingering stiffness of a long bed rest plagued my bones.

He chuckled softly as he slowly sat up. "You're probably healed by now."

Like flashbulbs going off, I saw Cyrus looming over me, blood on his hands. My chest split open like a cadaver for dissection. Nathan's stricken face when he found me in the alley.

One of the first things Nathan had explained to me about the Voluntary Vampire Extinction Movement was that they expressly forbid medical treatment for life-threatening injuries. I was dead when he found me. And here I sat. "You broke the rules."

His back went straight at my accusation. "Yeah, I guess I did."

I scooted up, wincing at the soreness in my unused muscles. I propped a few pillows behind me and drew the covers to my neck. "Why?"

I had a suspicion he rummaged a bit too long in the dresser for another T-shirt so he could think of an excuse. "I like to live dangerously?"

Of all the vampires I'd met so far, Nathan was the most serious, the biggest stickler for the rules. In the two weeks I'd been deciding whether or not to join the Movement, he'd called nearly every night with some new bit of information I'd never use, but that he felt was vitally important for me to know. He'd held Ziggy, the person who'd mattered most in his life, and watched him die when he could have easily turned him and spared himself the pain of loss. But he hadn't, because of his affiliation with the Movement.

Yet, he'd saved me.

"Why?" I asked again.

When he looked at me, his expression was somber. "I can't explain it."

"Let me know when you can." I made a move to get out of bed, but Nathan gruffly pulled the covers back over me.

"You need rest."

"I've had plenty of rest. I want to get up." I tried again, and he gripped my arms.

"Will you just listen to me and lie back down?" With a frustrated curse he handed me a clean T-shirt and turned his back.

"Something on your mind, Nathan?" I quickly slipped out of the soiled shirt and into the fresh one, pausing at the sight of the bumpy scar that bisected my chest.

His shoulders sagged with exhaustion. "This isn't the first time I've gone against the Movement. I'm on probation as it is."

I arranged the sheets around my bare lower half. "You can turn around now."

When he did, I saw him eye the scrap of bare leg that peeked out from beneath the covers. He quickly averted his gaze.

"Are you sorry?" What would I do if he said yes?

Nathan didn't answer immediately. "Carrie, when I found you, my only thought was to stay with you until you died. But it took so long. Just when I thought you'd actually… you'd pull right back. Honestly, I've never seen anyone fight so hard. But the damage was too much. There was no way you could have healed yourself. Not as new as you are." He sat on the bed, facing me.

"Did you look at the scar?" He touched the front of my shirt, just below my collarbone, and a jolt went through me.

"Yes." I couldn't manage more than a whisper.

He closed his eyes and didn't remove his hand. "He cut you from here—" His fingers slipped down, passing between my breasts and coming to rest on the hollow of my rib cage. He opened his hand and rested his palm against my stomach for a moment before tracing back to my neck. "To here. But it wasn't just a cut, it was like—"

"How a book opens?" I knew what it must have looked like to someone not used to such a sight. "You can pry the ribs apart pretty wide. But I'm in one piece now."

"I helped you along." He smiled and pointed to the nightstand where a stack of surgical texts rested. "Like I said, you're too new to heal something that serious."

"Nathan, how on earth—"

"If I told you, you probably wouldn't want to know. I didn't exactly have high-tech surgical instruments here." He motioned to the folding table, where the handles of rusty pliers jutted out from the first aid kit.

My stomach churned, but it could have been leftover nausea from the morphine. "Humor me."

"I used wire to hold your...sternum?"

I nodded at the correct terminology and let him continue.

"To hold it together." He looked away. "I had to wrap it around and around. I wouldn't go through any metal detectors, if I were you."

Wanting very much to change the subject, I cleared my throat. "Well, thanks for the advice. But if I couldn't heal the damage myself, why am I better now?"

He squinted at me. "You really don't remember that night?"

"No. I know exactly what happened. I just want to hear it from your point of view. You know, just to waste time." I leaned back against the pillows. "If there's something you need to tell me, I think you should just say it."

"You'd lost too much blood. Even if you had been conscious enough to feed, it would have just run straight through you. And you did die, Carrie." He sighed in frustration. "If I had known what would happen...."

My pulse throbbed in my ears. But more disturbingly, I could hear his, as if I had a stethoscope against his chest. "Nathan, what did you do?"

He looked me straight in the eye, and heat flashed through my body.

"I revived you the only way I knew how. I gave you my blood."

"What does that mean?"

"At first, nothing. I was desperate, Carrie. I thought my blood might speed your healing, that's all. Then, when I'd touch you to change your bandages, I started to see things, your memories. That's how I knew." He took a deep breath. "When you first became a vampire, you ingested some of Cyrus's blood. Your heart must have stopped at some point—"

"After one of my surgeries."

"That's when you became a vampire. When I gave you my blood, your heart—" He looked away and cleared his throat. "You were already gone, but that didn't seem to make a difference. The process repeated, as if you'd never been a vampire in the first place. I think I'm your sire now."

My mouth went dry, and for the first time in my life, I was rendered speechless. But not for lack of trying. I had plenty to say, but too many thoughts whirled through my head. One was relief that Cyrus's blood no longer pumped through my veins. But that wasn't much of a comfort when, a second later, I remembered I knew just as little about Nathan as ever. And even he didn't have a very high opinion of himself.

Of course, I knew it wasn't in Nathan's character to play the manipulative games Cyrus seemed to live for. But there had been attraction between us since the night we'd met.

That time seemed far away, and Nathan had almost become a complete stranger. He'd been guarded then, but I'd been able to glimpse the real Nathan at times.

But now he was my *sire*.

"I don't understand." My throat felt as if I'd just crossed a desert without a single drop of water. "Cyrus flatlined in the E.R. How did he survive without being re-sired?"

Nathan pinched the bridge of his nose between his thumb and index finger and closed his eyes. "Depending on our age and power, we can be dead for several hours while we heal, as long as our heart stays intact." He stumbled over the words, then cleared his throat. "If you were as old as he is, you'd have been able to survive on your own without a problem."

"So that's it, then?" I took a deep breath, my chest tight and achy. "You're my sire?" My tears were so sudden I didn't have time to hold them back.

Unfortunately, Nathan, not having been privy to the inner dialogue preceding them, misinterpreted my hysterical sobs. He swore and stood, and before I could stop him, he charged out of the room.

I threw back the covers and followed him, grateful for the length of the T-shirt. The hardwood floor of the hallway was cold, so I tried to tiptoe across. After two weeks of barely moving them, my legs had a hard time keeping up. I tripped over my own feet and crashed into the wall.

Nathan was at my side in two seconds, his face filled with anger and annoyance. "I told you to stay in bed!"

He scooped me up, cradling me roughly against his chest. He dropped me onto the bed a little less gently than I'd expect someone to treat a person who'd been practically dissected, then headed for the door again.

"Wait a goddamned minute!" I didn't sound as stern as I'd intended, partly because my face was buried in the pillow. I pushed up on my elbows to glare at him. "You're not going to do this, Nathan. You're just not!"

He met my furious expression with one of his own. "Do what?"

"Walk out!" I struggled to climb to my knees without exposing too much of myself. "You can't just go, 'Oh, by the way, I'm your sire, and hey, lucky you, I'm all dark and moody and too wrapped up in my own stuff to worry about your feelings!' It's not fair!"

"Life isn't fair, sweetheart. I'm *real* sorry if it hurts your feelings, but I don't want to stand here and listen to you work through your issues." He took a step toward the door.

"You don't even know what my issues are!" Regardless of the fact I knew he'd just put me right back, I got out of bed and followed him.

"Oh, I think I can guess," he said as he stormed into the kitchen and yanked open the refrigerator.

"Can you?" I watched him for a moment as he tried to remove the cap from a beer bottle. After he made several unsuccessful attempts to twist it off, I angrily snatched the bottle from him. "Well you're one up on me, then. Because I have absolutely no idea what your problem is."

I searched the silverware drawer. "Where the hell is your bottle opener?"

"Right here," he said, transforming his face. He yanked the bottle from me and punctured the bottle top with one of his fangs, wrenching it off and spitting the metal into the sink as his features returned to normal.

"I can't believe I'm tied to you on a cellular level now."

The comment only served to irk him more. "I'm sorry I'm not more cultured. I'll watch PBS. And cut people open for fun. Will that be better? Will you be less embarrassed to be my fledgling then?"

I probably could have cleared up the misunderstanding right then, but his whole attitude bothered me. I called him something very uncomplimentary and stomped into the bedroom. I started pulling out clothes and flinging them onto the bed.

Nathan followed me. "What are you doing?"

"I'm getting dressed. I'm going out."

"The hell you are!" His hand closed over my arm, and I yanked it away.

"Excuse me, I'm not your prisoner. You can't bully me into staying." I was so mad that my whole body shook. I found it very difficult to keep my human face on.

"Fine. Go out there and get yourself killed. This time, I'm not going to stick my neck out to help you." His Adam's apple twitched as he swallowed. The look in his eyes was so intense that it burned mine.

My heart pounding, I took a step backward. At the same time, he moved forward. The backs of my knees hit the bed, but he kept advancing. I slapped my hands against his chest to push him back, and he grabbed my wrists.

The surge of emotions that shot through the blood tie was astounding. There was no anger. Only incredible fear. Fear that I *would* leave, fear that I'd get killed, or worse, go back to Cyrus.

Even scarier was the naked desire that flared between Nathan and myself.

I knew I could fight it. At least, for a little while. I'd resisted Cyrus long enough. But I'd wanted Nathan before we'd shared blood, and my raging hormones wouldn't take no for an answer.

Neither would his, apparently. He jerked me forward, covering my mouth in a smothering kiss.

Though it wasn't tender, his kiss didn't set me on edge the way Cyrus's had. I didn't have to brace myself for a slap, or flinch from Nathan's touch.

He heard my thought, and annoyed hurt vibrated through the tie. His hands left my wrists and his arms wrapped around my waist, crushing me against him as his tongue slipped over my lower lip.

*Trust me.* His thought whispered through my head. But he didn't trust himself. I felt him attempt to block off his emotions, to feel nothing for me beyond physical desire. I sensed confusion in him when it proved impossible.

Then it hit me. *I'm his first fledgling.*

He couldn't help his urge to protect me, or his need to be close to me. That loss of control was what scared him most.

As if to prove he was still strong, still in control, he cupped my buttocks and pulled my hips forward against the bulge of his erection.

The giggling teenage girl part of me noted my new sire came with a serious upgrade.

Nathan heard the thought. I felt his lips curve into a smile against mine.

*This is how it's supposed to be.* Our blood tie wasn't evil. It wasn't a burden or something I had to guard myself against. The blood tie is a powerful bond, and it had been corrupted and abused by my previous sire.

*I* had been corrupted and abused by him. Nathan's blood in my veins and his hands on my skin eased the pain I'd felt since Cyrus had been my sire.

Nathan needed this, too, if only for the distraction. All of his thoughts were tainted by a sense of urgency. What could he focus on in the moment to keep the unfortunate realities of his past from intruding on the present? It made my head spin. I couldn't imagine living like that every second of every day of my life.

I gripped Nathan's shoulders as we tumbled into the same bed for different reasons. He avoided, I confronted.

"It's been a really long time since I've done this," he mumbled apologetically against my neck as his hands skimmed below my T-shirt.

His fingers raised gooseflesh on my thighs. I shivered. "You're doing fine."

Every inch of his body was as hard as it looked. There wasn't a spare ounce of flesh on him, and when he pulled his shirt over his head I didn't know where I wanted to touch first. My hands wandered restlessly over his smooth chest, his solid arms, the ridges of his abdomen.

Lying between my legs, he pushed my T-shirt up, baring my thighs, my stomach, my breasts. I pulled the shirt off and he rested his head against the curve of my stomach. When he kissed me there, I clamped my knees around his waist, my breath hitching.

With every gentle brush of his fingers, every stroke of his tongue against my flesh, he lost himself a little more in the act. His gratitude overwhelmed me.

Nathan sucked my nipple into his mouth, and I could only concentrate on his flicking tongue and the scrape of his stubble against my skin. I threaded my fingers through his hair and closed my eyes. Nathan crawled up my body, pressing kisses to my neck. "It's the most incredible thing," he whispered. "I can hear what you're thinking. Where you want me to touch you. Was it like that with—"

The instant he said it, my body went cold.

He cursed. "That was probably the dumbest thing I've ever said."

I wanted badly to cover myself. I was too exposed, too vulnerable. "It certainly wasn't smart."

"I only—" He shook his head. "You know you're my first fledgling. This is an entirely new experience for me. I'm not used to being the one who needs information. I'm usually the answer guy."

"I don't know anything about being a sire, Nathan. I have

no idea how it works. It's something you're just going to have to find out on your own."

He rose onto his knees and it looked as though he was going to get up from the bed. His denied need throbbed painfully through my own aching body, and I reached for him. I'd never been the initiator in sexual situations. Most of the time, I'd just gone through the motions, wanting to please for the sake of approval. Now I just wanted to make him feel something other than fear or anguish. And I really wanted him.

"What are you—"

I shushed him as I reached for the gleaming button of his fly. He took a sharp breath as the button popped free. I pulled the zipper down and slipped my hand inside his pants.

Despite the interruption, he was still hard. His erection jerked as my fingers closed around its substantial girth, and his shudder passed through me. I stroked him, my head reeling from the peripheral sensations that affected me through the blood tie.

He stood beside the bed to step out of his jeans, and I slithered across the mattress to grip the tight muscles of his thighs. He groaned when I rubbed my cheek against his hip, my soft breath teasing his straining cock. I gave in to his silent urging through the tie, opening my mouth to draw him in.

He tasted salty, but not unpleasant. I swirled my tongue around the swollen head as I sucked more of him in. As his excitement built, so did mine. When he grasped my hair and gently pulled me back, I knew he'd nearly reached the end.

Laying me back, Nathan relied on the blood tie to learn how I liked to be touched. He'd rush to fulfill my requests with eager hands and lips. He reveled in my responses. Not the way Cyrus had. Nathan didn't view my desire as a way to manipulate or control me.

This realization removed the last of my inhibitions. If I lost control with Nathan, I wouldn't lose a part of myself. I was so relieved by this that I came as he slid two fingers inside me. From the look on his face, he was as surprised as I was.

"Apparently I'm not as rusty at this as I thought." He sank between my legs, bracing his weight on his arms.

The movement of muscle beneath his skin fascinated me. "Watch it. I've got what I wanted. I could just decide I'm done with you and then where will you be?"

"Jerking off, like I've been for the past twenty years. But you're not going anywhere."

I slapped his shoulder lightly for his crude remark, and he reached between us and guided himself into the slick entrance of my body.

My lungs constricted as I stretched to accommodate him. I gasped, wrapping my arms around him. "Oh, my—oh."

He slipped his hands beneath my back and lifted me onto his lap. I held on to his shoulders as every long inch of him slid into me.

Leaning close to my ear, he practically purred, "Told you you weren't going anywhere." I buried my face in his shoulder as he flexed his hips. He felt solid and real, and his skin smelled faintly of soap.

"I've wanted to do this since the night you came into the shop." His voice was fueled by ragged breaths, and his words sent a shock through me.

It was nice to be wanted. Not for power or control, but wanted as a woman.

I pushed my hips down as he surged up and I bit down hard on my lip to stifle a moan. I tasted the blood my bite produced. Nathan leaned back, his eyes dark. He unconsciously licked his lip.

My heart pounded, echoing the throb of his erection that was buried deep inside me. Nathan's eyes never left the smear of blood on my mouth.

"Go ahead," I whispered. "I want you to."

He hesitated only a moment. Then he caught my lip between his teeth and licked the blood away.

When I'd ingested Cyrus's blood, I'd seen a vision of Nathan's past death. I could only imagine what Nathan saw when he tasted mine.

Whatever it was, it tore a fierce growl from his throat. He pushed me back on the bed and stretched my arms high above my head, pinning me.

*Pain.* In my blood, he'd seen pain.

The tenderness in his eyes overwhelmed me. "Why didn't you tell me what he did to you?"

I shut my eyes. "Why would you want to know?"

His lips brushed mine. There was nothing in the gesture but kindness, the love of a sire. His frustration and rage shook me to the core. "I could have made it better. I don't know how, but I could have."

I swallowed against tears. "You could make me forget."

With a sad smile, he nodded. "I'll see what I can do."

He moved within me, slowly. Over and over, he withdrew almost completely, then slid back in, gaining a bit of speed each time. Soon, he pumped against me so furiously, an explosion of breath escaped from me with each thrust. I clenched the sheets in my fists and rocked in time to his movement.

The familiar spiraling feeling, the sense of swiftly losing control, gripped me. I needed only a little push to make it over the edge. Hearing my silent desperation, he slipped his hand between us and rubbed my swollen clitoris. The stimulation was exactly what I sought. I arched up from the bed.

It was his name I cried when I came, his face I saw when I opened my eyes. The relief was so intense that I almost sobbed.

"That's it, sweetheart," he groaned against my hair. He abandoned the rhythm, plunging into me with more urgency than before.

"Come," I urged, clutching at his sweat-slicked back. He thrust almost too hard against me as he reached the end.

"Thank you," he whispered over and over when he could speak again. He kissed my lips, my forehead, anywhere he was able to reach.

When he laid beside me, I rolled awkwardly off of the bed, wrapping the sheet around my bare body.

Nathan frowned. "Where are you going?"

I suddenly felt cold, and oddly lonely. "The bathroom. To clean up."

When I got to the door, he spoke. "It was good we got that out of our systems. It was probably inevitable."

"Yeah," I agreed. Hadn't it meant anything to him? It didn't have to be serious, but he had to feel something more than just relief that it was over.

Exhaling in frustration, he leaned up on his elbow. "You know it did, Carrie."

His answer to my unspoken question should have comforted me, but it didn't.

I shuffled to the bathroom and snapped on the light. As I stared at my suddenly tired face in the mirror, a tear slid down my cheek.

*No, I don't know. And I don't know you, either, Nathan.* I turned away from my reflection, slightly disgusted with myself.

I didn't know him any better than I ever had.

# Twenty-Two
### ———⚬⚬⚬———

*I Left My Heart in San Francisco*

Though I dreaded the fallout from our encounter, the nights that followed were too busy to be very awkward.

During my recovery, Nathan had been feeding me his blood. With nothing to replace what he'd given, he'd seriously drained himself. Combined with the marathon insomnia and the energy he'd expended with me, he could barely get out of bed the next evening.

Luckily, I was able to contact his emergency donor. A perky suburban woman, she graciously dropped off neatly labeled and dated bags of blood. The first night, he was so weak I had to hold his head up so he could drink, but he improved quickly after that.

Ziggy's room was nearly packed up. Nathan had obviously been splitting his time between caring for me and repressing more memories. The only indication that the kid had ever lived in the apartment at all was the small collection of framed pictures on the bookcase in the living room. I rummaged through the boxes and brought out a few other items, tucking them away in places I knew Nathan would find them later. I wasn't about to let him forget Ziggy.

Little by little, I began to learn about Nathan's past. Not that he helped with the process. Occasionally, things would come to me in a flash of intuition from the blood he'd shared with me. That's how I learned the photograph hidden in the closet was indeed his wedding portrait, and the woman in it was Marianne. She'd been seventeen when they'd wed, and it had been a quickly arranged affair, owing to the bundle of joy that had already been on its way. But she'd lost the baby, and subsequent others, the first sign of the tumors ravaging her organs. The feelings of guilt and desperation that blanketed those memories was too thick to see past at times.

I didn't go to bed with him again, and neither of us mentioned what had happened before. I slept on the couch for a few days until Nathan recovered and took Ziggy's things to storage. One day he'd tossed me a clean set of sheets when he returned and said, "Ziggy's room is all yours."

Apparently, he wanted me to stay. Though I balked at the fact he hadn't bothered to ask me if I wanted to, I didn't argue. There was nowhere else to go, and no other place I felt safe.

After another two weeks, I wondered if Cyrus would ever bother me again. At first, it had been easy to assume he bided his time, waiting for an opportunity to strike. But I knew he wasn't patient enough to wait a full month.

The nights grew gradually shorter as spring approached. Renovations on the bookstore were nearly completed, and I found myself working with Nathan, cataloguing inventory in preparation for the upcoming grand reopening. Still, reading

ISBN numbers hardly kept my mind off the nagging feeling that any moment, Cyrus would come back for me.

It didn't help that, for the fourth day in a row, I woke to find Nathan beside me in the tiny twin bed.

I knew he wasn't asleep. "Nathan, what's going on?"

He leaned up behind me, propping his chin on my arm. "Max will be here tomorrow. We postponed the mission when I told him what happened to you, but the Movement is getting impatient."

"*We've* still got to kill Cyrus?" The calm feeling that had just begun to take root in me vanished. I rolled over to face Nathan, careful not to push him off the bed.

His expression confirmed my fear before his words did. "We better get it out of the way now. Before Max goes after the Soul Eater."

"Okay." I tried to smile and appear unconcerned. "What's the plan?"

I shouldn't have bothered with the facade. He didn't. "Don't get killed."

"How do we do that?" My voice wavered as a balloon of fear swelled in my chest.

He didn't answer right away. He toyed with one strap of the tank top I'd worn to bed, sliding it off my shoulder and back again. In the semidarkness of the room, he looked tired and defeated. "I don't know."

He was certain he'd lose me. His terror surrounded me in waves, terror that he'd feel the same pain over me that he'd felt over Ziggy. Over Marianne.

But Nathan would never admit he felt anything toward me but the obligation any sire feels toward their fledgling. It was a good thing, too. I wasn't sure I was ready to accept more from him.

I rolled over and let him pull me into the curve of his body. He locked his arms around me as if I would try to escape, but relaxed some when I laid my hand over his.

I wasn't ready to accept anything more than friendship from him because I wasn't ready to admit the depth of my feelings for him, either. As long as we both ignored our feelings, we could live, awkwardly but happily, in our dysfunction.

The workmen were just finishing up when we got downstairs that night. While Nathan engaged them in a fascinating conversation about wall studs, I went to the mailbox.

I dropped the assorted bills and catalogs on the counter, more concerned with the large padded envelope that had been stuffed in with them. It was addressed to Dr. C. Ames.

I waited until the workmen left before I presented the envelope to Nathan. "I'm not opening this. It looks like 'discreet packaging,' if you know what I mean."

"Very funny," Nathan said, snatching it from me. He ripped the brown paper open and caught the object that fell out. "This is yours. It's nothing dirty. I hope you aren't too disappointed."

It was another copy of *The Sanguinarius*. This copy was a little more beaten up than the previous one.

Nathan frowned and headed to the storeroom. "Near mint my ass! Bluebird45 is getting some seriously bad feedback."

"You bought this on eBay?" I flipped to a random page and started reading. "Man, you really *can* get anything on there."

The shop door swung open, and the bells, which Nathan had yet to replace, announced Max's shrill entrance.

Max was as young, confident and good-looking as I remembered. But I'd learned from Nathan that Max had a reputation as a merciless assassin. Judging from all the purple hickeys above the collar of his T-shirt, he was a merciless ladies' man, as well.

"I love this town, I love this town!" He jumped and grabbed the lintel of the doorway to swing inside.

"Have a good flight?" Nathan didn't look up from the stack of mail he browsed through.

"You better believe it!" Max grinned from ear to ear. "Listen, am I now in the seven-mile-high club, or does this just mark my seventh membership card?"

"Excuse me, lady present!" I turned back to the book.

Max sidled up behind me to read over my shoulder. "Whatcha doin'?"

"Not you," Nathan snapped.

I ignored him. "Reading *The Sanguinarius.*"

I turned a page and was greeted by a particularly gruesome diagram of the vampire stomach. "There is no way my insides look like that. I won't stand for it."

Max laughed. "It's amazing how many vampires are all caught up in that worthless book. Stake plus heart equals dead vampire. That's all you need to know."

"Actually, it depends on which heart you hit," Nathan said quietly. "There are two. Or should be."

A foreboding chill crept up my back. I studied Nathan's face. He looked away.

I frantically flipped through the book until I found a diagram of the vampire heart. I scanned the text on the opposite page.

The main weakness in vampyre physiology is the first of the two hearts, the original human organ. Rendered obsolete by the emergence of the seven-chambered vampyre heart, it now serves as the most efficient way to dispose of the creature.

Max, apparently oblivious to my sudden frenzied state, began to hum, and something about the tune grated on my nerves. It was disturbingly familiar.

To pierce the human heart with any implement is to render the vampyre instantly deceased by incineration.

"Nathan, why didn't you tell me?" Tears slid down my face as the physical emptiness in my chest made itself known. Or it could have been my imagination.

"I didn't want to frighten you."

"What?" I hadn't intended to sound so shrill and loud. I lowered my voice. "How dare you! This is my life. You should have told me!"

Max wandered away from the conversation, feigning great interest in the tape on the bare drywall on the opposite side of the room.

Nathan leaned in close. "How was I supposed to tell you something like that? For the past four days, I've stayed up while you slept, watching for any sign you were going to—" He looked away. "My blood runs in your veins. I know every part of you. If I didn't tell you what he'd done, I thought maybe…maybe nothing would ever come of it and I could forget."

Now I understood his desperate fear, and his certainty he couldn't protect me. But he had no right to keep me in the dark about my own mortality.

On the other side of the store, Max still hummed. The tune brought tears to my eyes.

*I Left My Heart in San Francisco.*

The heart that remained pounded in my chest as I ran to the door.

"Carrie, wait!" Nathan called after me.

I sprinted up the stairs to the sidewalk. The nights had grown somewhat warmer, and the rain that splashed the pavement didn't freeze.

For whatever reason, Nathan didn't follow me. While I hadn't wanted company, I certainly didn't want to think he'd just thrown up his hands and said, "Oh, well."

Not when Cyrus could kill me at any second.

I walked past the alley. Though my blood had long since washed away, I imagined I could smell it. My old, tainted blood, my former sire's blood.

It had been on his hands, his face, his clothes when he'd leaned over me that night.

The memory of the Soul Eater tearing through Cyrus's chest was suddenly so much clearer. Cyrus had told me the Soul Eater had killed his own sire. So he must have removed Cyrus's heart as an insurance policy. No one would betray someone who could kill them via remote.

Cyrus had taken my heart to ensure I wouldn't betray him. Did he think I would return to him?

As I walked, I periodically checked my skin to make sure it wasn't flaking away to ash and embers. Although he was no longer my sire, I knew Cyrus well enough to realize this was yet another installment of his torture. He could destroy my heart whenever he felt like it, and I'd never see death coming. All I could think of were Cyrus's memories of his father holding him down, cutting him open. His scar had faded but it mirrored my own. Did his father still control him with possession of his heart?

I walked around all night. Occasionally, I'd question *The Sanguinarius*. Why did we grow second hearts? Eventually, I settled on the most likely explanation, that the vampire heart was needed to push larger quantities of blood to our abnormally strong limbs. The old heart was rendered obsolete, yet somehow maintained a vital connection to our life force, even if it wasn't connected to us physically.

Ancient peoples believed the heart to be the seat of a person's soul. Maybe they were on to something. The fact I could be removed from this plane of existence if my human heart is destroyed appeared to prove their hypothesis. I promised myself I'd research it, if I lived long enough.

Several times I found myself nearing Cyrus's neighborhood and turned back. When the sun began to rise, I headed back to the apartment. My legs had grown tired hours before, but my anger propelled me to stay away.

Nathan hadn't come to look for me. Ziggy's van still rusted beside the curb, and I saw light in the living room windows.

Max sat on the couch, flipping through television channels with a bored look on his face. He held up a hand in a half-hearted wave to greet me.

There was no sign of Nathan. "Where is he?"

Max pointed down the hall. "He's been in there since you left. At least he stopped playing *Dark Side of the Moon*. I was about to go in there and fling the damn CD player out the window."

I stomped toward Nathan's bedroom, but Max's next statement stopped me.

"We're going in tomorrow night. Nathan didn't want me to tell you, but I thought you should know, seeing as it's your sire and everything we're going to off."

So Nathan hadn't told Max what had transpired the night

of the meeting. He must have had his reasons. Maybe Max was as fanatical about the Movement as Nathan had been.

"Why didn't he want me to know?"

"Probably because he's crazy about you and doesn't want you to get hurt." Max shrugged. "Or maybe he just thinks you're going to fuck everything up."

I laughed. "I'll bet it's the second one."

Max dropped the remote and patted the couch beside him. "Come, have a chat with me."

I really wanted to go into the other room and give Nathan a piece of my mind, but the way Max was looking at me told me that might not be a good idea. I sat next to him, bristling when he wrapped a companionable arm around my shoulder.

"I'm not getting fresh," he assured me. "I just think better with my arm around a beautiful woman."

I rolled my eyes. "Then think fast, before I remove that arm."

"Okay, okay." He chuckled. "Just let me give you some real quick advice. I've known Nathan for a while now. He hasn't had a girlfriend since, God, I think it was '84. And she wasn't what you would call a wild woman. I think she was a CPA.

"The point is, Nathan doesn't get attached to people, and when he does, he has a tendency to shut down. There's some scary shit in his past. I'm not even going to pretend to know the whole story. But he won't let himself get close to anyone. So, if you're thinking of going in there and tearing him a new one, keep in mind you might hurt him a little more than you intended to. And you'll just prove his 'love hurts' theory right."

I swallowed hard, remembering words Cyrus had spat in anger. "Max, did Nathan really kill his wife?"

It must have been a secret he was warned not to reveal, because he chewed his lip thoughtfully for a moment.

"Don't lie to me, Max. I'll know if you do." I lifted his arm off my shoulders. "Did Nathan kill his wife?"

Max sighed. "Yes. At least, that's what I've heard."

"But it wasn't his fault," I said, shaking my head. "I mean, he didn't mean to do it, right?"

"I wish I could tell you that, kiddo." Max's expression was heartbreakingly tender. "But he was a different person then."

I excused myself and headed for the room I'd only recently begun to think of as mine.

The couch springs creaked miserably as Max stood. "He didn't want you to go with us because he didn't want you to get hurt. That was his main concern. I don't know what's going on with you two, but don't waste the time you've got left. Take it from me, eternity gets pretty damn lonely after a while."

I lay awake for a long time, pondering Max's words, and the knowledge that at any moment, I could just poof out of existence.

It wasn't fair to let Nathan and Max risk their lives to kill Cyrus. Not when he'd just end up killing me, too. No matter how many times I thought it through, I came to the same conclusion. I should go to Cyrus and kill him myself. If he took me out in the process, the only loss would be me. And as far as I was concerned, I was dead already.

I listened until I heard Max turn off the television, then I crept into Nathan's bedroom. He woke immediately, bolting upright in bed. "Carrie? What's wrong?"

"Shh." I peeled off my nightgown and climbed in beside him. His arms closed around me and he pulled me beneath him.

This time, the only urgency came from his desire for me.

He touched me as though reassuring himself I was still there, we still had time.

We didn't speak. I think we were both afraid of making it mean too much. Perhaps Nathan thought to spare me the pain of his death. I know I would have done anything to spare him the pain of mine.

So when he kissed me, I kept the contact brief. When he slid down my body to tease me with his mouth, I didn't cry out his name. And when he finally spoke to ask me what I wanted, I didn't say I wanted him to make love to me. I told him to fuck me.

Angrily, he obliged. He spread my legs wide and plunged into me. Besides that, the most contact our bodies made was the slap of his hips against my thighs and the hard grip he had on my ankles as he held them high and apart. The bed shook and slammed against the wall, and I didn't bother to muffle my screams of pleasure. He came with a shudder that sounded like a sob and pulled me into a fierce embrace.

I kissed his forehead and held him tight. Who was I kidding? Trying to block off my emotions for him would be like trying to stop a leak in the Hoover Dam with a cork. I had to know that eventually, the cork would shoot out and my feelings would just gush everywhere, bringing nothing but death and destruction to the valley below.

Okay, maybe it wouldn't be that dramatic. But it was foolish of me to think that I could deny the bond created by the blood tie, or my feelings for Nathan that had existed long before our tie was created.

"Nathan," I said softly through my tears. "Nathan, I—"

"Please, don't say it." His words might have hurt me had I not felt the meaning behind them.

*Please, don't say it, or I won't be able to deny that I feel it. And I'm too afraid to let myself feel it.*

"I won't," I promised.

He laced his fingers with mine and raised my hand to his lips. "Thank you."

But when he fell asleep, I kissed him and whispered, "I love you, Nathan."

*Or Nolen. Or whatever. Even if I never get to find out who you are, I love you.*

Minutes after sunset, I slipped from his arms and dressed quietly. I didn't leave a note because I had no idea what I planned to do.

Only one thing was certain: by sunrise, either Cyrus would be dead, or I would be.

# Twenty-Three

### Welcome Home

My vampire heart beat loud in my chest as I approached Cyrus's mansion. The windows were dark, and for a wild, panicked moment, I thought I'd missed my chance. Cyrus had moved on, my heart tucked away in some box that was hopefully marked Fragile.

Then I saw a gentle glow in the huge, floor-to-ceiling windows of his study, and my heart sank further. Nothing would take this confrontation from me. It was time.

While charging through the front gate would have probably been the brave thing to do, I'd never prided myself on being exceptionally brave. It also didn't seem like a good idea to walk, barely armed, up to the gates of a heavily guarded castle and politely ask to be let in.

I patted my hip pocket, where I'd concealed a stake beneath the hem of my shirt. I didn't even know if I had the physical power to use one against another vampire, especially Cyrus, but at least I'd have something to jab into one of the guards if they got too close.

I followed the sidewalk around the end of the block. The entrance to the guardhouse was so far from the main gate that someone would naturally assume they were two separate residences. I passed the gate where Nathan and I had shared our secret meetings to plot Ziggy's escape, and I thought of Nathan, still asleep in his bed.

It seemed like all I had to do was walk into my room and Ziggy would be there, just like all those weeks ago. I glanced up the lawn. The lights were on in my old room. I felt an unexpected pang of jealousy at the thought I'd been replaced.

A thin figure picked his way gingerly down the lawn, toward the hedge maze. I recognized that profile.

"Clarence?" I called out. My voice echoed back at me in the cool air, and I gasped.

He squinted, then straightened quickly as recognition dawned on him. "Doc?"

My heart in my throat, I watched the old man scurry across the grass. The last thing I wanted was for him to break his hip. "Be careful!"

"Be careful," he mocked. "You're a damn fool, coming back here. They told me you were dead!"

From the pocket of his neatly pressed trousers, he produced a key ring covered with antique keys. After much muttering, he selected one and slipped it into the gate's lock. Instead of crumbling to dust, it actually swung inward with a minimum of screeching. A few leaves from the clinging ivy pulled off, but no one would notice the gate had moved in a hundred years.

"Get your ass in here," he scolded, glancing nervously up at the house. "Now, you got some explaining to do. Did you eat that boy?"

"What? No!" I said, a little too loudly.

Clarence shushed me. "Keep your voice down. The master's home, and he's been in a real bad mood since his daddy left."

"I thought the Soul Eater couldn't survive without his annual feeding?"

"Ain't nothing going to kill that bastard. Believe me, this isn't the first time somebody tried." Clarence shook his head. "What happened to the boy?"

"Cyrus killed him." I thought of the barrels in the basement and what Clarence had told me. "What did you do with him?"

"I didn't do anything with him. I had the night off. They probably burned him with the rest of them."

At least he wasn't crammed in some barrel. I pointed to the house. "Where's Cyrus?"

"In the study. He's been there since the night of the party, trying to avoid *her.*" His last statement was delivered in an accusing tone.

"Her? Dahlia survived?"

Clarence's face scrunched in an almost comical expression of disapproval. "Seems somebody told her she should find herself a vampire to turn her at the party."

I ground my teeth. It would be one thing to fight Cyrus, but Dahlia was way out of my league. "What about the guards?"

"They're trying to steer clear of Dahlia and the Master, but they'll find you if you go in there." He squinted at me. "You got backup coming, right?"

"No. I might as well stake myself right here on the lawn," I muttered, looking up at the looming facade of the house.

"I got one in my back pocket," Clarence offered. "This is gonna be ugly, isn't it?"

I nodded. "You might want to get out of here."

"No, when he's gone, someone's got to tidy things up around here," he said with a sad smile.

"You don't have to stay. I've got friends, we could help you get a condo in Florida or something. Anywhere you want."

"I ain't going nowhere." He made a halfhearted shooing motion with his hands. "I told you before. I come with the house. You give him hell, Doc."

I wanted to hug him, but I wouldn't ask him to lower himself to hug a vampire. I couldn't understand why he wouldn't jump at the chance for freedom. I also couldn't understand the strange compulsion people had to stay in their homes to face hurricanes and floods rather than evacuate. Fear of change, maybe. Or denial of their mortality. Whatever the reason, Clarence seemed to share their stay-put mentality, and I knew I wouldn't change his mind. I made him promise to stay near the guardhouse and not show his face until morning. I watched until he disappeared into the maze. Then I headed up to the house.

After spending weeks in close quarters with the Fangs and Cyrus's human groupies, the house felt downright empty. Apparently, he hadn't gotten around to replacing the numerous pets he'd expended for the feast.

The guards were there, though. The second I opened the French doors to the foyer, all hell broke loose.

Two bodyguards waited for me in the center of the room. No doubt they'd watched me as I spoke to Clarence on the lawn, because reinforcements—a lot of them—jogged down the staircase. Behind me, the front doors flew open.

I whirled to see Nathan and Max framed in the wide doorway. Relief and dread crashed through me. *I'm saved*, I thought. Then I thought, *We're all dead*.

"Don't put on the coffee, we're not staying long," Max announced with a wide smile.

"Get out of here, Nathan," I screamed as the first guard reached me. His hands crushed my shoulders. I grasped his forearms and fell backward, flipping him over my body as another guard came at me. I sprang to my feet and elbowed the next contender hard in the face. Blood spurted from between his fingers as he covered his broken nose. I punched him in the groin. When he doubled over I grabbed his shoulders and rammed the top of his head into my knee. He dropped limply to the floor.

I looked to Max and Nathan. Max had knocked out one guard and used a stun gun to put down another. Nathan was cornered by an opponent brandishing a stake. He tried to dodge it, but the blow landed the wooden spike in his shoulder.

"No!" I charged forward. Another set of hands closed on me. In my haste to get to Nathan, I gave a hard shove and sent the man flying into the wall. He crumpled like a rag doll.

I reached Nathan's side as he pulled the stake free and a torrent of blood spilled out. The guard pulled another stake from his belt and lunged, but not before I caught him. I bared my fangs before I realized I'd changed. If Nathan hadn't called to me, I would have bitten into the man's neck.

"Why not let her?"

Max and Nathan froze at the voice. I let go of the guard and turned.

Cyrus strode from the open doors of the study. His hair was half tied back in a disheveled braid, and his fur-lined robe seemed to swallow him up. Dark hollows beneath his eyes marred his pale complexion. He looked like he hadn't slept or fed in days.

"You've never had the chance to see her feed, have you, Nolen?" He smiled sadly. "It's something every sire should experience."

Arms gripped me from behind at the same time I saw guards grab Nathan and Max. I tensed, prepared to fight, but I felt the point of a stake against my breastbone.

My gaze met Nathan's and I heard his voice in my head. *Don't move.*

Max turned his face to look at Nathan. "What the hell is he talking about?"

Cyrus crossed to me, stroking the side of my face gently with the back of his hand. With the blood tie between us dead, I felt nothing but revulsion.

His eyes, one gold-flecked green, the other his own, icy blue, turned cold and hollow. "It really is over, then."

Howling in outrage, like a child whose mischief had been thwarted, he pounded his thighs with his fists. He rounded on Nathan. "Why? Why did you take her from me?"

"I'd like to know that myself," Max said through clenched teeth.

*Oh, God, don't let him turn on us.* I didn't know Max well enough to tell if he'd report Nathan's indiscretion to the Movement, or if he'd just be disgusted enough to abandon this mission.

Nathan sent me a comforting thought. *Don't worry, sweetheart. He's not going anywhere. We're going to get out of this.*

"You've got no one to blame but yourself, Cyrus." Nathan nodded in my direction. "You killed her in that alley. My blood restored her. Finders keepers."

Just as he finished his sentence, Cyrus struck him. Nathan's head snapped back and blood seeped from his nose. For a moment, I feared he would lose consciousness.

Cyrus shook his wrist, a pained look on his face. For hands so accustomed to violence, they were awfully delicate. "Finders keepers? Like the way I found your cast-off child and made him my own?"

Nathan struggled to break free, and would have managed, if four other guards hadn't rushed in to hold him. Vampires are strong, but not that strong.

One of the sentries brought his knee up hard between Nathan's legs. He doubled over with a grunt of pain.

"Cyrus, please, tell them to stop!" I cried.

My former sire snapped his fingers to the guard restraining me, and the stake at my chest pierced my skin.

Nathan stopped struggling immediately. Rather than panicking, he laughed. "Cyrus, you know staking her isn't going to do anything."

"Won't it?"

The wood pressed deeper, digging into my flesh. While it wouldn't cause me to ash-out and burst into flame, a wound to my remaining heart probably wasn't something to sneeze at. "Stop, please!"

*Don't beg him, Carrie. I can't stand to hear you beg.* Nathan's eyes were distraught. I looked away.

"Cyrus, knock it off," he growled. "Look, I'm playing nice."

"That's noble of you." Cyrus waved away the sentry that held me. "It's so nice that you'd defend her after what she did to your son."

Nathan shook his head. "Not going to work, Cyrus. I'm her sire now. I can see—"

I tried to hold back my memories from the night I'd fed from Ziggy, but in my panic, they overwhelmed me. They were powerfully vivid and painfully erotic. And I couldn't hide them from Nathan.

His anger swelled, but no more than I'd expected. *I wanted to tell you,* I thought firmly, but he didn't answer. Nathan purposely ignored the blood tie, and after decades of shutting out the Soul Eater, he'd perfected his technique. My thoughts bounced off him like tennis balls against a brick wall.

But he didn't show any outward sign of my betrayal. "She told me everything. Sorry to disappoint you."

"I really wish someone would have told *me* everything," Max snarled. "I'm probably gonna get marked for death just for breathing the same air as all of you. I don't know what's going on here, but this is fucked up!"

A frown creased Cyrus's brow. "Kill that one."

"No!" Nathan and I shouted at the same time. I felt some of his rage toward me ebb, like a stone lifting off my chest.

"Oh, you're going to bargain with me now? The two of you?" He laughed. "You should both know better."

More guards rushed into the room. In groups of ten, one group for each of us, they bound our hands behind our backs.

"Take him to Dahlia's room," Cyrus said, gesturing to Max. "The other two can join me in the study."

"We'll reconvene after," Nathan called to Max.

As if they were simply parting to spend their lunch hours in different restaurants, Max shouted back, "Sure thing. Get in a few good hits for me." Then, to the guards I heard him ask, "So, this Dahlia, is she eighteen?"

Half the guards following us remained outside and flanked the door at Cyrus's request. That still left us with ten on the inside, far too many for me, an inexperienced fighter, and Nathan, with his wounded shoulder, to take on alone.

"Afraid of me, Cyrus?" Nathan sniped as the doors closed behind us.

I eventually gave up trying to unbind my wrists. I could barely get the tags off a pair of new shoes. What were the chances I'd manage to Houdini my way out of a plastic zip tie?

The only light in the room came from the fireplace. I saw the elegant shape of Cyrus's profile against the flames.

He didn't look at us. "So it's come to this. You're here to take my life, when you've taken everything else from me."

What was he talking about? "I haven't taken anything from—"

"He's talking to me," Nathan said, his gaze fixed on Cyrus. "I'm not going to apologize for anything. You reap what you've sown."

"What I've sown?" Cyrus whirled around, his ruthless eyes shining in the firelight. "I've only done what every fledgling is bound to do by the blood tie. I've been loyal to my sire!"

Nathan laughed bitterly. "Don't use that tired excuse again! We have the same sire. I didn't lose my free will when he poured his blood down my throat!"

"The very thing I've been trying to convince you of for years!" Cyrus shouted at him, then turned to me. "I hope you will keep that in mind, Carrie, when considering what happened to his wife."

I glared at him but remained silent.

He circled us menacingly, like a shark in a feeding frenzy. "Did Nolen ever tell you what he did to his wife?"

"No." I couldn't look at Nathan. "But I know."

"Carrie?" Nathan's shock resonated through me.

*Max told me.* I wished I could reach for Nathan's hand. Something told me he wouldn't have taken it, though.

Cyrus leaned close to my ear. "I doubt you know the whole story."

He moved away suddenly, motioning to the sofa as though Nathan and I were dinner party guests who'd arrived unfashionably early. "Please, have a seat. I'll tell you all about it."

Nathan lunged forward. I had no idea what he'd planned to do without the use of his hands, but it didn't matter. Two guards grabbed him by the shoulders and hauled him backward.

Although his back was turned, Cyrus lifted his hand in warning. "I wouldn't, if I were you. There's no possible way you'll survive, and then who will protect your fledgling?"

He turned and pointed a taloned finger directly at me. "Believe me, I won't hesitate to kill her once you're gone."

"What's stopping you right now?" Nathan asked.

He didn't mean that. As angry as I knew he was that I'd fed from Ziggy, he wouldn't let Cyrus kill me. He was fishing for information.

Cyrus paused. "Nothing, I suppose. But it would be a shame to waste such a fun ride."

Nathan clenched his jaw at that.

"Oh, I see I hit a nerve. Tell me, Nolen, are you offended because you share that opinion, or because you have no frame of reference?"

"What I was getting at, dick, was why didn't you kill her in the alley? I don't think you'll do it."

I should have known something nasty was coming when Cyrus smiled. He walked up to Nathan and struck him so hard that I heard the bones of his face crack. Nathan's head swiveled to the side, twisting his body as he fell.

Cyrus rounded on me, his eyes furious. "I suppose you think you'll be spared? Saved by some lingering feelings I harbor for you?"

I nodded. "If you were going to kill me, you would have done it already."

He slapped me. "I no longer owe you my patience. I'd rip your throat out now, but I wouldn't want the taste of his blood on my mouth."

Kicking Nathan aside, he pointed to the sofa. "Sit."

I did as I was told to avoid inflicting any further pain on myself or Nathan, on the off chance he wasn't dead.

Seating himself in the wing chair facing me, Cyrus folded his hands in his lap. I noticed for the first time how fragile and bony his fingers looked. I wanted to snap them one by one. Or crush them with a hammer.

One of the advantages of no longer being his fledgling was my ability to think freely without him reading my every intent. Though I no longer had to block him from my mind, I'd never been able to disguise the emotions on my face. A slow smile widened his mouth as he watched me.

"You hate me, don't you?" It was a straightforward question, and harbored none of the sadness I remembered from our time together, when he'd asked me if I loved him.

I squeezed my hands into fists. "Does it matter? You say you're going to kill me, anyway."

Chuckling, he reached for something on the marble table beside him. "No, Carrie. I must concede. I was never planning to kill you."

The object he'd reached for was a sleek, lacquered box. It reminded me of the boxes Nathan sold in the shop to hold tarot cards and crystals, except this one looked much more expensive and was fitted with an ornate lock.

Cyrus pulled the box into his lap, resting his hands protectively over it. "Now, tell me what you know about your sire. I'm dying to hear his version of the story."

I had a good idea what was in the box, but I tore my gaze from it. "He didn't tell me anything. Max told me Nathan killed his wife. And when I—" I stumbled over the words I didn't want to say. "When I drank your blood, I saw what happened to him at one of your Vampire New Year parties. But I don't know how it all fits together."

Cyrus steepled his fingers in front of his mouth. "Yes, from what I understand, Nolen can be a very private person."

Snapping his fingers, Cyrus motioned to Nathan. Holding the box tight to his chest, Cyrus stood and retrieved a crystal champagne flute from a tray on the mantel. Instead of filling it with the sparkling green absinthe in the decanter beside it, he moved to where the guards hauled Nathan to his feet. "Shall you do the honors, or shall I?"

Nathan was unconscious. His head drooped forward, hiding the bloody mess that was his face. It was a miracle Cyrus hadn't killed him.

The thought had barely crossed my mind when Cyrus pulled a dagger from his sleeve and plunged it into Nathan's side.

"No!" I tried to stand, but with my arms tied, my balance was sorely lacking. I fell to the sofa and tipped sideways.

Cyrus filled the glass halfway with Nathan's blood, then wiped the knife clean on Nathan's soiled T-shirt. "Let's not overreact, Carrie. You knew he was going to die when he came through the front door. But he does need to live, for now. At least, until you can see what I need you to see."

He drew the blade across his wrist, letting the ensuing stream of blood mix with Nathan's in the glass. I thought they should have reacted violently toward each other, fizzing and foaming or separating like oil and water, but the dark liquid blended into one murky cocktail.

When it was full, Cyrus held the glass to my lips. "Drink it."

Closing my eyes, I smelled the familiar scent of Cyrus and felt the call of my sire. What would happen when I drank it?

The hard edge of the knife poked my throat, an insistent, dangerous pressure.

"Drink it."

Wetting my lips, I opened my mouth. *It's now or never. You wanted answers, you're about to get them.*

I gulped down the mixed blood of my sire and my enemy, and braced myself for the darkness that would consume me.

# Twenty-Four

### (Dis)Closure

The visions flew at me, two lifetimes of memories piling into my head at once. I feared I'd burst apart, unable to contain it all. Maybe that was Cyrus's plan. It was either that, or he wanted to make me mad with the emotions. There was fear, brief happiness, love, but above all, there was pain. I think I might have screamed, but I didn't feel my body anymore. I slid into the memories like a ghost, disembodied from the participants, a voyeur of pure consciousness.

One night in particular unfolded like a movie before my eyes. The night of the Vampire New Year. The night Nathan had been changed.

Cyrus sat at the table beside a woman I knew was named Elsbeth. She was his fledgling, I realized. They'd been together for just over two hundred years, but it was clear that he loved her far more than she cared for him. A brief glance at their posture, the adoring way he leaned toward her while she didn't bother to spare him a glance, told all.

It was the same room I'd seen through Cyrus's eyes when

I'd drunk his blood before, but I never saw Elsbeth's apathy, because he hadn't. He'd never been aware that she didn't love him. I almost pitied him.

In an instant, I shifted into his head. There had been an argument. He'd asked her for something, to do something she didn't want to do.

To give him her heart.

He'd meant it literally. He'd wanted her to willingly give him what he'd stolen from me. I would have been sick if I had a body left to feel.

Wrenching myself from his mind, I watched the doors to the room open. Nathan and his wife entered. I couldn't access her mind, but Nathan's was, for once, wide-open.

He recognized Jacob Seymour, the faith healer they'd traveled across the world to meet, but was surprised by the strange robe the man wore. And he wondered who all the people seated around the table were. Jacob's son, he knew. The handsome young man was Simon, and the woman seated beside him was his wife, Elsbeth. But what were they all doing here? Had they arrived too early and interrupted a dinner party?

When the doors slammed shut behind them, I felt his alarm. He *knew* something was wrong, in the way he'd known Jacob Seymour's promises were too good to be true.

He'd tricked Marianne, his beautiful Marianne, into hoping for a cure for her illness, because he'd wanted to believe.

*I wish I'd never brought her here.*

As the dispassionate faces seated at the table began to twist into their true forms, Nathan began to pray. But the Holy Spirit, Jesus Christ, and the Blessed Virgin all turned their backs, the way he'd turned away from them when his prayers did nothing to stop the cancer that ravaged his wife's young body.

"Nolen?" Marianne whispered, her already pale face white with terror.

I fled his mind as the monsters closed in on him. If I'd had eyes to close, I would have, but there was no way to avoid the sight. Nathan tried to shield Marianne from fangs and claws, but gnarled hands dragged him from the pack.

"This one is for me!" the Soul Eater roared. Then, propelling Nathan toward Cyrus, he said, "Simon, make your father proud."

Nathan struggled as Cyrus pulled him into his arms. He reached for Marianne, but the distance was impossible, and too many vampires blocked the way.

*This is hell. I am damned.*

I tried to block his panicked thoughts, but they were too strong. Cyrus slashed the buttons from the front of Nathan's shirt in one smooth motion. He splayed his clawed hand across the tanned skin that was revealed, stroking down, over Nathan's tightly muscled abdomen.

Marianne's screams were weak and growing fainter by the moment.

"Let her live!" Nathan begged. "Please, let her live!"

The Soul Eater considered a moment, then clapped his hands, a gesture I'd seen Cyrus mimic many times. The vampires who'd fallen on Marianne looked up, confusion showing as best as it could on their demonic faces.

"A change of plans," the Soul Eater snarled. "Out, all of you."

They cleared, grumbling their displeasure. Some hissed as they slid past their master. On the floor, Marianne moaned, her fang-marked limbs deathly still. Her chest rose and fell with shallow breaths.

Elsbeth scowled at her father-in-law. "You're always doing

this, Jacob. You change your plans without consulting any of us. It's not fair. I haven't fed in days!"

The Soul Eater grabbed her. "You'll find it much more difficult to feed when I snap your pretty head off your neck. Now get out."

"Father?" Cyrus still held his prize, but his attention was focused on Elsbeth.

"We'll let the sick one die on her own. With any luck, she'll live to see him killed." With a final nod to Nathan, the Soul Eater stepped out the door. "It's been lovely meeting you, Mrs. Galbraith."

Without willing it, I was once again in Nathan's mind. Marianne lifted a limp hand toward him, her eyes imploring him to help her. But he couldn't.

He was tired. Tired of chasing a cure from continent to continent, only to see one hope die after another. Tired of dreading her death, tired of the guilt he felt when he wished it would just be over. Perhaps this was his punishment. He turned his head away.

"It appears that it's just the three of us," Cyrus rasped against Nathan's ear. The feeling of another man's hands on him made the bile rise in Nathan's throat. He squeezed his eyes shut tight as those hands moved lower, releasing the button of his trousers. The cold fingers closed over him, stroking him to arousal against his will.

He sobbed a Hail Mary as Cyrus's fangs sunk into his neck.

*Please,* I begged no one in particular. *Please, I don't want to know this.*

So instead, I watched the frescoed ceiling, concentrating on the fat cherubs smiling down on the horrific scene instead of Nathan's screams of pain and terror.

The nightmare was sadistically long. After he'd broken him physically, mentally and emotionally, Cyrus left Nathan naked and violated on the freezing marble floor, small amounts of his blood leaking from a dozen open veins. He was dead by the time anyone returned.

The Soul Eater slid into the room with Cyrus at his side. "Very good, Simon. You've given him real potential." He knelt beside Nathan's abused body and cradled his head in his lap.

"I don't know if I'd call it potential. He'll only last until your next meal." There was an edge of annoyance in Cyrus's voice.

The Soul Eater stroked Nathan's arms lovingly. "No, I think I have other plans for this one."

He lifted his wrist and bit down hard, audibly puncturing the skin and veins. Then he pressed his wounded wrist to Nathan's slack mouth.

The blood slowly brought animation to Nathan's body. First, his mouth as he twitched his lips. Then his arms as they lifted to clutch at the Soul Eater. It took less than two minutes for the change to complete.

Alarm flared through Cyrus. I could feel it without entering his mind. "Father, think of what you're doing. Your blood is weak already. It will barely keep him alive. You won't be able to feed from him. Let me turn him, as we planned."

Nathan lurched to his feet, his eyes wild. Hungry.

The Soul Eater ignored Cyrus, focusing instead on his new child. "Look at you. You're parched. My old blood can't sustain you."

At that inopportune moment, Marianne cried out feebly. Like the moan of a dying animal, it caught the attention of the predators around her.

To his credit, Nathan tried to fight it.

"It will just get worse," his sire taunted. "The hunger will gnaw at you. It will drive you crazy."

Cyrus grew more anxious by the second. "Father, kill him. You can't survive another year without feeding."

The Soul Eater continued to ignore his son. "Nolen, please. You know she's going to die, anyway. Look at her. She's barely alive."

Contrary to what he said, the haze in Marianne's eyes lifted. I was glad that I couldn't see inside her head, to know what she saw when she looked at Nathan. "Nolen, what are you doing?"

He covered his face. "I can't."

The fatherly affection in the Soul Eater's tone vanished. "You will. You're feeling the hunger I have carried for centuries. If you think it hurts now, imagine how you'll feel in a week. In a month. Take her and ease your suffering, or I'll be sure you wish you had!"

Nathan's pain reached out and sucked me in. I'd felt hunger before, but nothing like this. The Soul Eater's blood was already depleted. The cells and tissue of Nathan's body tried to draw nourishment from the blood, but it was a by-product, stripped of the power needed to fuel his vampire flesh.

It was too much to fight both the hunger and the will of his sire.

Marianne screamed when Nathan grabbed her.

"I'm sorry. I'm so sorry," he murmured against her neck an instant before he pierced her flesh with his newborn fangs.

"I don't want to see anymore!" I cried, unaware I'd regained control of my body. But the vision didn't end.

The Soul Eater watched with perverse satisfaction as Nathan drained the last drops of Marianne's blood.

"Let her out of it, Cyrus!" The Nathan I saw before me in the vision hadn't spoken, but it was his voice I heard from the present.

"She needs to see!" Cyrus's words overlapped an echo of his voice as he spoke to the Soul Eater. "Father, kill him! He's fed, his blood is replenished. Feed from him!"

The Soul Eater shook his head. "He is too strong. Remarkably so. I couldn't possibly waste him. I do believe he will be of greater use to me in the future, through the tie. We must always think of the future, my son. I'll have to find another."

"There's no time. If you don't feed, you'll die!"

On the floor, Nathan rocked Marianne and sobbed.

Cyrus met his father's gaze, horror dawning on his face. "No."

"She's been a thorn in my side since you turned her." The Soul Eater strode to the doors.

"Father, no!" He gripped Jacob's robe.

Furious, the Soul Eater jerked the fabric from his son's hands. "Stop your sniveling, boy. Would you rather I take you instead? You'll find another. One who obeys. One more worthy of sharing our blood."

He kicked Cyrus backward, and before he could rise to his feet, the doors snapped shut, barring him from the outside.

"Elsbeth! Elsbeth!" He screamed until his throat grew hoarse. His talons gouged the wood of the doors, but they remained locked. The minutes slipped past, the wait unbearable. Finally, her horrified cries shattered the silence in the house, then just as quickly subsided.

The vision became grainy. I hovered in a void, surrounded by the sound of Nathan's weeping and Cyrus's enraged sobs.

"She's dying! Help her!"

I opened my eyes to the present to see Nathan struggling

against the guards that held him. A third stepped in to help, but he wasn't needed. As soon as I stopped gasping for breath and sat up, he calmed.

Sometime during the dream, I'd rolled from the sofa. My head throbbed and my back ached, from hitting the floor or as a result of some weird aftereffect of the sanguine cocktail, I had no idea.

Cyrus gripped my bound wrists and hauled me to my feet. His touch was purposely rough. "I hope that shed some light on our difficult situation here. And I hope you understand why I did what I did."

"To whom?" I snarled. "To Nathan? Or his wife? Or your fledgling? What exactly am I supposed to understand here?"

"That he's a killer!" Cyrus's rage was so sudden and violent, I trembled in fear. All the anguish of the past centuries curled into his words. The pain in his voice cut into me so deeply that I felt it myself, even without the blood tie between us.

As quickly as it had come, his anger subsided. In the defeated tone of a tired child, he spoke again. "He is a killer, and you left me to be with him."

"I didn't." I turned and looked him in the eyes, and the sorrow there stole my breath. "When you took my heart in that alley, you let me die. Nathan saved my life. It wasn't my choice."

"It doesn't matter. What's done is done. When he is dead, things can go back to the way they were." Cyrus snapped his fingers to the guards. "Kill him."

Nathan roared and rushed past the guards. With his hands bound, he could do little more than charge headfirst at Cyrus and knock him into the wall beside the fireplace. And that's what he did. The collision was loud, and it dented the dark wood paneling, but Cyrus recovered quickly, kicking Nathan to the floor. Laughing, Cyrus grabbed the fireplace poker from the rack on the hearth and raised it over Nathan's back.

Even if I warned him, he wouldn't be able to get out of the way in time. With a scream of rage, I yanked my hands apart. The plastic tie cut into my skin, but it broke. I was free.

Before the guards could react, I ran toward Cyrus, barreling shoulder first into him. We toppled onto the Persian rug, knocking over two chairs as we fell.

I grabbed a handful of his hair and tugged, forcing him to face me. "If you're going to kill me, just do it and leave him alone!"

He yanked free, leaving a white-blond lock twined in my fist. He brushed himself off and stood. "I don't want to kill you, Carrie. But it's out of my hands now."

Guards lifted Nathan from the hearth and threw him into a chair. He breathed hard. The jagged wound where Cyrus had stabbed him seeped fresh blood.

"What do you mean, it's out of your hands?" I asked. Another guard stepped forward to grab me, and I growled at him.

"Leave her," Cyrus commanded with a smirk. "I have a proposition for her."

I grabbed the guard and twisted his head to the side, exposing the pulsing artery in his neck. "You better start explaining or so help me God, I'll kill him right here."

Cyrus laughed. "What do I care? I have dozens more just like him."

*Touché.*

Out of frustration, I wrung the guard's arm until it snapped.

He sagged to the ground, howling in agony, and I kicked him forward, pinning his head to the floor with the heel of my shoe. "Talk, or you'll be cleaning brains out of this fancy-ass rug!"

"Very good. It's amazing you've come this far, with only him to learn from. The power in you...it's intoxicating." Cyrus moved toward me slowly. I took a step back, and the sentry crawled away, cradling his ruined arm to his chest. I backed into the marble-topped table. Cyrus kept advancing. "Think of what you could become, if only you'd come back to me. I could make you mine again. Drain your blood, bring you to the point of death and then fill you up again."

He stroked my cheek, his fingernail scoring a painful incision through my skin. I gritted my teeth to keep from wincing. "You never filled me up before, so I can't imagine you accomplishing it now."

"That's rather cheap, Carrie. I thought you knew better." He turned away from me to face Nathan. "I sent Father a rather interesting package last night. He should be receiving it any moment now."

Nathan shrugged. "Is this information in any way relevant to our current situation?"

"As a matter of fact, it is." Cyrus looped his arm around my waist and pulled me forward. "Since he missed his annual feeding and the victim intended for him is deceased, I thought it only fitting to send him a little takeout. Carrie's heart."

Nathan's calm facade wavered. "Why?"

"An eye for an eye." Cyrus pushed me aside. "And, to borrow another phrase, it will kill two birds with one stone. Carrie disobeyed me, and she had to be punished. Your life cost me Elsbeth, and I deserve something in return. If you thought losing your precious human boy was bad, wait until you feel the blood tie wither and go cold. Wait until you experience her death, with no way to prevent it. But I won't kill you, Nathan. You'll feel her death every day of your life, as I've lived with the pain of losing Elsbeth."

Disbelief froze me in place. I was going to die. Even if we killed Cyrus right now, the Soul Eater would devour my heart. I was dead already.

I opened my mouth to speak, but I couldn't say anything.

Cyrus patted my head in a mocking gesture of comfort. "Of course, I used a personal courier. I could call him back at any time, if you wished to make an arrangement."

A flashback of the night I'd exchanged my freedom for Nathan's life sickened me. "Let me guess. If I stay with you, you'll give me back my heart and let Nathan go?"

Clapping his hands, just like his father, Cyrus laughed. "No. Nolen is going to die, one way or another. But I'm giving you the choice to live. Stay here with me, become mine again, and I'll call off my father's feeding."

Without thinking, I lifted my hand, aimed for his one good eye and stabbed my finger hard into the socket.

He screamed in rage and lurched away from me. Blood trickled from beneath his hand as he covered the side of his face.

"I'm not going to be your prisoner again. I'd rather die," I snarled. And I meant it.

No matter what I'd thought he felt for me, I had only been to him what everyone else in his life was. A piece of property, a pawn. I hadn't played according to his rules. I'd broken down the order he cherished, and in doing so, I'd destroyed his feelings for me.

Maybe I had loved him, but I could live without love if it compromised my free will.

That's when I decided to make the most of what was left of my life. If I was going to die, I would go out fighting.

The remaining guards rushed me. If I'd been worried about the Movement's rules, I would have tried not to do too much damage. But it seemed that the best course of action would be to grab heads and twist.

I'd killed three by the time Nathan appeared at my side. His wrists bled where he'd broken free of the binding.

"I'm sorry," I said immediately, kicking back a guard.

"Don't apologize, get Cyrus!"

I looked up. He'd nearly reached the door. I leapt over the back of the sofa and blocked him. "Going somewhere?"

"Guards!" he shouted, trying to get past me and still hold his eye in place.

"Go ahead, call more in! I don't care. I'm dead." I stepped closer, pulling a stake from my back pocket. "And as far as I'm concerned, so are you. Now, you can go out like a little bitch with your bodyguards backing you up, or you can fight me until one of us is dead. It's your call. Unless you're afraid."

He dropped his hand from his bloodied face. His eye dangled from the socket on a cord of flesh. He pushed it back in and blinked to clear the blood-occluded lens. "I think I've underestimated you, Carrie." Then, turning to the guards swarming Nathan, he shouted, "Everyone out!"

I glanced at Nathan. He'd collapsed to the floor, but he was alive. I could feel his strength coursing through me.

Cyrus stepped back so the guards could file out of the room. I sprang forward and plunged the stake into his skull through his borrowed eye. The bones of the socket separated with a crack. I could have rammed the stake right into his heart to get it over with, but I wanted him to suffer.

"Whoops, was I supposed to wait for a signal or something?" The absurdity of the situation and my actions forced nerve-racked laughter from my throat. It died on a hysterical sob of despair, and I clenched my hands in front of me so hard I drew blood from my palms with my nails.

He pulled ineffectually on the stake protruding from his face. My shock melted away and I seized the opportunity to grab him and pin his arms behind his back.

"You know what's great about Nathan? His blood is ten times more concentrated than yours because he hasn't wasted it on a bunch of loser fledglings." I wrenched the stake from his eye, flinging droplets of blood across the room. Then I stabbed the sharpened wood into his back. "You know what? I think it makes me stronger!"

Despite the bravado of my words, my voice shook.

His legs crumpled beneath him and he tried to speak, but choked on his blood. I closed my eyes and took the deepest breath I've ever taken in my whole life. The part of me that still believed he could be good wanted to escape the part of me that wounded him in rage. Guilt tore through me for doing something so violent to a man I'd thought I might have loved, but my logical mind was stronger. Cyrus had earned this, and if I didn't kill him, he would repeat this sick game with other fledglings for an eternity. Summoning more courage, I twisted the stake and he gasped.

"Drop him!"

I looked up. Dahlia entered, pushing Max ahead of her. She surveyed the scene coolly.

"Go help your friend," she barked at Max, pointing at Nathan. "I want to have a word with Carrie."

The last time I saw Dahlia, she'd been running from a horde of hungry vampires. Now the air around her seemed to vibrate with unchecked power.

Panic shot through me. I'd had more confidence fighting Cyrus, because I knew I would die, anyway. I hadn't really given much thought to what would happen to Nathan and Max afterward. They might have been able to hold their own against Cyrus, but I was pretty sure that even together they were no match for Dahlia.

But Max was still alive. I guess that stood as testament to his way with the ladies. Hopefully it would get Nathan and him out of this mess when I'd burned to cinders.

Dahlia stood before me, her hands placed on her wide hips. "You marked me for death."

Gasping for breath on the marble floor, Cyrus tried to grab my leg.

"Stay down!" Dahlia made a sweeping gesture with her hands and he fell back, pinned by invisible hands.

I swallowed hard. "I didn't know exactly how the whole 'marked for death' thing worked. I thought he'd offer Ziggy to his guests, and turn you."

"And then I'd get eaten by the Soul Eater?" There was a surprising lack of anger in her question. She didn't accuse me so much as state a fact.

The least I could do was be honest. "Maybe. I thought Cyrus would change you, but as far as the rest of the plan went, you were on your own."

"As usual." She sighed. "It actually worked out better this way. I got my blood, I got my power—"

"And I'm assuming a random biker vampire got himself a very nice piece of ugly dragon jewelry in exchange for a few pints of blood," I interrupted.

Dahlia raised an eyebrow. "Very astute of you."

She must have released Cyrus from whatever spell she'd cast, because he climbed to his feet unhindered. Lifting a hand to his blood-streaked face, he pressed his remaining eye back into its socket. "You don't think I turned her, did you? I wouldn't waste my blood."

I expected Dahlia to fly into a rage or strike him down or

fall apart the way I'd seen her do before. But she just smiled. "Of course not. You never would have. You were just going to string me along until you got bored. Then you were going to kill me."

"Oh, but for a while you believed you had me," he said with a laugh. "God, but you were easy to manipulate."

Cyrus turned to me. "That's why I became so bored with her. The things I got her to do, Carrie. You thought what I did to you was bad."

"I really don't care to hear about it." No matter what had transpired between Dahlia and me, she didn't deserve whatever perverse torture he'd inflicted on her.

But she seemed genuinely unaffected by his taunting. "And I'd do it again. I got what I wanted. So did you. But you're not going to kill me," she said.

A strange buzzing started in my head. It was as if someone had turned on a television, but all I could hear was the high-pitched frequency noise. Dahlia's voice filled my head. It was nothing like the communication I'd had with Cyrus or Nathan through the blood tie. This was a different connection, watery and slightly garbled, and it made my skull vibrate with pain, but I could understand it enough to get her meaning. *"The package never left the premises."*

I saw her lips moving as she spoke to Cyrus, his superior expression as he answered her, but I couldn't hear their words. I shook my head as if I were trying to clear water from my ears.

*"Thank you,"* I thought back to her, my words ricocheting unpleasantly in my skull. *"I'll never be able to repay you."*

*"This doesn't mean I like you. We're not gonna go shopping for shoes or whatever the hell you're thinking."*

There was a moment of silence, then the buzzing stopped, then her next words were crystal clear in my mind. *"Kill him."* I saw her tremble as she turned to leave the room. *"He will kill me eventually. I need him dead. I'd do it, but I can't. Kill him, and I'll pay you back with your heart."*

So, she did love him. Not enough to trust him with her life, and she shouldn't have, but she did love him. She'd claimed it wasn't his power that had drawn her to him. I'd had a hard time believing that, but now it was apparent. What had she said to me before?

*Some things aren't good or evil. Some things just...are.*

I guess Dahlia just *was,* like a tornado or a tidal wave. A force of nature. I wasn't going to try to understand her motives beyond simple self-preservation.

She paused as she passed me on her way to the door. *"Make it quick. Don't let him suffer."*

Then she left. I was so busy watching after her in awe that I forgot she'd released Cyrus.

It was Max's shout that alerted me. "Carrie, look out!"

Cyrus clutched my blood-stained stake and rushed me with it. I leapt aside but lost my balance, tumbling onto my back. Without hesitation, he brought the stake down. I rolled away. The wood shattered as it drove full force into the floor.

Max started toward me, but I waved him away. "Stay with Nathan!" Though no longer unconscious, Nathan wasn't strong enough to fight off a swarm of gnats, let alone anything else that might come after him. And I still didn't trust Dahlia, bless her crazy little heart.

I jumped on Cyrus's back, using my momentum to propel him face-first into the wall. I reached forward to gouge at his ruined eyes and felt his teeth close on my forearm. My bones cracked easily in his jaws and blood dripped from my paralyzed fingertips.

*Oh, great. How are you going to fight with one arm, hotshot?* He lifted me over his head and flung me across the room. I landed hard.

He wiped his hands on his robe. "Having a little trouble?"

"No, no trouble at all." I hated the wheezing sound of my labored breathing. "Just pacing myself."

He laughed and held out his arms. "Come on, Carrie. Let's stop this foolishness. You know you'll never be able to kill me. There's too much between us."

He didn't sound as confident as he wanted me to think he was.

"I've already killed tonight. Maybe I've got a taste for it now."

"You killed strangers. Men you didn't know." He took small steps toward me. I didn't move, even when he put his arms around me. "Men who'd never touched you. Never been inside you. Men who'd never seen your most intimate thoughts and emotions."

I knew he was no longer my sire, but my heart—the proverbial one that couldn't be so easily removed—remembered when he was. "It didn't mean anything."

"It did," he insisted, stroking my hair. "You know it did. You felt things for me you couldn't ignore. You can't ignore them now."

"I felt things for you because you manipulated me into feeling them. And I don't feel them now."

I didn't love him, I'd never loved him. Not in the way he'd wanted. How could I have?

He looked more hurt by my words than by any physical violence I'd committed against him. "I loved you."

The admission froze me just long enough for him to get a better hold on me.

Nathan leaned up weakly on his elbows. "Carrie, get away from him!"

"Let her go!" Max got to his feet. "Don't move a freaking muscle, Carrie!"

I felt the sting of a blade at my neck. I'd been tricked.

"I did love you, Carrie. I still do." Cyrus's voice was strained, and a cold tear splashed against my neck. "Why couldn't you love me?"

*Love* wasn't a word I tossed around lightly, but with a knife at my neck, my priorities changed really fast. "Maybe I did love you."

"If you had loved me, you would have stayed with me. Why didn't you stay?"

I heard the same desperation in his tone as my pleading inner voice that criticized me every time I'd failed to please my father. The same desperation I'd seen in Cami, in the poor dead girl's eyes the night she'd asked Cyrus why he no longer requested her company. The dashed hope that had stolen across Dahlia's impassive face when she'd come to Cyrus's room and found me in his bed, in her place.

Cyrus really did want me to love him.

Though it pained me, I had to lie to save my life. "I'll stay."

"Carrie, no!" Nathan shouted, the look on his face as devastated as it had been the night Ziggy died. He was afraid.

*Trust me.*

I prayed Cyrus wouldn't see through my ruse. "I'll stay," I repeated. "But I have to know I'll be safe."

Pulling the knife away, Cyrus spun me into his arms and crushed me to his chest. "You'll be safe. I swear, nothing will harm you again."

"But I can't trust you." I took the knife from his hand, and he let it go willingly. "You've already sent my heart to the Soul Eater."

Cyrus released me from his embrace. "I'll get it back for you."

The relief on his face speared through my heart. *You can't feel guilty. He's got this coming to him,* Nathan told me. "I wish I could be sure," I said, both to Cyrus and Nathan.

His gaze flickered from my face to the lacquered box he had cradled so protectively earlier.

Cyrus's father tearing his chest apart.

Cyrus tearing mine.

I knew what lay in that box.

He smiled haughtily at me. "Of course, I knew you'd see reason and come back to me. But I also know you're not foolish. So I've brought some collateral."

He went to the table and lifted the box. "Here. Keep it safe until yours returns. But it will always belong to you."

"What is it?" I asked breathlessly as he slipped the box into my hands.

"My heart."

He pulled me to him and kissed me. I felt a tremendous sadness. I knew what it was to want love and have it constantly elude me. But Cyrus wasn't like me. Where I had forced myself to fill my life with other things, he had simply tried to force others to love him. In the end, his quest for power and control would be his undoing. Because now that he believed he finally had love, he'd left himself vulnerable.

I lifted the lid of the box with my hand that still gripped the knife. I hesitated only a second, fortifying my courage with memories of every cruelty Cyrus had ever subjected me to. Leaning back, I kissed his cold, bloody cheek. "I'm so sorry, Cyrus."

And I truly was. I was sorry he didn't have a better life, sorry he couldn't have been the man he should have been, and I was even a little sorry I couldn't make myself love him, for his sake. But there was no time for regret. I plunged the knife into the box, through the dried-up object that was his heart.

Cyrus screamed.

It was done.

The flames started at his feet, but instead of traveling up his body, they burned from the inside out. He threw his head back with an anguished cry as blinding white flames shot out of his eyes, mouth and nostrils. His skin melted away, revealing the raw muscle beneath. A raging wind filled the room, stripping his bones clean, but still his scream went on and on. I clung to the marble table to keep from being swept away.

Cyrus's bare skeleton hung suspended in the air. A ball of pure, blue flame burned where his heart should have been. Within seconds, the bones reduced to ash and blew away.

The wind stopped abruptly, and I fell to the floor.

"That was, by far, the coolest thing I have ever seen," Max said in awe.

"Shut up, Max." I heard footsteps, then Nathan knelt down and pulled me into his arms. "Carrie, are you okay?"

I couldn't speak. I could only sob.

He crushed me in a hug that would have been smothering if I could have stopped crying to breathe in the first place.

"It's all over," he soothed, stroking my hair. "You did good."

"We have to get her heart back from the Soul Eater," Max said quietly. "Is there someone around here who can help?"

"Dahlia," I said, wiping my eyes. Without questioning me,

Max and Nathan helped me to my feet, and we shuffled into the foyer.

Dahlia descended the stairs, her face streaked with tears. "Did you do it?"

I nodded.

"Then come get your heart."

She'd stuffed the grayish object into a Ziploc bag. She held it out to me, and I looked it over with uncertainty.

"That's the one," Nathan called. "I'd know it anywhere."

I took the bag.

"If I ever see you guys again, I'll probably kill you," Dahlia warned.

"Then I hope I never see you again," I said, and I meant every word.

I wanted to ask her if she'd stay at the mansion, or if she'd leave. More important, I needed to know if Clarence would be safe with her, since he'd rather stay here and die than face life outside these walls.

But Nathan and Max already headed toward the door, and I didn't feel like pressing my luck by hanging around any longer.

I didn't look back as we walked down the driveway, but I couldn't help imagining that Cyrus's freed soul glided through the watery afterlife beside me, all the way to the gate.

# Twenty-Five

❦

*Something Ever After*

It was a week before I could get through the day without crying. Most of the time, I stayed in Nathan's room, curled up beneath the covers of his bed.

Nathan stayed at my side when he wasn't overseeing preparations for the reopening of the bookstore. We didn't talk. I don't think I said a word to him until the sixth day, when my depression lifted long enough for me to decide that I had to ask about the vision I'd seen.

"How long were you married?"

Nathan sighed and lay on the bed beside me. "This is one of those unavoidable conversations, isn't it?"

"Yep." I reached for the mug of blood he'd left for me on the nightstand. It had begun to clot, but I drank it anyway, grateful that my appetite had returned.

Nathan cleared his throat. "Almost thirteen years."

"You loved her a lot." I laid my hand over his. *I'm here for you. Let me in.*

When he looked at me, his eyes were rimmed in red. "I love her."

The present tense shocked me.

He felt it, but he didn't apologize. "I don't want you to think I don't care about you. I do. The blood tie sees to that, I don't have a choice in that matter. But I can't let her go."

"You don't have to." A tear slid down my cheek. "Nathan, do you—" *Love me?*

"No." He knew what I'd meant to ask him. A glimmer of pain crossed his features. My heart should have turned to stone in my chest, but I knew he wasn't denying me. He was denying himself.

We lay in silence for a few minutes, nothing but tension connecting us through the blood tie. Finally, he rolled to his side to face me. "Now, there's still the question of where you stand with the Movement. Have you given that any more thought?"

*Of course.* I was about to tell him exactly where he could stick his precious Movement, but the words didn't make it past my lips before he spoke again.

"Because I'm getting out."

I suddenly understood the meaning of the phrase *You could have knocked me over with a feather.* "Are you serious?"

He laughed. "I've been on probation for more than seventy years now because I killed Marianne. I'll never stop being sorry for it, and if someone walked through that door right now and gave me the chance to switch places with her, I'd do it. But the Movement will never forgive me, and until they stop throwing it back in my face, I'm not going to be able to move on."

There was more. I felt it just below the surface of his regret. But I didn't push. There would be other days for that.

"That's a big change. I'll make one, too. I'll start looking for my own place," I said with a cheerfulness I didn't truly feel.

"No." His declaration was so vehement it scared me. Softer, he elaborated. "Carrie, you're my fledgling. I would never ask you to leave. I don't think I could survive if you did."

"It's not like I can't drop by and visit."

He grasped my hand. "Stay."

I knew he couldn't say what he really felt. He didn't know what he really felt. But I did.

A sire had to love his fledgling. It was a painful truth of vampire existence. It was what made the blood tie so unbreakable. I suppose it would have been nice if he would love me without the connection between us, but he was wounded and complicated. His emotional distance was almost a relief to me.

"You do know there will be consequences." Nathan rested his head against my shoulder. "If I leave the Movement, I'll be marked for death. If you don't join, you'll be, too."

"So I'll go from one death sentence to another. In fact, I've forgotten what it feels like to live without one." I set the mug back on the nightstand and wiggled down onto the pillows.

"What do you say we go out tonight?" he asked suddenly. "You haven't been out of this room for days."

"I could really use a shower," I admitted. "And it will do me some good to see some other people. Not that you're not fabulous in your own way."

"I'll go start the water." He bounded from the bed, a grin on his face.

"Wait," I called after him. When he stopped, I smiled sheepishly. "Bring me my heart?"

He nodded, but appeared confused. While I waited for

him to return, I rolled onto my side and waggled my fingers at the goldfish in the bowl. Before, I'd considered his three-second memory span a curse, believing that developing a new outlook on life so often would always end badly.

At the time, I'd never imagined that things might get better with each three-second change, just like I'd never considered becoming a vampire could turn out for the better.

Nathan entered the room, holding the steel box he'd purchased to keep my heart safe. Inside, it was wrapped in layers of gauze and cloth and bubble wrap, and it rested in a nest of foam packing peanuts. Only Max had been privy to the careful packaging, because I'd still been healing from the injuries Cyrus had inflicted on me. Since Nathan had padlocked the box shut and thrown away the combination, I had to take Max's word that it was safe.

Nathan handed the precious package to me, his hands shaking. I smiled. "It's okay. Cyrus's heart survived all those years in a wooden box. Too bad it didn't splinter and kill him."

Nathan cleared his throat and gestured to the box. "What did you want with this?"

I took a deep breath. "I wanted to give it to you."

"No."

"Hear me out." I pressed the box into his hands. "It's staying with you. Not because you're my sire. Not because of the blood tie. I'm going to stay with you because I trust you. With my life."

He looked away. "You know what I did."

"I do." Marianne's screams and pleas now haunted me, as well. "But I trust you."

Tears shone in his eyes, but they didn't fall. "Thank you. But I can't trust myself."

Later, when the sun had risen and Nathan slept at my side, I took his hand in mine. He'd started wearing his wedding ring again, either as a signal to me to forget about him or as an eternal punishment to himself. I guessed it was the latter.

But his self-inflicted penance was unnecessary. The Soul Eater was still out there, the Movement would soon enough learn of Nathan's defection, and God knew what else lurked on the horizon. I felt pretty confident that there was plenty of stuff out there to beat us down without his guilt having to plague us.

But I wasn't going anywhere.

I opened the drawer of his nightstand and slipped the box inside. I thought about my parents, and for the first time since their accident, I allowed myself to forgive myself. I'd come so far that I no longer recognized the person I used to be. I'd turned down the blind admiration and devotion Cyrus had offered me. I'd rejected his promises of power without consequence, because I now knew that a life without consequences was meaningless. And though I'd done things I wasn't proud of, I didn't regret them. In that regard, I was possibly stronger than Nathan.

Strength isn't about bearing a cross of grief or shame. Strength comes from choosing your own path, and living with the consequences.

And as long as I had the strength to keep living, I was going to do it without regret.

*New York Times* bestselling author

# KAREN HARPER

Julie Minton thought nothing of her
fourteen-year-old daughter, Randi, leaving
home earlier that morning to go Jet Ski
riding with Thad Brockman. But now
Randi and Thad are missing—and the
hurricane that hours ago was just another
routine warning has turned toward shore.

With the help of Zack Brockman,
Thad's father, Julie begins a race against
time to find their children—but first,
they must battle not only Mother Nature,
but an enemy willing to use the danger
and devastation of the storm for
their own evil end.

# HURRICANE

"Harper has a fantastic flair for creating
and sustaining suspense."
—*Publishers Weekly* on *The Falls*

*Available the first week of June 2006
wherever paperbacks are sold!*

MIRA®

MKH2307R